Tease
Immodesty
Blaize

EBURY
PRESS

1 3 5 7 9 10 8 6 4 2

First published in 2009 by Ebury Press, an imprint of Ebury Publishing
A Random House Group Company
This Edition 2010

The Random House Group Limited Reg. No. 954009

Addresses for companies within the Random House Group can be found at
www.randomhouse.co.uk

A CIP catalogue record for this book is available from the British Library

The Random House Group Limited supports The Forest Stewardship
Council (FSC), the leading international forest certification organisation. All
our titles that are printed on Greenpeace approved FSC certified paper carry
the FSC logo. Our paper procurement policy can be found at
www.rbooks.co.uk/environment

Typeset in Adobe Caslon by Palimpsest Book Production Limited,
Grangemouth, Stirlingshire

Printed in the UK by CPI Cox & Wyman, Reading RG1 8EX

ISBN 9780091930035

To buy books by your favourite authors and register for offers visit
www.rbooks.co.uk

Acknowledgements

Special thanks to those who inspired me: Robin and Bo
Boom, Paul O'Grady who gave me 'the bible', Basil Patt
Tura Satana and Satan's Angel.

Special thanks particularly to Ellen Taylor, Em
Dubberley, and, of course, Clare Conville and Gill
Green for the invaluable input, not to mention world c
afternoon tea meetings.

Thank you also to Andrew for humouring the af
burn of long writing hours.

A special mention goes to my showgirl 'sisters' all
the world who have shown so much support and ca
raderie; you all know who you are.

Last but by no means least, thank you to the true leg
of the burlesque stage who paved the way for othe
follow: Madame Vestris, Lydia, Peaches, Gypsy, I
Sally, Dixie, Zorita, Lili, Blaze, Angel, Tura, C
Frenchie, Ricki, Liz, Lottie, Jennie, Ann, and mor
many of whom are gone, but not forgotten. I swing a
to you amazing ladies and may the fire keep bu
bright.

For Ellen

Chapter 1

'Okay, girls, tighten me up and tie me off!' roared Tiger Starr, clinging to the wall with both hands. The energy in the dressing room switched instantly, the nervous undertow shifting through the gears into hyper excitement and bootcamp-like efficiency. Tiger's dressers Cherry and Brandy jumped for her corset strings. They each wrapped a length of the silk cord round their wrists and heaved smoothly in opposite directions while Cherry held her foot in the small of Tiger's back. This was the second tightening process of the night.

Tiger had been sitting in the corset for ten minutes already, flexing her ankles in her crystal-covered *pointe* shoes, whilst waiting for her internal organs to resettle themselves before going in for the last couple of inches with the corset. Her waist shrank eye-wateringly before everyone's eyes.

'Ooof,' exhaled Tiger, bracing herself against the wall, 'have you got that last inch?'

'Yeah, just gonna tie it off, that good for you?' replied Brandy.

'Well, I can't breathe any more ... perfect ...' Tiger gasped, wriggling uncomfortably. 'Holy cow ... okay,

Mario, it's time to batten down the hatches!' Tiger purred breathlessly to her hairdresser who was already hammering hair pins through the feet of the stuffed doves perched on her hair so that they nested firmly among her teased pink curls. She was now feeling the familiar warm tickle of butterflies in the pit of her stomach as Mario worked away at her immaculate coiffure as only a creative genius could. Tiger never liked her tension to show; only her stylist and best friend Blue could detect a faint tremble in her hands from across the dressing room.

'Geev 'em a shake, darlink,' Mario ordered. Like a good girl, Tiger shook her curls back and forth, flicking her head from side to side, testing any movement that might dislodge the birds on stage. Gone were the days of her wearing real doves. Bird shit in the hair was a price even Tiger was not prepared to pay for the ultimate in insanely glamorous accessories.

'Spray!' came her next command. On cue, everyone in the room covered their faces. Cherry paced evenly round Tiger wielding an industrial-sized aerosol can of diamond powder, spraying her liberally and smoothly. Tiger knew instinctively when to turn each limb so that every square millimetre of her was sparkling.

'This is your ten-minute call,' crackled the stage manager over the intercom.

'Oh god!' wailed Tiger. 'I almost forgot, but I have presents for you all!'

'What – now?' started Blue.

'Here. I want you to have them before the show starts! Just a little something to say thank you for all your hard work . . .' said Tiger hurriedly dishing out four small gift-wrapped boxes.

'You're kidding?' squealed Cherry.

'Well, I couldn't look like this without you guys,' she murmured softly, before passing a Fortnum and Mason bag to Blue. 'These are treats for the crew – can you give them out in the interval, darling?' she whispered. Cherry and Brandy had already ripped their presents open and were gasping at the expensive-looking sparkling pasties – bejewelled nipple covers – nestling in beautiful velvet-lined boxes.

'Jeez! Come on, guys, this is no time for unwrapping!' bellowed Blue impatiently. 'Chop chop!' he clapped his hands together loudly. Cherry and Brandy hurriedly put down their gifts, snapped to attention and swooped to collect all Tiger's pre-sets.

'Stilettos.'

'Check.'

'Diamond g-string.'

'Check.'

'Bath towel.'

'Check.'

'Fans.'

'Check.'

'Dress.'

'Check.'

'Liberace coat.'

'Check.'

'Let's go!' and off they whisked towards the stage with military precision, grinning from ear to ear. A wave of excitement surged through Tiger Starr as they left the dressing room and she hopped up *en pointe* in anticipation, her arches like taut little semi-circles in her ballet shoes. These were precious final minutes to psyche up for her opening night.

'Mario, get outta my hair,' she pleaded as the Italian hovered about her, pushing more pins through her curls. Tiger was purely focused on channelling her energy, and she couldn't care less about hair grips right now. Pre-show anxiety was a feeling Tiger had trained herself to embrace, and feel comforted by. Nerves gave her a mean adrenalin hit, which always gave her the edge when she made her entrance. Tonight she most definitely wanted her show to go that extra inch – for she had all her chips riding on this one.

Tonight her first number would be her infamous 'reverse strip'. Inspired by the late, great, burlesque star Lili St Cyr, with whom Tiger's grandmother Coco Schnell used to perform, it involved Tiger actually putting her clothes on, rather than peeling them off. People travelled miles to see the spectacle, especially as from the audience's vantage point, Tiger – ever the tease – never quite showed everything. Of course there was always the hope in people's minds that tonight her bath towel might slip just that little too much, and occasionally an overzealous fan would convince himself he had caught a rare glimpse of 'landing strip', but in reality Tiger's diamond-encrusted merkin was always firmly in place to preserve her last bastion of mystique. As far as Tiger Starr was concerned, that was the art of the true showgirl – to be mysterious, otherworldly and untouchable for mere mortals. If that meant people thought she grew diamonds down there, then that was just perfect.

For the show's big finale Tiger would lay on her *pièce de resistance*, playing the part of a 1940s *femme fatale* vixen on her giant vintage glitter telephone with spinning dial, accompanied by the 'Starrlets', her gorgeous troupe of sparkling, leggy chorus girls who paraded, slinked and kicked in exquisite symmetry around her. For Tiger's final dénouement, the Starrlets all posed on stuffed black panthers that had been automated to rear up and roar for the crescendo, baring their porcelain fangs. It was a camp fantasy that made *Lawrence of Arabia* look like a low-budget student pilot.

Tonight, standing in her dressing room, Tiger was as radiant and as ready for her close-up as ever. 'Blue, honey, whaddya think?' she asked her stylist with puppy dog eyes, reaching for a compulsive squirt of Chanel No. 5. Before each show Tiger would seek Blue's approval as a matter of course; not that she really needed it, but Tiger was curiously modest about her considerable charms. If only she saw in the mirror what others saw, she would realise that she could make a bin liner look like *haute couture*.

'You're stunning, darling,' answered Blue, giving Tiger the once over. 'I must say the boys are looking breathtaking tonight,' he sighed, ripping his eyes away from the sight of her incredible tits to smile at her reassuringly. Slowly he surveyed the towering glamazon standing before him. He took in her firm caramel skin, her miniscule waist spreading into full rounded hips. She had legs that could only be described as a masterpiece – long enough to reach her armpits, with powerful thighs strong enough to crack a pistachio nut. Her large, pert breasts, dressed with the most eye-wateringly expensive diamond-encrusted nipple tassels had the kind of delicious weighty bounce to them that was the preserve of only the most natural of assets. Her make-up accentuated her striking features, making her lips even more pillowy, her eyes more cat-like. Even her hair, cascading into her trademark powder-pink curls, looked as if it would have smelled of delicate rose powder. Put simply, she dazzled.

This was what Blue lived for. He had decided many years ago that what *he* lacked in physical beauty, he lived to hone in others. Although as a tall, strapping beefcake with a soft effeminate accent, a striking face often diplomatically described as characterful, and a garnish of impeccably designed stubble, he was pretty hard to miss in a room himself. He and Tiger had met seven or eight years ago when Blue was the reigning queen and Fashion Editor of *Below* magazine. He had decided to shoot her for a 'La Dolce Vita'-inspired story. Needless to say they had clicked as though they had known each other for a lifetime.

Blue ended up putting Tiger on the cover. When Blue had been usurped by a bitter rival, followed by the spreading of one too many vicious rumours alleging plagiarism and an all-round lack of talent for Blue to have any hope of finding another job in the industry, it was Tiger who had come to his rescue like an angel out of the mist. She had offered him a full-time job as her personal stylist and wardrobe mistress, and Blue was thrilled to have a welcome niche in which to let his true creative talents shine, away from the incessantly fickle politics of the fashion industry. Even though Blue found joining Tiger's hard-working team to be a thoroughly warm and fluffy experience, he had experienced one or two 'entry difficulties' in his professional relationship with Tiger's manager, Lewis Bond. But over the years, Lewis and Blue had developed a grudging respect for each other. Blue now lived with Tiger in the Diana Dors wing of her Regency London mansion, as much her confidante and occasional dog-walker as her professional eyes and ears. Tiger was without doubt his best friend; an honour for Blue, knowing how cautious she was about who she allowed into her inner sanctum. Although he had also seen many times just how generous she was with anyone she thought she could lend a hand to.

'Well, if Lewis doesn't crack a smile tonight at the sight of you then squeeze me into a unitard and call me a eunuch,' sighed Blue. 'C'mon, Mario, let's go sit with him out front and get him in the mood.'

'Oh god, Lewis! Where's he sitting?' Tiger quivered.

'Oh, he's charming the guests as usual, darling. Last time I looked he was taking care of Dianne Castrelli and the rest of the Vegas scouts; stage left, four rows back.' Blue knew that Tiger lived to please her manager. Lewis Bond was her biggest support – and her harshest critic. In fact, he was the only person in existence who could turn Tiger to ash at a glance, but then after fourteen years of working together, they understood each other like no one else.

'You just do your breathing, babe, get in your head-space,' said Blue with a comforting pat on her bum.

'Oh god, I'm on edge now. Did you pop your head in on the Starrlets? They happy?' asked Tiger uneasily. 'You gave them their first-night gifts?'

'Stop worrying, will you? Lewis' girlfriend has got them all fired up.'

'Georgia? Hmm, I'm sure she has. I bet she got Lewis fired up too while she was at it.' Tiger tried to see the good in everyone but even she sometimes wondered what her manager saw in such an arrogant and predatory girl like Georgia Atlanta. Each to their own she supposed. She could tolerate Georgia as long as she made Lewis happy – and as long as she left her attitude at the dressing room door and danced her arse off on stage. That was all that really mattered to Tiger.

'Right, I'm off. Enjoy it, darling!' trilled Blue, clapping his hands together with finality. 'It's gonna be a helluva show! The Starrlets look delectable. And as for you, my darling? Well, you could just stand up there and *fart* and they'd be cheering with you looking like that! Hey – you okay?' Blue stared at Tiger, concerned.

'Fine!' she laughed. 'Now bugger off!'

'But, babe, you look like you're going to be sick. Are you sure you're okay? You're not – *nervous* are you?'

'I'm just peachy,' reassured Tiger. 'That smoked salmon I had for breakfast must have been a little sketchy. I'm fine. Now scoot!'

'Okay, my darling, if you're sure. See you out there. Break a nail!'

As Blue and Mario disappeared excitedly to stake their seats in the audience, Tiger swiftly shut herself in her dressing room and leaned against the door to steady her wobbling ankles. Darn! She never liked anyone – even Blue who saw more than most – to see just how terribly nervous she got in the last couple of minutes. She gently reminded herself that the day the butterflies stop should be the day a true performer quits the job. Nerves were the one true mark that you really cared about your performance. She'd always thought that a performer without nerves was either arrogant or bored – or smashed – and what audience wants to see any of those on stage? As Tiger leaned at the door, she closed her eyes and used her final moments to take some slow, deep breaths, a generous slug of gin and tonic, and to channel the spirit of her idol, the queen of showbiz himself, Liberace. She would need him watching over her tonight, she thought, with the knowledge that the Vegas scouts and the entire population of London's critics were in the audience for her grand opening. She prayed her publicist, Rex, was out there entertaining them with his usual charm.

Rex Hunter had gone to the trouble of arranging the Royal box with waitresses proffering chilled Krug for the celebrities who were now taking their seats around him. The journalists he had stuck down in the press pit along with Tiger's younger sister, Sienna, who had just joined his PR agency, Hunter Gatherers, as his assistant. Any hack would be cynical if Rex tried the champagne treatment on with them – there was no point trying to butter them up. No, much more subtle to leave them with Sienna, who was down there happily flashing her long legs like a trooper. Whilst Sienna wasn't quite as gorgeous and enchanting company as Tiger – few women were in Rex's opinion – she did at least share some of her big sister's good genes. And she could turn on the charm – when she wanted to.

The press were certainly out in full force tonight, Rex thought, pleased with himself; all the dailies, the news channels, even the long leads, all waiting for Tiger Starr's latest offering. Rex would swoop on them in the interval when most of them would make a bid for freedom to file their copy and catch the next story of the evening.

In a way Tiger made his job easy. Her bold, sexy and unashamedly glamorous show was easily the hottest ticket in town. When Lewis Bond had first brought his new client to Rex for a PR strategy over a decade ago, Tiger Starr's reputation had preceded her; Rex had already heard whispers of the new girl on the block who was dancing and disrobing for princes, billionaires and movie stars. Considering few people under sixty had even heard of burlesque at the time, she was certainly whipping up quite a storm. But then, Tiger Starr was no mere burlesque dancer. She was a true star as her name suggested; a bombshell who exuded heat on a nuclear scale.

As Rex surveyed the press pit below, he noticed trouble in the form of one journalist, Lance de Brett. A caustic bugger on a good day, Lance had taken to sharpening his claws for Tiger's reviews, especially over the last year or so. Rex often wondered if he was one of these men whose dick shrivelled when faced with a powerful woman – after all, attack is known to be the best form of defence. Still, Rex's twenty years as a publicist had also taught him there were some journalists who had simply raised cynicism to an art form, and if Lance had just watched Jesus walking on water he'd have certainly given him a bad review for not swimming. A shame then, thought Rex soberly, that the bastard could still make or break a London show. Lance had given *Saddam the Musical* five stars in the *Telegraph* and the bloody thing was still running two years later. In a funny kind of way Rex was slightly in awe of Lance's unapologetic wickedness; it had clearly taken him all the way as a journalist.

'Careful! Take your foot off my dress! Who's got my drink?' a thick, Italian New York accent interrupted Rex's thoughts. Turning his head, he was knocked out by the sight of the infamous Libertina Belle, being escorted by at least six waiters, literally falling over themselves to help her to her seat. Perking up, Rex was suddenly pleased he had dressed for the occasion. With a deep olive tan and thick, dark hair now sun-kissed courtesy of a recent trip to the Bahamas, along with his toned stocky frame encased in slick Saville Row tailoring, Rex had definitely noticed more than the usual number of heads turning on his way to the theatre. He just knew the effort wouldn't be wasted on the immaculate Libertina Belle. Of course Rex didn't normally go for actresses – too devoid of personality he had always found. But there was something delightfully raw and brassy about Libertina Belle in person, despite her astounding classic beauty and the on-screen sophistication that suggested otherwise. Libertina was the first woman he had felt pure animal attraction for since . . . well, since Tiger. But since clients were strictly off limits, a rule Rex adhered to steadfastly, Tiger would always have to remain his favourite secret fantasy. But Libertina . . . she was fair game ready to be poached.

'Oi! Belle!' hissed Rex above the bubbling chatter from below.

'Rex! Baby, I had a funny feeling we'd see each other this evening,' winked Libertina as she took her seat.

'Ah well, aren't you the lucky lady.'

'So how's business, dahling?' Libertina fluffed her long raven hair and swilled back her Krug like a footballer's wife. 'Not bad, judging by the world's paps outside, hmmm?'

'Business is always good, babe,' boomed Rex. 'You're looking good for the cameras too, loving the hair wavy like that, babe. Fiery, like you.' He leaned in and continued in a hushed tone, 'Although you're looking a little tired – you should slow down on the work, babe, you know it can be a poison chalice being as in demand as you are.'

A flash of indignity blazed in Libertina's hazel brown eyes at this remark; Rex just relaxed and beamed care and concern back at her. Bingo. He always liked to make a really rude remark to a woman he fancied – he found this little trick made them feel insecure and eager to win him over by the end of the night.

'So, anyway! I keep hearing all about Tiger Staaaaarr back home,' drawled Libertina, changing the subject graciously, like a true pro. 'She's making waves from across the pond alright. I can't wait to see her performing in all her glory. I met her during New York Fashion Week last season and god, Rex, she looked amaaazing. The woman's a goddess!' she gasped. 'Oh Rex, look there's Elton on the other side, daaamn! He has his own box! Look, over there, Rex. You didn't say he was coming.'

'Oh didn't you know, Tiger's playing for a huge Vegas

deal tonight with the new Luxuriana Grande! Well, Elton had to come check her out of course, seeing as her show could be across the Strip from his this time next year!'

'Wow! That's incredible! Good for her! Oh, Rex, you have to take me over to Elton in the interval!'

'Anything, Libertina, anything,' murmured Rex.

Pulling his gaze from her glossy pouting lips Rex surveyed the buzzing crowd settled below. The scene was certainly set. Tiger had done well to get her show on here, thought Rex with sincere admiration. This was probably one of the most beautifully fitted theatres in Europe in fact, and originally built specifically to stage the works of Gilbert and Sullivan. But tonight's show would be worlds away from the opera.

The house lights began to dim. Soft murmurs of 'shh, shh' wafted on the air, amplifying the palpable excitement. Rex shifted around in his red velvet seat and started to wring his hands. Libertina squeezed Rex's shoulder from behind and leaned in, sloshing the last of her icy Krug down the back of his blazer.

'God, I feel nervous for Tiger. Make sure she comes out for the after party, I'd love to meet her again,' she whispered loudly in his ear before settling back in her seat.

Rex pictured Tiger waiting backstage right now, knowing how tense she would be, and he willed her to do well. If she pulled it off tonight and got the Vegas deal, that would mean everything to her. He crossed his fingers out of sight and focused on the velvet curtain ahead.

The heavy red swags parted. The first deafening brass stabs leapt from the twenty-piece big band arranged on stage. As the music swelled, the thousand-strong audience let out a huge appreciative gasp as a cascade of glittering showgirls poured from the wings, bobbing their way uniformly across the stage to the beat, led by their striking Viking-esque dance captain, Georgia. Each girl was poured into a 1950s-style gold lamé swimsuit with cutaways to show their glorious breasts, the ensemble topped off with a sparkling gold swimming cap. On stage, Barry, the first trumpet, could be seen cowering as the army of pneumatic, nipple-tasselled showgirls advanced on him with vigour.

Underneath the stage, wedged uncomfortably in the elevator underneath the trap door, trussed up in her glamorous Hollywood bedtime attire, Tiger's stomach churned. She hated this wait, she always felt she needed the bathroom right about . . . now.

'Ladies and gentlemen,' came the voice of God announcement, cutting through the excited gasps and rendering the audience rapt, 'welcome to the Savoy Theatre! Without further ado, please welcome on stage the star of this evening's show! She's the ultimate bombshell! She's our own national treasure! She's the incomparable, the one and only . . . Tigerrrrrr Starrrrrrr!'

The last words were lost as the crowd erupted in to something like the cheer that went up when Arsenal had slaughtered Chelsea the previous week. As the platform slowly rose, bringing Tiger up onto the stage through a haze of dry ice, the heat from the spotlight hit her instantly like the comforting rays of the sun. She trembled *en pointe* like the wings of a majestic butterfly as she felt the vibrations from a thousand pairs of hands clapping and feet stamping the floor, whilst her chorus girls paraded round her glass-fronted slipper bath on the central plinth. Looking out from the stage, Tiger was blinded by the lights, her audience merely a smoky chasm of black beyond the first two rows. A hit of adrenalin coursed through her as she elegantly fluttered across the plinth before stretching her strong gleaming legs into a positively leisurely arabesque. Immediately drawing her audience in with her feline gaze, she playfully prepared to take her bath, twinkling on tippy toe as she teased off her diaphanous bathrobe and satin corset, before bending over in a most suggestively supple manner to loosen the silky ribbons of her ballet slippers and reveal her cute red-painted toes. She beamed into the crowd, inwardly thanking her stars that she couldn't see the faces out there, especially tonight.

Fourth row from the front, slouched deep in his velvet seat and sporting his usual pinstripes, black Brylcreemed hair and a stubbled jawline that was more accident than design, Tiger's manager Lewis felt a tic start in his cheek, adding to his general air of a brooding Mafiosi. He kept one eye on the poker faces of the Luxuriana Grande scouts, hoping to detect a hint of a reaction. The deafening cheers of the glamorous crowds did little to sate him. Annoyingly, Lewis could hear Blue gushing on about the costumes right in the next seat, grating on him like a buzzing fly. Grabbing the nearest thing to hand, he jabbed his Mont Blanc pen violently into Blue's side, silencing him swiftly.

Flicking his attention to the stage Lewis watched Tiger carefully. He registered a spark of fire brimming in her eyes, detectable only to someone who had worked with her for a very long time. He knew she had entered what she called 'the zone' and he relaxed his shoulders a fraction. Lewis squinted as he scrutinised the Starrlets intently; a long line of shapely limbs multiplied and refracted across the stage. Ah, Georgia. His latest platinum-blonde fuck, up there leading the troupe; leaping into an effortless *jeté* with those long, long legs. An effusive dance captain, great on stage. No presence, but god she could dance. And boy could she give great head ... it was about the only time she shut up, he thought ruefully. If only she weren't so damn skinny. Lewis looked sideways at his Vegas guests to see a few of them scribbling furiously. Tapping his foot nervously in time with the drummer he forced his attention back to the magnificent scene unfolding on stage.

Streams of iridescent bubbles floated and winked around Tiger as she splashed about in her bath to the rhythm of

'Harlem Nocturne'. The frosted glass panel in the bath made no question of her nudity. With one hand Tiger lightly traced the silhouette of her breast. Arch the back! she reminded herself, exercising every last vertebrae to squealing point. As bubbles floated past her she burst them at her fingertips as the music swelled into a voluptuous chorus. On cue, she sank deep into the tub. Keeping her head carefully above the shallow water, she kicked up her legs into a vertical position, just as her thirty Starrlets took their positions too, synchronising with each of her carefully choreographed leg movements.

Waves of applause rolled over them as Tiger and her chorus girls expertly scissor kicked, posed, stretched, swam, and cycled their legs rhythmically through the crescendo with fountains of water jetting up into the air behind them, programmed in time with each kick and every crash of the cymbals. From her position down in the bath Tiger blinked repeatedly with the spray from the fountains and the glare from the lighting rigs above her. Holding her legs gracefully above her head in a muscle-burning splits position and counting the beats with gritted jaw, she wondered if she had remembered to leave some food out for her little terrier, Gravy. And breathe! she reminded herself as she emerged from the tub into full view with a glowing smile, kicking her feet playfully amongst the bubbles.

The Starrlets moved into a new tableau, preparing for Tiger to rise from her tub like a majestic Venus from her shell. With one hand Tiger clasped her fluffy bath towel across her front and tantalisingly patted herself dry. With the other hand she slid on her sparkling g-string in one long smooth movement, slipping it inch by inch over her taut thighs. With her back to the audience she dropped the towel as the g-string settled into the crease of her peachy buttocks. A cheer went up in the theatre. Facing the band nude like this, Tiger raised an eyebrow and shook her breasts as a playful 'hello'. A couple of bum notes rang out from the brass section. Pete on the double bass patted his heart faintly between strums. No matter how many times they saw Tiger's saucy flash, she never lost her ability to thrill.

Tiger knew now to step up the pace. She covered herself in fans of thick ostrich plumes and descended her plinth. Joined by a chorus of thirty flapping wings behind her she revealed and concealed her glorious hourglass figure, using the feathers to tantalise with the kind of expertise that made the enormous fans appear to be weightlessly and flirtatiously caressing her. In fact they were excruciatingly heavy, with a twelve-foot wingspan. They often gave her cramps in her hands, but she would never let the audience see that. She rotated the fans in turn through the air above her head in seamless figures of eight, then drew them fluttering slowly over her form. She used them as majestic peacock tails, cheekily revealing her *derriére*, but always using one of the fans to carefully conceal the right parts, constantly teasing. Diamond powder shimmered in the lights as it fluttered from the feathers with each swish. The audience sat in awed silence.

Tiger's sister Sienna sat in the press pit, impatiently tapping her foot. Just how did Tiger manage to make it seem as though you were in a room with her on your own, she wondered. Just as the *Mona Lisa* appeared to smile at you from anywhere in the room, Tiger always seemed to be shaking her breasts just for your eyes only. Their parents might have been ashamed of the way Tiger made her living and Sienna was certainly never one to give her sister credit, but even she had to admit Tiger was pretty awe-inspiring up there on stage. Sienna was also loath to acknowledge that she wouldn't mind some more curves of her own, but nonetheless found herself unfastening the top button of her blouse and rearranging the fabric to show some of her own cleavage. This was particularly out of character since she had always endeavoured to hide her bustiness throughout school. Yet now as she fiddled absent-mindedly with her blouse she wondered what it would feel like to be up there under the lights, holding the audience rapt. She did have longer legs than Tiger after all, she thought sniffily, even though she had been mercilessly teased at school for being way too knockery and completely out of proportion with her long scrawny limbs. Of course, Sienna would never, in her eyes, 'lower herself' to Tiger's antics on stage, but imagining herself up there was preferable to the reality of being stuck down here with all the bad-tempered journalists while her boss got to swig champagne in the Royal box with the celebs. Talk about being in Tiger's shadow . . . literally.

Sienna sighed as her eyes grazed across the crowded gathering of photographers, and dutifully checked they weren't taking any more shots. The protocol dictated that they were only ever allowed the first three minutes of a show to get their pictures, so that the artistes on stage could then relax into the performance and concentrate on pleasing their audience rather than thinking about their best angles for press shots and being blinded by flashguns. Sienna could see a couple of the photographers now gripping their cameras tensely, clearly frustrated by the myriad forbidden photo opportunities on stage as Tiger weaved her magic spell. As a ripple of gasps swept across the audience behind her, Sienna grudgingly stared back up at her sister.

Tiger was on the homeward strait and unleashing the full might of her seductive wiles as she dressed sensually for her audience in stockings, heels and her magnificent Dior cocktail dress, before mounting the riser for her final reveal. Her dancers had arranged themselves about her with their fans held in such a way as to entirely frame her beautiful face with enormous flower petals of ostrich feather. One by one and in quick succession the girls whisked away the fans for the final reveal. There stood Tiger rising from a sea of gold and fountains, draped in her final layer; the most colossal arrangement of rich pink feathers and ruffles, a replica of a cape Liberace had originally worn for his grand exit from a Fabergé egg back in the 1960s. With a flourish she swept open the cloak like a soaring bird to expose a lining entirely made of the fluffiest, floatiest feather fronds. Audience members in the first row caught a waft of Chanel No. 5 on the breeze.

On the blackout a cheer erupted like an explosion as the audience jumped to their feet to applaud. Oh lordy, thought Tiger, allowing herself some breathless panting while concealed by the blackout, they're already on their feet and they've got the rest of the show yet. Keep going, girl! As the spotlights found her, she held her breath, switched on the megawatt smile and took her bow, as poised as if she'd hardly lifted a finger. My god, I think Liberace is actually smiling upon us right now, thought Tiger, proudly holding her shoulders back and chest out for her first standing ovation of the evening.

Chapter 2

'You were only giving it ninety-nine per cent. It's not good enough. I need one hundred and ten per cent.'

'Look, I know I almost lost my footing near the phone, but—'

'You can't afford to operate at ninety-nine per cent. It has to be perfect, you know it makes all the difference.'

'Well, the audience were with me all the way—'

'That's a bullshit argument, Tiger. You shouldn't have slipped, for crying out loud, what were you thinking?'

'Oh come on – the bubbles from the bath had made the stage slippery! The stage clearly wasn't swabbed properly between numbers. I didn't stand a chance! It's not like I went down, thank god. No one even noticed but you – no thanks to your fabulous stage manager.'

'Not only that, Tiger, I could even see you breathing in the second number.'

'Is this a joke—'

'Listen, I don't want to see you out of breath up there. It should always look effortless, and that takes a lot of work! You have to work harder. Keep your mind sharp up there—'

'Lewis, come on! I worked so hard out there! I performed

my heart out! Those smiles were all genuine. Sorry three standing ovations clearly aren't enough for you.'

'You think this is about me? You've got it wrong, lady, this is for your benefit, not mine. And it's always been that way, make no mistake. I could just fuck off home and count the money. No, this is for your own good. I'm the only one who cares about you enough to tell you that wasn't your best performance.'

'Oh! You care! That's a new excuse for always tearing me apart! Well, you'd better be a good Samaritan in that case, and enlighten me – what *was* my best performance?'

'You haven't done it yet. You have to aim higher every time.'

'That's such a typical answer from you!'

'It's only right to tell you the truth. It's why we've come so far. You can't take your eye off the ball for a second. I only hope the Vegas lot didn't see that slip.'

'But . . . but that was a great show and you know it was good, you w-w-w . . .'

'Look, if you don't listen to what I'm saying then you don't deserve to do well. Do you understand that? This is all for your benefit you know. You can't afford to drop the detail for a nanosecond, it's what put you at the top, and it's what's keeping you here. You think you have no competition out there by now?'

'Oh, you wouldn't be referring to your charming girlfriend Georgia by any chance, would you?'

'Well—'

'Have you started wondering if maybe your ageing good looks aren't the only reason she made a beeline for you?'

'How dare you! She's not like that. And anyway, you're the one who handpicked her at auditions. I'm just saying there's always going to be someone newer and younger snapping at your heels, that's all.'

'No shit, Sherlock! I'm not worried about the competition. You might also have noticed that all the best dancers in the country are in *my* troupe! And like you said yourself, I put them there! So do I look like I'm the type to waste time getting anxious about n-new girls?'

'I'm just saying—'

'Oh, for god's sake, I c-can't deal with a post-show assassination barely five minutes after I've taken my bow. This is just so unfair! I can't think s-s-straight.'

'Great, now you're getting upset. I thought you were always the tough one, remember?'

'I'm *fine* th-thank you.'

'Let's just continue with this tomorrow. I'll give Pepper comprehensive notes for your rehearsal session in the morning. I'm off to the lobby to listen in on what the punters are saying, and I won't be at the after party. I've asked Georgia to make sure the girls don't drink alcohol under any circumstances. I also want you to get an early night. You have a heavy workload tomorrow before the next show and Rex has interviews lined up he'll tell you about. Oh, and by the way, there's a queue of fans building up outside the stage door in the cold for you. You might pull yourself together before you go down – stuttering in front of fans is not a good look.'

'Fucking hell, doll, I thought this was meant to be an after party, not a bloody autograph line-up,' moaned Rex, crunching on an ice cube irritably as his eyes darted about the packed lounge at L'Homard.

'You're my publicist. You should be pleased with your handiwork!' teased Tiger, handing a pen and freshly auto-graphed paper to the barman, just as Georgia, Frankie and Nikki staggered giggling from the bar towards the rest of the Starrlets, still in their seamed dance tights and clutching illicit bright blue cocktails. Tiger rolled her eyes to the heavens, and savoured her dirty Martini with deli-cate sips. She felt Rex's gaze still on her.

'You seen the ol' tank commando tonight? I'm surprised he's not here,' Rex probed.

'Who, Lewis? Oh you know him, why go to a party when there's more work that could be done!' laughed Tiger. 'Anyway he doesn't like it here, thinks it's too vulgar,' she mumbled, giving a cursory nod at the enor-mous giraffe head protruding from the gold-fringed velvet behind her.

'So he didn't want to at least raise a glass to you for pulling off an amazing show?' persisted Rex.

'Oh, he already came to see me in the dressing room back there.' Tiger had no intention of discussing Lewis's blow-by-blow critique of every aspect of her performance.

It was clear though that that her nonchalance wasn't fooling anyone, least of all a street-smart operator like Rex.

'Right,' he said with a dead-pan smile. 'That was just before you came to the stage door with puffy eyes?'

'Oh that – no I just got eyelash glue in my eye—'

'Oh cut the crap, I've heard you both at it hammer and tongs after the shows. Every time he – what does he call it – "gives you notes". Notes! Excuse for him to lay into you if you ask me.'

'No, no, you don't understand. Lewis just tells me the truth. He always has my interests at heart you know, I mean, we've travelled a long road together—'

'Look, there's quite a difference between constructive criticism and a gratuitous slagging, you know.'

'Okay, so the critique can get a bit relentless, I admit that.'

'So tell him to fuck off.'

'I can't! Try and see it from Lewis' point of view. He just assumes I listen to people telling me I'm a star, I'm fabulous, I'm this, I'm that, all the time. But you know me, I'm shy. I'm my own worst critic, and I don't hear the compliments. I don't think Lewis realises that. I think he sees his role as keeping me level headed.'

'Or bringing you down a peg or two. He's a bully.'

'No! He just has my interests at heart.'

Rex gave a cynical little snort. 'He's a control freak, babes. Let me tell you a secret. You know what all the stage crew say when they're working with other celebrities?

They ask, "So how bad's the manager, on a scale of one to Lewis Bond"?'

Tiger gasped and stifled a giggle. 'That's his job! Oh, darling, Lewis has been honing the "nasty gatekeeper" act for years! Duh! He's exactly the kind of manager every gal needs!'

'Really? You sure about that? Don't think the Starrlets didn't hear him kicking off at you earlier.'

'Oh right. News travels fast. I'll bet that came from Georgia. She probably had a bloody glass up against the wall listening in, cheering him on from the sidelines. Now if you *really* want to talk about control freaks—' Tiger leaned in to wave a manicured finger in front of Rex's bemused face '—from what Blue's told me that Georgia Atlanta's just Thatcher on rollerskates. She already has Lewis well and truly under the thumb!'

'Nah, she's harmless, babe. Just a stupid bit of fluff trapped in a supermodel's body. Just what kind of dumbass broad would choose Georgia Atlanta as a stage name, especially when her family are all Swedish, for Chrissake? Anyway, don't change the subject. Now listen to me.' Rex held Tiger's hand. 'You're a strong woman. But Lewis gets to you and you go soft as butter.'

'Okay, red card. You take that back. Anyway, I don't discuss *you* with Lewis. So I'm not going to start discussing Lewis with you. Can we just move on now? I was finally starting to enjoy myself and now this.' Tiger snatched her hand back.

'I'm only saying—'

'Please! No more work talk. And definitely not here in front of everyone. I've obviously already got bloody Georgia earwigging everything, it's humiliating. I'd like to keep the remains of my privacy if that's okay with you.'

An uncomfortable silence between the pair was drowned out by screeches and squeals of laughter as the party continued around them. Frankie and Nikki were now balanced precariously on one of the antique gold-leaf tables, performing a rousing accompaniment to Donna Summer's 'I Feel Love' to whoops and cheers from the backstage crew who had a cracking view up their skirts.

This was always Tiger's venue of choice for an after-show party. A members' club of the less pretentious kind, its glamour was of the most gloriously faded variety. Named after the infamous Dali telephone, L'Homard was crammed with exquisite bad taste, much like the artist himself, thought Tiger. An antique table-top held up entirely with empty stacked tortoiseshells nestled next to enormous gilt bird cages and diamond-encrusted animals, both of the plastic Bambi variety, as well as vintage taxidermy. Tiger's favourite was a large stuffed old British bulldog with wings. Hopelessly un-p.c., but you could hardly argue with something that had met its maker 150 years ago. At least it had been immortalised rather than left pushing up daisies. Floor to ceiling swags of sea green velvet and strings of tarnished pearls hugged the walls, practically holding themselves up with the dust and nicotine of an entire century. The ghosts of a thousand luvvies, drunks, and *bon viveurs* kept the place beguiling and homely; a good thing, since there was always a lot of adrenalin flying around after a show that needed dissipating and it was a sure bet that the club had seen much worse behaviour over the years than even Tiger could imagine. Hell, Oscar Wilde even had his own plaque of honour in the gents toilet – not that she had actually been to see it for herself.

'So who was that funny little guy waiting for you at the stage door back there?' asked Rex, ignoring the revellers.

'Johnnie? He's always there. Well, he's not actually called Johnnie . . . I don't know his name, but they call them stage-door Johnnies, you know. When they turn up at the stage door I mean—'

'Yeah, yeah, I may not live and breathe the theatre like you but I know that much. Christ. I've never seen this Johnnie guy before.'

'That's because you don't usually turn up to my shows unless some hot actress is coming who you fancy your chances with.'

'Not true . . .'

'Anyway, for your information, Johnnie's at every gig.'

'Every single one?'

'Religiously. Like, he must plan his whole diary around them. He came to see me on the Côte D'Azur, in Russia, LA, New York, – he even turned up in Sydney. Ask Lewis about it.'

'Woah. For real?'

'For real. He must spend every penny on it.' Tiger knew she had a colourful collection of devoted fans from far and wide, and Johnnie was the most conscientious by a long chalk. Tiger often felt guilty that he went to such lengths to visit her every show and often wondered if she should be offering him some kind of 'Loyalty Points' scheme; a signed picture for every London gig, a pair of worn silk stockings for Europe, front row seats for the Americas, perhaps ... One of Tiger's old burlesque pals and mentors, the willowy Mink Coates, used to give her stage door Johnnies 'exclusive' g-strings she claimed to have worn during her performance. What Mink didn't tell her fans of course, was that she actually kept a stash of cheap Soho sex-shop-bought g-strings under her dresser, the crotches of which she'd give a cursory rub on her French bulldog's chops before packaging them nicely in tissue paper to give away. It caught up with Mink one day when she was pursued as she left the theatre by one of her regulars, furiously demanding to know why his g-string was covered in white animal hairs. Needless to say she shrugged it off coolly as she wafted past, flagrantly dragging her black-and-white bulldog behind her and drawling as only she could: 'I'm Mink Coates honey, one hundred per fuckin' cent. What did ya expect me to have down there? Pubes or something?'

Tiger had simply adored Mink and had looked up to her – she had a good twenty years on Tiger but boy was she a siren – she was pure old school in that respect. An enigmatic tease with as much class as brass, she just knew how to wrap any man around her little finger. Young Tiger had worshipped her as one of the last in the breed of true old-school broads. She often wondered what had happened to her; Mink had left on a farewell tour bound for Moscow ten years ago, never to be seen again. Lewis used to joke that the Russians were big on fur and maybe she had been poached. But Tiger had often wistfully fantasised that she was living in the lap of luxury as some oligarch's object of fantasy. Lord knows she deserved some pampering after her many years of slogging it out under the hot lights.

'I like Johnnie,' declared Tiger, breaking from her fond memories. 'Being a devoted fan makes him happy, he always has a cheeky grin at the stage door. Such a sweet guy.'

'Hmm,' Rex mused. 'How do you know?'

'Know what?'

'That he's a sweet guy.'

'I just know! He always brings flowers, and he always wears a smile. Plus he's polite, you know, a real gentleman which makes a change.'

'Hah! Those are the ones you can't trust.' Rex flashed his most beguiling smile and popped a fat green olive into his mouth.

Tiger took a moment to look twice at Rex, holding back on a bitingly sarcastic retort, but her thoughts were interrupted as her eyes settled on the exquisite Libertina Belle. A vision in cobalt-blue Lacroix, she was ploughing her way through the crowd majestically, like Moses parting the Red Sea, tresses flowing like a raven-haired Botticelli figure.

'I knew I'd find you two at the bar! Tiger, dahhhling! You divine creature, my goddess. Su-perb!' she gasped.

'Ms Belle . . . *bellissima*!' Tiger declared, breathlessly air kissing the actress as Rex snapped to attention beside her.

'I believe we've met, darling. New York, remember?'

'How could I not!' replied Tiger coyly. 'You were wearing an original Dior New Look!'

'Wow, the girl knows her style too!' Libertina laughed appreciatively. 'Listen, Tiger baby, you were radiant tonight – no, bea-uuutiful. Dahling, you simply had everyone in the palm of your hand! Exquisite.'

'I wouldn't mind being in the palm of your hand, babe,' muttered Rex out of her range. Tiger jammed her stiletto into his foot. She had always been a great fan of Libertina Belle; a stunning actress from the same artist's easel as Monica Bellucci, who had risen from the ranks of trashy television drama to become fully fledged, bona fide Hollywood aristocracy. Tiger was extremely pleased to be on Libertina's radar as, ever modest, Tiger was still star struck around all her celebrity fans, and she certainly wasn't about to watch as Rex peddled his crap chat-up lines at the foot of screen royalty.

'Thanks, Libertina, I really appreciate your compliments,' Tiger declared with sincerity, having been secretly stinging after the slating from Lewis.

'Don't be silly, credit where it's due! That enormous vintage telephone, my gawd, how camp is that! How the hell do you get up there?! You certainly give new meaning to "on the phone",' Libertina roared at her own joke.

'Thanks!' laughed Tiger. 'It's a beast though, you know. It's high up sitting on that receiver and you know I hate heights. It really hurts my knees too, you should check out the bruises!' She felt an immediate affinity with Libertina, just as she had from their first meeting on the party circuit months ago. Tiger certainly never disclosed any behind the scenes secrets to any of her fans; that her performances involved any kind of effort, exertion, sweat or, heaven forbid, *bruises*. To show her human side was far too revealing – and Tiger usually steered well clear of intimacy like that. She could see Libertina obviously had the art of putting people at their ease down to a tee.

'Lemme tell ya, Tiger, women like us have to indulge the myth that we just appear out of nowhere like some permanently made up, primped and preened wet dream – heavens, I should know!' Libertina laughed vivaciously, flicking her mane away from her magnificent cleavage and holding Tiger's gaze intensely, just a moment too long. Rex crossed his legs as his eyes darted quickly between the two insanely glamorous women. It didn't take a rocket scientist to work out what was going through his mind as he watched them together.

'Well, I appreciate the feedback from an amazing performer like yourself—' Tiger started.

'Oh yes, dahling,' enthused Libertina, 'please, let's do the mutual appreciation thing. Listen, why don't we do numbers. Take my card, call me direct on my cell ... maybe when you fancy a bit more appreciation, huh?'

'Oh – oh of course, yes that would be great I'll – err – great! Let's do lunch!' Tiger blustered, suddenly coming over all bashful. If she wasn't mistaken, she felt a pang of desire. Tiger didn't usually find herself attracted to women, but then Libertina wasn't just any woman.

'Lunch? Oh I could think of something a bit cosier than lunch,' continued Libertina. 'Well, you have my number, it's your call. Use that big telephone of yours, hahaha! *Ciao bella bella*,' and with that Libertina Belle left the building.

Tiger barely had a chance to fan her flushed cheeks before Blue suddenly appeared like Elvis at a burger bar. 'Tiger! Did I just see the divine Ms Belle giving you her card!' came his excited voice piercing through the background rabble.

'Tiger just got what I think is commonly termed as "picked up",' explained Rex.

'Don't be ridiculous, she was being friendly!' snapped Tiger, aware that her stomach was awash with butterflies.

'Yeah right, she wants to talk feathers and tit tape,' said Rex petulantly, running his fingers through his thick hair, agitated. 'She was all over you like a cheap suit, Tiger.'

'Ooh, blow me, I never had Libertina Belle down as a lab technician,' cut in Blue. 'I'd always seen her out with men – h'mmm, such a great tit job, too. I thought it was all for the benefit of the boys.'

'No way!' exclaimed Tiger protectively. 'Those breasts are natural. I'm a woman, I can tell these things. There was no ridge at the top.'

'Oh Tiger, sweetheart, that's because she probably had them put in *over* the muscle. I'm tellin' ya',' insisted Blue.

'No way. I'd even put a bet on it. Our usual ten quid?' said Tiger.

'I'll hold you to that. Now, I've seen a cute barman who needs to meet me. So I'm going to get us all a Martini. Oh, by the way, your sister said to say "bye", she's had to go home. Said something about an early start in the morning.'

Blue rubbed his hands together and smoothed out his 'Leather and Lace' emblazoned muscle t-shirt before making a dive for one of the busboys, as Tiger turned back to Rex, settling into her barstool. Wow, she thought to herself, Sienna grab an early night? She must be taking her job seriously, thought Tiger, daring to be secretly relieved. She remembered how many times the managers of various members' clubs would call to sternly inform her that Sienna had blagged her way in yet again under Tiger's membership and had then been caught putting her Cosmopolitans onto other guests' tabs and powdering her nose indiscreetly – and that was before Sienna had even finished her A-levels. There was simply no broaching the subject with her though, the little tough nut she thought she was. Tiger knew she simply had to find Sienna a job the moment she left sixth-form college. Her theory was that instead of imposing more rules for Sienna to rebel against (since that seemed to be her favourite past-time of late), Tiger would find her some kind of golden opportunity that might entice her into knuckling down and applying herself. In particular, since their parents had died so suddenly, she had wanted to keep Sienna grounded. Tiger sighed and turned to Rex.

'So how is little Sienna doing at Hunter Gatherers' HQ?'

'Little? She's taller than you.'

'Yeah I know . . . but she's still my baby sister, even if she is a cat's whisker off six foot.'

'It's early days but she seems to be learning the ropes. You do know I would never have done this for anyone else?'

'Oh, I do, Rex, and I really, really appreciate you taking her on. I told you she was a bright young thing, she won't let you down, I'm sure of it. I know she's still young but I don't want to see her drifting aimlessly, not knowing what to do with her life. It seems so – so unfair, especially with what happened to our folks . . .' Tiger tailed off, not wanting to bring up the fatal car crash when everyone was trying to enjoy themselves.

'Hey. You don't need to say any more, I was there when you got the news, remember? It's gonna be okay. Trust me! I'm a nice boss!' Rex winked and squeezed Tiger's arm tenderly.

Tiger suppressed the nervous churning in her stomach as she felt Rex's touch and chastised herself inwardly. How could she let herself feel like this after a smooth decade of working with him? She had always prided herself on her professional relationships. She certainly felt she'd got the most out of her ten years working with Hunter Gatherers, who Lewis had hired just after Tiger really hit the big time. But Rex Hunter still had the power to mystify her. Whilst his charm was beguiling, Tiger could still be shocked at his toughness. He was certainly in the right industry, with sheer hard balls combined with the kind of inspired, wicked mind that made him the best publicist in the country. But after all these years she realised she knew little of his personal life, despite working so closely with him. To be fair, she hadn't actually probed; Tiger firmly believed in keeping business strictly business. But she found it an uncomfortable dynamic at times; Rex having to know so much about her, and her knowing so very little of him. At first she had thought he might be gay, what with the relentless obsessing about his appearance; he had once been late for a meeting because he had been pressing the creases in his 1940s three-button suit. In fact she soon discovered him to be quite the womaniser.

Happily, the past couple of weeks Tiger had seen an almost nurturing side to him with the way he agreed to take Sienna under his professional wing. It was an attractive quality; Tiger daren't admit to herself she felt the stirring of feelings that she had suppressed for so long. She knew that she could have any man she wanted – not that she often took advantage of that – but if she tried her luck with Rex? Well, as she had to remind herself so frequently, apart from ruining their work relationship, it was just such a darn cliché. Moreover, Tiger's last long-term relationship had ended just over a year ago, and badly. He had wanted commitment; something Tiger had been unable to give. Since then Tiger had been wary of getting tied up again. And Rex really should come with a warning label. With his history of womanising any relationship with him was probably just a heartbreak waiting to happen. She couldn't take the risk of falling for him and getting hurt again. Besides, if he really got close to her; well there were things in her past she could never take the risk of him, or anyone, finding out. Only Blue had that particular key, and Tiger felt secure in the knowledge that he would keep that box firmly locked.

Feeling suddenly sombre Tiger drained her gin in a ladylike fashion and looked around for Blue. She could see the party was more than in full swing, and was by the looks of things about to get messy. The Krug had obviously been finished off some time ago. Georgia and all the Starrlets were shitfaced. Even Tiger's dear, elderly choreographer Pepper appeared to have drunk the bar's sherry reserves dry. Lewis would be thrilled. Tiger finally spotted Blue, deep in flirtation with a tall, lean busboy, sloshing the Martinis everywhere as he haha'd, and darling'ed loudly at every opportunity. Tiger sighed inwardly and assumed he wouldn't be helping her home tonight. Having her best friend live in her enormous house was originally designed so Tiger wouldn't feel like she was rattling around on her own of an evening, but the reality of living with a gay man meant that they still felt like ships in the night when he was in the mood to play away – which was most of the time.

'I think I need to get to my bed, Rex,' Tiger announced, deciding another drink would definitely be her downfall.

'You sure I can't tempt you with one for the road?'

'No, not here, too many photographers outside for me to be seen trashed after my own show! I'll save that behaviour for private time.'

'You want me to call your driver?'

'No, it's okay, I already sent a message to the doorman for him to wait outside for me.'

'At least let me escort you to the car. It's swarming with paps outside.' It was one of the increasing problems of being a single woman with such a glamorous career – it came with an unwanted trail of journalists and paparazzi, eager to be the first to catch the next piece of gossip column fodder. Running the gamut of photographers was the last thing Tiger fancied now, after an exhausting night.

'Sure. Thanks, Rex, I appreciate the thought.'

'That's what you pay me for.'

'Oh. Yes, I suppose you're right. Well I should quickly say my goodbyes.'

'No, babe, there'll be a big fuss if they all think you're off. You just slip out, I'll tell the guys you're doing interviews or something. You've spoken to everyone by now anyway.'

'Okay, boss, you know best. Meet me at the door in three minutes.'

Tiger rose and slipped out to the lobby unnoticed. The cloakroom attendant nodded appreciatively and brought over Tiger's royal purple Yves Saint Laurent cape. With a flourish he swung it over her shoulders.

'Oi, careful, mate, you nearly had my eye out there.'

Tiger looked up and gasped. There stood Lance de Brett before her – tall, striking, and with an indecipherable expression. The cloakroom attendant bowed quickly, muttering apologies as he retreated to his cubby hole.

'Lance,' Tiger said nervously, shocked to see him popping up at her private club. 'Lovely to see you tonight,' she said coolly.

'Yeah, just been sittin' in the *fumoir* with Michael Caine. I'm covering his preparations for his latest role.'

'Sounds interesting,' she replied politely, standing tall, pulling her shoulders back.

'Yeah it is actually. Better than the shit I saw earlier at any rate. Some burlesque show at the Savoy. Know anything about it?' Lance moved in on Tiger, manoeuvring her up against the wall.

'Ha, ha,' Tiger responded slowly, rising to the bait like a cornered wildcat. 'And what show were you watching exactly? The bar staff?' Tiger resisted the temptation to unleash a torrent of curses at him, before continuing. 'Oh Lance, darling, that's what I love about you. I know I can always rely on you for a great review of all my finest performances, and I mean *all* of them.' She smiled enigmatically.

'Well, I hear the Vegas mob were watching tonight?' Lance raised his arm above Tiger's pink curls and leaned against the wall, bringing his face close to hers. 'You should be so lucky! That tired old stripping act may work over here but Vegas is way out of your league. And if you think I'm bad, you wait 'til you get any press coverage there. You're out of your depth, you'll get buried alive. Now that's a show I'd pay to watch.'

Tiger merely shrugged calmly, praying he couldn't hear her heart rattling out of her dress. It was strange to think that her relationship with this man had been the longest of her life – and the closest she had ever come to letting someone near her heart. Now all that was left was bitterness and anger on his part. Tiger had hoped they could have both moved on by now, but she simply wasn't going to let him push her around any more. Ignoring the lump in her throat she pressed onwards bravely. 'Nice to see you in a good mood, Lance. You been getting it lately?'

'Now there's a question. Tell you what, I can't read the time on my watch, could you do the honours?' Tiger locked her eyes on Lance's as she slowly pulled his wrist towards her face. Tiger knew if Blue had been watching he would have cursed her for ever having given Lance that watch as a 'Dear John' letter. She glanced at the expensive Rolex before looking back into his eyes, breathing deeply, and bracing herself to knee him squarely in the—

'Lance?' came Rex's booming voice. 'Mate! Good t'see ya! See the show tonight? Fuckin' genius!'

Lance spun round.

'Yeah, me and Tiger were just having a nice cosy chat about it. I was just asking her the time in fact.'

'Well, it's time for bed,' interjected Tiger, wringing her trembling hands behind her back, out of sight. 'Come on, Rex, let's dash. Nice to see you, Lance, as always. Have a lovely night.' Rex looked on bemused as Lance skulked off towards the gents. As usual, only Blue had ever known about Tiger and Lance's history . . .

'You okay, doll? You coulda cut the atmosphere with a knife just then.'

'Oh you know. Lance loves to see anyone doing well.'

'Ah he's a pussycat really,' lied Rex, 'he obviously just needs a shag. You sure you're okay, doll? You seem shaky.'

'Oh don't be silly! I'm just peachy, thank you,' Tiger purred. 'Right, brace yourself, darling,' she added, smoothing out her cape over her hips and rearranging the fabric over her *décolletage* in anticipation of the paparazzi. In one swift movement she grabbed the door and stepped into the night.

The whole sky was lit up in a glare of photographers' flashes as the paps caught their first glimpse of pink hair.

The cameras clicked frenetically, flashes strobing around them, the paparazzi hollering and cat-calling like market traders. Tiger kept her eyes low and her smile serene, and concentrated on keeping her balance. Rapidly the paps closed in on the pair, jostling with each other as they grunted and hollered. Tiger staggered on her skyscraping Guiseppe Zanotti heels as she felt a rough push to her shoulder. Her smile turned to fear as her eyes darted about the lenses closing in on her. Lance had well and truly shaken her up back there and she wasn't ready for a bear pit of photographers. Suddenly taking her upper arm in a vice-like grip, Rex rushed ahead of her, shoving force-fully through the horde and dragging Tiger to her waiting limo behind him.

'Get in!' he hissed, opening the door and holding his coat open to shield her. Cameras still flashed through the blacked-out windows as the Towncar pulled seamlessly into traffic with them both safe inside.

Silence fell between them. Tiger was still catching her breath. As she looked out of the window at the trailing lights of Piccadilly Circus, images of camera lenses swam on her retinas, merging with the mutating faces of Lance de Brett, Lewis Bond and Liberace, the effect making her feel a little dizzy.

'Let's get you home, little one,' said Rex quietly. Without warning, Tiger felt the familiar tug of lust towards him. Before she could give herself time to talk herself out of it as she had done countless times before, she lunged and grabbed firmly at his thick neck. She sank her tongue deep into his mouth, kissing him so hard he could taste the gin of her last drink.

'What the fuck—' Rex pulled away, but didn't have a chance to finish as Tiger straddled him, attacking him like a caged animal, ripping her cape off and sinking her mouth down on his for the second time. This time he reciprocated, kissing her hard, urgently thrusting his crotch up towards her. She clearly wasn't wearing underwear, and Rex could already feel her wetness through his trousers. He pushed her up against the privacy screen of the limo and pressed his weight against her, her thighs still gripping him. Feeling her nails clawing at his back and neck, Rex reached for his flies. Her instincts taking over, Tiger made a grab and pulled out his hot thick cock. Thank fuck he's got a good one, she thought to herself with relief.

Pushing him back into the seat, she lowered herself onto him without hesitation, and with a yelp of pleasure shoved his face into her magnificent breasts. She held on to the headrest behind him so she could pull herself hard against him and get him as deep inside as possible.

'Jesus!' grunted Rex, cupping her arse cheeks and parting them gently in his hands in time to her rhythm. 'Oh god, I never thought . . .' Rex's words trailed off as, feeling her sopping cunt start to pulse and tighten around him, he pulled Tiger firmly by the hair so he could watch her beautiful, exquisite face as she came all over him.

Chapter 3

'Oh yeah, faster!'

'God—'

'No talking, just do it!'

'Uhh.'

'Oh yeah, don't stop!'

'Aagh!'

'Yeah!'

'Ah ah ah ah!'

'Go on!'

'Uhhhhhh.'

'That was, like, twenty seconds faster than last time!'

Blue climbed off the treadmill, heaving gulps of air and tossing a filthy look over at his personal trainer Emily. He must have sweated all the alcohol out by now, he thought grumpily.

'Fantastic, we'll have you doing the marathon this time next year at this rate.'

'I'm not sure exactly what marathon you're thinking of, Em, but I reckon I already broke the Martini endurance record with flying colours.'

'Good party last night then?' asked Emily cheerily. 'I saw Tiger all over the papers this morning, they're all raving about the show. Everyone was there!'

'Oh the show was fabulous! Camp as tits. The party would have been fab too if only I could remember it,' Blue puffed, fanning his sweaty cheeks. 'I found someone's number in my pocket this morning, you know.'

'Good catch?' asked Emily.

'Hardly, I rang it first thing this morning expecting one of the young studs from the theatre and you know who I got through to?'

Emily looked blank.

'Alco-fuckin-holics Anonymous!' squealed Blue, most of the gym turning to stare. 'Honestly, can you bloody believe it? Must have been that barman I was chatting up. Cunt.'

A loud gasp escaped from the little old lady power-walking on the next treadmill.

'Sorry, madam, I cunt believe that just slipped out,' apologised Blue over his shoulder, before leaning in to Emily. 'Well, with friends like that who needs enemas, eh? I must be losing my touch in a big way. Emily, do you think I'm . . . am I turning into an old queen?'

Emily looked aghast. 'Blue, you wrote the rulebook!'

'Thought so,' he muttered. 'I'll end up on the shelf, I know it. I can feel it in my bones. My problem is I'm just weak when I get a dirty Martini down me. It clouds my bull-shit detector. I should stick to champagne.'

'Okay, sweetheart, I can see it's your time of the month. Listen, why don't you finish off on the mats yourself,' sighed Emily with resignation.

'That's a good girl, I owe you one,' said Blue, planting a big kiss on her cheek before mincing off to the crash mats, monogrammed towel slung artfully over his shoulder.

Blue wasn't actually sure why he had a personal trainer. It had been Tiger's brainwave originally. Blue always said he wasn't actually that fussed about training, claiming that as a stylist he had cultivated permanent pecs from always lugging around so many heavy shopping bags. Besides which, he preferred to create perfection in other people. Needless to say Tiger didn't buy his excuses. Anyway, she fancied having an occasional gym buddy to keep the boredom at bay while she was sculpting her own curves. Tiger simply loved her food, and the Catholic girl in her meant she was a sucker for the ritual of indulgence followed by penance in the gym. She also had this romantic idea that Blue would find the love of his life between the exercise bikes and the weights bars. Truth was, the only gay men who Blue ever saw at the gym he'd either already shagged, or wouldn't touch with Elton's.

'Hey, darling, how's it hangin'!' came a strained voice as Blue settled on a mat. Looking over he recognised his old make-up artist pal Dave Bourgeois who was sweating and trembling in a side plank. They had tried getting it on one boozy night years ago, never to be repeated since. It was a chemistry thing. That is, far too many chemicals.

'Oh get away, Davey, you're making me tired just watching you,' grumbled Blue.

'Wow, what a way to greet an old friend. Somebody get out the wrong side this morning?'

'Very funny. No, I'm just still pissed, and I'm a miserable drunk,' grunted Blue, making a feeble attempt at a press up.

'Hmm, say no more. How was Tiger's show?'

'It was dreamlike, Dave, dreamlike. Shame you couldn't come (grunt) so how were the Mobos?'

'Oh just the usual shake 'n' fake. I was with Chaka Khan this time, so I had a nice table,' replied Dave, progressing to stomach crunches.

'She's every woman, darling.'

'She's had every woman for breakfast. She was in a fabulous red leather catsuit last night. Tight.'

'Wow. That's a lot of leather.'

'You're telling me. So, (oof), any fit men last night?'

'Sore subject. Although Libertina Belle was there which made up for the (grunt) lack of eye candy.'

'Wow, did you get a close look at her? Haven't done her make-up for ages, I've often wondered how she's weathering.'

'Oh she's gorgeous, Dave, gorgeous. (Grunt) Although in my opinion she's had a bit too much collagen this time. All I wanted to do was lick her lips and stick her to the window.'

'Tut tut. Shame.'

'Oh bugger this,' grunted Blue. 'No more for me. I'm going for a shower. You got the papers today, Davey? Apparently Tiger got major coverage.'

'Oooh, yes, I've got a *Daily Standard* in my locker. She's on the front page. C'mon, I'll follow you out and get it for you, I'm cooked for today, too.'

With a synchronised flounce the pair made a break for the changing rooms, both compulsively eyeing their physiques in the mirrors as they passed. Blue already felt like he was having a fat day, but was even more horrified at his sweaty, blushing complexion. What an oil painting, he thought, shuddering. Only flushed whales get fobbed off with Alcoholics Anonymous, he thought to himself sadly.

Dave immediately dived for his locker, and, whipping his jogging pants off to reveal a fetching jock strap, threw the newspaper squarely at Blue.

'Nice, nice, like it!' nodded Blue, looking at Tiger's beautiful face staring up at him from the front pages, 'but god who's that next to Ti– Sharon Stone! Oh Dave, that's not a hair do, that's a hair don't!'

'Well, I'm not keen on Sharon's make-up either in that one I have to say. God, if I could get my brushes on her. Tiger looks amaaazing as usual. I must find out what red she uses on her lips.'

'Guerlain, darling. I should know, she gets through one a week! Leaves most of it on her champagne glass, bless her. In fact, last night she was probably leaving it somewhere much more intimate.'

Dave's eyes widened. 'No way! Whose microphone was she speaking into then? Dirty hussy!'

'Who d'you think! Who's in these gossip page pictures with her leaving L'Homard last night?'

'Rex? Nah, they've been working together for years – she could have anyone, surely not – Rex?'

'Mm, hmm.'

'But you were so drunk last night, how do you know?'

'Well—' there was a pause '—she certainly didn't come home last night.'

'No way!'

'Yes way. Oooh, saved by the bell!' exclaimed Blue, making a grab for his mobile which was now ringing loudly from inside his locker. Dave rolled his eyes at the interruption, feeling cheated of more salacious gossip.

'Lewis!' shrilled Blue. 'Yes . . . no I've no idea, I haven't seen her this morning. Isn't she rehearsing with Pepper? No . . . no . . . well I didn't go home with her, you see, she . . . er . . . I stayed out with a friend I think . . . no. Well I don't remember much, er – no. What? Vegas? No way! When? Oh my god, wait 'til she hears! Why? But I want to give her the news . . . oh okay then . . . no I won't, don't worry. Yesss boss. Speak later!'

'Aaaaagh!' squealed Blue to the entire changing room, dropping his towel and waving his mobile over his head. 'She got the Vegas deal! Oh my god, oh my god, ohmygod! Oh! Liberace, I'm coming home!'

Chapter 4

This morning it was the weathergirl's turn to rattle Sienna Starr's cage.

'Thick cloud cover over the city and a low wind chill means mild temperatures of around seventeen degrees. Don't get too excited though, we're in for a grey day in the city, with patchy rain through to the evening. So take your umbrellas to work with you today . . .'

'Bitch! Sort the weather out!' Sienna hurled the words at the portable tv, flicking irritably through the channels and wondering what the hell she was going to wear for work now. Her carefully planned fake Pucci dress would never look good against miserable rain clouds. Hearing the loud hiss of a pan boiling over in the kitchen she made a dash for the hob. As she stirred the steaming milk into her porridge oats, Sienna hurriedly rethought her dress strategy, deciding to wear her vintage Burberry trench coat – yet another Tiger hand-me-down – teamed with her trusty Topshop beret. Very resistance, *trés mysterieuse*, she thought, imagining her wafting past Rex Hunter in the office all leggy, lissom and chic. Phew, style on a serious budget certainly took some preparation, she thought, gulping her porridge, especially when thrown a curveball by some dumb dolly weathergirl.

Sienna hummed as she dressed, feeling unusually clear headed and refreshed from a good night's sleep. There was no way she was going to stay out getting drunk last night when she needed to make a good impression on Rex Hunter. It was bloody typical that she hadn't got her new job herself; as usual her sister Tiger had pulled strings on her behalf. Hell, she hadn't even wanted to work in public relations, but then as far as Sienna was concerned, anything that got her closer to the kind of glamour and celebrity that her older sister had been enjoying for years was well worth giving a go. It was high time Sienna had her own taste of the good life. Of course, the moment Sienna was introduced to the chiselled manliness of Rex Hunter, she resolved that PR had in fact been her true calling all along.

Standing at the mirror now, she checked out her lean svelte figure in her simple black polo-necked dress. A minimiser bra was doing its best to ensure her bosom wouldn't ruin the streamlined silhouette. She arranged her beret at a jaunty angle over her tawny cropped hair. She wondered if she shared the same natural hair colour as her sister, and realised she couldn't actually remember a time when Tiger didn't have her immaculately dyed powder-pink curls. In fact their dearly departed mum and dad hadn't kept pictures of Tiger past her baby years. They had always claimed Tiger didn't like to be photographed because she wore an eyepatch for a squint for years. A pirate for a sister? Seemed unlikely to Sienna.

Sadly she didn't remember her Grandma Coco – she

had only been four when she passed away – so Sienna had
been too young for the experience of family stories anyway.
Besides, dad had always enigmatically claimed that
Grandma was unsuitable to be around children. It had
been Tiger who had told Sienna about Coco having been
a burlesque star. How typical, Sienna had thought spite-
fully when she found out; typical that Tiger wasn't even
being original with her precious job; she was just copying
their Grandma! As Sienna now carefully arranged her short
hair under her beret, she wondered if Tiger had matching
collar and cuffs, having a good snigger to herself at the
thought of a pink muff, before concluding that if she knew
anything about Tiger's attention to detail, it was a given
that *everything* matched.

'. . . Tiger Starr brought the West End to a standstill
last night with the opening of her new show *My Bare
Lady*. Celebrity pals arrived in droves to cheer on the stunning Miss Starr . . .' The strains of the breakfast television news permeated the bedroom.

Oh bugger off, thought Sienna, suddenly annoyed that
her sister was managing to invade her morning without
even trying.

'. . . roadblock outside the Savoy as Miss Starr eventually left in her limousine having stayed after the show to
sign autographs for her legions of fans. We leave you with
a clip of last night's scene. I'm Emma Woods, and you're
watching EMTV Entertainment News.'

Oh go on then, let's see her prancing on telly, thought

Sienna, suddenly compelled to watch. There before her eyes was her sister, beaming from the screen, her face lit up with a thousand flashbulbs as she exited the theatre in exquisitely body-hugging vintage Mugler, flanked by the latest hot-young-thing actors. Immediately Sienna turned sour, soaking up the scene unfolding on the small screen. Dammit, if only she'd hung out at the Savoy and walked out on her sister's arm, instead of being made to escort the boring bloody critics out the tradesman's entrance, she thought. That should be Sienna Starr up there on that screen. 'Aaaand thank you, Emma, wish I'd been there myself!' The anchorman rudely interrupted Sienna's trance.

'And now for the sporting news. Wayne Rooney was the man of the hour when—'

Sienna flicked off the telly and sank to the floor in a sulk. Suddenly she didn't feel like such a *femme fatale* in her outfit. Who was she trying to kid anyway? She would always be known as 'Tiger's-Little-Sister'. Ironic, considering she was two inches taller than Tiger. Her gawkiness had always been a sore point for Sienna. All the girls in sixth form had literally clamoured to meet her glamour-puss sister whenever she visited Sienna, and afterwards the girls would taunt Sienna for being the clumsy, gangly top-heavy sidekick. Sidekick indeed! Tiger had to spend quite a bit of time encouraging Sienna to see all the good points of her physique, to embrace her blossoming bosom. But as far as Sienna was concerned, the taunts were all Tiger's fault in the first place; if she wasn't so much more beautiful, and so *nice*, people would prefer Sienna instead.

She took in her surroundings; the Marylebone flat that her darling sister had found so that Sienna could live in a nice area, the flat that her darling sister paid the rent on to get Sienna started in London, the flat that her darling sister had chosen for its restored fireplaces, high ceilings and antique floorboards; the flat with filthy grey dust sheets pinned up at the sash windows because Sienna simply couldn't bear to have any more Tiger hand-me-downs. Besides, her sister's raw silk curtains were so darn boring. Sienna wanted something cool and animal print. Giraffe maybe. Or even ocelot. She just couldn't afford anything on her meagre junior's budget right now. That would simply have to change, resolved Sienna as she tapped her talons on the floorboards, deep in thought.

Sienna certainly had no qualms about using her sister's generosity to get her on the next step of the ladder. She'd cultivated her mercenary streak from an early age. Tiger's sporadic visits to see her at boarding school certainly had their perks, as she used to bring all the goodie bags from the latest flash parties she had been to. Sienna regarded them as guilt offerings for not stopping her parents from sticking Sienna in some stone turret masquerading as a school in Hitchin. Tiger was busy in London on her own glamorous path to stardom. Didn't she have any idea just what going to boarding school in a town that sounded like a venereal disease could do to an ambitious young lady?

Sienna would always put Tiger's gifts to good use, shrewdly buying friends at school with promises of perfumes, scented candles, expensive face creams, trinkets, designer chocolates, champagne manicures – whatever the goodie bags proffered. She was especially in demand as a friend at Hitchin College for Young Ladies during London Fashion Week, when the gifts took on new levels of luxury. Sienna was never under any illusions that she was popular for any other reason. This of course never bothered her – Sienna had decided at a very early age that life was all about getting a result. Whatever it took. Looking at her watch, Sienna realised she needed to get a wriggle on if she was going to make it into the office early and get Rex's desk all organised and tidy ahead of his arrival.

Tiger drew the enormous duvet from over her pink curls and squinted at her mobile flashing merrily on the dressing table next to her. She gingerly checked her inbox. Seven missed calls from Blue, eight from Lewis. 10.05 a.m. Shit. Shit. Shit! She never missed a rehearsal. Pepper must be going crazy. Tiger dialled for Blue and braced herself.

'Youuuuu dirrrty girl!' roared Blue down the line. 'Oooh if walls could talk this morning!'

Tiger flopped back onto Rex's bed. Looking at her mussed-up reflection in the mirror on the ceiling she sighed dreamily.

'You're all over the papers by the way,' continued Blue casually, sensing her fragile state, 'and Lewis is going nuts that he can't get hold of you. Erm, he's got some news you might want to hear.'

'Oh god. I need your help then,' pleaded Tiger, rolling on to her front, 'I've let everyone down, I'm so late for Pepper in the studio. Could you come over, like *now* with the driver, bring me my *pointe* shoes, some false lashes and a catsuit? In fact, sling a headscarf and spare stillies in the bag too. Tell Lewis my phone died and I'll call at lunch.'

'Check, check and check. So where am I coming to?'

'What d'you mean where?'

'Where are you? I'd take an educated guess you're not in Elton's bed at any rate.'

'Oh right, oh I see. Yes, of course. Er, come to 555 Cheyne Walk.'

'Hmm. Whose house is that?'

'Don't do this, Blue.'

'I wanna hear you say it.'

'You still want your job tomorrow?'

'Gotcha. Need some shades?'

'You bet. Bags like an entire set of Louis Vuitton luggage.'

'Ha. I'll get you in showroom condition in a matter of minutes, my darling. I'm out the door. Be with you in thirty.'

'Oh and Blue?'

'Yes, darling?'

'Flowers – stop at Liberty and get the biggest bunch

of flowers for Pepper. I'm never late for her. Jesus, what was I thinking?' Tiger snapped her phone shut and rubbed her temples.

She sank back into the duvet and inhaled the delicious aroma of sex, sweat and aftershave on the sheets. Turning to Rex, snoring softly by her side, her heart took a little somersault and she kissed him tenderly. 'Wake up, sleeping beauty,' she whispered, fluffing up her hair before reaching under the Egyptian cotton sheets to give him a wake up call he wouldn't forget.

Sienna slumped into her chair at Hunter Gatherers' headquarters on Charlotte Street, exhausted already. The office was like St Pancras in rush hour and the morning hadn't even passed yet.

'Run off twenty copies of the Diamond Suisse account presentation will you, I just emailed you the PDFs, and then I need you to get Lou from World PR on the phone, she hasn't returned my calls and I need to speak to her. Just keep holding 'til you get her.'

'Sure,' Sienna replied wearily to Rex's second-in-command, Steve, a towering, charmless figure with porcine features – the exact opposite of the delectable Rex Hunter.

'Oi, Gareth mate, did you get the Tiger Starr press releases over to *The Times*? They need to get the feature wrapped up for the supplement. Oh and Kat, you're gonna have to put your foot down for copy approval if we're

gonna let Tiger do the . . .' Steve broke off from his direc-
tives. 'Shit, Sienna! Where's – didn't you get my bacon
butty?' he demanded from behind his desk, staring open
mouthed like a guppy at the space where his elevenses
would normally be.

'Um, I was running tight on time,' Sienna lied effort-
lessly over the desk divide.

'How come you managed to get Rex a pastry?' snapped
Steve, patting his generous gut.

Sienna blushed red and marched to Rex's desk. Grabbing the croissant she thrust it under Steve's nose.

'Good job he's not in this morning then. Here, you have
it,' offered Sienna tartly.

'Nah, I've lost my appetite now. Why don't you eat it,
you could do with a bit of meat on your bones anyway.'
Steve chuckled and winked over at Kat who appeared to
be fixated on Sienna's thigh-skimming hemline.

Sienna turned on her heel in silence and simply hitched
her dress up even higher, cursing inwardly whilst blushing.
The heating in the busy office was making her head itch
under her cheap beret. Fuck manmade fibres, she thought
angrily, trying to reach her itch with a pencil. Where the
bloody hell was Rex this morning anyway? She didn't
remember seeing any morning engagements in his diary
for today.

Sitting back at her desk she set about Steve's tasks and
stabbed the World PR switchboard number into her telephone.

'Lou Klein please . . . Hunter Gatherers . . . Yes . . . No . . . I'll hold thanks.'

Britney's 'Oops I did it again . . .' played through down the line as Sienna was put on hold, which wouldn't have been so bad if it hadn't been the extended pan pipe remix. She rolled her eyes and settled into her chair for the duration.

Chewing on her pen Sienna swivelled on her chair idly amidst the hubbub and stared over at Rex's vacant desk with a beady eye. Now where could he be? she mused, annoyed that he wasn't there to see her leggy display.

Behind his desk the wall was a shrine to Tiger Starr. Framed magazine covers, a photograph of Tiger in James Brown's show, funny newspaper headlines, a suspended scale model of the Boeing 747 infamously painted with her pin-up image. A small corner was devoted to Rex's highly treasured framed photograph of himself with his idol Ricky Hatton, taken in Las Vegas after another victorious fight. Sienna wondered what it would be like to be in Vegas with Rex. I bet he'd be fun, she thought, imagining herself there, all diamonds, fur and glamour at the craps tables. All eyes on would be on her, dressed in Gucci and with tanned skin sparkling under thousands of pounds of Bulgari – she would be on Rex Hunter's arm with Britney playing pan pipes in the backgrou—

'Morning all!'

'Rex!' squealed Sienna, cutting off her phone call as her

boss strode through the office. Her outburst was noted with raised eyebrows from Kat and a smirk from Steve.

'Heyyyyy! Mate, what happened to you last night!' teased Steve.

'Ah you know, went home, fed the cat, watched *Question Time* on telly,' laughed Rex with a wink. 'So what's in the dailies, how did we do?'

As Rex swept past Sienna without so much as a glance her way, she caught the unmistakable smug look of a man who'd seen some action the night before. It was a look she was beginning to know too well. Rex was a woman-iser, pure and simple, and every notch he clocked up on his bedpost was another cut to Sienna's heart. She felt so stupid. That bloody Libertina Belle, cursed Sienna – he'd been all over her in the theatre last night. A heavy pile of newspapers crashed onto Sienna's desk, sending her desk tidy with its content of Bic biros and paperclips flying across the floor. Rex stood in front of her.

'Scan these clippings and add them to Tiger's press book, there's a girl. File the actual paper articles in the "live events" cabinet. Your sister did us all proud last night, she'll keep us in Bolli for a while,' he said, before turning back to Steve. 'Mate, you up for a Bloody Mary at the Ritz? Call it elevenses, we can go through the Diamond Suisse strategy while we're there.'

Sienna flicked huffily through the papers, sure that she did her own special bit to keep the journos happy at the show last night. *The Times*, the *Telegraph*, the

Guardian, the *Sun*, the *Mail*, the *Express*, the *Independent*, all proffering Tiger's magnificent hourglass figure mid performance. 'Tiger Tiger burning bright', 'Tiger's Starry night', 'Night of a thousand Starrs', read the pun-soaked headlines.

'Oh and Sienna,' called Rex.

'Yes?'

'Fetch me an Alka-Seltzer before I go to the Ritz, will you. Cheers, mate.'

As Rex strutted off towards Steve and Kat, Sienna looked back crestfallen at the pictures of her sister, with scissors at the ready to cut out the articles. She stared at Tiger's beaming smile. Was she mistaken or could she just make out the distinct hint of a sneer?

Chapter 5

Tiger Starr's radiant face looks up from the newspaper page which is beginning to curl under the heat from the anglepoise lamp. A leather-gloved hand lightly traces the line of her pillowy lips, one finger now extending out to follow the line of her cheekbone with a barely detectable tenderness. The hand slowly takes up the scalpel knife lying in an orderly fashion next to the newspaper. Delicately, carefully, precisely, the picture is cut out, and its reverse caressed with a thin film of glue. The image is placed onto a welcoming scrapbook page and patted down gently.

The gloved hand reaches once more for the blade before hovering hesitantly over the newly arranged page. Leather-clad fingers begin to gently trace the line of her bouncy curls, pausing over her beautiful face. An intangible shudder of anticipation spreads through the room in waves, a room almost entirely covered in glittering images of Tiger Starr.

Chapter 6

'Ten Benson! Woooh!' squealed Poppy, waving the little gold packet over her head.

'Cool!'

'Where d'ya get 'em?'

'Dish 'em out then!' responded Emma, Claire and Marina excitedly.

'Listen, I had to go all the way across town in case I bumped into someone I knew. You owe me big time,' warned Poppy sternly.

'Aw, c'mon, you know you're the only one who'd pass for sixteen,' retorted Claire.

'Yeah, you'd never get refused with those bazookas,' giggled Marina, grabbing the packet and ripping off the cellophane to hand out the cigarettes.

'Bet you forgot matches,' chipped in Emma from under her fur-lined hoody. 'Come on, it's f-f-freezing out here, and we've got hockey next. I'll be an ice-block by then.'

'Hang on, I've got matches here, they're in the bottom of my bag,' muttered Poppy as she knelt on the wet grass and rummaged in her satchel. Pulling out folders and text books she finally located the small box of Swan Vesta. 'Are you guys looking out for any teachers?' she asked cautiously, looking up at the girls enquiringly.

'Yeah yeah yeah, anyway we'll hear the tennis court gate squeaking if anyone comes, don't worry,' reassured Marina.

One by one the girls struck a match and lit their cigarettes. They took awkward drags and eyeballed each other, each hoping they didn't look as clumsy as Claire who was flapping away clouds of smoke from around her face. Despite her lack of brainpower, she was the envy of the class, always bagging the hot boyfriends. However with her innocent, angelic face she figured she could procure a more sophisticated air with some accomplished smoking. Her pal Emma just wanted to keep the weight off, somehow she thought cigarettes and gum would do the trick. The popular girls of the class, Claire and Emma were a fearsome twosome, although Poppy secretly nicknamed them Thick and Thin. Marina was the most elegant of the girls, the one who everyone in the world wanted to be friends with. Marina loved Poppy for her combination of sparkiness, brains, and what she considered to be striking, rather than classic looks, but she also knew Poppy to be extremely insecure with her unusual features. Moreover, Marina found something about her rather intriguing and liked to include her in the group, despite Emma and Claire's stand-offishness towards her.

Emma broke the silence with a cough, struggling to quickly regain her composure. Marina looked over with amusement, exhaling a long thin plume of smoke. She had to be a natural, of course. Poppy simply spluttered loudly.

'Ugh, this is gross,' she cringed.

'Keep doing it you'll get used to it,' advised Marina.

'When do you start enjoying it then?'

'Well ... you're not exactly meant to enjoy it really, that's not the idea ...'

'Right. So what's the point?'

'God you're soooo clueless,' sighed Claire, rolling her eyes. 'Listen, if we smoke we get to look older and hang out with the older boys.'

'Aren't there cheaper ways to look older?' asked Poppy, wastefully dropping her cigarette and extinguishing it underfoot.

'You may have big tits, but some of us need a bit more help.' Emma scowled.

'Yeah, I've seen Mr Rogers checking out those puppies!' Marina winked.

'He always puts you in centre forward so he can see you running up and down the pitch, jiggling about,' sniggered Claire.

'Do I jiggle?' gasped Poppy, instinctively pulling her blazer tight across her chest. The group burst into fits of laughter. She hated being teased about her bust.

'Well, let's just say Mr Rogers gets his glasses all steamed up when you've got the ball,' said Marina, putting an arm around Poppy's shoulder affectionately.

'Yeah, you don't actually think you got on the squad

because you're a good player do you? Haven't you noticed that every time you're on we *lose* the match,' Emma grumbled.

'Cor, Emma's got her bitch stick out today,' laughed Marina. 'Whassamatter Ems, got your p-e-r-i-o-d?'

'Come on. It's obvious Mr Rogers has his faves.' Mr Rogers was their new gym teacher. He was Australian and a hunk. 'It's wasted on Poppy anyway by the looks of things. Look at the pictures of porn stars stuck all over her folder.' The girls all looked down at the pile of books and folders still lying on the grass next to Poppy's satchel, covered in black-and-white pin-up pictures.

'They're not porn stars!' gasped Poppy. 'They're movie stars! Marilyn and Rita!'

'What? But they're women! In bikinis! Ruffled knickers! Half naked!' taunted Emma. 'Whatever turns you on you lez. Lezzer! Lezzer!'

Without warning Poppy threw herself at Emma and knocked her to the ground, eliciting a sharp yelp. Claire squealed and giggled as Poppy struggled to pin Emma to the grass. Marina simply shook her head at the scene and elegantly finished off the last few drags of her cigarette as the two girls rolled around. Poppy grabbed fistfuls of hair.

'Argh! Get off my hair, I just had it permed!' screamed Emma, trying to push Poppy off her. 'Lesbian!'

'Slapper!' yelled Poppy waving a sorry-looking tuft of blonde ponytail in Emma's face.

'Take that back!' shouted Emma, her free hand leaping

defensively for her hair. As the girls wrestled on the grass a huge rip could be heard.

'My shirt!' squealed Poppy. 'You stupid cow, what did you do that for! My mum'll go spare!' Poppy sat back for a moment to survey the damage, giving Emma the advantage. In a flash Emma was straddling Poppy, yanking at her long plaits with one hand and grabbing at her exposed bra with the other. Claire and Marina had now piled in to separate the two amidst yelps and name calling. No one heard the loud squeak of the tennis court gate as Mr Rogers hurtled towards the fray.

Chapter 7

Tiger lovingly placed her diamond-encrusted merkin back in hibernation in its heart-shaped box, snapping the clasps shut with a flourish. Picking up a half-finished roll of tit tape and fondling it absentmindedly between her fingers, her green eyes gazed one last time over the carnage of the dressing room. Huge labelled trunks of costume were stacked next to hatboxes, make-up caddies, her feather steamer, jewellery cases and her lucky mascot – her vintage Jayne Mansfield hot water bottle. Layers of glitter and diamond dust were trodden into the gaps in the floorboards and worked into the pitted formica of the long dresser. Discarded cans of Elnett hairspray, dead flowers, used make-up wipes and a couple of empty Tanqueray bottles filled a black binliner. A defective pair of eyelashes still stuck to the mirror. Tiger had enjoyed her three months at the Savoy. The auditorium had been packed night after night; the critics were adoring, the venue were thrilled, the Starletts were on a high, the band was on fire, Rex was getting out the holiday brochures, Blue was in costume heaven, even Lewis seemed . . . happy.

An impatient little honk from Tiger's driver wafted up from the street below, signalling it was time for her to leave. Vladimir had been outside gently revving the black Lincoln Towncar for over twenty minutes and the bell-hops at the Savoy Hotel opposite were probably trying to move him on. Tiger scooped what she could under her arms and made for the stairs.

'Sorry, ma'am!' came a breathless panting. 'I was sent to ferry your cases to your car, but I'm new here and I got lost between dressing rooms. Can I take those for you?'

Tiger took in the strapping young security boy standing in the doorway. At a little under six foot he peered at her with coal black eyes. Eyes not unlike Rex's. Tiger felt an immediate twinge of lust.

'Wow that's very kind of you – er . . .'

'Mark.'

'Mark,' she sighed kindly. 'Look why don't I take the little caddies down myself, and if you could manage the heavy trunks that would be wonderful. Oh and careful with those hatboxes, you can't put anything heavy on them.' Tiger was already off towards the exit.

'Ma'am . . . um . . .'

Tiger stopped at the stairs and looked back at him.

'I'm sorry, but would it be too much to ask for a photograph? My mates won't believe I met you unless I have a photo,' he asked coyly, producing a small digital camera. Tiger laughed softly.

'Oh sweetheart, I haven't much scaffold or plaster on today, you wouldn't want to see me like this.'

'Oh no,' he retorted, shocked, 'no, you're wrong, you're

beautiful. Much more beautiful up close. Hey, I'm sorry, I shouldn't have asked—'

'Oh, come on,' said Tiger, sensing his shyness, 'let's say "cheese" then,' and they huddled up close as he held the camera at arm's length and managed to take a halfway decent picture of the two of them. Tiger even kindly signed some left over posters for his friends.

'So where are you performing next? I'd love to get tickets,' Mark puffed moments later as he humped the huge trunks of costume down the steep stairs with Tiger daintily clip-clopping her way down behind him.

'I have lots of one-nighters to do right now, but I'm supposed to be expanding my show for Vegas. Only thing is, it's a long way and I might miss England too much.'

'Oh my god, well I'd definitely make the trip over the pond to see it. Will it be all new material?'

'Well, if I decide to do it, then you can be sure it'll be something special.'

'I can't believe you'd even need to think about it!' exclaimed Mark, bringing Tiger's mountain of cargo to the foot of the stairs with a crashing thud, nearly taking his thumb off. 'Okay, ma'am, I'm gonna have these loaded into your limo in two shakes of a lamb's tail. You just sit back and I'll take care of everything.'

Mark held the stage door open for Tiger with a flourish. As she stepped out into the street she stumbled, nearly falling. Steadying herself she looked down to encounter a wall of white gladioli reaching to her knees.

'What the—' Mark immediately jumped to clear the towering pile of flowers.

'No, no, it's okay, sweetheart,' said Tiger gently, moving Mark out of the way and crouching down to retrieve what looked like a card on top of the pile. Opening the envelope slowly she found a newspaper clipping of one of her rave reviews. Tiger was silent for a beat. She looked up and carefully surveyed the street, tapping the envelope against her palm pensively as she scanned. Aha. There by a lamp-post on the corner of the Strand was the familiar squat figure of stage door Johnnie. He appeared to be hanging off the post as though awaiting a reaction. Their eyes locked across the crowded street. Tiger picked up an armful of the flowers and held them theatrically to her nose. Smiling, she stood and waved regally at Johnnie, cradling the bouquet. He patted his heart, punched the air and skipped gaily off in the direction of Covent Garden, his whoops carried on the wind behind him. Tiger laughed.

'You have a girlfriend, Mark?' she asked, turning to look into his lovely eyes.

'Um, well. . .'

'Here, take her a big bunch of these, okay? You'll get the best blow job of your life tonight if you do.'

Mark laughed. 'Thank you, ma'am. My boyfriend doesn't actually like flowers, but if it's okay, I'd love to take some for my mum, thank you.'

Tiger blushed. Of course. He was far too good looking to be straight.

'Sure you can, sweetheart. Help yourself. Bye, Mark, see you around. Vegas maybe.' Blowing him a kiss Tiger climbed into her limo with her own armful of flowers and shut the outside world out. She knew exactly who she wanted to give *her* gladioli to.

Tiger took a deep breath and flipped open her mobile. She had the number on speed dial. It kicked straight in to voicemail.

'Mr Hunter?' she purred. 'Tiger.' She waited a beat. 'Catch me.'

Tiger snapped the mobile shut. Cheesy. Dammit! She hated voicemail.

It had been weeks since Tiger had been with Rex. Not since their first time on her opening night. She had burned inside since then. After all those years of self denial, of playing the Ice Queen to his Zorro, she had finally unleashed within herself a terrifying kaleidoscope of emotion. Of course, business always came first and, fully committed to her Savoy shows, Tiger had only met Rex briefly for press and interviews; the atmosphere between them had been unbearable. Tiger felt like a strung-out puma around him; tense and fit to burst.

No wonder she had been receiving rave reviews, the only place she could vent her sexual energy was on stage. Once, she had received advice from her favourite old burlesque legend Satan's Angel, now sixty something. Angel had said to her, 'Tiger baby, when you're up on that stage, just imagine you're doing it all for your lover. That's what I always used to do back in the fifties. Brought the house down every time, honey.' Needless to say Tiger's audiences didn't know what hit 'em. Grown men bit their white knuckles and wept, women waited at the stage doors night after night for signed postcards, recipes and beauty tips. With Rex in Tiger's mind, the stage was alight with passion.

Of course, Tiger still had her new acts to rehearse while she did the evening shows at the Savoy, so she hardly had a second to even blink let alone socialise. And then Lewis was on her case every spare second trying to persuade her to do Vegas. To counter the sporadic platonic meetings, Rex frequently sent texts to Tiger of the single *entendre* variety which only served to send her into further paroxysms of lust. Despite keeping calm on the surface, she was already planning an extended repertoire for their next 'meeting' to top all others.

Tiger looked out of the car window. Vladimir seemed to be hurtling towards her Regent's Park palace at a good five miles per hour. Typical London congestion, she thought, irritably. She settled back into her seat and flipped open her mobile again.

'Lewis? Tiger. Just checking in.'

'Have you done the "get out"?'

'Yep, I'm all loaded out.'

'Good girl. Have you got all your costume ready for your show tonight?'

'Yeah, Blue's at home steaming and fluffing the poodle

costume. He's been revamping all the girls' puppy dog outfits ready too. It's the charity benefit tonight, right?'

'Yes. The diamante dog basket's already over at Hampton Court being rigged up. The stage was set up in the grounds last night, it looks great. Sparkling chequerboard, all a bit *Alice in Wonderland*.'

'Oh great, I've been looking forward to this one. I like a bit of *al fresco*.'

'Hmm. Sure you do. You only have time for a thirty-minute soundcheck tonight. Sorry, it's all I could get. They're putting on a red carpet catwalk show with Kate and Naomi and it's cut right into the set-up time. And I'm only putting on four of the Starrlets with you, the stage size is a bit tight as someone fucked up with the dimensions of the golden staircase – it's big enough to fill the gardens at Marseilles.'

'Jeez, Lewis, I forgot to check, did you sort the giant topiary poodles I asked for? You know I wanted them out by the maze to set the scene.'

'Oh god yes! I forgot to tell you, the charity is very pleased with you for that idea – they only managed to get Jeff Koons to make the giant poodles as a special art installation!'

'Wow! Amazing, I love his work! Will he be there tonight?'

'I would have thought so. I know the sculptures are going to be auctioned off to raise money, so brownie points go to you. This will attract some huge private collectors, and a wadge of cash for the charity; the art world's absolutely buzzing about it.'

'Fabulous! So when's my call time?'

'Well, Georgia's already down at the grounds re-choreographing with Pepper; she wants the girls to slide down that big gold staircase while you're being carried onto the stage in the dog basket by the butler boys. Your call time is 6 p.m. to load in, for a six thirty sound-check. Guests from eight, be ready for your photocall and champagne reception at nine, and you're on stage at eleven. You'll be expected for a private drink with the hosts after your show. I think Kylie's singing a couple of numbers, then they're all dancing 'til dawn.'

'Okay. Can you ask the spot operator to give me a lilac gel? It'll look best with the pink outfits.'

'I already asked, it's fine.'

'Great! See you at six.'

'Oh, Tiger?'

'Uh huh?'

'We need to sign on Vegas, time's running out.'

'Oh no, not Vegas again. Do we really need to talk about it any more?'

'I can hardly see what's to hesitate about, Tiger. You've wanted it for fifteen years. You're doing it. End of. See you at six.'

'Yes, boss.'

'I hate that.'

'Sorry.'

Tiger ended her call and sighed, knowing the Vegas argument was imminent that evening. Tiger just couldn't risk public humiliation at the hands of the critics. A Brit in Vegas was fair game at the best of times, and if Lance de Brett's malevolent words on her opening night had been a sign of things to come, Tiger had everything to lose. More than that, she couldn't quite put her finger on it, but she felt her confidence evaporating; ironic after having worked so hard for so many years for this opportunity. Why, when she seemed to have the world at her feet, did she feel so troubled?

Pushing all thoughts of the evening's show to the back of her mind she pulled the limo's privacy screen back.

'Vladimir, this traffic is ridiculous; can you just drop me at Rex's office round the corner, then take all my kit home. Blue knows what to do with all the trunks. That cool with you?'

'Yes, Ms Starr. No problem.'

Vladimir jerked the Towncar into a violent U-turn amidst crazed beeps and honks and within minutes safely deposited an excitable Tiger at the door of Hunter Gatherers' headquarters, armed with sweet smelling gladioli.

'Oh Rex, baby,'

'Argh, for fuck's sake.'

'Look it – it's okay. . .'

'Sorry, Vicky, this hasn't happened before . . .' Rex spat into his palm and pumped his cock furiously with his hand, muttering curses and willing it to get past marsh-mallow consistency. Fuck you, Tiger. Fuck you for messing with my head, thought Rex, breaking into a sweat as he pummelled away. Vicky rose from the palatial-sized bed and coolly pulled a Marlboro Light from the packet by the minibar.

'It's not me is it?' asked Vicky, standing by the open window, jutting her little tits towards Rex and trying to look sexy.

'Argh you stupid bitch, no! It's me!' Rex liberated his cock and flopped forwards onto the bed, concealing his excuse for manhood. Vicky looked visibly offended.

'Sorry. Sorry, look I'm just stressed out, babe, I shouldn't have taken the afternoon off really. I have a shitload of work to do before tomorrow, I guess I'm just preoccupied. Sorry, babes.'

'Yeah, I'm sorry too,' said Vicky quietly as she exhaled a long thin stream of smoke and tapped her nails on the windowsill.

'Here, put some clothes on,' muttered Rex, throwing a bathrobe lamely in her direction.

'What?'

'I mean, well you just look cold, that's all,' mumbled Rex, realising he had pissed Vicky off enough by now that he could guarantee she'd be deleting his number from her phone within the hour.

'Look, if there's someone else,' started Vicky.

'Babe, I only have eyes for you,' responded Rex, on

autopilot, as visions of Tiger swam tantalisingly before his eyes. Those magnificent bouncing breasts, that amazing arse, running his hands over her glorious hips and taut stomach as she mounted him like a rodeo champion. That roaring infectious laugh of hers, those voluptuous lips, swallowing up his helmet as her soft pink hair tickled his balls . . . Rex now felt his cock rigid, drilling a hole in the mattress.

Looking up he saw that Vicky had gone and locked herself in the bathroom, and he was sure he could hear her snivelling over the sound of the running shower. Great. Suddenly he hated himself. What was he doing here in a six hundred quid a night hotel suite, at lunchtime like some hooker's John? He ached with longing, he needed to be with Tiger, wrapped in her curves, smelling her perfume, tied up in her arms. Now her show was over he was ready and able to spend time with her. Properly. He'd waited this fucking long to meet his match, he wasn't about to blow it. Women are just women, right? A fuck's just a fuck, right? Well, Tiger Starr wasn't just any woman. She was a magnificent goddess, with an endearing vulnerability in balance with her formidable womanly power; and Rex Hunter was ready to rise to the challenge. And god, those tits! He was on his knees now, hand closing around his throbbing cock. Three strokes later he lay happily crumpled on the bed, satisfied and smiling like a smitten schoolboy.

*   *   *

Tiger tried to mask her horror as she looked at what lay before her on Sienna's desk.

'I knew you'd find it hilarious, bless her!' laughed Kat.

Tiger tried to smile but she was dying inside. Before them on the desk were pages of copier paper with every last square inch decorated with signatures reading 'Mrs Sienna Hunter', 'S. Hunter' and 'Ms Hunter'. Beneath those were a collection of pictures of Rex; not just any pictures, but ones that had been taken of him with Tiger at various events, which now had Tiger cut out of the frame.

'Look, Sienna will be back from her break soon, please put these back where you found them, Kat, she'll be mortified if she knows we've seen them,' begged Tiger.

'Oh relax, doll, she won't be back for an hour at least; she's off on an errand in St John's Street. Look, I'm putting them back now.' Kat patted Tiger on the shoulder.

'Okay, you know, it's just. . .'

'Yeah yeah, she's family, I know. Sorry. I guess I shouldn't have laughed, but honestly, the juniors we've had through here who've fallen for Rex – I never thought a smart cookie like Sienna would go for it as well!'

'She's smart you say?' asked Tiger, perking up.

'Yeah! She's alright, you know! She's been working hard. She made a few cock-ups at first but she learns fast. We give 'em some shit here, mind you. So many dolly birds pass through thinking it's all champagne lunches and networking . . . and Rex of course.' Kat rolled her eyes theatrically. 'We have to sort out the wheat from the chaff. But Sienna – she seems tough! The girl's got balls!' laughed Kat.

'Hmm. Well, great! Something inspired her finally!' said Tiger. Trust bloody Rex to be the object of her sister's crush. Damn him, she thought, suddenly feeling over-whelmed.

Tiger knew with a sinking heart that the right thing to do would be to step aside for Sienna's sake. Infatua-tion was painful at the best of times. Tiger couldn't bear to hurt Sienna by gadding about on the arm of her big crush. But could she really bring herself to give up the chance of happiness with Rex all because of what could be nothing more than a teenage fantasy? As Kat eyed up the flowers, Tiger's mind raced. She may as well face the fact that she was in danger of falling too deep, too quickly. Tiger knew deep down no woman could ever win the key to Rex Hunter's heart, least of all her. He'd never be ready for love. She would just become another of his many broken-hearted bitter lemons sooner or later, she was sure of it. She may as well nip it in the bud and save herself a lot of pain. She prayed Sienna had already seen for herself what a player Rex was. As Kat said, she was a smart girl after all. Tiger would just have to let Sienna have a clear path to sweet dreams for now, and hope sweet dreams was where it ended.

'Kat, can you just leave these flowers for Sienna, I thought she might like them,' sighed Tiger, reluctantly laying the gladioli on Sienna's desk. 'Oh, and give Rex a message that I called. I have something for him – a courier will drop it by later.'

'Sure, doll. Hmm, the flowers smell nice. Hey, break a leg for the gig tonight. Rex says it's gonna be wall to wall money and Hollywood.'

'It is? Yeah. Whatever. It's charidee, darling.'

'Oh cheer up! It's good to see you, lookin' gorgeous as always.' Kat slapped Tiger's bum heartily.

Once outside in the street, Tiger came over all faint and staggered across the road to the dining tables outside the posh hotel opposite. A waiter recognised her immediately and descended on her with the champagne menu and a little bow. Needing to calm her nerves she ordered a glass of Krug and dialled for Blue as she fanned her face with the menu.

'Dahhhhhling, I'm fluffing up your little poodle tail a treat!' came the drawl down the phone. Tiger was silent, trying to get the words out.

'Tiger? You there?' Blue sounded worried.

'C-c-c . . .'

'Tiger, calm, darling, it's okay. What's happened?'

'S-s-s . . .' Tiger thumped the table in frustration. Tears pricked her eyes. She was not going to cry under any circumstances. Survivors don't cry, she reminded herself as she hastily scrabbled in her bag and put her shades on.

'Breathe, darling, it's okay,' soothed Blue.

'I'm s-stopping this thing with Rex.' Tiger hurried the words out.

'What? But – you've hardly started! He's all you've talked about for the last three months! I thought as soon as the Savoy was done you guys were on and were going to spend some quality time together? He's absolutely besotted with you too! I've never seen him like it!'

'I knooooow!' she wailed plaintively. 'I just c-c-c . . .'

'What's he done? The slimy bitch, I'll kill him. Shall I come over? Where are you?'

'No! No, it's okay, it's not Rex's fault for once. Look I'll explain everything later. C-can you get a Rolex over to him at the Hunter Gatherers' office please? And a card, it needs a card. Just put erm . . .'

'The Rolex? Woh. Tiger, are you sure about this?' Blue asked, half laughing.

'Yes. Just put, "I love" . . . no, put, "It was fun. Back to business?"'

'Er – are you absolutely sure?'

'Yes.' Tiger snivelled daintily, composing herself. 'And put a little pawprint underneath.'

'If you say so,' replied Blue, sounding sceptical.

'Thank you. I appreciate it. By the way we have to be at this gig at six, and you need to load in costumes. God, I need tonight like a hole in the head. How am I supposed to go on and smile and be fabulous when all I want to do is lock myself in my bedroom and have a cry to Roy Orbison songs while wearing Rex's aftershave? I really need a hug.'

'Come home, darling. I'll be waiting for you. I'll get you in showroom condition for tonight, don't worry.'

Tiger snapped her phone shut and, realising an excited crowd was gathering around her taking photos with their cameras, dived inside the hotel to wait miserably for her Krug.

'Yeah! Amazing, darling!' squealed Blue, draping a gold silk dressing gown about Tiger's bare shoulders, as he escorted her to the dressing room. 'Lewis, did you see that actress in the audience start to take her clothes off too! Ooh, and did you see that chat-show host Bentley Berry down there too? You shoulda seen his face, classic! I bet he mentions it on his show next week!'

'Okay calm down,' said Lewis, closing the door of the dressing room and ushering Tiger to her seat. 'That was great. The audience are still going nuts, the client was giving me the thumbs up from across the room. I'll have to go and see her in a minute.'

'Oh the whole thing was fantastic!' gushed Blue. 'Did you see Georgia sliding down the banister, camp as Christmas!'

'Now, Tiger, the client wants you to join the celebrity guests and the charity CEO for a glass of champagne.'

'I don't think I can manage it tonight, Lewis,' she replied softly, starting to pack up her make-up caddy, 'I've already done my photocall with them anyway. I'll just tell Vladimir to be ready for half an hour's time, I'll be packed by then.'

'Hrmph. That's not what we agreed.'

'Lewis, don't. I can't. I won't be good company.'

'What's wrong with you?'

'Nothing.'

'Fine. Your choice. Blue have you brought all the costume back from the stage?'

'Ah. No, I'm missing the gloves and stockings. Where did you chuck 'em, darling?' Blue looked over at Tiger enquiringly.

'The gloves went behind me into the band – I think one of them went into the drum kit. The audience got the stockings I'm afraid.'

'Tsk, I can't believe Cherry and Brandy didn't spot them. I'll fine them both tomorrow.'

'No, no, it's okay, Blue, I think they were tied up with the puppy costumes. I know one of the tails kept pinging off.'

'There's nothing wrong with those puppy tails. Anyway that's not the point, the audience always try nicking any souvenir pieces of costume they see left on the stage. It's an unbelievable pain in the arse for me when that happens, I'm the mug who has to make everything again.'

'Whatever,' sighed Tiger, uncharacteristically apathetic.

Blue arched an eyebrow pointedly and turned to Lewis. He took the opportunity to theatrically usher Lewis out of the door, leaving Tiger to her thoughts.

'Did anyone catch your eye in the audience?' Blue whispered safely out of earshot of Tiger.

'Well there was this juicy blonde, she—'

'No no no!' hissed Blue testily, 'Listen, this is important. I think I saw Rosemary Baby in the audience.'

'Who? What kind of a stage name is that?' Lewis burst out laughing.

'You know, Rosemary! The ugly redhead! You know, the one who caused all that trouble with Tiger's pal Tiffany Crystal out in Vegas a couple of years back.'

'Really? But Tiffany's lovely!'

'Oh for Chrissake didn't you read about it? It made the newspapers! Tiger was up in arms about the whole thing. Tiffany tried to be her friend at first but she ended up nearly dying on stage one night at the hands of Rosemary Baby.'

'No shit!'

'Yes shit. First it was creepy things. Harrassment. Calls in the night. Heavy breathing and threatening voices saying things like "No one wants to see your bony ass and scrawny neck on stage."'

'What? But Tiffany's gorgeous! A legend in her own g-string!'

'Exactly. Oh, she just ignored it all at first. Had no idea who was behind it all, thought it was a silly prank. But then Tiffany started getting personal visits from heavies. Her husband hired protection for her and it seemed to get better. So anyway, Rosemary blags a part in the same show as Tiffany only she's way down the bill. Oh what was it called again? *Brief Encounters*, that's it. Great topless tit 'n' feather revue. I can't believe Rosemary managed to get a feature in it to be honest, even bottom of the bill. She must have been wiping the dust off her knees all around town, that's all I can say. So anyway they're doing a handful of tour dates with this show and when it gets to Vegas? Well, let's just say when Tiffany slipped down her huge glass staircase they found the top three steps doused in silicone spray; remarkably similar to the spray Rosemary was using to shine up her latex stockings.'

'I remember Tiger telling me about that now! Tiffany was in traction for weeks!'

'You got it. Well Rosemary was arrested, and get this! She claimed Tiffany was sending *her* hate mail, when everyone knew Rosemary was sending it to herself. The brass! Obsessed she was. Well in the end the useless cops couldn't prove anything, and Rosemary got off scott free. Probably got down on her knees again if the truth be told. So here's the thing. I'm sure I saw her in the audience tonight. You need to know this, Lewis, because I warn you, you don't want the likes of her anywhere near our Tiger. Rosemary Baby's just a bitter, washed-up never-has-been with an axe to grind with the world. I know it'll put the wind up Tiger off if she finds out she's been sniffing around. She never forgave her for what she did to dear Tiffany.'

'Sounds like a lovely girl. Hmm,' mused Lewis, 'Rosemary Baby. I'll remember that, thanks, Blue. Maybe I'll give Rex a call and he can give me the lowdown on what the papers said about her. Now grab that missing costume please before the locusts descend on the stage to claim every last dropped Swarovski.'

Blue scuttled off to retrieve the missing pieces of costume, worried that Lewis hadn't understood the seriousness of his warning. Rosemary Baby was a piece of work alright; as her name suggested, ugly inside and out with a face like a half-set jelly and probably a spare set of teeth in her cunt. Blue knew the jealous bitch would stop at nothing to stab a successful showgirl like Tiger in the back. Thank god Tiffany Crystal was alive to tell the tale. Blue only hoped Rosemary hadn't now switched her jealous, obsessive attentions closer to home.

Tiger sighed as she sat in front of her mirror, looking suddenly exhausted underneath all her make-up.

'You're preoccupied,' came Lewis' voice as he re-entered the dressing room, softly closing the door behind him.

'No, just tired. The Savoy – you know, I get post-show comedown after a long run,' sighed Tiger.

'Mixing pleasure with business is always a killer you know,' said Lewis slowly. 'You have the world at your feet, lady. Don't sacrifice that for cheap thrills with cheap men who are no good for you.'

Tiger looked at herself in the mirror aghast, and wondered how on earth Lewis knew about Rex – or was he bluffing? She turned to face him and their eyes met. She always got a feeling that Lewis could see right through her, though it surprised her to see there was no judgement in his eyes tonight, only concern. She wondered if he'd known about Lance too. It wouldn't surprise her. She pulled her shoulders back assertively, deciding now was the perfect time to change the subject.

'Lewis, I can't do Vegas,' she burbled.

'You're doing it. No discussion.'

'I'll be destroyed.'

'Come again?'

'Lance de Brett. He – let's just say he gave me a taste of what might come if the critics slaughter me.'

'Critics?' Lewis guffawed. 'Since when did anyone ever give a shit about critics! As if a critic could ever destroy you! I can see what's happening here Tiger.' Lewis leaned in over her dressing table. Tiger pulled herself up in her chair defensively.

'Sabotage.' Lewis thumped the table triumphantly.

'What?'

'You. Sabotaging yourself. You've worked your whole life towards this and now you can taste it, you're scared. Scared of success. The higher you go up the mountain the harder the wind blows, and you're losing your bottle. You wanted this so hard, now you've got it you can't believe it, can you? Now you want to break it all down again. You would have jumped at an opportunity like this ten years ago! It's no coincidence you've gone off the rails and started dabbling in a twat like Rex. He's not a *real* man. You need to step up, Tiger. You don't think you deserve success do you? You don't think you're good enough do you? You think—'

'Lewis, s-s-s-stop!' Tiger burst out.

'I'm just telling you the truth,' warned Lewis, standing and waving an index finger.

'Okay!' Tiger snapped, losing the will to argue.

'Oh and Tiger . . .'

'Yes?'

'I've got money resting on you, lady. I've got my life tied up in you. You're doing Vegas.'

'Okay,' said Tiger hoarsely, turning her face to the wall, her eyes burning.

'I'm going to see the client quickly before I go. We'll sign the Vegas papers in the morning.'

'Whatever you say. See you tomorrow,' she grumbled, an angry crease emerging between her eyebrows.

With that, Lewis was out of the door, leaving Tiger silenced, annoyed and alone with her confused thoughts. She crossly poured herself a large neat Tanqueray and took a swig, deep in thought. Looking around the room she saw a smoke detector above her head. She stood on her chair and squirted hair mousse into it, then retrieved a pink Sobrani from her emergency stash of cigarettes in her vanity case. Lighting it, she savoured her first puff, and chugged back more of the cool, bitter gin, trying to relax. She heard a loud rapping at the door and Georgia, Nikki, Frankie and Blanche all squealing their goodbyes at her. 'Bye, girls, see you at rehearsals,' Tiger shouted over her shoulder.

She stubbed her cigarette out and took out a make-up

wipe. Slowly, carefully she removed her mask layer by layer. Her shoulders dropped as she calmed down. The red lips came off. The eyelashes were peeled off. Tiger slipped down into her chair and rubbed gently at the eyeliner under her eyes. She held her hands demurely in her lap as she looked at herself barefaced in the mirror. Just a smudge of blusher remained. Gently she wiped her cheeks, pausing to sweep stray strands of pink hair from her face when something caught her eye in the mirror. She realised the door was ajar and she could just make out Lewis peering through the crack, rooted to the spot.

'Get out!' she screamed like a banshee, flying from her chair for the door with her arm over her bare face, feeling all her power gone.

'How dare you stare at me with that look on your face like I'm some hag or something! Get out!' She slammed the door so hard the plasterboard wall shook. It never occurred to her that Lewis was simply mesmerised.

'Ahem, Tiger?' he ventured through the closed door.

'Fuck off!' she screamed, throwing a stilletto at the door as an exclamation mark.

'Just to let you know stage door Johnnie's outside again. He has some flowers for you and a card.'

'Thanks so much for tonight, Sienna. I couldn't have got the presentation finished without you,' said Rex, itching to get away from the office so he could surprise Tiger after her gig.

'Oh, it was nothing. I had no plans for this evening anyway,' said Sienna casually, thrilled at getting a compliment from Rex Hunter.

'Well, the presentation should sock 'em between the eyes at any rate,' said Rex proudly, making his way to Kat's desk to pile up the documents.

'What's this?' he asked suddenly.

'Huh?'

'On Kat's desk? It's addressed to me,' he mused, puzzled.

'Oh right. Yeah, I seem to remember a courier coming earlier. It must have gone on the wrong desk. '

Rex was already ripping the package open.

Sienna took her time packing her bag and tidying her desk ready for the morning, wanting to spend as much time alone with her boss as she could.

Rex stared at the Rolex in his hands. He felt his jaw tightening. His throat went dry as he read the words on the accompanying card. Of course. Tiger was just a one-night thing. Yes of course, he kidded himself, she meant nothing anyway. A strangled little laugh escaped his lips as he tried to calm his churning stomach. He'd never felt like this before. Was this supposed to be what love felt like? He felt as though he had been punched. He felt sick.

'You alright, Rex?' asked Sienna, who was now buttoning up her coat. Silence.

'Rex? You okay?'

'Yeah.' A pause. 'Er – listen, did you say you had no plans for the evening?'

'Well, not as such. Why?'

Rex made his way over to her desk, pulling down the blinds on the way. He put his hands on Sienna's slim waist and gently turned her back to him.

'Er—' started Sienna,

'Shhh . . . I know this is what you want, babe.'

Silently Rex lifted up her coat and skirt, pulled her panties to one side and began to fuck her hard over her desk.

Sienna couldn't believe her luck. She knew at that moment that Rex Hunter must have fancied her from day one.

Chapter 8

'And five, six, seven, eight, kick ball change, Georgia, lift that leg!' barked Pepper, stabbing the air with her index finger in time to the music pumping through the CD player.

'And kick two, three, four, glide, and glide! Oh for god's sake, girls, will you watch those kicks. You're all over the place, it has to be sharp! Look here.' Pepper charged into the group of girls and manhandled them into position with her bony fingers. 'And! Snap, snap, kick, turn, kick! It's really quick, you need to be light as a feather. And look – your hands – they need to be graceful, not rigid. Grace is power, girls, grace is power! Right, take your starting positions, from the top again!'

Lewis sat tucked away in the corner of the rehearsal studio, sucking on a Murray Mint as he studied the Starrlets' progress proudly. It was dusty and hot in the mirrored room as the girls worked up a mean sweat, far from the glamour of the stage. But there was no doubt in Lewis' mind this was going to be a knock-out routine. Pepper was doing a fantastic job on the choreography as usual.

Lewis secretly loved sitting in on rehearsals and watching Pepper at work. He identified with her spirit –

she was an old-school ballbreaker who got results; with the chorus girls she was a strict mother hen in charge of her wayward chicks. Just as it should be. Lewis found it soothing to have a kindred spirit on the team who wasn't afraid to be unpopular in order to enforce high standards.

Pepper had certainly passed on to Tiger the kind of polished stagecraft that only came with years of experience. Of course, she was still the picture of elegant eccentricity even now in her eighties. Dressed in her leotard and floaty skirt, with white hair scraped back tightly into her trademark bun which gave her quite a becoming facelift, and with her signature slick of bright fuschia pink lipstick on pale powdered skin, topped off with a carefully pencilled beauty spot just above her lip, she had a vintage glamour that betrayed her roots as a 1950s burlesque star.

Actually, Pepper's colourful character was far more than skin deep. Lewis had found over the years that she could often be persuaded to unzip her lively past at the mere whiff of a good whisky. He had enjoyed many a tale of Pepper's days dancing with Tiger's late grandma Coco Schnell at all manner of classic old venues like the Alhambra in London's Leicester Square, the Gaiety on the Strand, the Friedrichstadtpalast in Berlin and countless Orpheum Theatres across the United States.

Pepper would recall the early days when complete nudity was so outrageous that the only way the girls could be naked on stage was to stand as still as a marble statue. The theatres billed the scenes as 'poses plastiques' and 'tableaux vivants'. One of Pepper's roles in *The Lady is a Vamp* back in 1954 was to balance in her birthday suit on a bicycle and stay still as she was shoved across the stage from one wing to the other, giving the men a quick flash as she whizzed by. In fact, Pepper claimed that Tiger's grandmother Coco drove the men nuts with the most sensual striptease in the whole show. Legend had it that one night she actually stopped midway through to ask a punter in the front row who was clearly having a wank if he'd like the band to play a faster rhythm to go with his flute solo.

Of course times change, thought Lewis wistfully, and what was once a *risqué* art form was now deemed high theatre by today's standards. With today's audiences full of aristocrats, high-society women, actresses, celebrities, ordinary folk and middle-class culture vultures, he had to remind himself that the audiences of yore in the burlesque houses would include the 'newspaper brigade', or to put it more crudely, the 'jack-offs' – and that the front rows always smelt of crotches and armpits. But, Lewis knew that when Pepper and Coco danced they garnered the star audiences even then. Pepper still proudly got out the odd newscuttings from their time in America, one of them showing Ronald Reagan staring up at their buddy, the legendary Lili St Cyr, suspended from the ceiling in her magnificent gilded cage. Pepper claimed she had been there herself that very night.

It seemed a shame that Pepper was Tiger's only means

of learning more about her own grandmother. Whilst Tiger rarely spoke of her parents, Lewis gathered that they had strongly disapproved of Coco's legacy and of Tiger following in her footsteps. Coco had been a Catholic of Italian descent, and so Tiger's mother Bridget, a staunch Irish Catholic, felt she was a disgrace to her faith. Nonetheless, when Coco had fallen ill Tiger's father Frank had insisted she come back from the States to spend her last months in England near her family, and finally that she be laid to rest with a Catholic service. That was fourteen years ago. It was later that very same year that Lewis and Tiger had made their own big connection.

Tiger often spoke of her theory that Coco had always known the path her granddaughter would take. Coco gave instructions on her deathbed to Pepper, requesting that she find Tiger at the funeral service and make her acquaintance. Whilst Tiger was guarded with the quirky old lady at first, over the years she came to embrace Pepper as her fairy godmother; a gift from Coco, and a constant reminder to Tiger that her grandmother was always by her side in spirit, cheering her on from the wings.

Lewis snapped back to the present day as the music in the rehearsal room stopped abruptly.

'Is there a problem, Georgia?' snapped Pepper.

Georgia rolled her eyes and sighed as she delicately smoothed her blonde bob and dabbed sweat from her glistening brow with her long slender fingertips.

'Pepper, this is really difficult without Tiger here, I'm

trying to get the girls' spacing right and give them a good lead but without her here . . .'

'It's out of the question, darling. Tiger's in New York overnight recording the Johnson Tyler show, you have to make do without her,' said Pepper gently but firmly.

'Yes, I'm all too aware of that.' Georgia smiled sweetly, glancing behind her at Lewis for a second, before continuing, 'It's just, well, maybe someone can mark Tiger's part just for today?'

'H'mm.' Pepper looked pensive. 'Who would you suggest?'

'Well . . . I could do it, I seem to have learned all her parts off by heart anyway,' proposed Georgia hurriedly.

'Well, if you think you can manage—'

'Stop!' roared Lewis, launching himself from his chair at the back. 'Georgia, what the fuck are you thinking! Get back in line,' he snarled, placing himself squarely in front of Pepper. 'No one takes Tiger's place, Pepper. Not ever, not even in rehearsal. Not even you, Georgia.' He turned back to face his stunned girlfriend. 'Or any dance captain for that matter,' he muttered hotly, before stalking from the room with a gust of air that set the window blinds swaying in his wake. Jaws could be heard dropping. A long silence ensued.

'Bleedin' 'ell, babes, you alright?' ventured Nicky out of the silence, moving to put an arm round a shocked and red-faced Georgia.

'Oh piss off,' Georgia half choked, half sobbed, pushing through the group of girls to chase after Lewis.

'Right, girls, I think we'll take two minutes for a water break,' suggested Pepper, unruffled.

'Fackin' hell, girls, have you ever seen Lewis that bad before? It's not like Georgia was trying to take Tiger's place,' squawked Frankie with her Essex twang.

'Yeah, possessive or what,' said Briony, contributing her posh accent to the proceedings. 'I reckon he's got a thing for Tiger anyway, it's written all over his face if you ask me.'

'Oh come on, they've just been working together for, like, *centuries*,' guffawed Blanche huskily. 'Anyway, it's obvious Georgia's got an agenda, why else would she "just happen" to know Tiger's parts?'

''Cos she's our dance captain, dumbo, it's her job to know what everyone's doing,' argued Frankie.

'Crap, Georgia would throw a banana skin in front of Tiger if she thought she'd get the chance to take her place,' retorted Blanche fiercely.

'Girls, may I remind you I do not tolerate gossip!' shrieked Pepper above the chatter. 'Bad backstage manners will get you nowhere. Desist the chitchat immediately. Two minutes then we'll move on. I'll go and find Georgia.'

Pepper's diminutive frame powered briskly out of the room. The moment the door clicked behind her, the Starrlets burst into an excitable rabble of gossip and conjecture.

'So come on then, it's not really a career path they teach you at school is it? When exactly did you decide you wanted to be an international showgirl sensation?'

The television camera zoomed in on Tiger as she sat on the couch cool as a cucumber under the hot studio lights, looking impossibly chic with little Gravy perched on her stockinged knee.

'Oh, Johnson, it wasn't really one of those Eureka moments, it was quite organic, I think it must have been in my blood from day one!'

'I can see that, but come on, tell us a bit about your background – did you go to stage school?' probed Johnson Tyler the chat-show host.

'Oh lord no,' laughed Tiger softly. 'No "jazz hands" for me.' The audience laughed with her. 'No, I did modern and Latin as a young girl, but I really got my passion when I ended up in Spain hanging out with the most incredible flamenco dancers. I immersed myself in the culture, the dance, the movement. In Spanish dance they call it *duende*, you know, where you become so consumed with passion when you dance that it's like being overtaken by a spirit, and your soul is bared – it leaves the audience mesmerised.'

'Ooh yes I'm feeling that right now as I look at you, you're very good at this *duende* thing you know,' quipped Johnson, winking at the audience who bellowed with laughter. 'So after the flamenco then what? You were kidnapped by strippers on the way?' More laughs.

'Oh no, better than that, my grandmother was a burlesque dancer in the fifties. So when I had to leave Spain for her funeral in England, I knew I wanted to use what I had learnt to carry on her legacy.' Tiger stroked her pink curls nervously. She had been briefed on the questions she would be asked, but was inwardly praying Johnson didn't go off script as he had a reputation for doing. She didn't need any more probing into her background than the official story she always gave. She reminded herself not to fiddle, and clamped her hands safely on Gravy.

'You're so modest, Tiger,' replied Johnson, 'as your grandmother was a huge name in England and America back then wasn't she? Coco Schnell, ladies and gentlemen, she performed in the same theatres as American burly legends Gypsy Rose Lee, Lili St Cyr and Ann Corio. Let's get a shot of her up on screen.' Johnson Tyler gestured behind him as a black-and-white photograph flashed onto the huge monitor behind his desk. The audience oo-ed and ah-ed at the beautiful image of raven-haired Coco in her sparkling gown slashed to the thigh with a long luxurious cape of fur and diamonds. Tiger felt an enormous twinge of pride, and grief, as she saw her grandma up there being revered all these years later. If only Coco could have enjoyed this moment of glory when she was alive instead of being ostracised as the black sheep of the family.

It made Tiger sad to think she was too young to have ever seen her own grandmother on stage, and even more so that her father forbade her to ask questions about anything to do with her career, as though he was ashamed of his own mother. Nonetheless, Tiger still managed to steal the odd moment to listen to her grandma's wonderful stories on the rare occasions she crossed the Atlantic to visit her family. It was true that many of the burlesque stars of Coco's generation longed to go 'legit' in those days and turn to more socially acceptable careers in acting, singing or ballet; yet here was Tiger, sixty years later, doing the same as her grandma, but as legitimate as 'legit' could ever be.

'Now that outfit would have been considered quite x-rated at the time wouldn't it, Tiger?'

Tiger looked coy, before replying, 'Well, you could be arrested for flashing too much back then, to see a belly button was naughty. Grandma used to tell me how the burlesque houses often had a red light concealed in front of the stage that would light up to let the girls know when the cops were in the audience. All the girls knew not to flash their beaver when that light was up . . . and of course with all those nudity restrictions that's where the pasties – that's nipple covers to you, Johnson – came into effect. It was a trend to have tassels on the pasties too, many of the ladies could spin their tassels in all directions to order. Jennie Lee, the Bazoom girl, was one of the most notorious for her tassel-twirling technique.' A huge roar erupted as Johnson Tyler calmly pulled open his blazer to reveal a pair of nipple tassels stuck to his shirt.

'Yes, I believe there's quite an art to spinning them, right?'

Tiger covered Gravy's eyes jokingly.

'Of course! But I'd take an educated guess you're not wearing a merkin too are you, Johnson?' asked Tiger huskily with a wink.

'Hoho! That's for me to know! Well join us after the break when we'll be interviewing Joan Collins, and Tiger Starr will tell us about her new Vegas show, ladies and gentlemen, and who knows, we may even get her to do a special shimmy just for you. Ladies and gentlemen, all the way from London, Miss Tiger Starrrrrr!' The crowd whooped and clapped and the cameras pulled back and panned across the huge television studio before cutting to the ad break. Johnson Tyler waited for the all clear to come through his earpiece, before leaning across his desk towards Tiger, upon whom the make-up girl had swooped to powder her nose and forehead.

'Spectacular, Miss Starr. Man, that's one cute as hell accent you have there. You look – my god, you look stunning,' horned Johnson. Tiger felt herself turn coy. Flustered, she dropped Gravy, who scurried off across the set, with several hefty production crew in hot pursuit.

'Oops!' Tiger exclaimed.

'Oh don't worry, we're all dog lovers here. I hope you'll join us in the green room after the show?' pressed Johnson. Tiger looked into his warm brown eyes, a little crinkly at the corners. At least he doesn't botox like the rest of showbiz, she thought to herself. Tiger spent so much time with Blue and his gay army that she found masculinity turned her on. A little 'me Tarzan, you Jane' made her weak at the knees. Maybe that's what had got to her about Rex.

Tiger spotted Gravy under a table, cocking his leg and making a steaming puddle as the production men huddled around and clicked, hissed and tried to entice him from under his hideaway.

'You know what, I'd love to join you after the show,' giggled Tiger, realising Johnson was decidedly sexy, especially with that salt 'n' pepper hair and strong jaw. There was definitely something of George Clooney about him.

'Great. I'm pleased.' Johnson beamed. 'Oh – hang on – okay we're counting down from sixty now. I'm gonna ask you about your Vegas show and then we'll wrap up your piece and bring out Joan Collins. You'll stay on the couch while we do her interview.'

Tiger smoothed her dress over her knee as one of the crew whizzed across the set to plonk a bewildered-looking Gravy back in her lap.

Back in her dressing room after the recording, Tiger dabbed some Chanel behind her ears as Blue fussed with her dress.

'Honestly, darling, I nearly wet myself when Joan walked on in that gold number, ohhh to die for,' he gushed as he hurriedly steamed creases from the hem of Tiger's silk Gucci gown. 'I need to ask John Galliano to whip you up something like it, that colour would be divine on you.'

'H'mm,' sighed Tiger wistfully in agreement, distracted

as she watched Gravy sniffing, then decanting on the other side of the room.

'Blue, have you taken Gravy for a walk today? He's peeing for England.'

'Huh, what did your last slave die of? We've been in between limos and meetings all day, when was I supposed to take him out? I thought you were being given an aide for this trip anyway.'

'I didn't bother with the aide, it's only an overnight job. Thank god Gravy didn't leave a parcel in the studio, that's all I can say.'

'Well he's so small they don't even cast a shadow. You could always plug him up of course. That's what Zorita used to do with her snakes you know, she'd plug 'em up so that they didn't shit during her shows, and when they died she'd just buy a new one.'

'That's just a rumour! Anyway, Gravy's my special buddy. I'm not plugging him up.' Tiger sniffed.

'More special than me?' Blue made puppy eyes.

'Well he doesn't get moody . . .'

'Yeah, but he can't rhinestone a bra and fluff a feather like I can.'

Tiger laughed and cooed over at the dog.

'Keep still darling, nearly done,' said Blue, rearranging satin over Tiger's breasts. 'Need to make sure you look pristine next to Joan in the green room,' he murmured to himself happily. A loud knock at the door made them both jump. Gravy growled.

'Miss Starr?' came a muffled voice.

Blue tucked the grumbling dog under his arm and pounced for the door.

'Oh hi, I was given this envelope to give to Miss Starr, it was left at reception earlier.'

Blue stared lasciviously at the young blond production runner standing before him who was craning his neck over Blue's shoulder to catch a glimpse of Tiger.

'And who are you, young man?' enquired Blue politely, puffing out his large frame to block the view into the room.

'My name's Brady.'

'Brady, I say.' Blue broke into a grin. 'Thank you so much, I shall pass this to Miss Starr. That sounds like a California accent to me. Nice. Will I be seeing you in the green room?'

'Sure, will Miss Starr be coming up?'

'Yes indeed. We'll be out shortly.' Blue winked and closed the door.

'Who was that?' asked Tiger.

'Eye candy. Tanned Cally boy. Yum. God I love it over here. Hey, I've got fan mail for you, hand delivered no less.'

'Thank you, darling.' Tiger took the envelope and ripped it open.

Blue watched her take the sheet of pink paper out of the envelope, stare at the page, turn it over, then turn it back again and stare some more. She looked up at him quizzically.

'Something the matter, babes?' asked Blue, snatching the paper from her manicured fingers. 'I know . . . where . . . you . . . live,' he read out loud. 'What the? What's with the cut-out newspaper letters? *Murder She Wrote* or something?' Blue looked at Tiger, bemused.

'That's what I thought!' laughed Tiger. 'Ah well, our "fan" is in the wrong country for now! If they truly know where I live then they'll know they have zero chance of getting past the paps in my driveway without being photographed. And then there's the full might of Gravy to contend with if they get in the house!' she laughed, scooping up all ten inches of her scruffy Yorkshire Terrier for a cuddle.

'Er, I'm not sure you should be laughing about this, babes.'

'Oh, Blue, lighten up, it's just some prankster. Either that or it's stage door Johnnie having a laugh. I wouldn't be surprised if he'd made the trip over here the little poppet! C'mon, champagne with Joan Collins and ol' silver fox Johnson Tyler is beckoning. You want to see Cally boy again don't you? Put that stupid letter in the bin.' Tiger swept out of the room, her silk dress whispering seductively against her stockings as she wafted. Blue quietly tucked the pink paper into the top pocket of his Gaultier jacket. He had a nagging feeling. He was hoping he had been dreaming earlier, but he was sure he had seen the unmistakably ugly face of Rosemary Baby in the audience.

*   *   *

Georgia followed Lewis anxiously through the heavy iron door of his cavernous Clerkenwell warehouse pad. He clapped his hands twice and the lights blazed on in the lounge area.

'Thanks for supper, it was nice,' he said, throwing his door keys onto the steel Conran coffee table with a clatter. Lewis had been in a funk with Georgia ever since the afternoon's rehearsal fiasco, and she had been trying to smooth things out ever since. She reckoned oysters and caviar at Scott's ought to do it. Despite her meagre dancer's wages, maxing out her credit card on supper tonight was worth it to placate Lewis. Secretly, Georgia was peeved with her stupidity in rehearsals earlier. How embarrassing in front of everyone, damn it. Lewis had seen straight through her attempt to impress Pepper with what she could do in Tiger's place. What was it Tiger had over everyone anyway? All Lewis' praise for her 'fire', 'heat' and 'stage presence'; well you could just learn that like dance moves, right? thought Georgia huffily. All she needed was a bit of arse padding in her dance tights and an expensive tit job and she'd be well on the way to sex goddess of the stage. Watch out Tiger!

Georgia heard Lewis smashing the shit out of a block of ice over in the kitchen. She figured the oysters hadn't worked their aphrodisiac magic yet. Wandering across the open-plan room to Lewis, she stood watching him with his Garrard diamond ice pick in one hand, shovelling shards of glacier into a fat tumbler with the other.

'Let me make you a nightcap, darling,' offered Georgia.

'Oh okay, go on then. I'll stick some music on,' replied Lewis. 'I'll have a dirty Martini. The shaker's there on the side. The gin's in the mini-fridge. Help yourself, there's vodka in the freezer too if you prefer.'

Dirty Martini. That's Tiger's favourite drink, damn her, thought Georgia crossly. Does Lewis *have* to like everything about her? Georgia carefully rinsed a Martini glass with vermouth, realising she would have to accept that the bond between Lewis and Tiger was simply the type that comes with working at such close quarters for so many years. But boy could it make a girl feel insecure.

'Smack My Bitch Up' blasted the music through the stereo system at deafening volume, making Georgia jolt and smash the glass on the kitchen floor. She looked despairingly at the mess as the heavy grinding techno bass lurched and thumped through the apartment, shaking the walls with every screech of the poetic lyrics. She took an executive decision to resort to Plan B immediately.

Georgia hopped over the dirty Martini carnage on the kitchen floor and ripped off her black tube skirt to expose her long lithe legs clad in silky Wolford hold ups, topped off with a pearl g-string. Only the best for Georgia Atlanta when it came to lingerie. She slinked her way over to Lewis as he stood by the stereo and before he had a chance to speak, she jumped on him and wrapped her legs about his waist, the way he always liked.

'Uh,' grunted Lewis, taken by surprise.

'I can't wait any longer, I just need your cock up me, baby,' breathed Georgia, feeling an instant hardening in Lewis' crotch area. Men are so predictable, she thought, relieved. Lewis clamped his hands round her sinewy thighs and threw her onto the sofa, unzipping himself to release his raging hard on. He thrust himself into her. Without a word passing between them, they sweated their way through several positions in quick succession.

Once safely on top, Georgia grabbed the sound system's remote and changed the music to her favourite, Prince. Fuelled with that night's oysters and champagne she performed like a seasoned acrobat, staying focused on the job of placating Lewis after today. He was one guy she wasn't going to lose for anything. He just knew the answers to everything, it was like nothing fazed him; plus he had a Titanium Amex card. Georgia loved his stormy ways, it kept her on her toes and longing to please him. Most importantly, he could help her career in ways other men just couldn't.

Georgia suddenly realised Lewis hadn't come yet. Her heart sank as she looked down to see his handsomely weathered face looking bored as she worked on his cock rhythmically as she sat on him.

'Look at me,' she whispered softly in his ear.

Lewis opened his eyes and stared up at her as she slowly rocked her hips back and forth.

'Say my name,' she whispered, pushing him deep inside her, 'say my name.'

Georgia grabbed his hand and placed it on her buttock, 'Just say my name,' she whispered urgently.

Lewis smiled awkwardly, and said nothing. His eyes closed and his hand fell away from her as the opening bars of 'Money Don't Matter Tonight' filtered into the room.

'Tiger, oh Tiger. Oh baby. Oh my.'

Johnson Tyler ran his fingers softly over Tiger's exposed back. He let out a soft moan as she skilfully massaged his cock, giving a delicate tug on his balls with her other hand.

'Argh. Oh Tiger baby. Oh that's too good.'

Seeing Johnson close to orgasm, Tiger pulled away with one last firm stroke.

'More champagne, darling?' she purred.

'No . . . no, no don't stop I was . . .'

'Oh darling, I like to pace myself, you know, savour every moment.' Tiger leaned in and spoke with her lips close to his. She smelled his musky scent, mixed with sweat. She closed her eyes and savoured the aroma. Hmm. Rex. Tiger guiltily pushed all thoughts of him aside and concentrated on Johnson. Maybe Blue was right when he'd suggested that the easiest way to get over one man was to get on top of another. It was certainly worth a try. In one movement she stood, unclipped the halter of her gown and let it slip to the floor with a swish.

'Oh. God. Tiger. Don't leave me hanging . . .' gasped Johnson, rising from the black satin sheets of the circular bed and reaching straight for her hips. Black satin sheets? Bachelor taste was still very much at large amongst men of a certain age, thought Tiger with a little chuckle as she slid from out of his hands and onto the bed like a prowling cat.

'Oh baby,' gasped Johnson, 'stay just there. That's an ass. God, you're perfect.'

Tiger rose up onto all fours and kicked her stilettoed feet playfully behind her as she felt Johnson approaching her from behind.

'Ooh that tickles!' squealed Tiger, arching her back as she felt Johnson stroking her buttock.

'Keep still, baby,' whispered Johnson. Tiger heard soft crinkling of paper. That doesn't sound like a condom wrapper, thought Tiger. Johnson had gone quiet, but Tiger could still feel tickling.

'What are you . . .'

She glanced over her smooth, bronzed shoulder. Sure enough, Johnson was racking up a line of white powder on her smooth bare arse.

Tiger rolled her eyes, sighed and flipped quickly and elegantly onto her back, her perky breasts rising like zeppelins.

'Oh shit! I said stay still, baby,' exclaimed Johnson, a half rolled hundred dollar bill mid air in one hand. Tiger gracefully swept up her long legs and wrapped them round his neck, pulling him towards her.

'Darling, my ass is an unspoilt landscape, I don't need

you racking up Colombia's finest on it thank you,' she murmured softly. Tiger was certainly no prude, having had her own chemical dramas in years gone by, but she had emerged on the other side a wiser woman, and now found the whole Class-A culture rather passé. She certainly wasn't going to be used as Johnson Tyler's serving dish.

'Aw c'mon, baby. It's a massive compliment. It's usually a blue pill,' said Johnson with a serious face.

'Oh thanks, that's a relief then!' laughed Tiger heartily. She couldn't be annoyed with such a downright charmer.

Johnson kissed her tenderly. Tiger suddenly felt relieved for the interruption. Deep down she knew she was still trying to get Rex out of her head. Thank god, she was better than this. Black satin sheets indeed! And cocaine! How eighties!

Tiger rose. 'I should leave, my darling. I have a long day tomorrow. Thank you for drinks and dinner and . . . I'm sorry, I just can't . . .'

'Yeah I shouldn't have – shit, what was I thinking – we're cool, aren't we?' asked Johnson, suddenly looking like a spoilt schoolboy in his high-tech playground.

'You bet. Look me up when you're in the UK and I'll take you out for dinner.'

'Okay, baby. You're a rare broad, you know, Tiger.'

'Well, if I do the job of a blue pill then I could make billions!'

They both laughed as Tiger smoothed her hair, dressed, and ran out to the warmth of her waiting limo.

Chapter 9

The gloved hand slowly turns over the front cover of the 'Funtime Playtime' scrapbook. The leaves of coloured sugar paper are turned over one by one, first blue, then pink, then yellow. Each page proffers another image of Tiger Starr, cut from a magazine or a faded newspaper. Beautiful smiles and sultry gazes radiate from each page; moments captured in time. The gloved hand reaches for a scalpel blade from the desk, and the blade is guided slowly towards Tiger's image. It is scraped deliberately and repeatedly over her heaving bosom in long, leisurely strokes, scoring the paper as she twinkles from the page. Trembling, both hands now methodically scratch gashes into her breasts, faster, shorter, faster, harder, faster; until all that remains is an ugly wound of sugar paper. The page now hangs sorrowfully from the binding by a thread, the picture a mass of angry slashes.

The gloved hand lays the blade down carefully, next to little piles of newsprint words arranged neatly on the desk. A sheet of wafer thin, translucent paper sits squarely next to an embellished packet out of which spills a pink writing block and matching envelopes. A small bottle of Chanel No. 5 occupies the last square of space on the desk. A pink envelope is selected and duly primed with a light spray of the amber liquid. Miniscule droplets of fragrance sparkle momentarily under the beam of light from the anglepoise lamp, before settling on the envelope. A deep sigh echoes through the room as it fills with powdery, floral notes of rose and jasmine.

Chapter 10

In the distance a lawnmower could be heard motoring up and down the playing field. The lively hum of chattering schoolgirls had been replaced by the soporific drone of the industrial floor polisher in the corridor, interspersed with sporadic shrieks of gossip barked in Polish as the cleaners noisily emptied bins and swabbed the parquet floor in the neighbouring classrooms. Poppy fiddled miserably with the novelty zipper on her Betty Boop pencil case, anxiously imagining the scene when she returned home. She had never had a detention before, and she knew her mother would be absolutely furious. Poppy prayed that Mr Rogers hadn't noticed the cigarette butts out on the grass earlier, or the unmistakable smell of stale smoke on her clothes. The ripped shirt was bad enough, but if her mother was told about the cigarettes, Poppy was sure to be grounded for the rest of her teenage years. That's if she wasn't sent away to boarding school like her parents frequently threatened if Poppy was naughty.

She looked over at Emma, who was still slouched sulkily in her chair, doodling on her A4 pad with a Bic biro. She'd been huffing and puffing solidly for the past hour. Flicking an evil sideways look at Poppy, she mouthed 'stupid cow'.

Ed Rogers looked up from his text book *Playing the Game: Bats, Balls and Boules*.

'Okay, girls, it's five-thirty, you may now leave. Please could you place your essays on the front desk for me.' He spoke in his Australian twang, deep and husky from all that bellowing on the sports fields. 'Your parents will be called by the secretary in a moment to let them know you are safely discharged.' He rose from his chair and turned to the whiteboard, upon which tonight's punitive essay title was written in marker, 'Violence is unladylike. Discuss'.

As he swept a rag in arcs across the board, erasing the legend, Poppy stared at his tanned, muscled calves. She idly wondered why he always wore long shorts, rarely track-suit bottoms. The chair scraped loudly next to her, and Emma rose. As she reached over to place her essay on the desk in front, she shoved Poppy's open pencil case onto the floor.

'Oops, sorry,' said Emma loudly, smiling slyly at Poppy as she sashayed from the classroom with a wave. Poppy leapt up to gather the pens and pencils that had scattered. Ed Rogers moved in on her. 'Let me help you with that,' he said kindly, crouching down and reaching out to pick up a couple of pens that had come to rest under the desk. Poppy was alarmed to find tears suddenly spilling down her cheeks and onto the bottle-green sweater that Mr Rogers had lent her to cover her ripped shirt. She snivelled in little spasms and frantically tried to rub her eyes dry with shaky hands. Crying in front of a teacher was so embarrassing, especially a man like Mr Rogers. She was fourteen now after all, no way was she a silly little girl any more.

'Poppy, I know you've never had a detention before,' said Ed gently, reaching to put a hand on her shoulder, 'and your parents have to be informed – those are the regulations. But let's just say . . .' He paused long enough for her to look up at him with her green eyes.

'Look, let's just be friends, Poppy. I didn't see anything like cigarettes and matches out there, for example. You get my drift?' He slowly slid the biros into her pencil case.

Poppy swallowed hard, stemming the flow of unwanted tears, and nodded as she knelt there on the parquet floor. She stared back at his kind face, as he casually ran his long fingers through his tousled golden hair. He was close. He smelled of washing powder.

'Your jumper, I need to give it back,' started Poppy.

'Oh that, don't worry. No, you just keep hold of it for the moment,' Ed laughed softly. 'Besides, you can't go home in your ripped shirt. Just one thing, Poppy,' he asked suddenly. 'Why were you rolling around the grass with Emma?'

'Like I said, we were just playing,' mumbled Poppy, feeling little butterflies in her tummy now that the tears had dried up. Wow. She was actually getting to keep Ed Rogers' jumper for a while. Wow. She reckoned she could sell it to one of her classmates for a heap of money, everyone fancied him.

'Playing? Emma was nearly ripping your hair out.'

'Um. Yeah. We've been watching the wrestling on telly?' Poppy ventured, unconvincingly.

'Well, you're better than that. You're not like other girls, you're not vulgar. Don't lower yourself to that.'

'Oh, sir, it was just that Emma – oh you wouldn't understand.'

'Are you being bullied?'

'Oh god, no!'

'You must say if there's something going on.'

'No, sir, definitely not, it was just a little difference of opinion. I got defensive, that's all. Sorry.'

'Did you hear what I said back then?'

'No.'

'That you're not like other girls.'

'Oh.'

'I mean it, Poppy.'

'Um . . .'

'You're special, never forget that.'

'Oh.'

'Don't be embarrassed.'

Ed reached out and rested his hand on Poppy's. She could feel herself trembling. She was confused. Her stomach churned with nervous excitement, but she was unfamiliar with the heady mixture of exhilaration and unease washing over her. The classroom was deadly silent. The cleaners had gone home, the gardener's work was done. Poppy's mouth felt dry. She didn't know where to look. She could feel Mr Rogers' eyes on her. Her mind raced. She wanted to hold his hand. Her friends would hate her for that. Should she say something clever? Her mind went blank. She opened her mouth. Nothing came out. Her small hand simply trembled under his. She cast her eyes down awkwardly and studied a small piece of fluff on her skirt.

Ed Rogers leapt to his feet and cleared his throat. 'Okay, Poppy, I'll take your essay. Have a pleasant evening,' he said coolly. 'See you for hockey Friday. Oh, and remember it's the match against Hazelbury next week. We want to thrash them. Those silly girls think they're going to be top of the league, so let's show 'em what's what.' He winked and showed Poppy to the door.

As she walked out into the corridor clutching her pencil case and books, she took a deep breath and braced herself for the furious confrontation she was about to have with her mother, who would be waiting at the school gates in her clapped-out old car. Poppy suddenly didn't care. Mr Rogers had just told her she was special, and she was wearing his jumper. She felt bullet proof.

Chapter 11

Tiger Starr's house may have looked unassuming from the outside – a neat Grade II listed stucco affair – but typically for Tiger, it was situated in the lavish surroundings of the Crown Estate, in the Outer Circle of Regents Park. It nestled comfortably opposite the Danish Church, and Tiger relished the view from her manicured garden: immaculate mansions with Corinthian columns and gargoyles reared up into view over her tree tops like absurdly elaborate facades, making her feel like she was tucked away on the set of some huge Regency drama.

Inside the house it was pure indulgence. Each room paid homage to a different country and decade. The dining room had the air of a 1920s cruise-liner bar, with dark punched steel wall panels, sleek leather banquettes and a streamlined minibar. The library might have come straight out of the Palace of Versailles with fancy gilded cherubs and glam-baroque scrolls. The parlour was all decked out in 1930s *chinoiserie* with black lacquer skirting, deep emerald satin walls, and a real cherry blossom in the corner. There could be no doubt that Tiger loved to submerge herself in different worlds.

The bedrooms were just as eccentric. One posed as a

1960s Michael Caine-esque bachelor pad with brown leather Eames chairs, chrome pendulum lamps and exposed brickwork. Another bedroom was a *frou frou* palace that mimicked the style of Diana Dors' mansion, with chintzy sage-coloured raw silk bedlinen, a chiffon canopy and a fluffy telephone. This particular room had been claimed by Blue the nano-second he had moved in six years earlier, and his framed prints of Bardot and Jayne Mansfield now adorned the walls, whilst piles of vintage '50s beefcake porn were stacked underneath the coffee table.

Tiger's own master bedroom had been styled as a sleek *Dynasty* fantasy, fully swagged in oyster silk, with rich gold fittings and the deepest cream shagpile. In fact, there was quite a production unfolding in her bedroom right now, as Libertina Belle straddled a blissfully docile Tiger, the exquisite pair bathed in a burst of Sunday morning sunbeam which streamed in through the sash window. Their soft moans harmonised with the bells that pealed out from the Danish Church, with Libertina's huge solid gold bracelets adding rhythmic percussion. A union of pink and raven manes were tossed about spectacularly as the symphony progressed into its fourth movement. Beethoven would have wept. The groans and sighs rapidly erupted into an almighty crescendo of ecstasy and arched backs, at which moment, a key rattled downstairs in the front door.

'Coo-eeee!' Blue could be heard calling up the sweeping staircase as he closed the heavy door behind him with a loud clack.

'My dahhhling, I don't want to leave you, but I must go,' murmured Libertina dramatically in Tiger's ear, as they lay entwined together in her huge bed, panting breathlessly. Libertina swept Tiger's pink hair away from her face, and softly stroked her flushed cheek.

'Please stay,' begged Tiger affectionately.

'I wish I could, dahhhling. I have to go for that reading for my next film. I'm sure I mentioned it.'

'On a Sunday?' protested Tiger.

'I made them squeeze me in before I fly to NYC first thing tomorrow,' Libertina explained.

'Okay, I wouldn't dream of holding you up,' sighed Tiger, making sure not to let her disappointment show. 'Good luck, beautiful lady.'

'Huh, luck has nothing to do with it. It's a done deal. The reading is just a formality, the part was written for me.'

'So no casting couch, then?' giggled Tiger.

'Honey, I *invented* the casting couch. *Ciao* bella bella,' said Libertina, planting a soft kiss on Tiger's lips, 'and give me a call, we should do lunch when I get back. We didn't do much talking last night and I want to hear what's happening in your world . . . properly.'

'Okay, lunch sounds perfect. Thanks for breakfast.' Tiger winked as she watched Libertina stepping gracefully into her dress and easing it up over her shapely hips.

'*Merda!*' cursed Libertina in Italian as she frantically tried to smooth out the creases of her miniscule Dolce and Gabbana number. 'I look like a bag lady!'

'Rubbish. You just look freshly fucked,' said Tiger. 'Perfect. Now, be gone! Wouldn't want you to be late!'

After a final kiss, Libertina grabbed her sheared beaver coat and ran out of the bedroom door, slamming straight into Blue. They squealed and apologised loudly in unison, and then Libertina was off towards her Ferrari in a flurry of fur and swishing hair.

'Sooooo . . .' started Blue, jumping onto the bed next to Tiger. 'You're just one surprise after another . . .' Tiger just smiled at him happily. 'You look like the cat that got the cream! Rex will be devastated!' he teased, eyeing up a long strand of raven black hair on the pillow.

'Rex will never know, will he?' answered Tiger, flopping back into her soft pillow and pulling the duvet up to her chin. 'Besides it's none of his business. Rex and I are history. Now I'm tired and hungover, so be gentle,' she lamented. Trying another man to get over Rex hadn't worked, so maybe another woman would work better. Besides, Tiger was very drawn to Libertina. She sensed that they could be friends as well as lovers and there was novelty in that alone.

'Sounds like you could use a little livener. I went out and bought the Sunday papers and orange juice for Buck's Fizz . . . you two didn't work your way through *every* bottle of champagne did you?'

'God no, well not quite – there's still some Krug chilling in the minibar.'

'Nice, I'll be right back. Oh, and Tiger?'

'Hmm?'

'Do you owe me that tenner?'

'What tenner?'

'Were they real?'

'Oh the bet. Er—'

'Be honest now?'

'Blue, they were a-*mazing*,'

'But were they real?'

'Oh okay, I owe you ten pounds.'

'Wooh hoo! Damn I'm good! I know silicone when I see it!'

'Good for you. Now go get the champagne.'

'Yes, ma'am. I brought up your mail from yesterday by the way.'

Blue threw the pile of envelopes on Tiger's duvet. Tiger had been avoiding the mail deliberately. In amongst the circulars was a pink envelope that bore a striking resemblance to the one she had been given in New York. Oh what the hell, she was still pleasantly alcoholised and glowing in the wake of Libertina, and she decided that whatever the envelope offered, she could handle it head on. Boldly she picked it up and ripped it open.

'I. Watch. You. Sleeping. You. Will. See. Me. In. Your. Nightmares.'

Tiger let out a snort of relief. Is that it? I watch you sleeping? Impossible, she thought to herself, flicking her eyes over to the heavy sash window. Nightmares? What kind of a threat's that! She held the paper to her nose. It smelled of Chanel. Tiger heard Blue clinking glasses loudly as he wobbled up the stairs with the tray of champagne and juice. Quickly she stuffed the pink letter under a cushion.

'Breakfast is served!' announced Blue as he swept through the door. Gravy followed and jumped up on to the bed, tail wagging ten to the dozen.

'I won't crack any "hair of the dog" jokes,' promised Tiger as she cuddled the little ball of fur tightly.

'Hold your horses, babes, because breakfast in bed wouldn't be complete without . . .' Blue paused, picking up Tiger's stereo remote control. 'Disco!' he squealed, as 'Ring My Bell' blasted out through the speakers. 'Who needs *Songs of Praise* when we've got the seventies!'

'Oh my head,' groaned Tiger.

'Here. Get this down you.' Blue jumped on the bed and wafted Buck's Fizz under Tiger's nose like smelling salts. 'Ring my bell, ring-a-ling-a-ling,' he sang tunelessly, leaping up and swinging Gravy in the air as he minced round the luxurious bedroom, swigging champagne to the thumping music. 'Now this is my idea of Sunday Mass! Amen!'

Lewis' eyes adjusted to the bright daylight as he exited the cinema. Finding himself a space at the bar he flicked through the pages of his programme idly, whilst keeping one eye on the world that passed by outside on the south bank of the Thames. The National Film Theatre was running a month-long retrospective on one of Lewis' favourite actors, Robert Mitchum. He knew Tiger would have dearly loved to watch *Night of the Hunter* that afternoon, what with Mitchum being one of her all time favourite idols, but Lewis had the boundaries of their relationship strictly defined. A Sunday movie accompanied by Tiger would stray into the 'personal' zone too much. Instead he had sent a bored Georgia off to Sloane Street for some sponsored retail therapy whilst he indulged in movie classics on his rare day off.

Lewis felt unusually relaxed staring out of the window and people watching. He watched as the resident batty old flute player twiddled his melodies between the passing tourists like Methuselah on Ecstasy. People hovered at the rows of second-hand bookstalls to choose dog-eared thrillers for fifty pence a go. Hoodie boys sped by on their skateboards. A skinny blonde stringbean picked her way awkwardly over the cracks in the pavement in unfeasibly high heels, all flailing arms and legs. Lewis gave a double take as the girl came into focus and he realised it was in fact Georgia stumbling over to meet him as arranged. What on earth is she wearing, he thought grimly, rolling his eyes in their sockets.

'Hey hunny!' screeched Georgia as she piled through the door into the bar, laden down with bags of shopping. She clattered her way past chairs and tables towards Lewis, before dropping her bags at his feet and throwing her arms around his neck dramatically.

'Wait 'til you see what I bought!' said Georgia excitedly.

'Yes, I can see!' said Lewis, looking her up and down and noting that she was in an entirely different outfit than the one she left in this morning. It looked expensive. It didn't exactly suit her frame either. And what was with the platform skyscraper heels? They made her skinny legs look like golf clubs. Georgia fished in her purse and retrieved Lewis' Amex Titanium card, and pressed it into his palm.

'Thank you for today,' Georgia whispered in his ear, 'I desperately needed some smart new clothes, thank you. Hey, I even bought a little something for us to share when we get home later,' and with that, she proudly reached into one of her bags, and waved a lacy thong under Lewis' nose.

'Very good, darling. Can I get you a coffee or something?' asked Lewis, hastily putting his credit card back in his wallet, wondering how much that bootlace masquerading as underwear had cost him. He daren't ask. He simply turned to the bartender.

'I'll have an espresso and a . . .' Lewis turned to Georgia.

'Glass of champagne please,' she replied automatically. 'So, how was the film?'

'Good.' Lewis nodded.

'What was it again, a thriller or an action movie?'

'Film noir.'

'Film what?'

'Film – never mind.' Lewis folded his programme and tucked it in the inside pocket of his jacket.

'Do you like my outfit?' asked Georgia, waving her hand over her dress; slim fitting, grey, over the knee, and tightly belted with cute button details. On Georgia it certainly looked sleek and, well, very straight. Lewis decided it would benefit from someone of Tiger's shape to carry it off better.

'Actually I spotted you from outside,' he replied, side-stepping her question, 'it's not your usual style is it? Who's it by?'

'Dior.'

'Oh, one of Tiger's favourites.'

'Really?' said Georgia in a clipped tone. 'Well, Tiger couldn't fit into this, it's a US size zero.' She sniffed.

Lewis wasn't sure how to respond to that, and instead just watched as the waiter placed the drinks in front of him. He chugged back his espresso. Pow, the caffeine hit his bloodstream in a shot. He remembered when he used to live on the stuff. Twenty of these a day would keep him on an even keel. But back then he was putting in twenty-hour days too; though not much more than he was working now, being Tiger's 'back end of the horse' as he put it.

Fourteen years ago Lewis was an ambitious thirty-year-old high flier heading up a huge soft commodities division for the global investment group Mayall Plc., trading coffee, cocoa, sugar, nuts and spices on the futures market. He bought companies and factories for millions and just occasionally managed to sell them for billions. The kind of people he dealt with on Colombian coffee plantations were the kind of people who made the wicked world of showbiz look like the Teddy Bears' Picnic. With so much money at stake, the business of commodities had its intrinsic dark side. Out on the road men would die; blown up in Russia, or stabbed in Cuba, and in the office your colleagues would be your worst enemies, ready to stab you in an entirely different way.

Lewis used to train hard every morning in the East End boxing ring; he believed that maintaining peak fitness was what gave him the stamina to snare his opponents in the boardroom at the end of a long day, when their mental reflexes were flagging. Not only that, but punching the crap out of someone first thing in the morning released Lewis' primal instincts, so that taking on adversaries in the office felt positively civilised. His gruelling schedules took him across time zones and continents, and with his notorious mental resilience, he was well regarded for taking tough negotiations in his stride.

Then along came Tiger Starr. No amount of punches and blows dealt him by knuckleheads in the ring could prepare Lewis for the hit between the eyes when he was confronted with the vision of Tiger pelting towards him backstage at the Duke of York's Theatre in London like a crazed wildcat. She nearly knocked him over as she made a bid for freedom through the stage door.

'Ooff! Watch yourself, lady!' Lewis had yelled fiercely.

'Are you investing in this piece of crap too? Tell the

director to keep his fucking hands to himself. I'm outta here as of five minutes ago!'

Lewis had then watched bemused as Tiger struggled violently to free her ballet-cardigan sleeve which had entangled itself in the iron bar of the fire exit door. Her curses turned the air blue. Menacing Cuban sugar plantation owners had nothing on this hellcat, he remembered thinking. Lewis had eventually calmed Tiger down, liberated her sleeve, and had sat with her outside on the concrete steps for some fresh air. Tiger was unlike anything he had ever seen. She had a huge mane of untamed pink hair, almondine eyes in a striking shade of green, and an olive colouring that confirmed she was definitely not entirely of English descent. Lewis wondered where on earth this creature had come from. He couldn't put an age on her. She had the body and face of a girl in her late teens to early twenties, but she spoke with the knowledge and wisdom of someone quite older. As she managed to relax, her breasts stopped heaving and her face softened. She looked, quite simply, extraordinary.

Lewis carefully explained to Tiger that he had been brought in to invest in the show. He was a personal friend of the producer, Camelot Mackie, who had called on Lewis to lend a further cash injection. What Lewis hadn't mentioned was that Camelot's offer was timely; Lewis secretly had idle cash from an illicit backhander at work. He figured that ploughing some of it into an interesting project; a remake of Gypsy Rose Lee's infamous film *Lady of Burlesque*, adapted from her novel *The G-String Murders*, turned the cash into good karma. Supporting the British arts had to be a decent thing to do, surely. Deep down Lewis knew that nineteen out of twenty West End shows never made their money back, but he had fancied the diversion from the intense world of commodities and hey, just looking at this beauty in front of him convinced him his decision was already paying off. It was good for him to remember there were other things in life than commodities and cash.

Lewis used his well-honed skills of negotiation to convince Tiger to move on from the incident with the director and resume her rehearsals. As Lewis watched her dance on stage he was captivated. She was raw, on fire. She was sensual and knowing; yet untouchable, at times even coy. The way she moved, and the way she made him feel like he was the only person she was dancing for, had him hooked like a drug. Off stage she was detached and defensive. She had a story there was no doubt. But once on stage, there was something hypnotic about her that left audiences fixated. This woman was the real deal from the inside out – a class act.

Tiger lasted another week before leaving the production for good, after she caught the director in the dressing room one lunchtime, chewing at the crotches of the girls' panties. Tiger's departure pretty much killed the production and *Lady of Burlesque* closed after poor previews.

The spell had already been cast and Lewis had made

his decision. He left his job at Mayall, unsure of exactly how to make it in show business, but knowing there wasn't a contract in the world he couldn't negotiate, and that he simply had to work with Tiger Starr. His colleagues mocked and laughed like old biddies over the garden fence. The odd one actually patted him on the back and congratulated him for the transition from 'City Boy' to 'Stripper's Pimp'. However, a gut feeling told Lewis that the last laugh would be his.

Lewis set about moulding Tiger. He saw a way to channel her raw passion into a more high gloss, more commercial version of herself. He was travelling against the tide at that time, for back then, any kind of erotic entertainment either involved lots of neon Lycra and splayed legs, or it had to be intellectualised as 'edgy', 'gritty', or 'subversive' by goatee-stroking feminists in order to be regarded as art. As for the proper old-style showgirl 'tit 'n' feather' revues – well they had been experiencing their own wilderness in Britain for simply decades. Lewis therefore focused Tiger on all the gloriously glamorous, expensive, chic and camp elements of her shows; why shouldn't erotic entertainment tick all those boxes? After all, he thought it should be for women as much as men. Lewis was intent on bringing back big budget, unashamedly glamorous, theatrical erotic shows that didn't have to masquerade as anything but that. Shows that would put the notion of the Goddess centre stage once again.

Lewis listened carefully to Tiger's vivid dreams, visions

and ideas for flamboyant tableaux and elaborate costumes. He helped her source the best costumiers from Paris to New York. She went about smoothing any rough edges, taming her hair into sleek and shiny curls, softening the bright pink into a more powdery hue. Lewis agonised that subconsciously he hadn't moved on, that he was just dealing in a far more specialised commodity, but he came to view his role as the gardener nurturing a new rose; he watered it, pruned it, tended to it, and watched it blossom gloriously.

Tiger had taken some time to relax into the concept that Lewis wanted nothing from her, other than a straight business relationship. He needed to prove to himself he could rise to the challenge and make his new life path work, and all he asked was that Tiger co-operated and took every opportunity they both worked towards. Once Tiger had defrosted, they were a formidable team. Both self-confessed workaholics, they needed no encouragement. Before long, Tiger was the toast of London, this 'girl from nowhere'. She performed at the hottest celebrity events, fashion shows and society balls. She worked liked a demon behind the scenes, creating bigger, more opulent shows each time, shaving away at the product, making each show smoother and glossier than the last. Lewis' performance had been pretty spectacular himself, he had picked up the reins quickly and was like a duck to water. He ate theatrical negotiations and contracts for breakfast, and fast grew a reputation as a ruthless manager. Lewis was happy with that. His job was to protect the welfare of his *artiste* after all, and boy were there sharks out there who wanted a piece of Tiger.

His final piece of the puzzle was to find her a fantastic PR, who could handle the increasing pile of press enquiries that were landing at the door. He needed to find someone who could weed out the crap from the decent stuff, and help protect Tiger from the trickeries of ruthless journalists who had their own agendas. Lewis just read piles of newspapers and magazines, focusing on actors and personalities who he thought had solid profiles as respected artists, away from gossipy celeb-driven rubbish. Then he would call their agents, posing as a journalist, and ask who represented them for PR. One name kept popping up – Rex Hunter. When Lewis met Rex, he was pleased to find that he had a similar work ethic as Lewis and Tiger. Like most people, Rex was captivated by Tiger, and was delighted to come on board immediately. He fitted into their industrious little team seamlessly. Though recent events had led Lewis to wonder whether he'd been right to hire Rex at all.

One thing Lewis made sure of was to allow Tiger space to breathe when the climb got too intense. He guessed she hadn't had much time to herself in the past, sensing she'd spent most of it surviving. He learnt that Tiger had been sleeping on someone's sofa when he met her that first day at the Duke of York's Theatre. Yet every day she would make it across town to audition after audition, determined she would find work. The irony was, landing the lead in that West End show would have set her career up very quickly, but Tiger was having none of it for as long as she was compromised by the sleazy director. Lewis admired her principles. There was never going to be a casting couch in Tiger's world.

Outside the close-knit professional relationship, Tiger was guarded about her past. All Lewis could glean was that she had left home at a young age, and somehow ended up in Spain living with gypsies. Tiger hinted that she drank heavily at that time, and Lewis suspected something stronger too. Tiger had returned to England a little before Lewis met her, to spend time with her grandmother before she died. Since Coco had been a burlesque star of the fifties, Lewis guessed she was obviously a huge influence on young Tiger. Beyond this story however, she was zipped up. Even when her parents had died and Tiger had rearranged her life to be able to look after Sienna – paying for her education, securing her a job, paying her rent – Tiger had barely shed a tear. She seemed to find intimacy tough in general, and she was a closed book when it came to her personal affairs.

Lewis and Tiger had walked a long, intense road together from a bizarre, chance meeting; each of them had transformed immeasurably since that first day. Lewis was still no closer to unravelling Tiger, but one thing they had was a fundamental understanding; one based on trust and absolute mutual respect. Tiger knew the risk Lewis had taken with her in changing his life path, and equally the other way round. They had a unique, unspoken bond that transcended, and in some ways, contradicted conventional friendship. They were unquestioningly equal, they depended on each other, yet kept so much of their lives private from each other. To this day, Lewis couldn't even say how he felt about Tiger on a personal level – it was something he dared not even think about. One thing he did know was that he had felt an alarmingly sharp stab of resentment when he heard the gossip of Tiger and Rex's dalliance. He knew Tiger must have had relationships over the years, but she kept her romantic affairs fiercely private. Lewis had been secretly happy with that arrangement too. He told himself that he felt bad for Tiger; that Rex simply wasn't good enough or deserving enough of her, although Lewis couldn't pinpoint exactly why – after all, Rex had been honourable and hard working enough over the years. He just didn't seem to be the right man to be standing by her side. Recently Lewis had simply resigned himself to the knowledge that after fourteen years of working together, and as refined, honed and flawless as Tiger had become, she still left him mystified, exasperated, and utterly captivated.

'Bloody hell, you haven't been listening to a word I've said!' squeaked Georgia, sitting before Lewis at the bar, rapping her long nails on the chrome counter and pointing to her empty champagne glass plaintively.

*   *   *

Blue topped up Tiger's champagne as the end credits of *Columbo* rolled on to the plasma screen. They hadn't moved from the bedroom all afternoon.

'I wonder if there's any old re-runs of *The Love Boat* this afternoon?' asked Blue, flicking through the cable channels.

'Ugh, I have heartburn,' hiccupped Tiger.

'Dump a brandy in the Krug, that'll sort you out, babes.'

'No! No more. I have loads to do tomorrow,' protested Tiger.

'Relax! We said we'd have a break today,' reassured Blue, 'anyway, spare a thought for me, I've got like a million bugle beads to sew onto your costume tomorrow ready for your next gig. You are still doing the new rocking horse aren't you?'

'Oh for Prince Romano? Yeah, the horse is in the workshop being finished. I'm having extra plumage fitted. I'm so excited, it really looks like a proper Arabian stallion.'

'I suppose I'll have to sort out its saddle upholstery?'

'Aha, no I'm one step ahead,' proclaimed Tiger proudly, 'I sent the workshop the fabric samples from the costume you put together. They're doing a beautiful quilted silk cover embroidered in gold to match my corsetry.'

'Hmm, get you, Miss Organisation! Okay, well all the more reason for me to relax today and then I'll get cracking tomorrow,' and with that Blue knocked back his champagne theatrically.

'Blue . . .'

'Yes, babes?'

'I'm a bit nervous about the new Vegas stuff we're working on.'

'Oh behave.'

'No really, they're over for the development meeting next week. It's the "work in progress" meeting thing.'

'Oh relax. We've had the glitterball costume on the go for over two months now! Jeez, that reminds me I need to get down to the studio and see where Valerie and Hartley are with the outfits.'

'I'm not worried about that! The director has seen the designs anyway, he'll understand if they don't have every single crystal sewn on. I'm just really nervous for some reason. It doesn't seem rational, I mean we have amazing routines taking shape, and I know the Starrlets are gonna look amazing. Pepper's using ten of them, and the rest are resident chorus girls from Vegas. I guess I just feel a bit hassled myself. You know, I have to get the new rocking horse piece right for the Prince Romano show in a few weeks, and yet I can't seem to get my mind off Vegas. I just feel uneasy about the show. I can't put my finger on it.'

'Run it by me again, which pieces made it to the final cut for Vegas?'

'The directors are still finalising it – there's more acts to agree on. So far they have confirmed the Starrlets for the Poodle act, the *Alice in Wonderland* act, and the fifties carwash with rhinestoned Rolls Royces, and they've put together the male troupe for the big James Bond medley I wanted. I'll do the film noir telephone and the Cleopatra bathing in asses' milk as my headline numbers, plus the big Busby Berkeley-style piano number. They've secured two of my favourite features too, Minnie Diamond is doing an adagio act in which she's the pendulum in a huge Venetian clock, and Viva La Diva's doing her Napoleon act, with dressage on a live stallion, Lipizzaner style. Oh, and of course I'll come out again to perform the glitterball Fabergé egg as the grand finale. Lewis thinks they're really close to agreeing to let me have the water feature with programmed fountains for that one, like Liberace used to have behind his rotating piano. Lewis says it's busting their budget, which is why it's taken so long for them to sign it off. They're figuring out a way for the glitterball egg to rise from the pool so it looks like it's being pushed up by water jets.'

'Woah. But the opening won't be for—'

'Nine months, I know. But it's creeping up so fast. They start teching in three months, can you believe?'

'Jeez. I must admit, after the Savoy, a year ahead sounded like plenty of time.'

'Exactly!' Tiger looked suddenly tired and anxious. 'Oh, I think this champagne is making me giddy,' she whimpered, fanning her face frantically.

'Oh, babes, come on, you've got it all under control. The whole team is on it. Lewis has all bases covered, plus you get to work with the Vegas Philarmonic on the score, the art director's the best in the biz, you've got the best of the Hollywood lighting designers, and you get on with the director, right?'

'Well, naturally. He's amazing, he's done all the epic shows, but—'

'No buts. You have a crack team, and besides . . .'

Blue paused as he registered a crinkling beneath him as he leaned back onto the pillow.

'What's this – Tiger?'

Tiger blushed. 'Oh it's just another silly letter. I was going to show you.'

'Oh really?'

'It's nothing.'

Blue ripped the envelope open. 'I watch you sleeping?'

'Yeah, as if.'

'You will see me in your nightmares? No way. Tiger, this is plain old creepy.'

'I know. And that's *all* it is. Just a sad old bloke, or, or . . . or a practical joke or something. Ha bloody ha. Johnnie knows where I live, maybe it's his stupid idea of a joke.'

'But what if someone really has been here at the house?'

'It's just a bluff. Some weirdo. Anyway, let's go eat. I can't sit here worrying, it's making me feel sick. There's seven whole hours of Sunday left, let's make the most of it.'

Blue felt distinctly troubled about this new letter and wandered over to the sash window three storeys up, wondering if someone could really have got up there. He tapped his fingers uneasily on the windowsill, remembering the letters Rosemary Baby used to send to Tiffany Crystal. Within moments, however, thoughts of roast dinner clouded his mind.

Chapter 12

Sienna waved the waiter away, deciding his presence would distract from the full impact of her strut across the restaurant towards Rex Hunter. She felt all eyes on her as she strode forcefully across the black-and-white marble floor, doing as her sister had taught her and making the most of her assets. Today Sienna was capitalising on her deliciously long, coltish legs. She had always considered them a drawback, following ten long years of being called 'Twiglet Legs' by her classmates; at least until Tiger had taught her to embrace her gawkiness along with her unwanted bustiness and turn it to her advantage over the last couple of years. Tiger liked to call it 'accessorising the outfit god gave you'. So, with Sienna's newly honed air of confidence, along with her butt-skimming Moschino Cheap 'n' Chic dress that Tiger had just bought her, she sensed every pair of female eyes clouding in envy as they watched her passing, and every man's gaze travelling up the seams of her carefully chosen vintage silk stockings. The morning power-meeting clientele at The Wolseley was well known for being an intimidating blend of fashionistas, film producers and hedge-fund managers. Excited to be attending her first power meeting, Sienna now felt a sense of achievement at being admired by such a discerning bunch. Even if she was only Rex's Junior, she was on her way.

As Sienna approached her boss, she saw that his eyes were locked onto his BlackBerry. Damn him, thought Sienna, peeved that Rex had missed the spectacle of her entrance. She dropped her vintage scuffed leather attaché case – another Tiger hand-me-down – onto the white tablecloth with a thud. Rex grunted without looking up, as he continued to briskly tap out an email.

'Err, Rex?' Sienna nudged, gently.

'Hmm . . . wait . . . okay done.' Rex finally stood up and popped his BlackBerry into his inside pocket, 'Sorry doll, just had to get an urgent email off before the *Mail* supplement goes to print. *La Boheme* at the National got incredible write ups from the previews so I persuaded the *Mail* to give it a colour feature in "Cultural Week". Gate-fold. I got Lance on the job yesterday. I've played a blinder again, doll, busting through the week's column-inch targets as usual.' Rex didn't even register Sienna's new outfit. Typical man, obsessed with his column inches, Sienna thought to herself. She leaned in to kiss him, but Rex fended her off with a handshake.

'Daytime is business, doll,' he whispered, clocking her immediate pout.

With immaculate timing Lance de Brett loomed up at the table.

'Damn, I thought I was early for once!' said Lance,

pumping Rex's hand cheerily, and leaning in to air kiss both Sienna's cheeks. Sienna threw a sarcastic glare over at Rex, and pulled up a chair to sit next to Lance.

'Actually I think we're all a few minutes early,' said Rex. 'Shall we kick off with a Bloody Mary?'

'Perfect! That'll blast the cobwebs away,' replied Lance as he caught the waiter's eye. 'Three Bloody Marys, please, make mine very spicy,' he ordered. The waiter smiled and nodded before melting away. Actually, Sienna loathed tomato, but was too polite to say anything. She was just thrilled to be having her first proper brunch meeting, and with a top cultural journalist like Lance de Brett, no less. Wow, if only my mother could see me now, she thought to herself wistfully. Her smile faded as she then wondered if Rex would have brought her to the meeting if they weren't sleeping together. She pushed those thoughts to the back of her mind.

As Rex grilled Lance about his last night's mischievous exploits, Sienna's eyes darted around the restaurant, becoming aware of one, no two ... no three, slightly nervous-looking young girls sitting bolt upright at their respective tables. Each of them wore very new looking outfits, and were fervently scribbling notes as their bosses held court with their clients. One of the girls on a neighbouring table looked up from her pad. Her big brown eyes locked with Sienna's for a moment. They both smiled tentatively, recognising a fellow assistant when they saw one, before looking away again awkwardly. Sienna began to wonder how many Juniors like her – and like the other three Junior Girls in the restaurant – had passed through Rex's office . . . not to mention his bed, over the years. She shuddered involuntarily.

'Got those details down, Sienna?' asked Rex.

'Yes of course! Erm, how do you spell that?' Sienna knew she'd been caught daydreaming again. Rex shot her a look, and wrote the name 'Bob' on her notepad, very slowly. Sienna flushed immediately, and was relieved that the waiter had arrived to unload three tall Bloody Marys from his tray. She braced herself and gulped the slippery cold tomato concoction before her anxiously.

'We were just talking about Bob Bell, from the "News of the Screws",' explained Lance kindly for Sienna's benefit, as he scribbled a phone number on her pad. 'Bob asked me to pass Rex his private number last night when we were out on a social. He's taken over from Camilla Walker as editor you see, so the next time one of Rex's footballing clients gets caught using a mobile phone as a gay sex toy . . .' Lance paused for a comedy wink at Rex, before continuing, 'He has a direct lifeline to Bob so he has a chance to stop the story – or maybe even do a trade off for a better one.' Sienna smiled weakly, aware of an intense burning sensation in her throat.

'Don't look so shocked, Sienna, you'll get to learn everything about this sordid little business very soon, don't you worry!' laughed Lance.

'Er, actually, I think I just got your extra hot Bloody

Mary,' rasped Sienna, trying not to cough. Lance and Rex guffawed, and Sienna felt Rex's foot kick her under the table. He winked at her. Sienna relaxed in her chair a little.

'Okay, hand that over,' said Lance with a smile, reaching across to swap the drinks. Sienna wondered if he actually had a rather charming side underneath his intimidating exterior. She gave him a swift once over as he reached for her drink.

'Nice watch,' she suddenly remarked, sucking her breath after catching a flash of Lance's wrist as he swapped the glasses across the table. 'Rolex Daytona. Nice.'

'Wow, you notice everything, lady,' Lance smiled, uncomfortably pulling his shirt cuff down.

'Oh yes, I know the real thing when I see it. It's the most expensive and legendary model. Rex honey, didn't you buy one like that recently?' asked Sienna proudly. Finally she had a brownie point. Observant. Yeah, Rex would appreciate that, she thought to herself. Only her darling Rex wasn't smiling.

'Mate, not being funny, but may I?' Rex motioned over at Lance's watch. He grabbed Lance's wrist and peered at the watch face.

'Hmm. Exactly the same as mine. Ten points to Sienna – well done. So, Lance, when did you, err, buy this?'

'Uh . . . let's see . . . about a year ago.'

'You bought it?'

'Yeah. You buy yours?'

'Yeah. Few weeks ago.'

Lance and Rex stared at each other intently. Sienna felt the air turn hostile. She glanced from Lance to Rex and back, waiting for one of them to start laughing. Their expressions remained inscrutable. Sienna nervously took another slug of her thick, slimy Bloody Mary as she puzzled over what had just happened. She felt faintly lightheaded as the vodka coursed through her bloodstream.

Rex was the first to break the silence.

'So, you have the mark of the Tiger. You kept that quiet for some time.'

'Touché,' replied Lance smoothly.

'It was just business.'

'Natch.'

'Now I understand the shitty features,' said Rex, breaking into laughter, 'I can't believe I didn't suss that one out, I'd have thought it would be too much of a cliché. Mate, she must have chewed you up and spat you out.'

'Nah, she's just a pussycat. Anyway, all in the past.'

'Yeah, sure. She said something about "trouble in paradise" about a year ago now I think of it. She was all over the place for about a week. Couldn't get her to concentrate on anything. That was you? Mate, I reckon she got to you baaaad! Now I tot up all your swipes, and those snide remarks you wrote in . . .' Rex tailed off, suddenly aware of Sienna's eyes boring a hole through him.

'So anyway, what a coincidence, we bought the same Rolex. Sienna babes, what do you do when you birds wear the same dress to a party, eh? Does one of you have to leave? Or do you fight it out?' Rex was left talking to Sienna's back as she stalked from the table and sped off towards the restrooms.

Safely in a cubicle, Sienna locked the door behind her and plonked herself on the toilet seat lid, biting her lip to stop herself from unleashing a torrent of foul curses. She leaned forward with her head in her hands, trying to clear her thoughts after the barely veiled revelation back there. She racked her brains, trying to work out when Tiger could have seduced Rex. Her mind reeled. She concluded that Tiger must have taken him for sport, knowing that Sienna was already in love with him. Had Sienna really made it that obvious? When had Tiger found out? Had she actually gone all the way with Rex? Ugh, the thought was too much. Tiger would have to pay somehow. Why couldn't she just stick to the celebrities and millionaires she had falling at her feet? Why go for darling Rex of all people? Sienna sat in her cubicle, burning in resentment. Tiger would have to pay somehow.

Angry thoughts spilled over as she remembered how Tiger was always too busy flitting round the world and building her precious career to rescue her own little sister from horrible boarding school with its nuns and stodgy dinners and cold showers. Then when Mum and Dad died a couple of years ago in the car crash, oh, then Tiger was all over her like a rash. Paying for Sienna to stay on for sixth form, taking an interest in her grades, wanting to come to parents' evenings, reading her reports, even sticking her nose into her romantic affairs! Not that there were many. She'd even wanted to have Sienna come live with her and Blue – play happy families – but Sienna was having none of it. Blue? What was he going to be, her fairy godmother? No, she'd persuaded Tiger to pay the rent on her own flat instead.

All Sienna knew now was that she had to pretend she had fallen for Rex's barely coded talk back there. Sienna Starr was on her way up and nothing was going to stop her, she just had to force herself to look upon this as a little bit of sand in the suntan lotion of life. She would see to it that dear sister Tiger paid for her actions somehow. Suddenly Sienna missed her mum and craved a hug. Feeling her eyes well up, she took a deep breath, pinched the bridge of her nose, sniffed, and waltzed out of the cubicle with a flourish.

There stood Junior Girl with the big brown eyes from earlier, digging around in her obviously fake Louis Vuitton as she stood in front of the mirror. She pulled out a hairbrush and smiled over at Sienna.

'Wow, I was admiring your dress earlier. I saw you come through the restaurant. It looks amazing on you. Who's it by?'

'Moschino,' replied Sienna, tightly.

'Oh. I guessed it looked expensive,' said Junior Girl, looking crestfallen at the imagined price tag.

'Well . . . actually my sister bought it for me.'

'Oh my. Lucky you, I wish I had a sister like yours!'

'No, you don't. She's a bitch.'

Sienna swept from the restroom on her long legs, leaving Junior Girl open mouthed and flustered, hairbrush mid air.

Blue stood back as the small bright blue wooden door buzzed open. As he climbed the near-vertical set of narrow stairs, he could hear his art director Hartley barking orders above the thudding beat of the radio that ricocheted through the small building. Blue stuck his head round the door as he reached the first floor, to see ten or so teenage-looking girls and boys arranged around a huge mound of crinolines splayed out on the uneven wooden floor, surrounded by hundreds of glass bowls full of small square mirror pieces. All along the walls sewing tables reared up, interspersed with dressmaking dummies upon which were pinned various biro-marked *toiles*. The work team kept their heads down in concentration as they applied the mirror pieces to the crinolines, a couple of them grunting in time to the music. The air was thick with the familiar singed smell of hot glue guns mixed with the spicy cedar aroma of moth deterrent.

Hartley sprang forward to greet Blue warmly with flamboyant air kisses. 'Oh Blue, it's a hive of activity in here,' he puffed, scooping up yards of fabric in his arms and looking harassed. 'We're already halfway through the mirrorball skirts, twenty down, twenty to go!' He motioned towards the students.

'So I see!' said Blue. 'Looks promising, you've got a lovely shape on them, they look just like my drawings. How long did the crinoline cages take?'

'Got through about two a day.'

'Mid thigh?'

'Of course, I know you need them saucy. I had that Georgia bird in for the *toile* fitting. The design works beautifully, a perfect half-sphere crini, and with the bumless mini bloomers underneath they look cute as hell, especially with Georgia's long pins. You could see her butt cheeks when she bent over.'

'Well there's a revelation. I didn't know the bony bitch actually had an arse. So have you started on the bustiers?'

'No, the skirts are taking a lot longer than we planned. The mirrorball panels were pinging off after the glue had set, so we had to make the crinis again with a coarser fabric. Don't worry, we factored in some contingency. We'll still have them done to deadline.'

'Can't you bring more staff in?' asked Blue, looking fidgety.

'Blue, they're fashion students. Gimme a break. They all think they're bloody Dolce and Gabbana already. Glueing five billion pieces of mirror to chorus-line costumes isn't their idea of the giddy heights of *haute couture*. They weren't exactly banging the doors down to do this one.'

'Students, huh? Well, boys and girls, you should all be so lucky to be working on this gig at all,' shouted Blue, addressing the room theatrically, 'Erté would be creaming himself at these artworks. Oh, Hartley, I knew we should have given it all to Valerie again.'

'Blue, she's working her way through three hundred thousand rhinestones for Tiger's costume right now. She's slam up against it. I can assure you she hasn't got time for mirrorballs. Go upstairs and see for yourself,' said Hartley, suddenly looking worn and creased.

'Okay, babe,' replied Blue. 'Sorry, I do trust you. It's just that – well – my bits are really on the chopping block here.'

'It's cool, I know this is an important one. Just leave the worrying to me.'

'Thanks, Hartley, appreciate that. C'mon then, let's go and say hi to Valerie.'

'No, it's fine, you go ahead, I gotta sit here and go through the glitterball prop specs on the phone with the sculptor. We need the prototype delivered for this Monday presentation thing of Tiger's. You go up, Val will be thrilled to see you, she's on good form. Oh, and Blue? I meant it when I said not to worry. It's all in capable hands. Have we ever let you guys down?'

Blue secretly loved the fact that Hartley was such a dependable rock in the sprint for the finishing line. While Blue spent time whipping himself into an artistic frenzy when he created something new for a show, Hartley could always be relied upon to be working steadily in the background, seeing to it that the rest of the production wasn't falling apart at the seams, quite literally. As a team they were like coffee and cream, or gin and tonic as Hartley fondly liked to think of it.

Of course, some of the costumes Tiger and Blue dreamt up between them needed a qualification in advanced engineering to construct, and combining the artistic vision with the practical workings was Hartley's area of expertise. He had overseen whole set designs that were less complicated to resolve than Tiger's costumes and props. He once joked that Howard Hughes would be left scratching his head if he saw some of the wire-work cages underneath Tiger's enormous feathers, all to give them the impression of being floaty and light. People were often surprised if they picked up one of Tiger's gowns and realised how heavy they were with all the layers upon layers of fabric, crystals, feathers, underwiring and steel stays. In fact, Tiger often judged her costumes on a scale of naked to Liberace. If the costume wasn't big enough to warrant counterbalances in her heels like Liberace famously used to have, then it wasn't deemed elaborate enough.

Blue was now puffing and panting his way up the second set of even narrower stairs, having bid his farewells to Hartley, who could be heard faintly from the other room, barking down his mobile at the sculptor. Blue clung to the rope fixed along the wall for safety as he hoisted himself towards Valerie's private studio. That was the problem with these ancient mews houses – charming though they were – they were built for a generation of people who used to be half the size, certainly half of Blue's proportions, at any rate.

'Valerie's Art House' was now legendary; for over fifty years she had been sewing her fingers to the bone in this amazing little building. It was as though every thread and stitch was infused with the atmosphere of ancient Soho. Valerie had personally clothed entire operas, classical ballets, drag shows, Hollywood movies and musicals. Most of all, she loved a showgirl; she worshipped Tiger, and regarded every item she made for her as 'a piece'. Never 'a costume', but 'a piece', in the way a work of art was 'a piece'. Valerie didn't stitch for just anyone, and she would simply ignore a potential new client if, god forbid, they made the fatal mistake of asking for 'an outfit' to be made.

Blue knew the new piece must be a real humdinger for Valerie to be up and working in the daytime; she was a nocturnal creature by habit, and would usually wait until dusk before opening up the blinds and the big skylight to let the light of the twinkling stars into the top floor of her studio. She once said that the sounds from the old knocking shops at night back in the 1950s used to give her a good rhythm to stitch to during the night. Those days were long gone of course. Soho had cleaned up, and was now full of production companies, coffee shops and vintage boutiques. Against all the odds, Valerie's Art House had withstood the redevelopers, and remained nestled in Soho's backstreets; a beacon of glorious history in a newly

Starbucked district. As Blue got to the top of the rickety wooden stairs he rapped loudly on Valerie's door.

'Blue! Come here, young man, and shake my hand.' Valerie beamed the second Blue popped his head through the door. He minced over as Valerie elegantly extended a long bony finger from her hunched position in her big old moth-eaten chair. He shook it gently and curtsied for the stylish, platinum-haired dame before him.

'My, my, you are looking well, *ma petite*,' gushed Blue.

'Well, I'm still here,' laughed Valerie, 'it's the diet of feathers and rhinestones that keeps me going. Speaking of diet, you look like you've been at the fairy cakes since I saw you last, dear.'

'How's that for a welcome! Well never mind the cake, just a fairy would be nice. Actually I've been so busy with Tiger I haven't had a chance to get myself into the gym,' explained Blue, breathing in the cedar-scented air and glancing around at the shelves on every wall, stuffed to overflowing with fabrics and trimmings in every colour and pattern imaginable.

'Ahh, dear, dear Tiger, I do hope she's keeping you in check my sweetheart. I take it you're up here to see the progress on her new piece?' asked Valerie, her pencilled eyebrows arched questioningly.

'Yes indeed!' enthused Blue. 'As well as to see you of course . . . so do I get a sneak preview?'

'For you, dear? Anything,' said Valerie as she uncurled from the corset she held in her lap. Blue looked down and gasped.

'Oh Val. Oh Valerie, Valerie, Valerie. Exquisite!' Blue held his breath as he studied the sparkling article before him. Every shade of pearlescent crystal, in all different shapes and sizes snuggled up next to real diamonds, all swirling in intricate patterns that flowed with the curves of the corset. It sparkled like nothing he'd ever seen.

'It's special isn't it,' sighed Valerie, running her long fingertips lightly over the diamonds, 'I had them flown in from Antwerp like you asked. It goes in the safe at night.'

'Oh Val. Shall we keep it and do a runner? To Necker Island, just the two of us? No one need know. We could live off this for years!'

Valerie cackled, and waved her hand at the mannequin on the other side of the room.

'Just take a look at the train to go under the osprey fantail. I haven't started the rhinestones yet, but that's the base over there. I shall ask you to bring in Her Ladyship for a second fitting very soon.'

Blue approached the mannequin across the room like its long lost lover, narrowly missing knocking over a precariously balanced tower of jars filled with buttons, bugle beads and crystals on his way.

'Look at these ruffles,' he breathed, ogling the huge sea of rich, pale oyster-coloured silk fabric before him.

'I know, they were an absolute bastard to sew.'

'Language, Valerie!'

'Oh but they were, dear. I lost count of how many hundreds of metres of fabric they used up. The crystals are going on the underside of the train so that the audience will see a wall of sparkle from the front, and then pure ruffles from behind. I'll still apply rhinestone between the fabric layers though, so that when Tiger kicks the tail up, the crystals catch the light from behind. It'll move like the sparkling waves of the ocean under a hot sun. Soft. Womanly. Perfect to offset that huge glitterball and perfect to harmonise with the fountains as they spray. Then when she removes it and uses it as her blanket, the ruffles will mould to her curves. Oh Blue, it will be alive and breathing when it's finished.' Valerie sighed deeply, and closed her eyes for a moment.

'Well, it's even more than either of us could have imagined. Tiger's going to flip,' said Blue wistfully.

'Ooh I almost forgot to ask,' added Valerie, coming to life again, 'have you had the osprey fantail back yet? Hartley needs to construct the wirework for it to slot into this corset.'

'Hmm no, it's still being reconditioned. It's costing us a bloody fortune too, especially now that you can't get osprey any more.'

'Yes and thank goodness, there must have been a lot of herons with cold bums back in the day,' laughed Valerie. 'I remember some of those showgirls used to be covered from head to toe in the stuff. But there's nothing now that can replicate that wonderful feather texture. Shame.'

'There's no doubt this will knock the socks off Vegas when they see this. You know what, Valerie darling?

This is how the *Birth of Venus* was *meant* to be – a rotating ten-foot glitterball rising up out of the floor upon jets of fountains, opening up to present Tiger inside her red velvet-padded Fabergé egg interior like the bird of paradise she is. Ooh, I'm getting goose bumps, look!'

'But wait, Blue – you should use that as the title for the whole show – *The Birth of Venus*! How camp! I can just see it in lights!'

'Oh, Valerie, pure sacrilage! The finale will be something like the rape of Botticelli by Salvador Dalí on the way to Studio 54. Genius! God, I have to tell Lewis to suggest that title before Monday's meeting!'

'Ahhhh, but do you know how Venus came to be born, my dear?'

'No, but you're going to tell me, right?'

'Basically, Uranus' son castrated him and threw his cock into the ocean, dear. So the sea was fertilised and then out popped Venus from her giant cockleshell somewhere off the coast of Paphos! That's Cyprus in case you didn't know. Of course the shell was a metaphor for the vulva, which would in theory make Tiger's Fabergé egg glitterball a huge great cu—'

'Oh Jesus and Mary Chain! Well, I'm certainly not telling the Americans that! Let's just keep tight lipped about it.'

'Tight lipped?'

With that, Valerie and Blue dissolved into hysterics.

'Darling,' Valerie wheezed, 'thank god Venus didn't emerge from a bearded mussel that's all I can say!'

Blue's shoulders shuddered with dirty sniggers. 'All this genitalia talk is usually my job. Get back to your rhinestoning, wench!'

Valerie settled herself back into position in her chair, breathless. 'Oh my goodness, I'll never be able to watch the show without giggling now!'

'For god's sake don't tell Tiger we had this conversation,' said Blue, 'or she might . . . clam up or something.' The pair erupted again.

'Enough already!' protested Valerie, soberly taking a deep breath. 'Now stop, I just can't keep my eyes on the rhinestones like this.'

'I'm sorry, darling, maybe I should leave you to it – stop distracting you, huh?'

Valeria looked thoughtful for a second. 'Oh what the hell,' she laughed with a wicked glint in her eye. 'Do you fancy a quick glass of sherry with me before you go?'

'Now that's like asking Tiger if she fancies getting her kit off. Of course, where is it?'

'Over on the bureau there.'

'Wonderful,' sighed Blue as he reached for the sherry decanter. 'God, I'm so easily corrupted. I can see this is turning into the perfect afternoon. Now, back to Uranus . . .'

Rex grunted and climbed off Sienna. He whipped off his condom, turned to face the wall and began snoring loudly.

Sienna often lamented that for all his sexual charisma, Rex was an incredibly selfish lover. She had limited experience where men were concerned, and all of it bad, but for the first time she was relieved that Rex was at least consistent. This was Sienna's big chance. She rolled out of Rex's bed and padded through to the sitting room to her handbag. She fished out her mobile by the light of the moon.

Tiger would have to pay somehow. The thought had been playing in her head all day like a stuck record. Tiger would have to pay somehow. All day Sienna's mind had drawn a blank as to how to wreak her revenge. That is, until Rex had taken her to La Perle Noire in Soho for oysters and champagne. They had bumped into Blue weaving his way back home to Regent's Park after an apparently boozy afternoon. As Blue and Rex made small talk, Sienna had slipped into one of her daydreams again, finding herself staring at the window display of the Trashy Lingerie sex shop. As she zoned out on the tacky bondage gear in the window, she was suddenly reminded of one night when a tipsy Tiger had confessed to her that she had tried her hand as a dominatrix in New York.

Sienna remembered it so well – how could it have slipped her mind? It had only been a couple of years ago. Their folks had just died and Tiger was eager to spend time with Sienna, cheering her up. There in her parlour, Tiger had lain all stretched out and fluffy in her robe after she had introduced Sienna to Kahlua milkshakes – sisterly bonding she called it – and in this unguarded moment told her a rare story about her early performing days. Tiger had her gorgeous friend Tiffany Crystal staying with her that night, and Tiffany had brought some rancid-looking bird with her called Rosy or Rosemary or something, who Tiffany had befriended, apparently out of sympathy since the ugly old bag's personality was less than sparkling. Sienna recalled she also had terrible snaggle teeth when she smiled and a hilarious affected posh accent that broke into a Yorkshire burr every five words or so. Apparently the two girls were doing a tour that stopped in London for a couple of nights and Tiffany was taking the ugly one under her wing and coaching her as she was rather hopeless as a dancer. Tiger had thought it a great idea that since Tiffany was in town, she should come to dinner, meet Sienna and brighten the evening up. Probably all part of the sisterly 'bonding' thing, no doubt.

Tiger and Tiffany had settled in for the night to tell Sienna their funny stories about the smell of the grease-paint; the ugly one had already drunk too much and after trying to show off by attempting a cringe-inducing splits in the middle of the parlour, now thankfully appeared to have passed out on the *chaise longue*. Tiger then regaled Sienna and Tiffany with a very interesting little tale about her early days. How she was auditioning in London every-where. Every day. Burlesque didn't pay the bills back then. Acting bit parts came and went, chorus-line work put a bit of bread on the table and extras work beckoned;

although she drew the line at podium dancing in naff clubs. Tiger just couldn't seem to find a balance. Then a friend of a friend of someone's girlfriend reckoned Tiger could earn a pretty packet as a dominatrix. You didn't have to have sex with the guys or even strip, and you got to dress up, hone your acting skills, and get your boots licked and toilet cleaned in the process, so the girl had said.

Well, Tiger thought it sounded great as a money spinning stop-gap until the perfect West End part came along; better than temping in an office any day. She even figured out a name straight away. It was suggested by the friend of a friend of someone's girlfriend that a dominatrix's name should always start with 'Lady'. Then an 'a' should be tagged to the end of her first name, followed by the words 'mistress of the . . .' then add the name of the most expensive power tool in her tool box.

Tiger settled on 'Lady Tigra, Mistress of the Cheese Grater'. Since she didn't have a toolbox, or even a power sander, she figured her cutlery drawer would have to make do for inspiration. Of course, she decided if she was going to do something, she would do it properly; and that meant going to New York to be Lady Tigra, where she had heard all the best whip crackers worked. After all, if you want to be the best, you have to learn from the best. She could earn a packet and return home with her spoils. Besides, she didn't want to run the risk of having a client come in for a spanking or to be bottle fed who she recognised . . . her doctor or local MP, or something. So off Tiger went to the Big Apple – open minded, open hearted, and brimming with possibilities of what to spend her new stream of income on. Decent lodgings, for a start. And some beautiful new dance costumes. And maybe even some nice new books; she was quite the bookworm when she had the chance to curl up on her own.

Lady Tigra lasted all of three days. As she rolled around on the floor one lunch time in virginal white Chantilly lace underwear, wrestling with a sweaty Hasidic Jew in lime green Y-fronts, Tiger knew she would never be cut out for the job. She had just about managed to make enough to cover her flight back to London.

As Sienna now punched Bob Bell's number into her mobile she hoped she had rehearsed her own 'Hollywood' version of Tiger's story in her mind enough to make it seedy, shocking and absolutely sensational. A spoonful of 'sex for money shocker', a dash of 'auto erotic asphyxiation', a liberal sprinkling of 'sick, drug-fuelled orgies' with the distinctive flavour of 'brutal mistress' should do the trick, thought Sienna, rather pleased with herself. The line on the other end picked up and a gruff voice answered. Sienna's stage was laid out for her performance. She nervously cleared her throat, heaved a deep breath and took the plunge.

'Mr Bell? I'm so sorry to be calling at this late hour. We've never met but I have something I think you're going to be very, very interested in. I hope you have a large cheque book.'

Chapter 13

Blank canvas, blank canvas, blank canvas, blank canvas, blank canvas, Tiger chanted in her head as she selected a charcoal-coloured eyeshadow from her make-up caddy. This was her mantra before any kind of performance. Tiger had been told by one of the first directors she worked with that when Liza Minnelli had a show, she would focus the entire day around that night's performance from the very second she woke up. Tiger had considered this to be excellent advice, and adhered to it strictly in her own way. Starting with her own blank canvas – a clear face, and a clear mind – and slowly building towards her grand presentation was a delicious ritual for Tiger.

Blue popped his head in the door.

'Sorry to interrupt, babes, what time shall I send Cherry and Brandy in to dress you?'

'Oh, give it forty minutes. I've only just started putting my face on.'

'No worries. Lewis and the Luxuriana mob will be here soon. Can't wait to see it.'

'Hmm. Well, it'll be interesting. First time with the props.'

'They know that, don't worry about it.'

'Yeah, I know.'

'I'll be back in forty, babes. Oh, and I have a little surprise for you.'

'Oh? Don't tell me Valerie finished the corset already?'

'You just get back to your eyelashes. All I'll say is that you'll be feeling a million dollars when I'm finished with you.'

'Huh. That's only five hundred grand these days.'

'Damn inflation. Make it a billion.'

'That's more like it.'

'See you in forty.'

'See you. Love you.'

Tiger turned back to her mirror and tightened her silk dressing gown about her waist. She felt weird putting on a performance in the daytime for a scathing panel of suits armed with notepads. Still, this was the acid test for the Vegas finale routine. There was no way Dianne Castrelli would sign off millions of dollars of the promoter's budget for an epic water feature if she thought the act wouldn't work. Lewis had arranged for today's demonstration to be installed in the Hippodrome. Formerly 'The Talk Of The Town', it was one of the few venues with a hydraulic stage lift, and flies high enough from which to work Tiger's huge glitterball prop. The Hippodrome also happened to be most fitting, in that it was a beautiful old, faded venue which used to house circus shows, followed by music hall entertainment a hundred years back. An observant eye would be able to spot the huge iron hooks set into the walls that were used to chain up the elephants.

Of course, when Tiger had excitedly discovered that in the Hippodrome's circus days elephants would slide down an enormous waterfall the height of the proscenium arch into a huge water tank, Lewis had been extremely quick off the mark to stress that under no circumstances was he asking Dianne Castrelli for a troupe of elephants. Tiger knew that it was always a battle between the artist and the producer to strike a happy medium that satisfied both creative vision – and budget – a battle that Lewis was forever stuck in the middle of. She also knew that if she wanted elephants, she would bloody well find a way of having them. As it happened, she thought diving tigers would be much more appropriate. Hell, if they were good enough for Siegfried and Roy, then they were the obvious choice for Tiger Starr. After all, this was for Vegas, baby. First base was getting Di Castrelli to agree to her water feature.

Blank canvas, blank canvas, blank canvas, chanted Tiger inwardly as she expertly blended her eyeshadow. She worked her brushes like an artist used gouache, blending, daubing, blending some more, then methodically working thick mascara into her false lashes layer by layer. She hummed as she worked, gaining energy as the layers went on. Rapidly she sculpted her cheekbones with highlighter and contouring powder. Razor sharp, she thought to herself, pulling back from the mirror and sucking her cheeks in for a second while she admired her handiwork. Her breathing deepened as she drew in her lip line with a steady hand, before filling in her lips with glossy red. She sprang up to apply a final dusting of diamond powder to her cheeks and eyelids with a flourish. She smiled to herself and shut her eyes as she soaked up the first familiar tingle of butterflies. Great, we're on the ride now, she thought to herself as she bent over to shake out and fluff up her pink curls.

'Now that's what I call a view!' came a familiar voice.

Tiger squealed in surprise, and immediately straightened herself, flinging her hair back violently and swinging round to face the intruder with a vicious glare.

'Rex! Who let you into . . .'

Tiger felt a surge of butterflies. Her heart pounded. She didn't know whether it was the nerves, or seeing Rex unexpectedly like this. He looked stunning in an immaculate tan Italian suit, with a delicious shading of stubble on his jaw. Damn, he even smelled good; Aqua di Parma, thought Tiger as an intoxicating waft of fresh bergamot and lemon filled her dressing room.

'Hey, kiddo.'

'You know I hate that,' said Tiger tetchily, 'anyway, what are you doing in here?'

'Listen doll—' a beat '—I'll cut to the chase – we have to talk.'

'Not now, Rex, not before the presentation,' dismissed Tiger.

'But this is really urgent.'

'Well, why didn't you just call?'

'It's sensitive. I need to discuss this with you face to face and since you've been avoiding me lately . . .'

'I don't know what you mean. We work together. I'm on the phone to you five times a day. I don't need to see you.'

'Look. This is urgent,' Rex repeated insistently.

'I'm sure whatever it is can wait until this evening. I'll meet you around six?'

'No can do, the thing is—'

'Oh wait, don't tell me, it might interrupt a date you have planned with my own *sister.*'

'Well, well, well, I didn't think you were the jealous type. In fact I thought blowing hot and cold was more your style . . . in every sense.'

'That's disgusting. I have a really important performance to do right now. Lay off with the mudslinging in my private space.'

'For chrissake, Tiger, we need to talk. There's a story breaking with the *News of the World.*'

'I beg your pardon?'

'It could damage you.'

'The 'News of the Screws'? Oh pull the other one. I've done nothing.'

'We really need to talk through your options. And you do have options, so long as we act fast.'

'I've been straight with you from the start, along with

Lewis. Someone always reckons they have a story on me, and you know it's always been some false alarm.'

'Well, *someone* bears you a grudge—'

'Rex, shall I remove you from this dressing room myself? Let's discuss this later. Don't ever dump shit on me before a show, and certainly never in my dressing room.'

'You got it, lady. I don't need your help to leave, don't worry. You call me when you're done. But speaking as your paid advisor, be warned. This won't wait.'

'Fine. I hear you. Loud and clear.'

'Oh, and some girl gave me this to give to you as I was on my way from the stage door.'

Rex held out a pink envelope. Tiger blanched.

'Aren't you gonna take it?' Rex asked, pushing the envelope under her nose.

'Thanks, I'll open it later,' said Tiger, forcing a smile. 'It'll be a fan or something.'

'Yeah, whatever.'

'Oh, Rex?'

'Yep.'

'What did she look like?'

'Who?'

'The girl who gave you the envelope?'

'Oh, I dunno, she kind of ran past. I think she works here, looked like she was wearing a staff t-shirt. Red hair, bit of an old boiler.'

'Oh. Okay, cool, thanks.'

Rex left the room. Bastard, thought Tiger, invading her

dressing room like that. And looking so handsome. Her heart ached. Shit, now her head was all over the place. Anxiety. Longing. Fear. Desire. Guilt. Confusion. Lust. Panic. And who the fuck was dishing out these stupid anonymous letters? Surely it was a wind up. Tiger paced, still holding the pink envelope in her hand. What was Rex on about, anyway? A story in the tabloids? About what? She hadn't done anything really newsworthy lately – at least not in a scandal sense. No drugs, all that was well behind her. There had been no married men, no secret gastric band, no sex tapes, no covert boob job. Maybe it's some elaborate kiss 'n' tell, wondered Tiger. Probably some guy from years ago who was stony broke and fancied making a cool ten grand from a fabricated encounter. Yes, of course that was it. Oh let them, thought Tiger, calming herself. As long as they give a good report on my technique, she thought, smiling to herself naughtily. If that's the only way they can earn money then she just had to feel sorry for them.

Looking down at the envelope she wondered whether or not to open it. Oh what the hell, it's not like things could get much worse this afternoon. She ripped the paper open.

'I. Know. Your. Secret.' Tiger froze. The four little words on the pink paper burned into Tiger's retinas like a branding iron. Her mouth went dry. Her mind raced. What secret? Most people had secrets – parts of their past they'd rather not be publicly revealed. Who sent this? The same person who was selling a story to the newspapers? Tiger told herself it was simply a shot in the dark. Oh lord, maybe someone had discovered about her liaison with Libertina. Tiger panicked. Libertina was firmly in the closet, convinced it would damage her career if the Hollywood mafia knew she was batting for her own side. But Tiger wondered, did anyone really think that was scandal any more? Newsworthy perhaps. But surely it had to be more. Could the letter writer really know about Tiger's *real* secrets? Tiger shuddered before making a sign of the cross and hastily mumbling a Hail Mary. How on earth was she going to get through her performance with a mammoth stab of fear now lodged in her heart?

Lewis sat with Pepper, Blue and Rex to his right, and Vince, Johnny T and Dianne Castrelli from Las Vegas to his left. The tension was palpable as the lights dimmed. This motley crew were not easily impressed.

'I got Tiger into the osprey fantail and the new corset,' hissed Blue. 'You wouldn't believe what strings I had to pull to get them finished for this meeting . . . 'scuse the pun.'

Lewis grunted absentmindedly. He couldn't give a crap about the costume – after all, Tiger could make a coffee sack look good. He just wanted her on form, and he had just received a weird text message from her to say she really needed to 'kick some ass'. That's all it had said. Lewis had seen Rex sniffing around Tiger's dressing room earlier, and knowing that Rex had the diplomatic skills of a gorilla with a hard on, Lewis dreaded to think what he might have been saying ... or doing to her by way of encouragement back there. He'd hoped that whatever had been going on between Tiger and Rex had fizzled out but now he felt the tic start in his cheek as his paranoia started to get the better of him.

Lights flooded the stage, and the opening bars of 'Carmina Burana' blasted through the room as the magnificent ten-foot glitterball rose, spinning above everyone's heads. It was certainly a rousing start. So far so good, thought Lewis, as he nudged Di Castrelli.

'If you just imagine the pit as the pool,' he shouted over the fanfare, 'the fountains would be pushing up the mirrorball at this point.'

Dianne nodded and jotted notes in her pad.

There was a collective gasp as a door swung back from the glitterball to reveal Tiger perched upon a bird swing like an albino bird of paradise, set against red padded interior upholstery in the style of the Russian Czar's Renaissance Fabergé egg. The sparkle from the diamonds on her corset was blinding. She looked like a jewel in a crown.

'Holy Cajone!' cheered the normally poker-faced Vince and Johnny T in unison. Dianne Castrelli continued to scribble furiously in her notepad.

Ten of the Starrlets were lowered to the stage on rope swings, each wearing their sparkling mirrored crinolines as Tiger nimbly swung down from her glitterball, using a huge suspended velveteen tassel. Her long silk ruffled train undulated wildly behind her as she rotated. Tiger looked like a gazelle mid pounce as she flew through the air; pure elegance in motion. 'Carmina Burana' reached its infamous crescendo as Tiger was finally lowered to the floor in an arabesque. Lewis detected a steely expression on her face, tense and fiery.

Lewis leaned in to Di Castrelli, shouting in her ear: 'She'd be on the central plinth in the pool at this point with the fountains in synchronised jets.' The three Americans leaned in together to confer. Lewis looked to his right. Blue had his nails in his mouth, Pepper was tapping her dainty foot as she scrutinised Georgia and the Starrlets, and Rex looked on mesmerised. Lewis eyeballed Rex suspiciously, deciding he had a distinctly lecherous air today. Rex smiled over at Lewis and stuck his thumbs up. Tosser, thought Lewis resentfully as he curled his lip and looked away to concentrate on the stage.

The music segued into a dramatic, filmic John Barry number as Tiger lifted her enormous circular fantail like a peacock, and paraded majestically with the girls, as they broke into leggy kicks behind her. She had a predatory air as she stalked regally across the stage, shimmering with every movement. Lewis knew she was wound up, with a forceful tension in her limbs that he recognised from her early days on stage. Lewis glared back over at Rex, narrowing his eyes as he watched him licking his lips at the Starrlets. His hackles went up. He had trusted

Rex as a solid part of the work team for all these years; that is until he overheard Tiger enthusing about the shape of his penis with Blue in one of the intervals at the Savoy show. Lewis had been appalled to think of Rex's great hairy paws on his elegant Tiger; what on earth was she thinking? Lewis couldn't watch her on stage that night without seeing her differently somehow. She was too good for Rex, she must have lost her head. Tiger was too much woman for someone like him to handle and Lewis wasn't surprised to see Rex move on to her sister like some sleazy Lothario. Now, Lewis was damned if he was going to let Rex anywhere near any of the young Starrlets, and certainly not his girlfriend Georgia. Lewis kept his eyes on the stage, realising he had been clicking and unclicking his pen angrily, much to everyone's irritation.

Deftly, Tiger unclipped the huge osprey fantail from her corset to use it as a feather fan. Only this was no gentle wing flapping. Tiger used it as a fighting fan. Slicing the air, she span it in extreme circles over her head like a Japanese warrior as she thundered towards her audience. She then unclipped her matching osprey headdress and used it in tandem. With fire in her eyes she slashed powerfully through the air in synchronised circles. It was a spectacular display. The energy was untamed. The Starrlets could be seen glancing sideways at each other on stage. Pepper looked confused.

'She's moved away from the choreography!' Pepper

complained into Lewis' ear. 'She's moving into the girls' space! Absolutely apalling discipline!'

Lewis turned to look at Rex with an accusatory glare.

'What the hell did you do to her in the dressing room? She's all over the place!' Lewis hissed over at Rex.

'Nothing, mate, what's the problem? She's doing great! This is fucking electric!'

Lewis settled back in his chair, unable to face Rex. Lewis knew he was right. It really was electric to watch, that old Tiger fire; that heat that turned Lewis on to her in the first place. Her glamorous shows had polished some of that rawness away over time. He'd never seen her so worked up in the last ten years. So this was what she meant by 'kicking some ass'.

Tiger was down to her pasties and diamond g-string as she moved through her blanket dance, writhing and slinking amongst her bed of ruffles like a cat on heat. It was pure animal sexuality. The costume looked breathtaking as it moulded with her curves. Tiger looked at ease as she used her trusty old flamenco tricks to manipulate the enormous train of ruffles, with her army of Starrlets behind her, now swinging like exquisite twinkling pin-up dolls on their own suspended perches. As the music increased in pace, Tiger leapt with each cymbal crash, and purred with each saxophone slide. The muscles in her thighs glistened as she worked up a glow. With a final dramatic jump she gripped onto the velvet tassel hanging from the glitterball above her and wrapped it about her waist with a flourish. On cue the huge prop rose, spinning wildly in a glorious spectrum of sparkles.

'What on earth is she playing at?' murmured Lewis as he realised Tiger had adopted the pose of Jesus on the cross with outstretched arms as she ascended towards the flies, rotating with the glitterball, and shaking her hair as it tumbled down her back, with her diamond-encrusted pasties and merkin glittering blindingly under the lights.

'That's just madness. Controversy for the sake of it. Jesus was definitely not in the choreography. Fucking disaster,' Lewis muttered to himself, pinching the bridge of his nose tightly. 'Rex, I want a word with you later,' he muttered. 'This wasn't supposed to be the friggin' resurrection. I think Tiger just screwed up. A hunch tells me you had something to do with it. They're gonna cut this number entirely after seeing it like this. Do you know how much that blasted prop cost?'

'Mate, that was genius, what's the problem?' replied Rex, smirking. Lewis looked over at Blue, who was staring with his mouth agape. Pepper had her hand held over her mouth. Lewis' heart sank. He held on to his seat as the Starrlets finished their crescendo with the music reaching its rousing finale as Tiger disappeared from view into the flies in a final flash of blinding lights.

The silent pause was long and pregnant. Dianne Castrelli, Vince and Johnny T huddled together.

'Okay, Mr Bond,' opened Dianne with her usual stern expression.

Here it comes, thought Lewis, bracing himself.

'I can see your vision.'

Cut to the chase, thought Lewis, I can take it.

'I think we can make the water feature work.'

Okay, now give me the 'but', thought Lewis, let's get it over with.

'In fact I think it will be quite stunning.'

Okay, now she's going for the bad news. Come on, baby, don't be a coward.

'I have to say, this is pretty spectacular stuff, Lewis. It's still camp, but it's original, set against the more traditional showgirl pieces. In fact, I'd use the word "artful".'

Huh? thought Lewis.

'Yes, it's very artful, it reminds me of a painting. Umm . . . I'm trying to think of the name . . .'

'Renaissance?' chipped in Blue hopefully, casting his mind back to his afternoon with Valerie.

'Yes . . . the painting eludes me.' Dianne smiled. 'Never mind, I'll remember it later. Now, if we can rethink the religious references at the end, I think we're really on to a winner.'

Lewis kept his face straight and nodded thoughtfully,

'That was quite an incredible performance you know,' said Di, lowering her voice and looking around at the rapidly nodding Vince and Johnny T. 'Now I heard some rumour flying around that Tiger wanted diving Siberian tigers?'

Lewis clenched his teeth, wondering how on earth Tiger

had managed to get her ridiculous request past him and direct to Dianne.

'Really?' Lewis coughed, smiling politely. 'No, no, no, I think that must have been hearsay—'

'Oh, but it's a fabulous idea, Mr Bond. Let's discuss it. We'll need to check out the insurance implications but I think tigers shouldn't be a problem. Ahh, Bosch! That's who I was thinking of – that finale will look like a modern day *Garden of Earthly Delights*, with Tiger as Eve, rising to the skies surrounded by naked beauties, majestic animals, rising to the great disco ball in the sky. Isn't that poetic?'

'Ooh, all we'd need then is for Liberace to parachute in through the ceiling,' muttered Blue with a sigh.

'I might just ask my people to check out availability for white Bengal tigers instead,' continued Dianne, looking eager. 'Siberian tigers are so *passé*. Do you think Ms Starr would prefer white tigers?'

Tiger emerged in the wings after her presentation, realising with a sinking feeling in the afterglow that she had taken her baggage right out onto the stage and waved it about in the spotlight for all to see.

'Jeez, what happened back there with the fans?' asked Nikki as Tiger caught up with the chorus line, who were patiently waiting for her.

'Whaddyamean?' asked Tiger.

'I mean, well, wow I've not seen you use them like that before! You were a warrior!' breathed Nikki admiringly.

'Cor, yeah I wouldn't want to be on the wrong side of you!' laughed Frankie.

'Hmm. Come on, girls, lets just take our bows, eh,' sighed Tiger, preparing for a deafening silence.

As she demurely walked out in front of the stage her audience cheered, whooped and clapped. As Tiger bowed, allowing a smile to creep across her face, she could see Pepper jumping up and down, Rex leaning back and whistling loudly, even Lewis clapping loudly and cheering. Tiger caught Di Castrelli's eye; she proffered a big wink, accompanied by a knowing nod and a beaming smile. Tiger breathed an enormous sigh of relief and allowed the sound of clapping and cheers to ring loudly in her ears as she bowed once more.

Chapter 14

Cheers and screams surged through the air as Poppy raced round the pitch with lungs burning, arms outstretched, hockey stick held high in the air, and the wind blowing sweaty ringlets of hair away from her flushed, elated face. Hundreds of pairs of feet stamped on the metal boards of the tiered seating either side of the pitch as hands clapped frantically along with the cheering. A few low boos rang out from the losing team. All of a sudden Poppy was swept up into the air as several pairs of hands jerkily hoisted her above their heads to celebrate the winning goal in the last ten seconds of the match.

'Put me down!' squealed Poppy, laughing her head off. This just made her team mates spin her round even faster. Poppy looked anxiously around from her vantage point for Mr Rogers, hoping he had watched her scoring that crucial goal. She caught him out of the corner of her eye at the sidelines, standing tall with legs apart, arms crossed, nodding and beaming, his thick blond hair tousled in the breeze. Their eyes locked for a second. Yesssss, thought Poppy, he would be so pleased with her! She knew this would make up for the shame of the catfight last week; she knew she could prove she was a good girl at heart.

Back in the locker room after an extremely rowdy bus ride back to school the last remaining girls were stuffing their damp gym skirts and muddy hockey boots into their kitbags. The air was thick with Impulse body spray and 'Red Door' eau de toilette.

Poppy felt a hand on her backside and jumped round with a start.

'Emma! You made me jump!'

'Ha! Why, who did you think it was?'

'Well not you for a start, you've been a bitch all week.'

'Yeah I know, actually Marina had a bit of a go at me tonight before the match. She told me I had to say sorry to you. She said she thinks I've been mean. We are supposed to be on the same team after all right?'

'I'm not just talking about hockey.'

'I know, I know. Look, can we forget all that stuff from before? You know you nailed 'em good and proper tonight, Pops!'

'You know I hate "Pops".'

'Whatever, that tackle was fierce! You shoulda seen that cow's face when you got the ball, she started hopping to make it look like you'd got her in the shins, it was classic!'

'So I take it we're mates again.'

'Yeah, only 'cos you put us all in Mr Rogers' good books though. Even if you do keep shaking your boobs at him. God he's so gorgeous when he's smiling.'

Poppy blushed and smiled to herself as she reached in her bag and felt the green sweater she'd had in her kit bag all week. It had obviously been a lucky charm for tonight. She decided maybe she wouldn't give it back straight away.

'Listen, I'm off, Mum's waiting outside,' said Emma. 'You need a lift? Your mum does night school on Wednesdays, doesn't she?'

'Yeah, but it's okay, I could do with the walk home, I'm still buzzing. It's a nice enough evening, the sunset'll keep me company.'

'Okay, if you're sure.' Emma gave her a look as if she was mad. 'See you tomorrow. Triple maths – can't wait.' And with that Emma skipped off out of the locker room, kitbag and satchel slung over her shoulder.

Poppy pulled on her own blazer hurriedly as she realised she was the last one to leave as usual. She flicked the light switch of the locker room before pulling the door shut behind her. Making her way out of the sports block she paused to tie up her shoelace. A hand grabbed her shoulder as she knelt down. Poppy sprung up, alarmed, and as she span round came face to face with Ed Rogers.

'Well done, Poppy, you were really fantastic tonight,' said Ed.

'Oh, thanks, it was – it was so much fun.' Poppy blushed, suddenly wishing she'd put some mascara back on after her shower.

'Tell you what, why don't you come to my cabin for a minute? I could show you the designs for our new team strip.'

'Oh, well – sure, I've got a few minutes.' Poppy's heart

raced. Five minutes with Mr Rogers! Wait until she told Emma, Claire and Marina! Thank goodness Mother wasn't waiting for her at the gates tonight, there was a god after all, she thought excitedly.

Ed's cabin was cramped, with team photographs, trophies and medals on all the walls. Any spare wall space was filled with scribbled match schedules and typed class timetables. Poppy perched nervously on a stool and looked around. In the corner stood a grey locker out of which was spilling what looked to be Mr Rogers' own kit, underneath piles of school sweatshirts. She figured the new team strip samples must be in there too.

'So, Miss Adams. You've been a very good girl today. Would you like to be the first to try on the new sweatshirts?'

'Cool!' said Poppy, wondering where she should change.

'Well, why don't you just slip out of your blouse. I won't look.'

Ed turned to the locker and rummaged amongst the piles of kit. He hummed happily. Poppy took her blazer off, and went to undo her top button. She hesitated. The girls would think she was a slapper if she told them she had taken her blouse off in front of a man, whether he was looking or not. She thought better of it.

'Mr Rogers, shall I go to the girls' changing room?' Ed turned to her and stared at her quizzically.

'Why do you need to do that, Poppy? You're safe with me. Don't you trust me?'

'Oh yes, Mr Rogers, yes of course. It's just that, well—'

'You're okay with us being here together, aren't you?'

'Of course, yes.'

'I don't invite just anyone into my cabin you know.'

'Oh thank you! I mean, well, great, I'd love to try on the new stuff if that's cool with you.'

'Yes, it's fine with me, Poppy. Well then. Let me help you.'

As Ed fumbled with Poppy's top button, his breathing became heavy. His face hardened in concentration. Poppy's excitement turned to alarm. What was he doing? He wasn't smiling any more. Had she upset him? Maybe she'd offended him. The last thing she wanted was to disappoint him.

'It's okay, Mr Rogers, let me undo—' Poppy didn't have a chance to finish, as Ed ripped her shirt open, exposing her ample bosom spilling from her cheap peach satin bra. Poppy gasped, and fearfully held her arms up to hide her breasts. Ed locked his arm about her waist and reached for the wall with his other hand to turn off the cabin light as he firmly yanked her body up against his.

Poppy hobbled through the common. The night was closing in. Mother would be getting home about now. If she hurried, Poppy would only be a few minutes late. She wondered if Mother would be able to tell. She would kill Poppy if she found out what had happened, she would be in deep, deep trouble for leading a man on. She'd definitely be sent to boarding school if it ever got out. And how on earth would she explain another ripped shirt? Mother would think she'd been fighting again. Poppy knelt down by a large oak tree and retrieved a tissue from her bag. She spat in it and scrubbed at the dried blood on her thigh. Tears filled her eyes. She was hurting and confused. Her friends must never find out, they would hate her. They would say she deserved it for drawing attention to herself.

She scrambled to her feet and started to hum manically as she walked, hoping to drown out the vicious cackling voices in her head. She choked her tears back, anxiously singing the words to 'Somewhere Over The Rainbow' as she struggled home alone in the dark.

Chapter 15

'I'm so sorry about what happened, Sienna,' comforted Rex.

'Unfortunately, it's just not a simple scenario – the media world's a complicated beast,' he sighed, turning back to his laptop.

'So, hang on, let me get this straight. You told Tiger to tell her own side, right?' persisted Sienna.

'No, no, no. Bob Bell's sub ed called me to warn me the story was going out. He gave me twenty-four hours to get Tiger to spill the beans in her own words. He had his own agenda.' Rex turned from his desk to face Sienna.

'Look, I'll give you the abridged version. Some sewer rat journo's got a lead on a scandal; I still don't know how, I always thought Tiger was snow fuckin' white and water fuckin' tight. The journo has gone to New York to dig around and he probably offered a big pay-off to some crackhead, grudge-bearing dominatrix bitch for spinning a yarn about Tiger. Probably put the words in her mouth himself. Sewer rat journo then sticks in a load of his own fiction which is disguised in the final article with the words "our source said . . . blah." The newspaper gives your big sis the golden opportunity to 'fess up in her own words

– in the process they may also bluff her to hopefully give even more away. In the meantime the newspaper goes back to crackhead bitch and the original lead whoever that was, and says, "I'm cutting your fee," from say, twelve grand to three; for example, telling each that there's a better story from another source. Crackhead bitch gets screwed over, the original lead gets screwed over, Tiger gets screwed over, the winners are sewer rat journo and the newspaper. Got it?'

Sienna looked astonished. Rex's face softened. 'Hey, babe, I know she's your sister, and it must have been a shock to find out about her being a former dominatrix, but this is a rough business, and I'm in a difficult position with you working here. You wanna learn, right?'

'Right,' squeaked Sienna.

'In fact, I know you're probably thinking your sister hid her head in the sand over this, but you know what? She handled this the right way.'

Rex failed to mention that the night they had their crisis meeting after the Vegas presentation he had urged Tiger to tell her story in her own words as a damage limitation exercise. Tiger had been incensed that Rex couldn't see that the story had been wildly sensationalised, and he had worked hard to bring her back from the brink of a furious rage. He even thought she might have hit him at one point; he hadn't seen such anger burning in her eyes before. He had to admit that he'd been massively turned on. He could have fucked her there and then over the dinner table if he didn't think he'd end up with a London Ritz fine silver fork stabbed into his neck.

Tiger had given Rex the strict instruction to let the story run in all its fabricated glory. She stressed that she adhered to Katharine Hepburn's infamous mantra – 'Never complain, never explain.' Shortly after, she'd mumbled something about 'could have been worse'. Rex knew that for someone who took her clothes off for a living, however artful or glamorous, Tiger fully accepted she would always be subjected to people of a certain insecure mindset taking the moral high ground against her, and she vowed never to waste time attempting to convert such bigots or hypocrites. Instead Tiger voiced her instinct that with the great adage 'today's news is tomorrow's chip paper' in mind, the story would merely add to her mystique over time. As long as she gave it no credence by commenting, she would maintain her dignity.

Rex had to hand it to Tiger, she played her hand well, and her theory worked. Even Lewis, who had been furious at Rex about the story – like it was his fault – eventually conceded that Tiger's strategy was spot on. Even though she had been really quite shocked at just how elaborate and seedy the story had been made, especially as the reality of a pathetic little three-day failed adventure was poles apart from what had been painted, Tiger was prepared to ride the storm. She had also let it be known that she had her suspicions about the culprit – she simply didn't buy the 'random dominatrix with a grudge' as the informer.

Tiger remembered her pal Tiffany had brought the ghastly Rosemary Baby along with her the night they had all swapped their funny stories to cheer Sienna up shortly after the death of their parents. Tiger had a gut feeling even back then that Rosemary Baby was just a skidmark on the g-string of the showgirl world and was amazed that Tiffany was offering to bring her into her circle. After Rosemary was then arrested on suspicion of causing Tiffany's accident in Vegas, Tiger had had her card marked. She was definitely a prime candidate for the source of the latest little drama.

Rex had been all ears when Tiger filled him and Lewis in on her hunch, this Rosemary certainly seemed quite a piece of work. Ultimately Tiger figured she may never get to the bottom of the news story, but the twist in the tale was that whoever the guilty party was had unwittingly done Tiger a favour. Incredibly, both Lewis and Rex had been inundated in the last day or two with enquiries for Tiger to make guest television appearances, attend radio panels and provide cultural comments once the initial shock had passed. Business had never been so booming.

Rex realised Sienna had been quiet for a few minutes. She looked pensive. He felt a strange mixture of feelings towards her. Sienna Starr had simply been a revenge fuck that had gone awry. He wasn't really into her sexually at all – certainly not the way he was with Tiger. Neither had Rex bargained on Sienna moving a load of her stuff into his prized bachelor pad; she had obviously very naively taken his pillow talk to heart. The problem was, to finish with Sienna so soon would be madness – it would be so obvious what his motives had been all along. Plus there were a few perks to having her around. She provided sex on tap, she was always available to massage his ego, and she gave him no hassle about the odd 'business trip', so he could still service his little black book on the side when he got bored with her.

The only grit in Rex's oyster was the unbridled lust he still harboured for Tiger. He tried not to torment himself too often, and kept himself from meetings in her presence pretty easily, she was always so busy anyway. Yet just having her on the phone several times a day could set him off. He loved catching her when she was on the run, then he would break off mid sentence to snatch a couple of seconds listening to her breathing heavily as she raced to her next engagement. Once he had a wank to her velvety voice as she read out her annual order for her hosiery sponsor. He had made her repeat the word 'gusset' until she had slammed the phone down in pique. Rex Hunter and Tiger Starr were meant for each other, they were a perfect fit, or so he had thought. Tiger was the one woman he would have settled down for – he never in a million years considered that the feelings wouldn't be reciprocated. Even her name would have sounded right when he finally made her his. Tiger Hunter. Synchronicity.

Rex reasoned that it was perversely fitting that Sienna Starr should help to numb the pain of Tiger's reckless rebuttal. In a funny way he had begun developing some fondness for Sienna; and after the *News of the World* debacle he just felt sorry for the kid, even though empathy wasn't his forte, particularly in family matters.

Rex Hunter had never had any siblings. That's not to say he hadn't frequently longed for the support of a brother or sister whilst his father was kicking seven shades of shit out of him most evenings. If his mother had stuck her neck out for him once in a while it would have made a nice change he had often thought, but the bitch had to go and leave him after 'falling down the stairs' face first onto a burning hot iron. An ambulance had taken her away. Rex Hunter saw his father leaving the house a week later in a suit. He remembered seeing curtains across the street being twitched. There were only two occasions he would ever be seen in a suit, and Dad hadn't mentioned anything about a wedding. Most importantly, Rex knew to keep quiet and play the game to take care of business. He didn't hang around too much longer after that, he ran away to London on the eve of his thirteenth birthday. His father never came looking. Fittingly, Rex viewed his current job as a PR guru with a similar philosophy; playing the media game to take care of business. With that thought he snapped his attention back to his office and the job of slowly educating Sienna in that very game.

'Babe, it's bound to be a bit raw when something like this is happening to your own sister,' sighed Rex, looking over at Sienna earnestly, 'but from a professional point of view it's excellent experience for you to learn from. It can only benefit you long term. You'll get this with other clients in the future, I promise you, maybe a lot worse. So you'll learn how to play the game properly now. That's what you want, isn't it?'

Sienna's face brightened. 'Oh you mean, I'll be allowed to deal with clients of my own soon?' Rex smiled, noting how quickly she could look on the bright side.

'Well, not just yet, but I don't see why I can't slip in a little promotion if things keep going well like they have been. Let's get past your birthday first, then I'll take a review. Good to see you're turning it into a positive. Well done.'

'Cool!' beamed Sienna.

'Babe, that's an expensive-looking dress you've got on there,' Rex remarked, changing the subject. 'Is it new?'

'Oh! This! Er, well . . .'

'And Louboutins if I'm not mistaken.' Rex was already guiltily imagining Tiger on her back with her legs in the air wearing only those towering stilettos.

'Hmm, sexy outfit!' he murmured. 'Your sister must have bought that lot for you I'm guessing. I know the Hunter Gatherers' intern wages aren't good enough for Louboutins!'

'Er, yeah! That's right. Good old Tiger.' Sienna grimaced, the full humiliation of being fobbed off with a measly few grand for her story by Bob Bell finally sinking in. She could have had herself a nice little nest egg by now if only she hadn't been so naive. To add insult to injury the story had barely touched the sides; Tiger had bounced back like the jammy cow she always had been. If anything she was even more of a mysterious *femme fatale* now, damn her. Rex was right about one thing. At least Sienna now knew exactly how to play the game for next time.

'Oh my god, did you read that bit about the men in nappies?' shrieked Frankie, slapping the table as she creased up with laughter.

'Ugh, it was the cheese grater thing that made me throw up,' giggled Samara.

'Yuk! And all the orgies? Sick! I just can't believe it's the same Tiger,' screeched Frankie, her voice getting louder by the second.

'Shhh, girls! Bloody 'ell, people are staring!' admonished Nikki, looking round sternly at the group of girls as they all tucked into their lunchtime *prix fixe* meal of steak frites.

'I agree.' Blanche nodded. 'Show some respect. We're all on the Tiger Starr payroll. She's our boss. I love being a Starlett, I get chatted up loads, all the time.' The girls all gasped, 'yeah'-ed, and nodded madly in agreement. 'And let's face it, being a Starrlet pisses over being stuck in some bland West End musical doing eight mindnumbing shows every single week for a crappy four hundred quid. If we were in "Shitty Shitty Bang Bang", none of us would be able to afford nice lunches in French restaurants like today you know,' continued Blanche gravely, 'and we wouldn't be as cool. As it is, all the girls want to be us. Why d'ya think it's so hard to get in to the harem!'

The girls all agreed loudly in unison.

'Well, I've got news for you,' announced Nikki. 'Our new girl, Honey Lou, over here has yet to sample the delights of the West End,' she pointed out, smiling over at the pretty, fresh-faced, mixed-race girl at the end of the large table.

'No way!' said Frankie. 'You've not done a proper run yet?'

'Er, no,' said Honey Lou coyly.

'Wait for this, she's straight from the Rambert School.' Nikki winked.

'Bloody 'ell, Tiger doesn't usually take girls straight out of dance school,' cackled Frankie, 'says they need to get the poles out of their arses and find their passion!'

'For god's sake, she doesn't exactly put it like that,' interjected Briony in her cut-glass tones, 'anyway, Honey Lou's the new girl, we need to make her feel one of us, not like some student understudy.'

'Exactly, girls, and let me tell you; I saw Honey Lou's audition piece. I can assure you . . .' Nikki paused for dramatic effect. 'She's one hot, sexy byatch on stage!'

The girls all whooped as Honey Lou blushed and chewed awkwardly on a mouthful of minute steak.

Within seconds, the girls reverted back to bondage story swapping, and although desperate to join in, Honey Lou decided she was far too embarrassed to mention how her parents had gone ape when Tiger's story was splashed all over the *News of the World* at the weekend. They had been dubious about her being a showgirl in the first place, and she knew how hard it was for them to steel themselves to congratulate her for making it into the Starrlets straight after graduating. They knew being a showgirl was all she'd ever dreamt of since school. And everyone knew how good you had to be to become a Starrlet. Tiger took great care to handpick her girls, and her criteria were so different to those of regular theatrical shows.

At dance school you were taught to blend in with the rest of the chorus line, but Tiger looked for personalities and sensuality. She wanted her troupe of Starrlets to be as legendary as the famous Crazy Horse girls. She also worked with Pepper in the auditions to 'undo' some of the classic poses taught in dance school, and introduce more period movement and kitsch poses, with some of the exaggeration and campness that the old Paris shows had. Tiger even made the girls arch their backs at all times so their crotches were always directed away from the audience. If Margot Fonteyn had seen the postures of the Starrlets she'd be spinning in her grave.

If the girls were lucky enough to have a re-call, they would then be made to wear cumbersome, heavy headdresses and the tightest corsets to see how they could dance and high kick with so much restriction. Honey Lou had nearly fainted in her audition, her corset was pulled so tight. She had got to the point of seeing stars, but she was determined to go the distance and make her mark. Honey Lou had always dreamed of working with Tiger Starr, and to see her heroine splashed all over the tabloids in such a cheap story had distressed her, especially as now, after the glory of her big achievement, her parents were even less keen on her being a Starrlet. As Honey Lou finished her last mouthful, Frankie was asking for the dessert menu.

'Steady on, Frankie, you'll get a right old barge arse if you keep eating like this,' said Nikki.

'I've got a fast metabolism, I can eat what I want.' Frankie sniffed.

'Not if you keep packing the bread away like you were back there,' teased Nikki with a sparkle in her eye.

'Oh sod off, you lot. You're just jealous that I've got hollow legs.'

'Speaking of which, where's Georgia?' asked Blanche. A barely detectable murmur swept round the table, more of a groan than appreciation.

'Oh she's with Lewis and Pepper this afternoon learning our routine for the rocking horse show,' replied Nikki.

'Shame, I hoped she'd give us more of the gossip on the *News of the World* thing. I bet Lewis has a load of inside information!' said Frankie.

'Yes, well, knowing Georgia, she's always one step ahead on any gossip that might bring Tiger down,' snapped Blanche.

'Oh? Know something we don't?' asked Frankie.

'Nope. Just a hunch,' replied Blanche tartly.

'Well, we've all had a laugh today but let's not get carried away. We know Tiger's no hooker. My mum and dad said you should believe none of what you hear and only half of what you see,' proclaimed Nikki.

'Yeah,' agreed Samara, 'my folks still think Tiger's alright you know. I think my dad secretly fancies her.'

'God, don't tell your mum,' gasped Frankie.

'As if!' muttered Samara.

'Right. So let's just move on, Tiger's been good to us, now's our chance to show our support. Right girls?' asked Nikki.

Honey Lou sighed, wishing her parents were as cool as Nikki's and Samara's.

'Yeah, you're right,' conceded Frankie, 'anyway, Tiger's doing this four-day press junket in Vegas soon, and I wanna be on that plane with her! She can only take four of us you know!'

'Well in that case Georgia's a definite, so that leaves room for three of us . . .' said Samara.

'Ooh I'm keeping everything crossed. I heard it's a private jet! Can you believe it?' cooed Frankie.

Honey Lou quietly sipped at her Diet Coke, knowing that as the new girl it was a long shot that she'd be chosen. Even if she was, her parents were hardly going to let her go after this week's scandal. Still, she could dare to dream. After all, it had been a dream to be a Starrlet and here she was. She just hoped at the very least she could hold on to her prize now she had it.

Tiger carefully tucked a rogue strand of coiffed pink hair underneath her Chanel headscarf and with immaculate manicured hands grabbed her shades before heading for the front door, python handbag in tow. Her nail technician had already been to the house that morning to sharpen her talons, along with hairstylist Mario, brandishing his hot tongs. In fact Tiger had spent the last few days hibernating and restoring herself, sweating it out on the exercise bike in her basement for hours on end and kicking the crap out of the punchbag as she let her mind take a wander. On top of the press story the anonymous letters had kept coming. One thing Tiger despised was cowardice, and whatever mysterious game playing was afoot was starting to grate. She was determined not to let the first tendrils of paranoia creep into her mind. A good hard workout was the ultimate therapy in her opinion. After all, the best way to fight back was to come into the outside world looking fucking fabulous.

On autopilot, Tiger stopped mid-clack in the flag-stoned hallway to check her handbag for her keys, purse and mobile. Pausing for one last check in the hall mirror before she faced the predatory paps at her door, she saw that a flower had dropped from its stem on to the stone floor, dead. All good things come to an end, thought Tiger wistfully. The beautiful flowers had arrived first thing

Monday by courier, a huge basket of expensive, richly scented orchids. Tiger picked up the accompanying card from the basket once more.

'Darling. I read the story. You should have called me . . .' Tiger turned the card over. '. . . I simply have to see you again. This time I'm your slave. Love Libertina x'

Tiger smiled to herself, feeling a twinge of lust. She put on her shades to hide any dark circles about the eyes, took a deep breath and ran out of the front door gracefully on her Gucci power heels, barging firmly past the frantically snapping paparazzi who had been camped outside and waiting for her first public appearance since the weekend. As the photographers called out her name and jeered and cheered, Tiger wondered if they had actually been expecting her to emerge from the door in a catsuit, whip and a leather-peaked cap or something. As she pushed past them with a dignified smile, a little voice called out her name. She turned for a second to see stage door Johnnie standing there holding a small posy. The photographers were snapping Tiger's every move. Taken aback to see him outside her house with the photographers, she managed to politely mouth a thank you at Johnnie and grab the little posy before diving elegantly into the already purring Lincoln Towncar which pulled away swiftly with Vladimir at the wheel, leaving behind the flashing cameras in its wake.

'I'm vibrating, do excuse me,' said Blue as he pulled his mobile from his back pocket. 'Darling, I'm in McQueen, where are you? Just get Vladimir to pull up outside, I have some things for you to try on . . . well hurry up then!' Blue snapped his phone shut and handed an armful of garments over to the cute new sales assistant he'd been flirting with for the last half hour.

'Okay, she's pulling into Bond Street, pop that lot into her fitting room.' Blue smiled, before mincing over to the headscarves and pulling out a few different colourways. Hearing the familiar clip-clop of stiletto on shop floor, Blue emerged from the back of the store to greet Tiger.

'Darling, you finally made it out into daylight, congratulations!'

'Oh very funny,' said Tiger a little tetchily, whipping off her shades before giving Blue a quick squeeze.

'So what have you found?' she asked, sweeping her eyes along the rails.

'What haven't I found more like, it's hard to narrow it down, the collection is so beautiful. There's a pile of things in the fitting room ready for you. I'm feeling the Hitchcock, Kim Novak vibe for you a bit with this season,' mused Blue, smoothing his micro-pencil moustache.

'Oh look!' gasped Tiger, laying her hands on an exquisite embroidered dress coat artfully draped over a mannequin.

'Hey, I thought you wanted me to find day wear.'

'Oh yes, but just look at this. Oh and look!' Tiger was now at the rails, caressing a full length, one-shouldered black gown. 'You can just tell how this is going to hang when it's on – curves, curves, curves.'

A couple of people in the store were staring at Tiger, recognising her despite her rudimentary disguise. Blue rolled his eyes and turned to the sales assistant.

'Sorry about this, looks like the kid in the sweetshop over here is gonna be trying on a few more things.'

'Oh no problem. I can see most of the collection working for Ms Starr, to be honest. It must be hard to choose.' The sales boy nodded kindly.

'Well if you can't beat 'em, join 'em,' sighed Blue, diving for one of the rails opposite.

After a few minutes Tiger sidled up to Blue.

'Darling, there's this boy, he seems to be following me, watching me,' she whispered.

'Something unusual in that?' muttered Blue.

'Not like that,' she hissed, 'he doesn't fancy me, look at him! There's no way he's straight.'

'Ohhh, he's cute!'

'But he followed me into the shop I think. He might be a journalist. We should leave.'

'What? But you haven't tried on your—'

'I don't care, let's get out of here,' Tiger pleaded.

'Oh stop being paranoid, get a grip,' Blue whispered back irritably. 'Get back over there and get that gown, you've done nothing wrong.'

Tiger hesitated.

'Go!'

Tiger skulked back to the rail, and furtively selected a black and red gown.

'Excuse me, ma'am?'

Tiger jumped and spun round to find the young boy at her shoulder.

'Can I help you?' she asked curtly.

'This may come across a little forward but . . . is he your partner?' The boy motioned over at Blue.

'What? Oh god no. He's my stylist. Why?' Tiger asked suspiciously.

'Oh wow. Right.' The boy looked relieved. 'Erm, my name's Richie. I was wondering if you could introduce me?'

'For real?'

'Sorry, it's just I noticed him coming out of a boutique down the road, only I was too shy to—'

'Don't tell me it's the thing to cruise down Bond Street now,' Tiger laughed.

Richie looked embarrassed. 'Oh, look I'm sorry, this was a mistake, I shouldn't have—'

'No no! Hey, I'm sorry, that was a bad joke.' Tiger softened, realising he was definitely no journalist. He was a beautiful-looking lad, softly spoken with a touch of Eastern Promise about him. Richie's boyish beauty made quite a contrast to Blue's beefy frame and eccentric face; they'd make a handsome couple, decided Tiger. She kindly took his hand and sashayed over to Blue.

'Darling. This is Richie.'

'Richie. Why hello, I'm Blue.'

'Very pleased to meet you . . . erm . . . uh . . .'

'Richie spotted you from afar didn't you, darling,' prompted Tiger helpfully.

'Thanks, yeah . . . up the street.' Richie smiled. 'Only I was too shy to say hi, so I went through your friend here – er, Tiger – instead. At least I figured you had to be friends to be shopping together.'

Blue puffed his chest out a little, unused to being chased by fit young men but taking to the experience like a duck to water.

'I've seen you in the Ray Bar, haven't I?' continued Richie.

'Yes, sometimes if I have meetings on the east side I'll pop in.'

'Yeah I thought so, I've seen you there a few lunchtimes.'

'Hmm, I don't remember seeing you there, and I'm sure I'd have remembered *you*.' Blue leered.

'That's 'cos you're probably always too busy checking your reflection in your Martini,' muttered Tiger.

'Excuse my friend,' said Blue, steering Tiger's shoulders towards the dressing room. 'In fact, you try your things on dear. Richie and I can have a little chat while you're busy.'

The boys gassed and gossiped like they had known each other for years. As Tiger tried on her clothes in her fitting room she cursed, looking in the mirror at the size tens looking loose on her. She needed the next size down, dammit. Where were her breasts disappearing to? And that peachy butt? She stuck her head round the door, and seeing Blue and Richie mid flow, decided to leave it for today. She really wasn't in the mood. What she needed was another run. The latest pink letter was making her toss and turn at night, so maybe some more time on the treadmill would give her a chance to figure out the culprit.

As she left the fitting room, Blue and Richie were kissing their goodbyes.

'Wow, looks like the start of a beautiful friendship,' remarked Tiger as Richie skipped off into the sunset hues of Bond Street.

'You bet. We've swapped numbers. I'm taking him to Old Compton Street tonight,' sighed Blue.

'Already?!'

'Darling, a boy like that's almost too good to be true. Gorgeous, and smart too! I'm not letting this one go.'

'Let him go? You've only just met! You'll scare him off!'

'No, I'll show him off more like. Best wear your earplugs when I get home tonight, babes.'

Chapter 16

The gloved hand gently lays a sealed pink envelope on top of the pile of neatly folded clothes filling the suitcase. A faint hint of Chanel still hangs in the air. On the wall rearing up behind the suitcase are pinned newspaper cuttings and photographs, all of Tiger. Some are yellowing, with the edges curled from long days of lazy sunshine filtering through the window; others have fresh, bright colours. Some have been ripped, as though another figure has been removed from the picture – anyone who might be standing with her. New cuttings are pinned over old ones.

Glossy photographs pinned amongst them depict Tiger in her gowns, arriving at and departing the next glamorous event. Some have been scratched, so the face is no longer visible. Some white flowers are pinned to the wall, still arranged in the bunch with their stems reaching for the ceiling as though they have been hung and dried right next to Tiger; their beauty withered, faded over time like the newspaper images.

The hand reaches for the drawer in the bureau and slowly pulls it open, revealing a glistening Smith & Wesson knife amongst the pencils and pens. A cloth is plucked from the drawer before the knife is carefully picked up and its blade slowly, deliberately polished with the cloth. As the metal glints, catching the light of the anglepoise lamp, it sends a shaft of light onto the wall, cutting across the myriad images of Tiger.

In a flash the knife is hurled at the wall of pictures. It slices through the air, spinning on its axis before plunging through layers of newspaper and sticking in the wall. It quivers there before the weight of the handle pulls it down, and it drops. Silently it lands in the suitcase upon the clothes, next to the pink envelope as if by design; an eerie portent.

Chapter 17

Georgia slunk around Lewis' apartment in a thoroughly bored fashion. She turned the stereo up a notch to drown out the sound of Lewis tapping away relentlessly on his laptop. She had thought that going out with Lewis Bond would be all limos, fine dining, society events, the odd entrance by helicopter thrown in, and maybe even a movie role by now. She hadn't expected Lewis to be – well – to be *working* all the time. And she certainly hadn't expected him to be so disinterested in her own career.

Tiger, Tiger, Tiger was all Georgia ever heard. Why hadn't Lewis offered to be a manager to Georgia Atlanta, his own girlfriend? It just didn't make sense to her. All the other men she had jumped into bed with had given her stuff. Hell, when she had gone to hang out on the Côte D'Azur straight after dance school, she used to be taken on to the yachts all the time and if she was lucky enough to be chosen to go to the master cabin for a night of fun, she knew she would always walk out with an arm full of diamonds, a nose full of cocaine, and a purse full of cash in the morning. Georgia certainly didn't see anything wrong with a simple exchange of luxury goods, and, boy, did she make sure she was in tip-top racehorse condition for the men at all times – smooth, tight, sleek, and flawless. Whilst she had never been the most beautiful yacht girl in St Tropez, Georgia's infamously long Viking legs and sinewy frame had always been the honey that attracted the bees, and, boy, did she know exactly how to work a pair of itty-bitty hot pants. The problem was, none of the yacht-owning Russian oligarchs, Chinese gamblers or oil traders gave two shits about helping Georgia Atlanta to further her career; and Georgia knew she couldn't make a living on the yachts for too much longer before it drove her insane. The sun, smiles and champagne formed a very thin veneer. Besides, she wanted her own pots of cash at her own say so, not when some sun dried old prune decided she was worth having a poke with his shrivelled dip stick. No, she simply had to find her own solid career before she got caught in that rut.

When Georgia had elegantly sailed through the tough auditions to be a Starrlet six months ago, she knew if she was smart, she would have to zero in on the head honcho behind the scenes immediately and get her feet firmly under the table; sure enough within days she had her long legs wrapped round the thankfully handsome Lewis Bond. In her experience, things always slipped into place once she'd fucked the boss. Luckily, Georgia loved her older men; they had much better sexual technique, better stories, and they were past playing games like the young boys did. Lewis Bond was certainly easy on the eye, with a brooding look of Al Pacino in his *Heat* days. Despite being in his forties, Lewis was also still in amazing shape with incredible stamina between the sheets when she could drag him away from his work. He might only have millions in the bank rather than billions like the yacht owners, but Georgia knew that Lewis Bond was a bona fide catch, unlike some of the sweating little old pricks Georgia had put up with on the Riviera. Most importantly she was relieved, if not a little surprised, that Lewis and Tiger had never got it on; thank god she didn't have to compete in that area too. Although with Georgia's extensive experience with her Côte D'Azur clientele she had racked up a few tricks of the trade she knew could drive pretty much any man crazy in the sack.

Georgia decided it was high time her and Lewis made more of a public statement as a couple, thinking perhaps she could somehow coax Lewis towards spending more time on Georgia's career endeavours if they had a more 'official' relationship. Certainly the odd snap in the gossip pages and diary columns as a handsome couple would put her on the celebrity map. In fact, she had always planned from day one that Lewis would be the key to building her public profile; she was distinctly frustrated that it hadn't happened yet. Georgia nosily sifted through the pile of invitations slung carelessly on Lewis' coffeetable with the junk mail.

'Lewis honey, why don't we go to a party tonight?'

Lewis grunted from across the room without looking up.

'I said let's go out tonight,' repeated Georgia loudly.

'Turn that crap off, I can't hear you.'

Georgia pointed the remote over her shoulder and flicked the sound system off.

'Well, it's just that you have all these invitations to posh events, how come you don't go to any?' Georgia persisted.

'Boring.'

'What do you mean?'

Lewis sighed and closed his laptop with a snick. He looked straight over at Georgia who looked like a petulant gangly child curled up in his enormous sixties leather couch.

'If you must know, they don't do it for me. I leave those things to Tiger. It's work for her, she needs to be seen out and about once in a while; keeps the gossip rags happy and she gets to see some old faces for a bit of a gas. She turns up, gets photographed, has a glass of warm champagne, listens to the gossip, and then leaves. What am I gonna do there? These things are generally teeming with fashionistas, celebrities and vacuous, talentless clothes horses masquerading as 'models', 'actresses', 'presenters' and 'stylists'. I don't work with these people, I work with producers, agents, corporations and all the other folks at the back end of the pantomime horse.'

'Okay grumps, so it's all *passé* for you, but I still haven't been to any good society parties since I joined the Starrlets. I think it sounds like fun. Can't we just go out for one night?'

'You'll be bored, trust me.'

'Okay, so if it's all rubbish we'll just leave, and I'll treat you to a nice nightcap at Annabel's.'

Lewis looked at Georgia through narrowed eyes before nodding his head slowly.

'Okay then, you've got yourself a deal. Take your pick. Nothing too naff please.'

'Well, I heard Tiger saying she was going to some gallery event tonight so let's go there.'

Lewis shot a stern look at Georgia. 'I work with Tiger, I don't socialise with her.'

'Come on!' pleaded Georgia. 'Otherwise I won't know anyone and you'll be stuck talking to me all night . . .'

'Oh god. Good point. Okay fine, the gallery it is. God knows what I've let myself in for.'

'Yay!' Georgia punched the air.

'Well, you'll need to call the Hunter Gatherers' offices and speak to Kat. Ask her to rsvp on my behalf and tell them that I'm attending with a plus one.'

'Er – I'm not just a plus one you know, I have a name.'

'For god's sake. Is it really that important?'

'I'll put both our full names down,' Georgia insisted. 'Oh, and Lewis?'

'Hmm?'

'If I'm going to make an impact I'll need to buy a new dress. This afternoon.'

'Tiger!'

'Over 'ere, Tiger!'

'Tiger, to your left please!'

'Tiger, this way, smile!' She struggled not to blink with the flashes as she stood before the wall of paparrazzi.

'Tiger, straight in front!'

'Lift your head up, Tiger, straight ahead!' Tiger shifted on her feet slightly for a new pose.

'Over 'ere!'

'To your right, Tiger!' She felt her jaw tightening and her cheekbones tensing as she tried to hold her 'pap' smile a little longer.

'This way, Tiger, give us a smile!' God she recognised *that* face. That was . . .

'One more straight ahead please, Tiger!'

. . . Rosemary Baby? Surely not.

'This way, Tiger!' What was Rosemary doing amongst the crowds? Tiger was convinced she had just seen her staring from the other side of the velvet ropes with that big ol' ugly face of hers, fixated.

'Yowsers! To your left, Tiger!' Tiger's smile faded as she felt her stomach churning. Was that really Rosemary? Why was she here tonight? What did she want?

'One more over 'ere, luv!' Tiger nodded politely and pulled away from the throngs of paparazzi at the entrance of the Paula de Paulson gallery. She motioned for Lewis, Blue, Georgia and Richie who had been hanging back to follow her in. As Georgia stepped up she smiled at the photographers, expecting them to take her picture, seeing as she was one of Tiger Starr's group. The paps had already moved on to their next bill-paying fodder, some new actress who was already tottering along behind. Georgia's embarrassed, blushing face went unnoticed as a trio of leggy hostesses appeared out of nowhere and descended upon Tiger, greeting her warmly and ushering her inside.

'Blimey. Does she get that everywhere?' whispered Richie up at Blue, who gazed into his big doe eyes with a warm smile as they were led inside.

'This is an industry party, darling. It's work,' explained Blue. 'Tiger is always on show for work. Around Waitrose? Not so much. Although the paps do hang about Regent's Park for her when they're feeling optimistic, maybe hoping to catch her jogging in a tracksuit. Although that's about as likely as sighting the Loch Ness Monster,' he said, patiently standing in line in the huge white marble reception until the hostesses had finished their small talk with Tiger. 'So a party is work then?' breathed Richie, almost in amazement.

'I'd describe it as an event. I mean it's not exactly a '*party*' party is it? It's not like she's being paid to pop pills and get wankered.'

'Yes, I hadn't thought of it like that I suppose,' mused Richie.

'Hang on, you're a photographer's assistant,' said Blue, quizzically, 'you're in the media world, you should know how it all works!'

'Oh! Well, it's all new to me actually; I haven't been

doing it for too long,' stuttered Richie, looking a little embarrassed. 'I guess I never like to talk to the photographers too much about things that go on outside the studio, I – I worry I might come across as unprofessional if I pry.'

Blue instantly melted. 'Sorry, darling. I didn't mean to . . . it's just, well I need to get to know you so much more. We both have so much to learn. This is just the beginning.' Blue squeezed Richie's hand.

'God, listen to Barbara Cartland over here,' complained Georgia bitchily from behind. 'Anyway, move up, boys, those ladies are taking everyone's coats.' Georgia wriggled out of her new leopard-print trench, and held it out regally for one of the hostesses.

'The cloakroom is over there, madam,' said the hostess politely before protectively whisking Tiger's silk cape away.

'What am I, pleb class or something?' fumed Georgia.

'No, you're just not Tiger Starr,' retorted Blue. 'Oh give it here for god's sake.' He scooped up Georgia's trench and stalked over to the non-VIP cloakroom.

Georgia turned to a bored-looking Lewis for support, who merely shrugged and wandered off to catch up with Tiger, who was now being escorted up the huge staircase towards the star artworks by an eager busboy.

'My, my, that's a charming dress you're wearing, is it Westwood?' asked Blue as he returned and handed Georgia her cloakroom ticket.

'Yes,' huffed Georgia.

'Red Label?'

'Yes, how did you know?'

'Darling, I'm a stylist. It's my job to know,' explained Blue patronisingly. 'Besides, you may have noticed Tiger is wearing a remarkably similar Westwood Gold Label tonight.'

'Really? Oh, I didn't see her take her cape off.' Georgia smiled.

'Of course you didn't.' Blue smiled back.

'Well, I'm sure Tiger wouldn't fit in *my* dress at any rate.'

'Maybe not,' Blue beamed, continuing, 'And the dress does suit you I must say.'

'Oh! Oh thanks!' said Georgia, pushing her breasts out a little.

'Yes, I just love how Westwood gives shape to those girls who don't have any in the first place,' Blue said and immediately turned to Richie. 'Champagne, darling?'

Richie nodded and the pair waltzed up the stairs, leaving Georgia standing alone with a foul expression.

When Blue eventually found Tiger after a lap of the whole gallery, she was with Lewis looking at one of the installations. She was sipping her champagne, statuesque in her tight cream lace cocktail dress, and looking unusually ill at ease.

'Hey darling, you okay?' asked Blue cheerily.

'Oh, you know,' sighed Tiger. 'It's the same old shake and fake.'

'What's the matter? You don't usually mind these events. It's a stunning gallery. Have you been round yet? Beautiful art. Some of the special installations are fab. There's one next door you're gonna *love*.'

'Oh come on. All these media whores are just knocking back Cristal and talking about what nail shape they're going for this season. That could be the *Mona Lisa* up there and they'd still be more interested in discussing whether squared-off nails were *passé* enough to be ironic yet. Before you came up, I just saw some drunk heiress stumbling over to a Damien Hirst piece in the middle of the room, thinking it was a huge canapé display. She made a grab for it, then knocked it over. It smashed into a thousand pieces. It was cleaned up with a dustpan and brush like a dropped cocktail glass.'

'Probably the best place for it,' Blue joked. Tiger wasn't laughing. Blue regarded her through narrowed eyes; she looked distinctly wound up.

'Oh Tiger darling, that's why we used to love coming to these things together – we used to have a laugh at everyone posing, pouting and scrabbling up the social ladder wearing their latest it-bag and sample sale finds, then we'd scoot off to Horse Meat Disco in our ball gowns for some proper grimy Vauxhall fun to the wee small hours. Remember?'

'Oh, I don't know, sweetie, I'm sorry. I think I lost my sense of humour somewhere outside. I swear I saw ...' Tiger trailed off, looking round at Lewis who was leaning in, listening.

'Oh, don't mind me,' he said. 'You carry on, I'm all ears. Actually I thought you'd been a bit off lately. Especially considering you've got some great things going on right now.'

'A bit off? Oh thanks,' deadpanned Tiger. 'I can see you haven't honed your witty repartee for some time.'

'Wow, you really have lost your sense of humour, babe,' said Blue, raising his eyebrows over at Lewis in sympathy.

'Let's just have this conversation later, okay?' snapped Tiger.

'What is *wrong* with you?' hissed Blue out of the side of his mouth.

'Oh, nothing. Just forget it. I'm sorry I'm not good company. I'll take myself home after this drink. I have long rehearsals tomorrow anyway,' Tiger mumbled.

'No way, babes. I'm making you go to the fashion party after this, and then when we get home later, I'm coming to your room with a good Cognac and – well, I think we need to have a girl talk.'

'No, you have other commitments, darling. Honestly, don't worry about me. I'm really not in the mood for another party anyway.'

'No way!' protested Blue. 'Richie can go back to his own place tonight. You're coming out. Everyone wants to see you there. Besides I'm worried about you. Don't think I haven't noticed the recent weight loss.'

'What weight loss? I'm the same as always,' Tiger lied.

'Babes, you're losing your arse. Big mistake. We gotta sort that out for a start.'

'What was that about a fat arse?' asked Georgia loudly as she came sachaying towards the little group, champagne flute in hand.

'Ah, here comes the entertainment,' said Blue, smiling over at Georgia and raising his glass to her in a sarcastic gesture.

'What's that all about?' whispered Tiger.

'Never you mind,' muttered Blue through his clenched smile, 'I just have a bad feeling in my gut about that girl.'

'What, Georgia? Nah, I think she's alright deep down. I thought she was a bit dodgy at first too, but she makes Lewis happy. I reckon she's harmless. I think she just tries a bit hard, that's all. It's probably all Lewis' fault. Can you imagine going out with him? He probably gives her marks out of ten and performance notes every time they have sex.' The pair had a private little snigger into their champagne.

'Did I miss the joke?' asked Georgia, wrapping her arm possessively around Lewis.

'No, darling, we were just talking about the installations actually,' replied Blue.

'Oh, right.' Georgia scanned the room. 'I don't get them I'm afraid. All this arty shit, I think it's all just a marketing ploy. They're all just clever businessmen these artists.'

'That's quite a sweeping statement, Georgia,' countered Blue provocatively.

'Okay then. You tell me what that one means over there,' she challenged. 'You see it? The naked bloke hopping from foot to foot under a spotlight.'

'Oh come on, we're supposed to be having fun,' moaned Blue.

'No. Come on, Mr Know-It-All, deconstruct it, I dare you.'

Blue was silent for a few seconds as he swilled his Cristal in his mouth. He took a deep breath. Lewis, Georgia, Richie and Tiger all leaned in, eager for his response. Blue took a few more moments, adjusting his stance theatrically. He began:

'In a literal sense it references torture methods, with the artist attempting to recreate the alarming muscular spasms achieved over a long period of time of being constricted in a small area; whereas metaphorically the artist's nakedness refers to our own struggle for dignity, with the artist's silence symbolising the process of being stripped bare, whilst masking the ultimate truth via our loss of communication. The black bandages about his face are a damning historical reference to slavery and hence the violence we inflict upon our own kind, whilst the shaft of light is the oxymoron binding the whole piece together, at once an investigative measure, yet simultaneously a graphic symbol for our redemption, and ultimate ascension. Against a textured backdrop of modern cultural icons, celebrities, fashionistas and drunken social climbers, liggers and blaggers, the audience is subsumed into the artwork to provide the setting of hypocrisy, materialism and apathy prevalent in our modern culture.'

Georgia was silenced and took a moment to gulp her champagne loudly. Richie looked stunned. Lewis cleared his throat. Tiger burst out laughing.

'Where on earth did that come from!'

'I knew I could make my baby smile.' Blue winked in her direction.

'I need a cocktail,' snapped Georgia in defeat, dragging Lewis with her over to one of the waiters circulating with silver trays full of mojitos.

'Blue, I'm impressed, I feel a new career for you coming on,' said Tiger, warming a little. 'Right, Mr Art Critic, please provide your analysis of Mary Dubonnet's installation of *Girl, interrupted*,' she asked, mimicking holding a microphone up to Blue's mouth and looking over at a tall pile of filthy mattresses in the opposite corner with a woman precariously balanced on the top one, apparently asleep. Blue braced himself, a smirk creeping across his face as he slipped into his groove.

'Well, at a first glance it appears to be a simple modern reconstruction of the 'Princess and the Pea' fairytale. However on closer inspection, the pea clearly relates to the clitoris, and the piece reveals itself to be at once about a woman's literal distancing of herself from her own sexuality; the mattresses are representative of society's overly multi-layered and complex taboo systems, whilst the audience is left uneasy with the uncertainty of whether the princess can feel the pea through the mattresses, thus providing the central sexual tension of the piece. Perhaps this is a message to us all that the artist clearly needs to masturbate more often.' Both Tiger and Richie were now clutching at each other and giggling.

'Now it's your turn, Ms Starr,' announced Blue. 'Go take a look at the Esther Williams piece in the next room in the huge tank and give me your critique.'

'Wow, I haven't seen that one,' said Tiger excitedly as she moved into the next room, starting to enjoy the game. As she approached, she stopped dead in her tracks. Before her was the most incredible scene of an extraordinarily beautiful woman swimming in a huge tank of fish, naked except for hundreds of yards of pearls strung about her, trailing and undulating around her as she writhed and propelled herself around the enormous tank with her white hair billowing out around her, each strand caressed by the water. Tiger was mesmerised. As she drew nearer, she let out a piercing scream, and ran to press her face against the tank.

'Blue! Look, it's Ocean!' Blue stood back and scratched his chin. Of course. He knew he would recognise that exquisitely muscled figure anywhere. It was indeed Ocean, Tiger's real-life mermaid confidante. Every girl needed one. The pair had met in New York way before Tiger's now well notorious three-day foray into the world of domination.

Tiger was tapping manically on the tank, creating a stir

amongst the party goers. Ocean was up at the glass looking confused. Realising Ocean would have blurred vision through the water, Tiger scrabbled in her purse, retrieved a red lipstick and scribbled backwards as best she could on the glass in huge capital letters, 'It's Tiger! Talk 2 me!' Cameras flashed as Tiger defaced the artwork. Blue rolled his eyes and yanked her back from the piece, nodding and motioning at the burly security men who were steaming forwards towards her. Within seconds, there was a huge splash as Ocean appeared ten feet up at the surface of the huge tank. 'Hey girrrrrl!' she shrieked in her fabulous throaty Brooklyn accent. 'I shoulda known the pink hair belonged to you!'

'Oh darling Ocean, I can't believe it's really you. I didn't even know you were in town!'

'Tiger baby, I'm only meant to come out of the water for air, so just tell me where I can see you after.'

'Well, come to a Dolce and Gabanna party with us when you finish. Get a cab to Whitehall, and where you see the velvet ropes and photographers, just walk up and tell the door bitch you're with me. You're officially my guest as of ten seconds ago.'

'You got it, baby! See you there!' Ocean took a deep breath and plunged back into the water, darting and swirling amongst the fish like a vision.

'Blue? Let's cut loose, ' declared Tiger. 'We're going to the party. Let's get our coats. Oh, by the way . . .'

'Yes, darling?'

'I tried to tell you earlier . . . I don't know if I dreamt this, but I'm sure I saw that crazy redhead amongst the photographers earlier.'

'Who?' Blue asked, knowing exactly who she meant. He had spotted the unmistakable face too.

'You know, that psycho Rosemary Baby who was stalking Tiffany Crystal all that time ago?'

'Oh *that* Rosemary Baby. Noooo. You must have been dreaming. No, I'd recognise *that* face anywhere. Come on, let's go.'

Of course Blue had seen Rosemary, but he wasn't going to tell Tiger that and add to her worries. It didn't matter how much she tried to hide it, Blue knew Tiger was spooked by the pink letters and the press story. So was he.

'Oh my god! There's someone pissing in the coke room!' came an almighty screech from the other side of the toilet cubicle. Tiger tutted and curled her lip by way of reply, smoothed her dress over her hips and burst through the door ferociously.

'Eeuww, Tiger Starr!' shrieked a lanky brunette as Tiger exited the cublicle, catching a whiff of the brunette's pungent champagne breath on the way past.

'Tiger, it's me! Katie Jakes!'

Tiger gritted her teeth and spun round, knowing full well who the talentless actress was, and realising she couldn't get away without a bit of polite small talk before getting back to the party. Tiger switched on her professional smile mid turn.

'Katie, hi, how are . . . Sienna?'

Tiger gasped as she caught sight of her sister, half hiding behind Katie.

'Hi, sis,' said Sienna meekly.

'Oh my god! It's so funny seeing you here. Sienna said you were at some art thing instead, we had no idea you would be coming!' squealed Katie.

'Evidently,' said Tiger. 'So, Sienna, how did you meet Katie? I had no idea *you* were coming to the party actually?'

'Rex got me an invite,' replied Sienna flatly.

'Oh my god, isn't Sienna's dress divine?' garbled Katie loudly like a gameshow host. 'In fact I spotted her across the dance floor because of her Fendi shoes. Major.'

'Why, look at those, Sienna,' remarked Tiger. 'Very chic, very expensive. Rex is treating you well I see.'

'Yes.' Sienna blushed. 'Anyway I was here on my own and Katie was friendly enough to—'

'Bring you into the toilets for a line of chang? How original,' said Tiger, raising an eyebrow.

'Don't be silly, Tiger!' laughed Katie. 'She just needed . . . ah, she just needed a Tampax, didn't you, darling?'

'Lovely. Well I'll see you in the party then,' said Tiger, boring a hole into Sienna's eyes before turning on her heel. She knew that even if she marched Sienna from the toilets that very second, her sister would still find a way of sticking coke up her nose. Tiger just hoped that her special glare would be enough to make Sienna feel too guilty to want to get high. As Tiger made her way back into the blaring noise of the party, she seethed inside. There was no way on earth she was going to let Sienna turn into some dismal coke fiend like so many of the talentless social climbers and bitter has-beens on the media circuit. She wondered if Rex knew what Sienna was up to. Tiger needed to have a word; ask him to keep an eye on her, without him accusing Tiger of trying to meddle in their relationship. As she crossed the room to find her table Tiger tried to keep her anxiety down. Sienna's renewed friendship with cocaine was one more thing on a long list of troubles for Tiger right now.

The party unfolding was quite a scene. All around her, towering Italian models, head to toe in exquisite couture cosied up with an elite selection of designers, fashion editors, actors and rock stars as cameras constantly flashed in all corners and every alcove. The beautiful people writhed and slinked as Grace Jones worked her way through a phenomenal rendition of 'Warm Leatherette' up on the stage. One of the pretty young busboys walking by with rock solid pectorals and a six pack paused to offer Tiger a Martini. He was clad only in skimpy red shorts with 'Lifeguard' printed in white across his tight buttocks. My god, I could swipe my Amex between those cheeks, thought Tiger as she liberated one of the cocktails and watched him stalk away haughtily. She wondered if Blue had familiarised himself with the busboys yet, seeing as he'd sent Richie home over an hour ago.

Tiger crossed the packed dance floor towards Ocean and Blue, garnering quite a few nudges, stares and camera flashes herself. Her pals sat gassing at her table, along with Georgia and Lewis whom Tiger had not entirely been in the mood for when they rocked up. Lewis had shot Tiger a rare apologetic look when they arrived, signalling it hadn't exactly been his idea to attend either. Boy was he under the thumb, Tiger had thought to herself, wondering if maybe he was getting a karmic kicking for his controlling ways over the years. Tiger quickly decided she didn't want to tell anyone about the Sienna incident right now; she couldn't face airing any drama in front of her pal Ocean, who was just here for some fun.

'Girrl, this has been, like, so amazing spending time with you!' yelled Ocean over the music, grabbing Tiger's hand close as she slid into her seat. Even under the unflattering nightclub lights, Ocean looked like a wild beauty with her huge tangle of untamed white-blonde hair cascading down her back, and her rippling toned shoulders and arms lending her a seductively tough edge. Even in this imposing banqueting hall, with hundred-foot-high ceilings covered in rich artwork, and surrounded by fashionistas, foie gras and fawning, Ocean had swept shamelessly through the room bare footed and topless but for her hundreds of strings of pearls covering her breasts and her shimmering satin skirt with long fishtail . . . naturally.

Ocean was truly special. She always insisted she was

a real mermaid. She literally swam with the fish. Tiger had first seen her swimming in a huge tank in Coney Island many moons ago when they were hired to perform in a show called *A Fish and Feather Fantasy*, with Tiger being asked to perform an homage to Elvis Presley's cousin 'Evangeline the Oyster girl', and Ocean to perform as the rivalrous 'Divena, the Aqua-Tease'. Tiger had been mesmerised by Ocean's beautiful underwater striptease from the very first second, and Ocean had felt a mutual affinity. During their run, Ocean was being bullied and trailed in the tank by a giant barracuda with a grudge; and Tiger was always on hand to offer her a warming pep talk before each show. The two girls developed a close bond and had remained firm friends ever since.

'We mustn't leave it so long before we meet again, honey! But listen, I gotta cut loose in a minute, I was only in town for tonight's gig, they're flying me back to the Big Apple tomorrow,' sighed Ocean, adding, 'Anyway I gotta shower all the fish shit off when I get back to my hotel too. It's a world of glamour I tell ya.'

Tiger smiled. 'I miss you, Ocean. You're a true friend. Old school.' The girls high-fived each other and giggled.

'Listen. Babe. You just call me. Anytime.' Ocean looked squarely at Tiger. 'Lemme tell you somethin', kid. You seem distracted tonight, but you have all this great shit goin' on, I mean, Vegas man! You hit the big time, kid, an' I'm proud of you! Look how far you've come! Right now, you gotta do right and take care o' *you*.' For Ocean, growing up on the streets of Hell's Kitchen as a child, true friends she could trust were like gold dust, and she was fiercely protective of anyone who was a 'keeper' in her life. Tiger appreciated her concern right now.

'Ocean, it's cool. I just think a couple of things are niggling me right now.'

'I kinda figured.'

'But hey, they don't call me Tiger for nothing,' she said, brightening for her friend, 'I can take care of myself, no problem.'

'Listen, just one thing, girl. What's with your twin over there?'

'Twin?'

'The chick in the dress? Your hoochie mama dancer girl?'

'Georgia? She doesn't look anything like me!'

'Girrl, she's trying. Check out the pin-curled hair. The dress. The shoes. The make-up. It's all your style, your look. And it doesn't suit her.'

'Oh, I was unsure about her at first too, but I think she's harmless. It's probably just a coincidence.'

'Okay, here's the thing.' Ocean lowered her voice and leaned right in to Tiger's ear. 'I bet that's not where she draws the line. You know what they say, "keep your friends close, keep your enemies closer". She's your lead dancer, she's bumpin' your manager, and now she's turning up at your parties an' tryin' to rock your look. She wants your life, girrrl. And by the looks of it she doesn't even have the sense to grit her teeth and be nice to you. You watch out for that one. I'm tellin' ya. I've been round the block, I've seen it happen before. You watch her.' Ocean squeezed Tiger's hand once more.

Tiger leaned in for a big hug. 'I don't know, darling, I think there's something weird in the water right now.'

'Girrrl, you protect yourself, that's all I'm sayin'.'

'I hear you. Thank you, sweetheart.'

'Oh. And listen. You'd better have, like, the *best* seat in the house for me on your opening night in Vegas. I ain't missing that for the world!'

The girls kissed their goodbyes and Blue left the room to escort Ocean to her cab. Tiger was left feeling unsettled. She looked over at Georgia. Was Ocean right? Was Georgia really that calculating after all? Tiger knew she had ambition; that's what she had liked about her in the auditions, ironically. Tiger watched Georgia carefully as she now snuggled up to Lewis' starched collar and fingered the lemon twist in her Martini in a provocative manner. Lewis squeezed Georgia's thigh. Tiger felt confused. She felt something like a strong pang of jealousy but rationalised that was an impossibility and quickly pushed it to the back of her mind. Tiger had so far always been careful not to socialise with Lewis outside the work environment and tonight she was surprised to encounter him being relaxed with another woman; at least as relaxed as Lewis ever could be. She saw a rather different side to him under different lights. Charismatic. Fun. Tiger suddenly shook her head and heaved a sigh. Her head hurt with too many thoughts. All in all she was having a lousy night, with the sole exception of seeing Ocean. She quickly messaged Blue to ask him to stay at the entrance and hail Vladimir. This party was over for Tiger.

Blue read the message as he paced outside the club. He gave a little nod as he recognised stage door Johnnie near the velvet ropes. They exchanged kind smiles, and Blue wondered what present he had for Tiger tonight. Sometimes he brought chocolates or a slim volume of poetry with the usual bouquet. As Tiger's Towncar crawled up Whitehall to meet him, Blue could hear people calling out Tiger's name behind him. She must be on her way out, he thought, giving Vladimir a quick thumbs up through the car window before popping his head back into the venue to retrieve her. As Blue approached through the reception he saw a short, stocky, shaven-headed male leaning in to Tiger's curls and whispering something. Tiger drew back violently and regarded him with furiously arched eyebrows.

'It wasn't a spatula, for your information,' spat Tiger loudly. 'It was a Black 'n' Decker 18 volt hand vacuum, don't you know? Anyway, that's old news, why don't you come up with something more original?'

'Eh, baby!' reasoned the bald guy in a thick Russian accent, realising the pair were garnering an audience for him to play to. 'I just fancied a leetle fun, I heard that was your speciality! Come, let's have fun!' he laughed. At that moment, Blue saw Georgia opposite, mobile in hand as though she had come out from the party to make a call. She was watching the exchange intently with a sly smirk on her face.

Blue immediately steamed over and pushed the bald guy forcefully from Tiger's path. Yanking her arm he pulled her towards the door. From the corner of his eye he saw Georgia wearing a huge grin, her phone now pressed to her ear.

'Ow! Blue, you're hurting me!' grumbled Tiger.

'Gotta get you out of here, darling, this is not a good scene,' muttered Blue, tightening his grip. He pushed through the doors and towards the purring Towncar.

'Miss Starr! I have a surprise for you!' called out stage door Johnnie, rushing forwards towards Tiger, who had managed to free herself from Blue's grip. Johnnie shoved a bouquet of flowers in her face, complete with a small pink card poking from a pretty matching pink ribbon. Tiger glared at Johnnie, and he recoiled slightly in surprise. She was usually so friendly.

'I thought you'd like pink roses this time instead of the gladioli.' He grinned, waiting for her to smile. Tiger stood deadly still, staring at the flowers. She felt her head throbbing, thoughts pouring in from all sides. A crowd was gathering.

'Pink?' she snarled. 'You like the colour pink do you?' she shrieked, suddenly ripping the flowers from Johnnie's hands. Cameras immediately started flashing as she lashed out at him with the bouquet and swiped for his face with her long nails. 'You're the one watching me sleep are you, you pervert?' she growled. 'I see you're hanging out at my home now anyway. I s'pose you have some big secret of mine you want to reveal too, do you?'

Johnnie held his hands over his head, shouting for her to stop. The flashes continued frantically and the crowd tripled in size within seconds. Blue grabbed Tiger firmly by the shoulders and dragged her backwards. The cameras continued snapping and a hum of excited chatter swelled within the crowd.

'You don't scare me, you freak!' howled Tiger, pointing furiously in Johnnie's direction as she staggered backwards in Blue's grip. As the crowd progressed to heckling and goading, the paparazzi surged forwards, closing in on Tiger's wild face as Blue opened the car door and bundled her in.

With Tiger shaking on the backseat, the flashes popped relentlessly through the blacked out windows until the car had pulled safely away. Blue put his head in his hands and gulped for air. He just sat for a moment, trying to make sense of it all. He waited for Tiger to speak, say something, anything. She just sat and shook. Stage door Johnnie had just tried to give her some flowers back there. Blue had no idea what had happened in Tiger's head, but to the outside world, she just looked like the next drunken celebrity assaulting a well meaning fan. The paparazzi had captured every detail.

'J-j-just take us h-h-home, Vladimir, th-thank you,' stuttered Tiger.

'Tiger, we have to talk,' said Blue firmly. 'What the fuck's wrong with you tonight? You're spinning out. You need to tell me everything, babe. And I mean everything.'

Tiger looked across at Blue with watery eyes and a trembling lip and tried to speak. Unable to say anything she looked away. She didn't drop a single tear or utter a single word the whole journey home.

Chapter 18

Oh come on, you can't keep it a secret any more!' giggled Sienna, fidgeting in the cream leather seat of the huge Sikorsky S-76 helicopter as she pressed her nose up at the window, watching as lush green fields and hedgerows rolled by beneath.

'Wait, you'll see!' laughed Rex from his seat opposite. 'Just enjoy the ride. Have some more champagne, birthday girl. How does it feel to be nineteen?'

'The same as it feels to be eighteen, silly,' said Sienna. 'Except no one's ever treated me to a surprise like this before.'

Rex leaned forwards and topped up Sienna's glass, letting it fizz over enthusiastically.

'Careful!' she tittered drunkenly. 'It's going to my head as it is!'

'Whoops. Must be the altitude making everything bubble over,' murmured Rex, planting a soft kiss on the inside of her wrist, deep down wishing it was Tiger here with him sharing the view.

'Ooh, I feel a little . . . lightheaded!' Sienna gasped, fanning her pretty face.

'Okay, babe, how about you open a couple of presents then?'

'Oh wow, you mean there's more? I was having such a good time I didn't even think about presents!'

'Well your present from me will be revealed when we land,' said Rex. 'In the meantime Tiger gave me this to give to you as she knew she wouldn't be here for your birthday.' He held out a small, beautifully wrapped gift bag. Sienna's face turned stony.

'Yeah, work's always more important for Tiger.'

'Just wait 'til you open it, babes, she said she'd chosen something special. It's bound to be expensive knowing her. She's always very generous.'

'Yeah. Well, money can't buy everything you know,' grumbled Sienna, taking the bag and ripping it open. Inside was a small velvet box. Sienna took a deep breath and wished for diamonds. She opened the box and stared. There nestled an exquisite Gucci watch fashioned from minature solid gold horse bits. Sure enough, diamonds framed the square watch face, which was tiger eye . . . naturally. It was stunning. Sienna snapped the box shut and chucked it unceremoniously on to the walnut table.

'Aren't you gonna show me?' asked Rex.

'Er, no. It's nothing special,' replied Sienna, quickly totting up how many thousands she could get for it if she sold it on eBay.

'But Tiger said she'd chosen it carefully – is it a ring?'

Sienna paused for a moment before replying. 'No. It's a watch,' she said, looking straight at Rex's wrist. 'I think she gives those to people she wants to get rid of doesn't she?'

'I don't know what you mean, babes,' said Rex dismissively. 'Come on, have some more Cristal.' Sienna chugged back her whole glass of champagne and screwed her face up as the fizz hit the back of her throat.

'Yeah. More bubbly for the birthday girl, bring it on,' jeered Sienna, slurring her words a little.

'Come on, babe, this weekend is all about you. Enjoy.'

'Oh? Somehow I get the feeling my sister has still managed to make it all about her . . . this time because she's *not* here! Bitch. Sending me a gold diamond watch in her absence. She hasn't even called me. Next time I sell another story on her I'll make sure it's a fucking—' Sienna gasped and clamped her hand over her mouth. She looked over at Rex who for once was silenced. The helicopter swung round dramatically on its flight path.

Ladies and gentlemen, we remind you to please remain seated until the fasten seatbelt sign has been turned off. The local time is now 11.30 a.m. We hope you had an enjoyable flight, and we trust you will have a great stay,' the purser said with a friendly grin as he stood at the head of the cabin.

Honey Lou felt butterflies in her stomach and looked out from her small window. Heat waves emanated from the tarmac as the aeroplane taxied slowly along. She couldn't quite believe she was in Las Vegas on a private jet with Tiger Starr, no less.

'What are you doing?' asked Blanche from her seat next to Honey.

'Pinching myself.'

'Whatever for?'

'Oh, you know, just to check it's all real.'

'Oh, Honey Lou,' Blanche laughed softly, 'there's *nothing* real about Vegas.'

Once Georgia, Nikki, Blanche and Honey Lou were esconced in their quarters at the Luxuriana Grande, the room hopping started in earnest. They had an hour before their final costume fittings, and this was taken up with checking that none of them had a better view, a bigger hot tub, or an extra plasma screen in their room than anyone else. Honey Lou was beginning to feel relaxed with the girls, like she was finally starting to fit in. Nikki, she decided was the fairest and kindest, and Blanche she thought was the prettiest and most ladylike. Georgia didn't really engage and spent most of her time either making calls or hiding her head in a magazine. But that didn't bother Honey Lou, she was just determined to have a fabulous time.

The Starrlets met Blue and his seamstress for their fittings in his suite. It was enormous. Honey Lou's eyes darted everywhere. She couldn't quite believe it had more rooms than her entire family home back in London. If only her parents were here to see it. Honey Lou's father had been against his daughter making this trip, especially after the shit storm in the newspapers after Tiger lashed out at one of her fans last week, but Honey had found a totally unexpected sympathiser in her mother, Lila, who quite out of the blue confessed she'd always fantasised about working as a croupier in Vegas, ever since she had watched a television programme of her idols Diana Ross and The Supremes doing a Vegas gig in the late sixties. It had all looked so showy! Lila was adamant that her daughter should take the trip, on the condition that Honey Lou reported back and told her every fabulous detail.

Honey couldn't imagine her mum ever believing the hotel room she was in now; it even had its own dance floor and split-level lounge, for goodness' sake. The views were simply breathtaking; the whole of the Strip seen through twenty-foot picture windows. Honey sneaked a photograph with her phone and quickly texted it home to her mum while Blue was busy sticking pins in Georgia's g-string.

The costumes were beautiful, with intricate crystal bras and thongs, and each Starrlett was allotted a slightly different headdress, with many shades of dyed feather from deep cherry through to fiery orangey red. Each costume included huge, unwieldy backpacks with wide feather sprays built in and the girls were allowed ten minutes each to practise parading in the room, getting used to the way the feathers dragged them back by the shoulders. Honey Lou immediately had blisters beneath her armpits from the stiff, heavy-duty straps, but she didn't like to say anything since this was only for the press junket. It wasn't like she would need to dance in the costume for any length of time yet.

The Starletts were given their itinerary for photo calls that afternoon, and then the press interviews the following morning during which they would be presenting and flanking Tiger as she took the Q and A sessions at the hands of the entertainment press and broadcasters. The girls were excited to see Tiger's costume. They had wanted to ask her lots of questions on the plane, but she had seemed unusually subdued, and slept deeply for pretty much the entire flight before being whisked away by Lewis the second they hit the airport. All Blue would reveal was that she would be in a couture gown in Jessica Rabbit red, rather than anything feathery. She needed to look 'Hollywood glam', so Blue had said, rather than looking like she was about to step onto stage. Once he had secured his final pins in the girls' costumes, he chivvied the Starletts off to another room to get into hair and make-up, while he directed the seamstress on the necessary alterations ahead of the photo call.

'Cor, were those g-strings tight or what!' muttered Nikki once they were safely in their dressing room and well out of earshot. 'Either that or I need to go on a diet, shift some of the weight off my hips.'

'Actually mine had to be taken in slightly,' said Georgia smugly, stretching a wig cap over her scraped-back hair.

'Don't worry, Nikki, mine was tight too,' said Blanche, shooting daggers at Georgia who was now pulling on her sleek long black wig. Honey Lou looked over at beautiful Blanche and sighed. She had the sort of figure she would kill for, reed slim yet with soft curves and distinctly knockery.

Honey Lou turned back to her make-up station and brushed her own black wig, deep in thought, wondering where they would all be taken tonight. The Starrlets had been told by Lewis on the aeroplane that they would be expected to make appearances at various venues during the evening. Even though she had only been in Vegas less than twelve hours, Honey Lou knew it just felt right; as though it was a home from home already.

'Fuck it!' yelled Georgia, springing up from her stool. 'I've spilt red nail varnish on my Danskins! Oh crap! Ohhh! Honey Lou, could you get me another pair from Blue while I clean all this mess up? Cheers, babe.'

Honey looked up in disbelief. She had only just managed to tame her afro and pop on her wig cap, surely Georgia couldn't expect her to leave the dressing room like that, especially without a scrap of make-up on yet?

'Er, could you make it snappy? It's not like we've got all day,' ordered Georgia. Not feeling very assertive in a wig cap, Honey Lou bit her tongue to keep the peace, and scrabbled in her holdall for a headscarf to cover her head.

'Like, now!' yelled Georgia. Honey Lou jumped to attention, dropping the scarf and hurriedly making for the door. She cursed under her breath as she made her way down the corridor, hoping no one would see her, especially not Tiger. She wanted to make a good impression all the way.

Reaching Tiger's suite, Honey Lou tentatively knocked at the door. There was no answer, although she could hear loud music blaring. Blue must be in there, she thought to herself. She knocked again, louder. After what seemed like minutes, Honey decided she would have to leave empty handed. Georgia could jolly well sort her own tights out. That moment, the door swung open. Tiger looked terrible. There she stood in the doorway in the most unbelievable shimmering red gown, which she barely filled with her noticeably diminishing frame. Her hair was scraped back beneath a thick hair band, revealing alarmingly sharp cheekbones. Big black bags circled her eyes, which were puffy as though she had been crying, and her normally silky olive skin looked pale and pasty. She looked gaunt, worn-down and haggard. She certainly hadn't looked like this on the aeroplane; she had looked glamorous and fluffed up as always, and she had hidden her body under a chic shift dress.

Tiger shrieked, her hands immediately jumping to hide her face. Honey gasped, her hands immediately jumping to hide her wig cap.

'Excuse me, Ms Starr, I didn't mean to interrupt.'

'No, no, I thought – I'd been expecting Blue, th-that's all,' stuttered Tiger.

'Coo-ee!' came Blue's familiar voice from across the corridor. 'I got the cucumber! It's a nice big one! Ooh, Honey Lou, what are you doing here?'

'Sorry, I didn't mean to—'

'You'd better come in, quickly' urged Tiger, motioning Honey through the door. 'I'm having my dress taken in. Blue was just fetching me something for my eyes, I think the air con is drying them out. Please excuse my appearance, I'll be in full make-up for the photo calls this afternoon and back to my old self again, don't worry.'

'Oh! Oh, but I only came for an extra pair of tights for Georgia, she ruined hers,' Honey explained anxiously as Blue shoved her into the suite.

'And she's too grand to come herself I suppose?' asked Blue.

'No, I offered to help,' mumbled Honey Lou.

'Hold the door!' came a breathless yell from outside. It was Georgia. 'Bloody hell, Honey, I could have got the friggin' tights myself, what took you so long?' Georgia demanded as she barged into the suite. Tiger stiffened visibly and grabbed for a towel to hide her face.

'Christ, Tiger, what happened to you? You look like a five-pound bag of shit! You wanna borrow some of my Touche Eclat or something, cover up those eye bags?' asked Georgia. Honey Lou died of embarrassment at the cruel dig and vowed she was running no more errands for Georgia.

'What a generous offer,' replied Tiger modestly, addressing the room and dropping the towel to her side with resignation. 'It's amazing how the air con plays havoc with your skin,' she laughed nervously. 'But I have some cucumber here, that should do the trick, thanks for the kind thought all the same, Georgia.' Honey Lou decided there and then that Tiger was the most dignified and beautiful creature she'd ever met.

Sienna stretched out her long thin legs on the satin divan and yawned as she basked in the warm glow of the sunbeam cutting across the bed. She could faintly hear Rex singing in the shower. She made a grab for her throat to check the necklace was still there. Emeralds, to match her eyes. Rex had presented it to her as they landed in the exquisite grounds of Cliveden stately home after he had made her a fully initiated member of the mile high club, or Half Mile High if that was the helicopter equivalent.

At first Sienna had thought she'd truly blown it, opening her big mouth about the Tiger press story. Perhaps it was the champagne that had gone to both their heads, but Sienna swore it was almost as though her ruthless behaviour had actually turned Rex on. After the initial shock, he had fucked her like he'd never fucked her before; bent over across her seat right behind the pilot, like a wild animal up there in the beautiful sunset sky. She had never flown in a helicopter before, and it had been one ride she would never forget.

Wearing her new necklace, which perfectly complemented the classic black Yves Saint Laurent gown she had bought for the occasion with the last of her *News of the World* earnings, Sienna had felt like a princess for the night as she was helped down from the helicopter by a butler, and escorted to the main entrance which was illuminated with flame-bearing torches. The beautiful Italianate mansion was where they ate five exquisite courses that night, but Rex's *pièce de resistance* was booking them both into the Spring Cottage by the bank of the Thames, where Christine Keeler had famously stayed in the early sixties. Sienna was too embarrassed to admit she had no idea who Christine Keeler or John Profumo were – neither history nor politics were exactly her strong point – but she got the impression it was a big deal so she nodded at everything Rex said and hoped he wouldn't ask her opinion about the whole thing. She thought it sounded kind of romantic, whatever the story was.

Today Rex had booked Sienna in to have a whole day of pampering treatments in the spa. If only her school friends could see her now, she thought, as she rose from the bedsheets and wrapped herself in a fluffy bathrobe. She lazily wandered through the opulent room to the picture window and meditated for a moment on the breakfast that the butler had wheeled in only ten minutes earlier. What a birthday. If this wasn't a sign that she was climbing the ladder then nothing was.

'Hey, what's cookin'?' asked Rex as he wandered in from the bathroom, wrapping a towel tightly about his waist.

'Well take your pick. There's an exotic fruit platter, fresh juice, fresh smoked salmon, the works.'

'Great, I sure worked up an appetite after last night,'

said Rex, patting his sturdy, toned stomach and picking up the newspaper. 'You trying out the pool today, babe?'

'I hope so. After my massage maybe,' replied Sienna, tucking herself into a large upholstered antique chair and popping a juicy slice of fresh papaya in her mouth.

'You still have your emeralds on. Did you sleep in them?' asked Rex absentmindedly, flicking to the sports section of the newspaper.

'Of course,' murmured Sienna dreamily. 'I'm never taking them off.'

'Great. Glad you like 'em.'

'Rex, I—' Sienna looked at him, nervously biting her lip before continuing. 'I think I'm in love with you.' There. She'd said it.

'Ooohhh!' yelled Rex, clapping his hands together triumphantly. 'Arsenal beat Manchester! Boner! That calls for an extra celebration,' he cheered, waving the newspaper over his head triumphantly. 'Shall I get my dealer to courier over some coke for tonight, babes? Yay! Go Gunners! So what d'you reckon?'

'Oh. Oh, okay then. Er, sure. Why not,' replied a crestfallen Sienna, as she clutched desperately at her emeralds.

'Well, open it then!' insisted Libertina, tottering over to Tiger's perch by the edge of the Hanging Gardens of Babylon-styled rooftop pool.

'Oh darling, you really shouldn't have,' murmured Tiger.

'Yes I know I shouldn't have, but open it and you'll see

why I changed the habit of a lifetime,' laughed Libertina, leaning against one of the white Doric columns, looking just like a Roman goddess dressed in an aptly chosen short white draped dress, with her raven hair pinned loosely in a classic bun. 'I guess I feel bad that I just left you so suddenly back in London. I couldn't have you thinking I was a one-night-stand kinda lady.'

'Oh bull, you just wanted to come up and check out my penthouse suite didn't you!' teased Tiger. She didn't like to admit that she had felt more than just a little slighted that Libertina had made off so quickly that first time they had slept together. Even though Tiger didn't normally date women, Libertina had fired up a burning lust in her right from their chat at the after-show party. Tiger had no idea where the affair was taking her, but she was curious to see where the ride took them. Libertina was, in her eyes, an extraordinary woman. Tiger felt safe with her, as though she had found a kindred spirit; someone who knew the truth of what it took to survive in this vicious industry.

'Listen, honey, I made it over from the Big Apple between shoot days just to see you! Now that's dedication!' continued Libertina. 'Anyway, I thought we should have our own private party. And after the last twenty-four hours you've had, you deserve a treat. Trust me, I know these publicity things are a bitch, I hate doing them when I have a new film out. I'm happy to give you any tips you need, baby. Now, you still have the press interviews tomorrow so I can recommend you're well oiled for those, dahhling. I never do them sober. Fancy a Manhattan?' Libertina cracked open a bottle of bourbon.

'You know what? I'd rather just have a bourbon on the rocks,' replied Tiger with a glint in her eye, gently tugging on the ribbon tied around the large square velvet box in her lap. She flipped up the lid and gasped. Inside was the most beautiful brooch depicting a roaring pouncing tiger, studded in sparkling intense yellow diamonds. It was huge. Magnificent. In fact it was so ridiculous Tiger was speechless for a moment.

'Ya like it?'

'Oh Libertina, I just can't accept this, it's far too extravagant,' Tiger said breathlessly, ogling the exquisite craftsmanship.

'That's no kind of answer! Dahhling, it was made for you!' Libertina pressed a drink into Tiger's hand. 'The diamonds came from an Australian mine you know. I was told the design's a one off. Vintage. Rare as rocking-horse shit. Like you. Baby, it's yours, please take it. It would mean everything to me if you wore it out some time. It'll be our secret. I know your heart belongs to another, but we can enjoy ourselves while this lasts, can't we?'

'Oh fucking hell!' wailed Tiger suddenly jumping up, sending the velvet box tumbling from her lap to the floor with a thump.

'Holy cow, what did I say?'

'Ohhh! It's Sienna's birthday today! I meant to call her!

Oh why am I so forgetful!' Tiger stamped her heel in frustration before slumping back onto the poolside lounger, head in hands.

'You can still call her now can't you? It's gone midnight but she'll understand.'

'That's the problem, I forgot about the time difference. It's nine in the morning in England . . . the next *day*.'

'Oh, fuck her, she's your sister, she'll understand. You gave her a present, right?'

'Yes but . . . she's funny about me missing things. Now she'll hate me – I didn't even call.'

'Screw her! She's a frosty bitch to you from what I can see. Frosty the friggin' snowman. You're always helping her, and she's an ungrateful cow. You're just breeding a diva.'

'I can't help it, she's family.'

'Hey. I'm half Italian. Don't talk to me about family. Anyway, proper family is two-way traffic you know. She doesn't appreciate what you've done for her. *I* know how tough it is to make it and what *I* had to do to get here. I don't know your story, baby, but I can recognise a fellow traveller when I see one. I see the pain in your eyes, and I see the fire too. Sienna has to go find her own fire. You can't do it for her, you've done more than enough already.' Tiger felt overcome; as though Libertina had just reached inside her.

'Actually – we have more in common than you think,' Tiger said slowly, swirling the ice cubes in the bottom of her tumbler. She was well aware she was straying out of her comfort zone, opening up like this. 'My grandma was half Italian so I share that heritage with you ... never mind that my father was ashamed of Grandma – poor dear Coco – but here's the thing, my folks did this really terrible thing to ...'

'Wait. Stop. Tiger, you're shaking.'

'It's okay, I—'

'No. You don't have to tell me anything you don't want to. You wouldn't want this to be the liquor talking!'

Tiger smiled. 'No. No it's not the liquor, but thank you. Maybe you're right. Some things should be left unsaid.' Tiger sighed and shook her head sadly. 'Thank you,' she whispered.

'What for?' asked Libertina.

'Just for being straight with me.'

'Straight?!'

Tiger laughed out loud. 'You know what I mean! Just ... thanks.'

'You're a fantastic lady you know, Tiger. Never forget that. I've never bought diamonds for anyone after a first date, I can tell you *that* for nothing.'

Tiger laughed again. 'Oh darling, I don't know what to say, the brooch is exquisite. I simply haven't the words, so ... thank you. I'll wear it tomorrow.'

'Ugh! No way, if you waste it on those vultures I'll kill you, wear it on the red carpet to my next premiere.'

'Wow, is that an offer of a date?'

'Might be.'

'In public? So – are we . . . ?'

'No. Whatever I may feel about you, I know this isn't serious for you,' Libertina said firmly.

'I beg your pardon?'

'Like I said. Your heart's with someone else. I can see it a mile off. And you're waiting for a Mr Right, not a Ms Right.'

'Oh?' Tiger asked, bemused. 'Did you have someone in mind? Who?'

'Like you need me to tell you.'

Tiger felt confused by Libertina's words. Why was she blowing so hot and cold on her? Was it really that obvious that she still thought about Rex all the time? Tiger knew she could never be with Rex now he had moved on to Sienna. That possibility was utterly dead and buried.

'You've gone quiet, dahhling,' said Libertina, slowly strutting over to Tiger. 'Come on, this is supposed to be our private party, remember? Let's have some fun,' she purred, crouching down and lightly touching Tiger's arm. A smile curled at the corners of Tiger's mouth as she looked at the beautiful woman before her.

'How can I refuse an offer like that?' Tiger smiled. 'Life's too short, and you're too sexy,' she murmured, rising and slowly undoing the zipper of her red gown, letting it drop to the floor. Libertina sighed deeply as she rose to survey Tiger's beautiful body.

Without another word, Libertina turned and slowly

slinked her way into the pool in her white draped dress, which became transparent immediately as it became wet. Looking behind her over her bronzed shoulder she nodded for Tiger to follow. Tiger picked up her bourbon and slipped elegantly into the water behind her, sipping the amber liquid as she let the warm water lap against her skin. She felt warm all over, inside and out as the whisky worked its magic. Libertina stood before Tiger and caressed her breasts and her bullet-hard nipples.

'You gotta keep the curves, baby,' taunted Libertina softly, 'Don't go all LA on me or you won't see me for dust. Now give me that glass,' she murmured, her lips close to Tiger's. She took the drink and retrieved an ice cube. Without a word she pushed Tiger against the poolside. Tiger gasped as she felt Libertina trailing the ice cube under the water against her inner thigh, taking her time to reach her clit. Libertina pressed the melting ice cube there, massaging it gently between her lips. Tiger sighed as Libertina leaned in to plant long deep kisses on her luscious mouth, and as the ice cube melted away to nothing, slipped her fingers deep inside Tiger as the pool fountains rained cool water upon them under the warm blanket of the starry desert sky.

Tiger had no idea, as she came to a shuddering climax, that a small pink envelope was being pushed under the door to her suite.

Chapter 19

Gorgeous? Check. Smart? Check. Funny? Check. Well hung? Big smile. What a catch, thought Blue as he snatched a good look at Richie from across the table. Now Tiger had become a virtual recluse since Vegas it was a given that she had turned down her invitation to the opening of M, a new restaurant in Mayfair, saying she wasn't in the mood for socialising. Blue had therefore decided to come with Richie instead. The glitterati were certainly on show tonight for the launch, and the restaurant was absolutely buzzing.

At a first glance M looked like any other chic, luxury restaurant, with an abundance of expensive 'glam-baroque' black and lilac glass fittings, velvet walls and colossal jet chandeliers, until it became clear that the proportions and perspectives of the whole interior had been very cleverly manipulated to give the diners the experience of being either very small in some parts of the room, or oversized in other parts. Blue had already got utterly confused in the gents, the inside of which were entirely decked out in beautiful etched mirror arrangements and complemented with expert lighting to give a kind of ever-decreasing *Through the Looking Glass* effect. Blue just couldn't work out what was door and what was wall – even the ceiling looked confusing – and in an attempt to get out he had accidentally shocked a well-known actor minding his own business on the can. Eventually Blue had made it back to his table in one piece, wondering whether it made any difference to tackle the restrooms sober.

'Fancy a digestif?' asked Richie, motioning for the waiter. Between them, the pair had already polished off a tray of complementary dirty Martinis, a bottle of pink champagne and several bottles of good Pomerol, and it looked as though Richie was still going strong. Blue convinced himself it was an age thing. His own hangovers got worse with every party that passed, but hey, it wasn't every day he took his boyfriend to the opening of the hottest new restaurant in town so why the hell pass up a good Cognac?

'Sure, if you're having one, that'd be dandy.' Blue beamed, starting a game of footsie under the table.

'Two large Remy's please,' ordered Richie as the waiter whisked over, 'and a large espresso for me,' he added loudly to make himself heard above the hum of the well-oiled diners. The waiter nodded and disappeared.

'Blimey, babe, sounds like you're in the mood for staying up.' Blue winked, feeling a little drunk but on the whole faring well. He was enjoying himself tonight. He couldn't quite believe how close he and Richie had become in such a short space of time. At first he had a nagging feeling that it was almost too good to be true, until Tiger had told him to stop being so paranoid and just to enjoy it.

Blue found it cute that even though Richie was gorgeous *and* cool as hell he was still keen to learn, and because of the age thing, not to mention being a good six inches taller, Blue found himself being rather protective of his new beau. He had even offered to use some of his old magazine contacts to snag Richie a position assisting a high-profile editorial photographer, which would help Richie get his foot in the door of the notoriously fickle fashion industry. Blue had never heard of the photographer Richie was currently assisting, and he had been quite brutal in explaining that just because one has a camera, it does not entitle one to call oneself a photographer. But despite Blue's generally catty and cynical commentary on life, he was just a simple soul who liked to look after people, and since Tiger seemed to be distancing herself even from her inner circle of late, Richie filled the gap a treat.

One thing that particularly pleased Blue was that Tiger approved of Richie. Even though she and Blue stayed out of each other's love affairs, Blue still valued her opinion highly, and since Richie was shaping up nicely to be 'the one', it would be a logistical nightmare if she didn't get on with him. Luckily Richie seemed to love Tiger too; in fact he had spent all evening asking about her.

As the last glass of wine really kicked in, Blue felt a little morose as the hubbub continued around him. Talking about Tiger all evening meant that he suddenly realised how much he had missed their closeness the last few weeks.

She had definitely withdrawn a little. Even though Tiger had always liked to be able to retreat into herself from time to time, and would often have an introspective few days, she'd definitely not been firing on all cylinders for quite a few weeks now. At first Blue had assumed she just wanted a few days' breathing space, but she had become increasingly distant. She was starting to be a little snappy with her team, even Gravy. Lewis had been furious about last week's incident with Johnnie, and had incorrectly assumed she had been completely drunk. Ever the professional, Tiger had fared well in front of the press in Vegas last week, yet seemed almost a ghost of herself when she wasn't performing for the cameras. Blue was particularly bothered about her losing two dress sizes. He knew exactly where every single garment was in the dressing room at home, and he knew she had sneaked a couple of her gowns and costumes out to alter them a couple of days ago. Tiger Starr was known for her hourglass silhouette, and to lose it would be commercial suicide. He couldn't quite put his finger on it, but he felt like she was pushing him away when she most needed to be protected, and he didn't like it one bit. In the past they had shared everything and he knew that they had both shared secrets with each other that they'd never tell a living soul, even a lover. In all these years he'd never known her to be like this. He wanted his soul mate back.

'Penny for them?' asked Richie

'Huh?'

'Penny for your thoughts.'

'Oh, sorry. What were you saying?'

'Nothing, you've just been deep in thought for a few minutes.' Richie smiled, as the waiter returned with the brandies and coffee.

'Oh. I guess it's all this talk of Tiger. I've just realised that we haven't really spoken properly – you know, as best buddies – for a while now.' Blue took a hit of Remy.

'Is she okay?' asked Richie.

'Well, that's the thing. I shouldn't say this, but . . .' Blue looked around to see who might be listening in. He needn't have worried, the kind of celebrities who were dining were far too interested in talking loudly about themselves to notice if a herd of wildebeest came sweeping through the room, let alone what someone might be saying on the next table. Tiger would have hated this crowd.

'It's okay, you know you can trust me,' reassured Richie.

'Well, I guess I can tell you. I'm worried about her.'

'Why? Does she need help?'

'That's the thing. I don't know. She's not talking to anyone. I don't think for one minute it was the bad press that upset her. She's way too tough to let that dent her armour. But I just have this nagging feeling . . .'

'Go on?'

'She got a few letters. You know, anonymous ones. They started a few months ago.'

'Threatening?'

'Yes and no.'

'How many?

'Well, I'm not sure. I just have a suspicion she's had a lot more than the few she's told me about. It's weird, at first she wasn't bothered and laughed it all off as the work of a practical joker. I was the one who was more worried. But now . . . you see, the thing is . . . I know she has—' Blue paused dramatically. 'Oh God! What am I saying! It must be the alcohol!' He drained his Remy and looked panicked.

'Oh darling, relax! You can confide in me,' said Richie softly, placing a hand on Blue's arm comfortingly. Blue felt better for the gesture.

'Waiter? Another large Remy for my boyfriend please,' ordered Richie, smiling caringly as he squeezed Blue's arm affectionately. 'Now, what were you saying?'

Chapter 20

Plumes of hot sparks and metal shot into the air against a postmodern symphony of hammering and drilling which echoed through the cavernous workshop. Tiger gingerly picked her way across the floor through the half-built constructions and industrial flotsam and jetsam. She tiptoed nimbly on her heels towards the enormous gilt rocking horse over in the corner, carefully leading the way for Pepper to follow daintily behind her. A peal of loud wolf-whistles rang out as the banging ceased.

'Couldn't they be more imaginative?' tutted Pepper, patting her neat white ponytail and looking around at the paint-stained sculptors, welders and workmen who had all downed tools to take in the glorious view. 'They should be letting off an air raid siren for you, dear,' she sighed at Tiger who was in full bombshell mode, wearing the tightest of black Chanel dresses and showing off a smooth pale caramel *décolletage*, with the fabric nipping in tightly around her teeny waist and elegantly tapering to a trim of chantilly lace at the knee. Her coiffure was fluffed to full volume, softly bouncing at her shoulders and she wore matching baby-pink hand-stitched kid leather gloves. Nude seamed stockings and five-inch pale-pink ponyskin stilettos with mink pompoms at the heels completed the knock-out ensemble.

'Howdy,' said the sculptor working on the rocking horse as he turned towards Tiger and pushed his goggles up onto his crop of thick, blond wavy hair.

'Wow,' replied Tiger and Pepper in unison, Pepper craning her neck to take in the beauty of the huge prop behind him, Tiger running her eyes up and down the sculptor.

'You're new here?' asked Tiger as she immediately racked her brains to think if she had any other props that needed to be made any time soon.

'Just started. Bob,' he proffered, quickly taking off his protective gloves and holding out a mucky hand.

'Tiger,' 'Pepper,' replied the ladies in turn, each accepting the grease-stained handshake warmly.

'Tiger, just look at this. This is to *die* for,' breathed Pepper, moving immediately towards the horse, and running her hands over its planed and flocked flanks. Tiger's eyes were locked onto Bob. He ripped his gaze away to address Pepper.

'Oh, I was just smoothing off the last few inches of the rockers with the angle grinder. Watch your hands if you're getting close, ma'am, I wouldn't want you to accidentally hurt yourself on a jagged edge now,' said Bob, rattling the weighty rockers. The horse shuddered a little in its rearing pose. 'There's still some wax rub on the gold leaf scrolls too, so watch your clothes.'

'Thank you, dear, I'll be careful,' replied Pepper, slowly walking around the prop, patting it as she went. Tiger immediately slipped off her heels and hitched up her skirt.

'May I?' she asked.

'Why sure, ma'am, it needs christening!' laughed Bob, tucking his thumbs into his belt loops and standing back to admire Tiger mounting the horse. She swung her leg up and over and landed in the saddle with a satisfying thump. A murmur swept around the workshop. Bob threw a look over at the other prop makers who all cleared their throats and found something important to fiddle with at their workbenches.

'Whoa, I'm struggling here,' laughed Tiger, kicking her legs frantically, while the horse threw her back.

'Ah, yes, the balance. That's something we have to fine tune while you're here. It's just a matter of an inch to the front or back, to find where your centre of gravity is in the saddle.' Bob pushed her forwards in the saddle gently, his big warm hands almost encircling her waist. Tiger's back arched automatically. 'Then if the horse lists to one side once you're off, since it's not symmetrical in its rearing position, we'll just conceal some weights in the rockers so it sits dead centre when it's at rest. It's the final little tweak. It'll be ready by the end of the day.'

'Hmm, they've thought of everything, darling,' said Pepper, as Bob enlisted two lucky welders to help him shift Tiger and the horse into the exact position of perfect balance. Once it was all bolted firmly into place, Tiger let out an almighty 'yee-hah' and flung herself back and forth on the prop. Pepper watched the horse rocking majestically on its arc, its sparkling jet crystals on the velvety finish winking in the light. The horse had flaring nostrils and bared teeth, and its mane swished as it moved. Pepper half expected it to whinny and bray.

'Oh, Tiger dear, it's magnificent. You look like one of the horsemen of the apocalypse,' she gasped. 'You should have trumpets and pipers and banging drums when you enter the stage, darling. Prince Romano is going to love it.'

'Oh you have to try it, Pepper, it's so much fun up here!' squealed Tiger like a child in a toy shop, her troubles forgotten for a moment.

'What? You're joking, dear, I don't do animals or wheelchairs, thank you.'

'Wow, this is going to be so much fun, I can't wait for the show,' enthused Tiger, looking down at Bob and grinning from ear to ear.

'Neither can I,' he murmured under his breath. Pepper heard him. She regarded Bob with a wry look – she recognised a smitten young man when she saw one.

A smile curled across her face as she fondly remembered her days touring the States when the men used to chase after her like wolves on heat. Back then she and Coco had worked out a great way to convert the amorous attentions of their lovers into cash by way of General Motors stock which they requested from all the men they dated. Tiger's grandma Coco had wisely bought a huge brownstone just off Central Park next to The Pierre off the proceeds. Pepper, the more hedonistic of the two, had drunk most of her income away in New York's Chelsea Hotel with Dylan Thomas in the early '50s, although in a moment of sobriety she had the good sense to buy a small *pied à terre* in London's King's Road in the '60s before her youth, the stocks, and the money ran out.

The King's Road had changed somewhat since then, and in addition to the Sloaney young ponies, it now saw gold diggers, celebrities, investment bankers and smug tweed-wearing Californian wannabe's in its streets who pushed past Pepper as though she were some wizened old dear. They were too arrogant and self absorbed to consider that Pepper could tell them stories about her life that would make their jaws drop, moreover that she could drink them under the table in five seconds flat. Pepper could certainly teach some of those phonies a thing or two about how to be a *real* lady. If ever there was a woman after Ava Gardner's heart, it was Pepper.

She smiled once more as she watched beautiful Tiger jump down agilely from her horse prop and elegantly slip her heels back on, patting down her hair with one hand and smoothing out her dress with the other. Now there was a real woman. That undertow of pure sexuality, whilst maintaining the tease that she would never actually give it away. Although judging by the almost tangible sparks flying between her and the sculptor right now, Pepper wondered if Tiger might be making an exception to that rule this afternoon.

'I must leave for my lunchtime poker game over at Big Annie's. I heard she won big money a few nights ago which I intend to relieve her of today,' announced Pepper.

'Okay, darling, but what do you really think?' asked Tiger, clutching at Pepper's satin dress a little needily.

'You heard me back there. It's going to be knockout. But now we have to work out how in hell you're going to take off your stockings while you're riding that baby. There's not much time left to get it right.'

'We have a few days before it's sent to Cannes. It's just a case of balance. I've been practising on that big old stuffed polar bear in my house anyway. And the rest of the routine is all finished, rehearsed and perfect. Have faith in me, darling,' pleaded Tiger. 'I know it will be fabulous, it's just too much fun not to be.'

'Well, I'll share in your enthusiasm. I'll see you in rehearsals with the girls tomorrow, *ma chérie*,' and with that, Pepper kissed her goodbyes to Tiger and Bob, and made her way towards the door to grab a black cab into town for her poker game.

Tiger's mobile buzzed from inside her handbag and a text message flashed from Blue to signal that he was waiting outside with Vladimir to take her to her press interview across town.

'I must be going, Bob,' said Tiger slowly, licking her lips as her eyes ranged over his sturdy torso. He was tall and broad, with beautiful golden skin and the palest blue eyes, a little crinkly at the corners.

'Before you go, ma'am?'

'Yes?' asked Tiger, looking up at his handsome face.

'I need you to sign off, so we can despatch the prop tomorrow.'

'Oh sure, just give me the paperwork.'

'This way, ma'am.' Bob led Tiger to a small Portacabin set into the corner of the huge workshop. Tiger's heart started pounding, her stomach fluttered with nerves as he opened the door. She found herself checking for any sign of a wedding band as he held the door open like a gentleman. All clear. She wondered if she dared to steal a kiss. How presumptuous, she thought, chastising herself. Though she was a free agent – Libertina had made it more than clear that what they shared was little more than a fling or at best a friendship with benefits. Bob closed the door softly behind him. Tiger froze, unable to walk any further as sheer excitement washed over her. Dare she make a move? So shamelessly? Bob was spectacular looking, with that incredible body and those thick blond curls that Tiger longed to run her hands through, never mind the way he had firmly patted his big hands on the horse's flanks . . . and hers back there. Tiger's thighs tensed at the thought, and a second wave of anticipation hit her stomach.

'Ma'am? Are you okay?' asked Bob, watching Tiger, who was curiously rooted to the spot. In a nanosecond Tiger had turned and pounced. Bob stiffened in shock before reciprocating passionately, immediately grabbing for her hair with his grease-stained mitts.

'Oh darling, don't get me dirty, I have to be in Knightsbridge straight after this,' whispered Tiger as she quickly unsnapped his overalls and tugged at them, reaching within the elasticated band of his grey Calvins for his already rock-hard cock. Bob took a moment to lift Tiger onto the desk where all the paperwork sat, leaving greasy smudges on her taut thighs. Tiger helped him yank her dress up, trailing her mink-trimmed stiletto over his smooth back as he bent over her. She nuzzled into him, lapping up his warm scent as he moved in to caress her neck with his hot tongue. As Tiger ran her kid gloves over his back, her mouth watering in anticipation of a good lunchtime spank, she caught a glimpse of a face at the window. She froze.

'Stage door Johnnie!' she screamed. Bob recoiled. 'How did he find me *this* time? Ohmygod I have to go,' garbled Tiger.

'What the?'

'Oh shit dogs. Oh baby, we could . . . oh hell. Oh this is all wrong, I have to go. I'm sorry. Fuck it!' stuttered Tiger, jumping up and grabbing her handbag. 'Shit shit shit!' She turned back and scribbled her autograph right across the now-crumpled despatch forms. Within seconds Tiger had bolted from the building to a rousing chorus of cheers from the workmen as she dodged past, frantically tugging her hemline to sit at her knees. Outside, Tiger stopped to gulp some air. There sat Vladimir in the

Towncar as it purred calmly in the fresh air of the no-man's-land of Tower Hamlets, waiting to rescue her. Thank god, she thought, jumping inside.

'Blue? I swear I saw Johnnie. How did he know where I was? I'm sure he's been sending the letters. He must be. There's no other explanation.' The words poured out as Tiger panted. 'Vladimir, drive round the block once, before you go to Knightsbridge. I need to look for someone,' she ordered. Blue delicately wiped an oily smudge from her chin.

'Calm down, darling. I didn't see Johnnie out here. You must have been mistaken.'

'Blue, it was him! I'm sure of it. It's getting creepy now. He seems to know where I am all the time! I mean, who *tells* him this shit? He must follow me.'

'He's harmless, and you're paranoid,' Blue sighed.

'Okay, so how do you explain the pink card in the bouquet last week?'

'Well, most girls like pink. It's a fair choice of colour. God, you were in a weird mood that night.'

'Then how about this. Johnnie knows where I live. He was outside my house after that press story with a posy. He always finds out where all my shows and appearances are. Think about the letters. "I know where you live." "I watch you sleeping." "I know what underwear you have on today." "I know your secret." And what about that one that arrived in *Vegas* . . .' Tiger trailed off, remembering she hadn't been telling Blue about the latest little batch.

'Woah there. What's all this new stuff?' exclaimed Blue, pulling a hip flask from his satchel. 'I don't think you've been giving me the whole story. Now, have a nip of gin and calm down. I calculate we have around thirty minutes before we get to Knightsbridge and you are going to tell me about every single pink letter that you've kept quiet. Got it? And only then can you tell me how you came to have grease and gold paint on your chin and your – your thighs.'

Tiger nodded and swiped the hip flask from his hands with a wicked glint in her eye.

'Did I hear the word "lunch"?' asked Rex hopefully.

'Well, it's 12.45, so I guess—' started Sienna.

'Great. Driver, change of plan. Could you swing round and take us to The Ivy, please,' he ordered. 'I'll ring 'em now, babes, and make sure they have a table.'

Sienna sighed. Dining out again. She would have to get her butt down the gym soon – she had definitely noticed her size 6 outfits feeling a bit snug. Sienna had never had to worry in the past about what she ate, but she figured the constant flow of champagne and being driven everywhere might have something to do with her recently expanding in the arse department.

She looked out of the black cab window as it crawled through the throngs of tourists on Shaftesbury Avenue and finally conceded she was struggling to keep up with Rex. She did her best to be indispensable, both as an employee and as a lover, but it was starting to wear her out. Rex never stopped. All his business seemed to be done over breakfast, lunch or dinner, or on his mobile in between breakfast, lunch and dinner. And then he would continue in the evening after dinner, networking or buttering up editors and clients alike at members' clubs and parties. It was almost a relief when he went away on his numerous little business trips so she could put her feet up at home, have a face mask, slop around in her pjs, and give her professional smile a rest for a night.

Of course, Rex was incredibly discreet where work was concerned; he was the consummate professional. In fact no amount of alcoholic or chemical substance ever seemed to touch the sides with him. Sienna found it slightly scary how he managed to remain in control at all times. Rex had a knack of getting his associates completely kaboobied by the end of a meeting, but he always worked his charm to the very last second, and he always remembered absolutely every word and every promise that had been uttered. Sienna guessed that kind of dedication was what made him one step ahead in business. Every media personality wanted Rex Hunter behind them. So did every woman, sighed Sienna, trying not to think about all the actresses, models and PR girls who seemed to chuck themselves at him on a daily and nightly basis right in front of her. It would help if Rex would introduce her as 'my girlfriend' once in a while, rather than as 'my assistant'.

As the cab pulled up at The Ivy, Rex clocked the usual smattering of paps outside.

'Hmm, wonder who's in today?' he muttered to himself, peeling a note from the large wad in his inside pocket and throwing it at the cab driver. 'Keep the change mate. Right, come on, Sienna let's see what's on at the circus.'

He charged through to reception and greeted the *maître d'* like an old friend.

'Come on, babes, we've got our usual table,' said Rex, ushering Sienna into the restaurant. She had learnt never to look around at the people in a room when she entered, or she would look like a star-fucker or a tourist. Instead, she now waited until she was settled at her table, seat or space at the bar, before having a quick survey of the room just before reaching for her handbag; and then if she saw anyone she wanted a closer look at, she would take out her compact and hold it up in their direction so she could stare for a few more seconds whilst looking as though powdering her nose. Any more staring or surreptitious glancing was strictly off limits, in fact, the said celebrity would then have to be studiously ignored until they got up to leave, at which point generally the whole room would stare for the duration of their exit.

Safely at her table, Sienna flicked her eyes around. A high-profile radio presenter and a comedian sat to her right. She didn't bother with her compact.

'What do you fancy?' asked Rex.

'Oh, I haven't looked at the menu yet.'

'No I mean to drink. Bolli or Stolli?'

'Um, actually I might have some water, thanks.'

'Water? Jeez, fish fuck in that stuff. Choose something else.'

'No really. It's a bit early for me. I'm okay with a Perrier. I'll have some champagne with you later.'

'Hmm. Whatever you say. Bottle of the Bollinger Grand Annee Rosé please and thanks,' ordered Rex as the waiter swooped. 'Ahh. Can't beat a bit of pink,' sighed Rex, rubbing his hands together and studying his menu.

'Well, if it isn't the two lovebirds,' boomed a familiar voice.

'Lance! Mate! To what do we owe the pleasure?' said Rex cheerily. Sienna rolled her eyes and curled her lip from behind her menu. She wasn't sure about Lance any more. He'd obviously had sex with her sister for a start – ugh – and he also intimidated Sienna the more she got to know him. From sitting in on meetings with him and Rex it was quite evident from his monologues and critiques that Lance had a mind like a steel trap, and a mischievous streak verging on merciless. Sienna wondered whether Tiger was brave or just stupid to have got close to him. Though her sister obviously liked intelligent, witty men. From what Lance had hinted, she sensed the pair had enjoyed a long relationship, long enough for Lance to have felt burned by Tiger finishing with him. It was weird though that Tiger had never mentioned him once, though they didn't often share confidences.

Sienna certainly found she couldn't relax around Lance, and she never knew whether to take him seriously or if he was pulling her leg. Rex had told her she would have to get used to people like that in the PR business. Sienna just found it exhausting keeping up with it all.

'Who are you here with, mate?' asked Rex.

'Oh I'm sitting over the other side in social Siberia with Devon Sexton's manager,' Lance said under his breath, crouching down to Rex's level.

'Oh? Where's Devon then? She's a bit of a babe that one.'

Sienna scowled over at Rex.

'Well, I've got this big feature on her now she's got her "Devon Rocks" tour coming up. Her bloody management won't let me near her until they've given me the official Hollywood story. Honestly, mate, they're all so bloody media trained these days, I can't get a single interesting scrap of gossip out of them. Not like the old days.'

'Yeah, I'm on the other side though,' protested Rex, 'and believe me, most of the "talent" out there can't string a sentence together. The managers have to give 'em a script to stop them gabbing on to sharks like you about how many pills they necked at the weekend.'

'Well, bollocks to the manager, I'll just insist on taking Devon to lunch somewhere miles away, the Fat Duck or something, so we have a long journey; she'll run out of the official story in about ten minutes flat. Then we make friends and I'll talk about my new puppy or my mum or something, then I'll move in for the kill on the way back when she's forgotten I'm a journalist and thinks we're best buddies.' Lance paused and looked at Sienna whose mouth was open as she listened. 'Are you writing this down? Good for you to know the tricks.' Lance winked in her direction. Sienna smiled and hastily buried her head back in her menu.

'Mate, can you sit with the little lady for two minutes while I go and decant?' asked Rex.

'Sure. My pleasure!' replied Lance as Sienna looked up like a rabbit in the headlights. Before she had a chance to politely decline, Rex was off to the gents and Lance was already in his chair and leaning in.

'So how is the delectable Miss Starr?'

'I'm good thanks,' replied Sienna self consciously. 'You?'

'How's Miss Starr Senior?' asked Lance, ignoring Sienna's question.

'Yeah, er, she's good I think. She's in Cannes next week doing a show.'

'Cannes eh? Who's that for?'

'Some royalty, or something. I don't keep up to date I'm afraid.'

'You close to Tiger?'

'Well, she's my sister.'

'That's not what I asked.' A smile crept across Lance's face. Sienna looked nervous. Lance backed off. 'Okay, so let's just kill time. I've always wanted to know, where did she get her stage name?'

'Why don't you ask her yourself?'

Lance arched an eyebrow at her.

'Oh that's right, you don't really talk any more do you.' Sienna smirked. 'Well, let's see now. She always says she chose "Starr" because she used to like watching the stars as a kid whenever she felt lonely. She says she believed there was one up there for everyone.'

'Whenever she felt lonely? I know it's a long way to Tipperary but it aint exactly the Gobi Desert.'

'Excuse me?'

'Ireland. She grew up in Ireland, didn't she?'

'Er, no! We grew up in Hertfordshire.'

'Darling, I'm sure you've worked this out by now, but I have known your sister in the biblical sense. She once told me on a late boozy night about growing up in Clonmel, after I introduced her to my greyhound Paddy, from Ireland.'

'Oh yeah, 'cos my sister has such a strong Irish accent – how silly of me not to notice.'

'Well, okay maybe there's no accent, but—'

'Look I think you're confused. Sure, Mum had Irish parents but she was born in Kilburn. After she met Dad they lived in Hertfordshire, like, forever 'til they died.'

'No, I definitely remember . . . ah. You know what, sorry, I must be thinking of someone else.'

'You're right about that.'

'So go on, you were saying about her stage name.'

Sienna had learnt enough from her time at Hunter

Gatherers to know that she shouldn't crawl into the detail with a hack like Lance so she simply repeated the fiction that 'Tiger' had been her sister's nickname for as long as she remembered. In fact, because of the age gap between them, she couldn't remember her sister being referred to as anything else. In fact her parents hardly mentioned her at all throughout Sienna's childhood.

'So . . . hang on, how can you be a Starr too in that case? I'm confused.'

'It's quite simple really. I just liked Tiger's stage name better than our boring family name and I decided to change it after our mum and dad died.'

'Yeah, I heard about that. Must have been tough to lose both your folks like that.' Lance paused. 'You changed it from what?'

'Oh nothing special. I thought Starr sounded – well, like a movie star. It was an improvement on my old name, put it that way.'

'Which was?'

Sienna stopped and took a deep breath. She managed to look at Lance straight in the eye.

'Why all the questions?'

'Just curious! A choice of name says a lot about someone. I'm interested! You know me, I'm a journo. I get paid to be nosey. C'mon . . . it's just harmless fun to kill the time!' Lance winked and put his hand on Sienna's arm. She tensed.

'Relax! So come on, what's your family name?'

'I don't want to say.'

'Something to hide?'

'No.'

'Sounds like you have to me,' Lance goaded.

'Oh for god's sake. It's Adams!' The diners on the surrounding tables looked around at Sienna. She lowered her voice. 'Sienna Adams. Satisfied?'

'That your real name?'

'Yes!'

'Why the big secrecy over that?' Lance shrugged.

'I don't know . . .' Sienna looked uncomfortable as Lance stared at her intensely. She felt like he was already reading her thoughts. Her shoulders dropped and she turned her face to him.

'Oh alright, If you must know I got bullied at school. They all used to . . . sing the theme song from the Addams Family.' Lance stifled a laugh. Sienna ignored it and continued, 'I've had a – a thing about it ever since. Look, don't laugh, I'm really touchy about it. *Really* touchy. School wasn't – it was bloody awful if you must know.'

'Oh darling, I'm sorry. Truly I am.' The waiter appeared at the table with more pink champagne. Sienna watched as he let the cork out with a sigh. She was pleased at the distraction.

'I got bullied too if it makes any difference,' said Lance as the waiter disappeared.

'Yeah? What for?'

'I used to get chased around the football pitch with penknives and called "Daddy Long Legs".' Lance smiled.

'Oh yeah? Well, I got "Twiglet Legs".'

They both looked at each other and burst out laughing.

'So is Sienna your real name?'

'Yes!'

'Well, after all that secrecy I'm not sure whether to believe you.'

'What?' she replied, looking alarmed. Wild horses wouldn't get her to reveal that along with adopting Starr as her surname, she had dropped her dorky Christian name in favour of her middle name. Unlike the name her parents had given her, Sienna Starr was a name destined for stardom. Now her heart was beating loudly as she wondered how on earth Lance would come to know her real name.

'Well, Sienna,' started Lance. 'For all I know, you could be called Wednesday.'

'Huh?'

'Wednesday Addams?'

'Oh ha bloody ha,' said Sienna, realising with relief her leg had been pulled yet again. Where was Rex anyway? she thought irritably, realising he'd been gone for an age. Sienna looked over towards the restrooms to see him bowling over towards them mighty cheerfully. A table of attractive women stared at him as he passed and nudged each other. One of them made a 'phwoaar' face. Sienna was really fed up now.

'What took you so long, Rex?' she asked as he approached.

'God, women, they all turn into nags don't they,' remarked Rex, taking back his seat. 'You're too young to be a nag, Sienna, tone it down, babes.' Sienna sighed and turned to her menu once again.

'Okay, I'm off,' announced Lance, 'be good, you two.'

'Yeah, see you, mate. Have fun with Devon and er – don't do anything I would,' said Rex, winking. With that Lance disappeared back to his table, humming the *Addams Family* theme song as he went. Sienna fumed underneath her forced smile.

'What's the matter?' asked Rex, sensing her tension.

'Nothing, it's just – Rex? Is that . . .? Oh for goodness' sake, so that's why you were gone so long. Will you wipe your nose, please?' Sienna bristled as she passed him her napkin. Rex waved it away laughing, and took a huge wet sniff followed by a swig of champagne. Sienna sat there simmering. She couldn't believe he was on it so early in the day. How did he manage it?

Rex was now making eyes back at the table of ladies.

'Rex, don't embarrass me. And why are you getting high now anyway?' she snapped. 'I thought it was something we did together – our special thing. Since when did you start doing it in the daytime?'

'Babe, I've been doing chang longer than you've been alive. Now quit with the nagging, you're turning into a bore,' he retorted, washing back his vintage rosé.

The words stung. Sienna felt well and truly out of her depth in every way. She decided she really should have some champagne after all, and leaned over to pour herself a glass. Her mind kept flicking back to the exchange with Lance. Something just didn't sit right. Why was he so interested in her and Tiger anyway? And that weird comment about where she grew up, arguing with her as if she wouldn't know what country her own sister had grown up in. Okay, so there were ten years between them, and Tiger was always away at boarding school but her folks told her everything about Tiger she needed to know; not that there was anything that interesting.

God, Sienna hated how Lance had a knack of wheedling information out of people; she mentally kicked herself for giving in to him. There was no question, she had to harden up; learn from the tough guys. She'd dipped her toe and got eaten up for breakfast by Bob Bell. Now it was time for her to find a way to prove she could really play with the big boys. Then Rex wouldn't find her such a bore, would he?

'Mwah! Mwah! Thank you, darling, that was a fabulous interview, thank you for your time. I must say you're looking exceptionally well today, Ms Starr,' Lydia Appleby muttered. It was her first compliment of the meeting. Tiger took a deep breath and looked sideways at Lewis who gave a barely detectable nod and wink. That was a tough interview. It was supposed to be a huge feature on how a British national treasure was making her mark on the most American of institutions, Las Vegas, although one would think it was about Tiger's personal life, the way Lydia had been digging around for gossip like a kid on an Easter egg hunt. Tiger had fielded her questions like a pro, always aware of how her words could be twisted, and always making sure to drag the subject back to her new Vegas show. For once, she was pleased that Lewis was there in the background with his ears pricked as usual, particularly since Rex was a no show, unusually for him. He was normally keen to police any major interviews himself.

Tiger wondered if Lydia's choice of venue today – the infamous and opulent Les Trois Petits Cochons tea rooms in the heart of Knightsbridge – had been chosen to distract her and lull her into thinking it was a gossipy coffee morning. Lydia had stuck to her story that she wanted the accompanying photographs to be somewhere quintessentially European, and seeing as Tiger was reknowned for her fabulous figure, she felt it would be something of an irreverant celebration of that to feature her in amongst the exquisitely decorated cakes. She was certainly right on that front, the cakes verged on artworks and were delicious; Tiger felt entirely happy spending an afternoon surrounded by sugary confection.

Tiger had, in fact, declined to mention to Lydia that she often came to Les Trois Petits Cochons to hide away quietly with a book and a delicious coffee éclair for an hour between meetings, whenever she had the opportunity. The kitchen staff would even send small boxes of macaroons outside to Vladimir while he waited in the limo. Tiger simply loved the vaulted ceilings and enormous gold chandeliers and the mezzanine level with its sweeping gold staircase and rich purple velvet chairs. It was all so fancy and overtly decorative with its filigree duck-egg blue and gold wallpaper; it made her feel like she was sitting right in the middle of a doll's tea party. It also reminded Tiger of happy times spent in the beautiful rich old cafés of Budapest when she spent a month there in a show at the State Opera House. No, there was no way she would mention to Lydia that she was a regular here, or her occasional peaceful breaks would turn into autograph-signing sessions.

'We'd like to take the shots now, near that display by the window,' said Lydia, motioning over at the lanky, whiskery photographer who had already lit the corner and was now flapping a test Polaroid, while his assistant played around with the lighting, trying to adjust one of the reflectors by an eighth of an inch without disturbing a pile of iced fancies. Tiger immediately recognised the photographer as Kris Stewart, some new hotshot on the scene who had already shot everyone from Bowie to Beckham. She walked over and shook his hand warmly to break the ice. Lewis buggered off for a pot of lapsang souchong on his own. Shoots always bored him senseless and he was happy to leave Blue to do what he did best. Blue was already chatting with Kris and having a careful look at the Polaroids.

'Darling, it's quite muted – candy-box 'fifties colours –

you might want to pop a black hat on so your hair isn't disappearing tonally,' he whispered over at Tiger. 'It'll balance out the Chanel dress perfectly too.'

'Okay, darling, choose me something from your magic box,' said Tiger as she eased into the shot between the huge displays of cakes.

Ageing, dried-out ladies with expanding waistlines, bundled up in Bulgari diamonds and other spoils from their failed marriages, were nudging each other at their tables and winking sourly over their teacups at the action unfolding, while Blue disappeared out to the car to retrieve some accessories. A crowd was steadily gathering outside. Teenage girls huddled together and chattered about Tiger's outfit, as young men pressed their noses up at the glass hoping for a flash of stocking top. Tiger looked over and batted her eyelids for the boys, who excitedly jostled for the best view.

'Okay, Tiger, another test with you in shot please, and – *click* – thank you,' said the photographer, retrieving the Polaroid and holding it under his armpit while it developed.

'So, Vegas here we come eh!' said Kris as he waited. This was always the small talk part where the good photographers tried to get a rapport going before giving their directions.

'Yes, not long now,' replied Tiger brightly, turning as she heard a tapping at the window. One of the boys outside was getting a little forward. She winked and smiled.

'Well, this shot is as far from neon and casinos as possible,' laughed Kris, peeling back the Polaroid.

'Oh, but that *is* what they want of course, isn't it!' agreed Tiger, hearing the tapping at the window again. She turned and the boy outside drew a heart shape in the air with his index finger. The ladies on the tables nearby were tutting loudly and scowling as best they could through their botoxed brows. Tiger put her finger up to her mouth to the young boy as a 'shhhhh'.

'Right, this is looking gorgeous now, I just need to give you a little more cheekbone then we'll go for it,' said Kris, sounding happy with his shot.

'Okay great, but I just want to pop on a hat if I may. Blue will be back in a few minutes with a couple for me to try.'

'Fine, no probs,' said Kris, as he motioned for his assistant to tweak a light. Tiger heard the tapping again, this time louder.

'Hmm, they make them cheeky these days,' she remarked.

'Heh heh, ah you never know, maybe they're just after a bit of cake frosting,' said Kris.

'Yeah right,' snorted the up until now mute assistant.

Tiger's mind whizzed as the tapping on the window progressed to banging, and the old ladies were emitting loud, plummy Wimbledon Village-style 'Well *really*'s' in Tiger's direction. There was only one way to shut the naughty boys up, Tiger decided. She scanned the tall piles of cakes and located a dish of cream-filled choux buns. This ought to silence them, she thought, and she threw a bun towards them as they tapped madly on the window, forgetting that the reason she had never made it into the netball team at school was entirely down to her lamentable aim. Tiger gasped in horror as the cake sailed past the window, hitting one of the particularly unattractive lunching ladies' brigade squarely in her rock-hard sandy blonde coiffure. The room fell silent as cream dripped from her dry hair. Her thin lips pursed so tightly they resembled a cat's bum. Tiger bit her lip and braced herself for a torrent of braying abuse. Instead she watched as a wicked gleam came into the old lady's eyes, she screwed up her face, grabbed her jumbo Florentine and threw it like a frisbee. Tiger ducked as it flew by, a shard of almond nearly taking her eye out. The sticky biscuit hit Lydia in the face with a 'thok'. Lydia looked shocked for a moment as she stared at the cream-covered old lady, who was now struggling to stop laughing.

Tiger and Lydia scooped up everything they could lay their hands on. So did the entire tearoom. Macaroons, buns, croissants, cakes, strawberries, profiteroles and tarts flew through the air in all directions. Tiger laughed like she hadn't laughed for months. Crumbs rained upon her hair and cream spattered her dress, and she howled with laughter as she took aim. Kris Stewart clicked away frantically, unable to believe his luck as he moved around capturing the action.

Everything blurred in a creamy haze before Tiger's eyes, but she could just make out what appeared to be a team of security guards parting the crowds, with Lewis at the helm. A huge lemon meringue flew through the air from behind and hit him in the face. Tiger looked behind her to see a horrified Lydia with her hand over her mouth. The two women looked at each other, then fell about in hysterics. Tiger slipped in spilt cream and went down laughing all the way.

'Okay, time for a sharp exit, young lady,' boomed Lewis' voice as he appeared from above, scooping Tiger up from the floor and carrying her through the carnage to the back entrance, led by the security men.

'Most bodyguards take a bullet, darling, but I took a pie. Now that's what I call devotion,' huffed Lewis as he dripped meringue all over Tiger's Chanel dress. She held on to him tightly and snuggled blissfully into his strong arms, letting him carry her into the street and all the way round the corner to safety.

Blue had been watching the drama unfold from outside and he now stood by the Towncar bewildered and still clutching a pile of hatboxes. His eyes widened even more as he watched Lewis staggering from around the corner with Tiger curled up in his arms, the pair looking for all the world like newlyweds in love, as the outrageous cakefight continued without them in the tearooms. Not wanting to interrupt the moment he carefully popped the hatboxes back in the trunk of the Towncar and made off for some solitary retail therapy.

*   *   *

Tiger perched herself on one of the tall brown leather stools of Claridge's *fumoir* and brushed crumbs from Lewis' lapel.

'Well, Rex is gonna have his work cut out for him that's for sure, patrolling the press after today's little scene,' remarked Lewis with a smirk. 'About time he put in some hard graft.' Lewis had been less than pleased with Rex's recent sloppy record on the press front; never mind the piss-poor performance on the bad stories. For example, where the hell had he been today for Tiger's interview? Rex needed to be reminded that no one was irreplaceable. 'You don't seem too concerned?' noted Tiger, slightly surprised at how laidback Lewis seemed to be about the whole afternoon's debacle. Lewis' mobile buzzed. He checked and saw that it was a text from Georgia. He tutted and deleted the message without reading it.

'Oh it was only Georgia, she can wait.'

'No, silly, I meant about this afternoon!'

'Oh right!' said Lewis, slightly embarrassed. 'Ah well, how bad can it be? It's hard to see how a journalist could get too serious about a cake fight. Everyone seemed to enjoy themselves and the magazine will cover any damages.' He paused. 'Besides, I know it was Lydia who got me with the pie. So she owes me one,' laughed Lewis, as Tiger scooped up a smear of lemon filling from his sleeve and sucked it from her finger. She let her eyes linger on Lewis as he chuckled to himself. He had such a gorgeous smile, she thought to herself. She'd never really noticed before;

she couldn't remember him laughing very often with her at work. A waiter suddenly appeared with napkins to help them clean up.

'No thanks, do you know how expensive this cake is?' exclaimed Lewis as he shoo-ed the bemused waiter away before turning his attention back to Tiger. 'Anyway, one thing I *am* concerned about is *you*.'

'Me?' asked Tiger, brushing crumbs from her shoulder. The last thing she wanted to do was explain about the letters. She'd already been through it once today with Blue. Lewis didn't really need to know, anyway. Blue would look out for her.

'So come on then. What's up?' pressed Lewis. 'You've been so withdrawn lately. You're losing weight. And today was the first time I've seen you laugh properly for weeks. What's going on? Oh, you've missed a bit,' he said, pointing at a smudge of cream on Tiger's wrist.

'I'm not hungry,' she replied, holding her arm up to Lewis' mouth. He held her delicately and licked the cream from her skin slowly. Tiger was shocked to feel a warm wave of electricity. Lewis' lips lingered over the soft under-side of her wrist. He closed his eyes for a moment then looked up at Tiger. Their eyes locked for a split second. Instantly they pulled back from each other and reached for their drinks. Tiger gulped her dirty Martini, Lewis swigged his Whisky Mac.

'So come on then, what's up?' continued Lewis. Tiger fiddled with her napkin, wondering if perhaps she should tell him everything after all. Lewis' mobile buzzed again.

'Oh for Pete's sake, what does she want?' he muttered under his breath, deleting the text.

'Hey, it's okay if you wanna go and call Georgia outside, I'm alright here on my own for a bit,' offered Tiger.

'No. Georgia can wait. She probably only wants my credit card number anyway. I want some time with you now.' Tiger raised her eyebrow at the comment. But the mobile was buzzing again. 'Oh, this is ridiculous, what does she want? Sorry, Tiger, I'm just nipping out, I'll be two minutes.' Lewis strode out of the bar, leaving Tiger perched and nursing her Martini. So he really *is* under the thumb after all, she mused, fiddling with the olives in her glass. Or maybe he just fancies a quiet life away from work and lets Georgia lead the way once in a while. Either way, Tiger was fascinated. So rarely did she see any personal side to Lewis. She blushed to herself as she recalled feeling his heart beating under his shirt when he had carried her in his arms earlier. She tried to push it to the back of her mind.

'Right,' came Lewis' voice as he came back into the bar, 'I've just seen a load of paparazzi outside – they've obviously got wind of the fracas earlier and someone's tipped them off that you're here,' he muttered. 'I've told Vladimir to wait out front as a decoy, and I've asked the concierge to have another car waiting out back for you. I'll take you down in a minute. Sorry about this. Drink up and we'll go,' Lewis ordered, fully back to working mode and breaking the spell ... whatever it had been back there. But if only Tiger had told Lewis about the letters, and if only Lewis had known what was waiting at home for her in that morning's post, he would never have let Tiger out of his sight. It was turning out to be quite a day.

Chapter 21

Keys. Purse. Moleskin. Scarf. Cashmere cardigan. Make-up bag. Air tickets. Freshening wipes. Moisturiser. Passport . . . Bingo. Sienna opened it up and looked in the back. Pah! Only Tiger would have a great passport picture, thought Sienna bitterly. Now, the name is . . . Starr, Tiger. No surprises there, Lance. Hang on, place of birth . . . Clonmel? Sienna suddenly felt lightheaded.

'Everything okay in there?' shouted Blue as he came into the lobby.

'Er yes, thanks!' replied Sienna, stuffing the passport back in Tiger's Hermés handbag before swinging round and holding it out to Blue. 'Sorry, darling, I couldn't find them. It was just a faint hope that I might have put them the wrong handbag absentmindedly after the strategy meeting at the office yesterday. I guess I must have lost them after all,' said Sienna. 'Where shall I put this?'

'Oh leave it down there with her cases. I'm sorry you can't find them – god, if I had a pound for every pair of sunglasses I've lost,' tutted Blue. 'Were they expensive?'

'Nah. It's okay, I'm sure they'll turn up,' said Sienna, her hand flying to her own bag to make sure her sunglasses weren't visible in there. How embarrassing would *that* be.

'Well, pleased to catch you before you go, wish Tiger good luck for me.'

'Yes of course. She'll be back in, like, three minutes if you hang on. Gravy doesn't like being walked too long when it's raining. Actually Tiger's been a bit quiet the last few days, it might be nice if you said "hi".'

'Er . . . no, I really have to dash, I have a cab with the meter on,' replied Sienna hurriedly.

'Oh, I can give you some money. It would be nice if you two could catch up.'

'No no, I'll be late for work otherwise.'

'Oh, alright then. Are you okay? You look a little pale.'

'Yeah yeah, just in a hurry that's all.'

'Well if you're sure . . .' replied Blue, walking Sienna to the door.

'Thanks, appreciate it. See you guys when you get back.'

'Okay. Mwah, mwah, darling,' said Blue, half to himself as Sienna was already out of the door into the early morning mizzle and running towards her waiting black cab.

That was easy enough, thought Sienna as the cab rattled the short distance back towards Marylebone. She knew Tiger would have to have her bags packed and passport at the ready for her morning flight to Cannes, and she also knew Tiger liked to take Gravy out to stretch his legs just before they travelled. All Sienna had to do was huddle down and wait in the cab until she saw the pink hair bobbing past, then dive into the house, fob Blue off with some lame story about losing something, then raid Tiger's handbag. The only problem was she hadn't bargained on what she had found.

Dad had had lots of sayings, and he had once told her, 'Be careful of asking questions you don't already know the answer to.' Sienna had always thought it a ridiculously stupid thing to say, since why *else* would you ask a question? Only now, she understood perfectly what he meant. Sienna was shocked. Her parents wouldn't have lied to her. So what was Tiger doing, being born in bloody County Tipperary? It was possible her mother had given birth while she was in Ireland visiting relatives, but it was odd that no one had mentioned it while Sienna was growing up. She couldn't even remember any visits back to Ireland during her childhood. If there was family back in Ireland, mother had long since lost contact with all of them before she died. Lance's words rang again in Sienna's ears from their conversation at The Ivy . . . that Tiger had told him she grew up in County Tipperary. Could she be adopted? Could it be that the bitch had lied to Sienna for all these years and they weren't bound by blood after all? Perhaps Lance might just be useful to her now. Sienna wasn't fussed about loyalty at the best of times, let alone loyalty to someone who wasn't even real family.

'Tiger, what on earth is wrong with you, you've hardly said a word since you got here.'

'I'm f-f-fine.'

'Look, you're on in half an hour. Prince Romano's already

here having his champagne and toasts. If you can't do this I need to warn Lewis, he's down there with the Prince and the guests.'

'No!'

'No what? No you can't do it, or no don't tell Lewis?'

'I'm f-fine. Just look out for m-me. Okay?'

'Well tell me what's wrong? You're stuttering. You've had another letter haven't you?' The feathers in Tiger's enormous plumed headdress quivered as she shook her head miserably. She tried to breathe deeply in her tight corset but only managed shallow panting.

'No, just . . . just be a f-f-friend to me, okay?'

Blue felt terrible, watching Tiger in such a state. She only ever stuttered when she wanted to cry. Blue knew she must have had another pink bombshell delivered, and despite feeling like wringing her neck for not telling him, he simply took her into his arms and gave her a long, hard squeeze.

'Right, lady. Gin. Tonic. Chanel. Lipstick,' he said, lining up the pre-show ingredients on the dressing table. 'Cherry and Brandy are in place by the stage to receive your costume. Just throw it all stage right. The Starrlets look unbelievable. The best pony girls I've ever seen if I do say so myself. Now you've got to do *your* bit. Just get out there and be the best you've ever been. Get in your headspace. There's no room for baggage on stage. You hear? No baggage. Not even a soap-bag.'

Tiger nodded feebly and forced a smile.

'Good girl. I'm leaving you to do your breathing. I'll be back at the five-minute call to take you down.'

Tiger waited until Blue had left the room before reaching for her vanity case. She pulled out the pink piece of paper and read it slowly again, as though reading it for the hundredth time would make the words change.

'LOOK. Forward. 2 your. canNES. show. I. love. shoot.ING. moving. Targets. BANG BANG X' Tiger reached for the gin bottle and took three large swigs, neat. She screwed her face up as it burnt the back of her throat, and then pounded the dressing table with her fist. 'That's the spirit,' she muttered to herself, 'nobody tries to intimidate Tiger Starr. Bloody psycho.' She ripped the letter in two and chucked it in the bin, before reaching for her lipstick and applying a perfect slick of radiant red. With one last pout in the mirror she felt ready to take on the stage.

Sienna paced round her flat agitatedly. Another of her father's favourite naff sayings was 'Be careful what you wish for, or it may just come true.' Sienna had spent all these years hating and envying Tiger in equal measures. The cocktail of intense jealousy mixed with the rejection Sienna derived from the feeling Tiger hadn't cared about her dorky sister during her childhood gave her the bizarre bitterness of unrequited love and rivalry in equal measures. Of course, Sienna would never arrive at that analysis herself. Instead she recalled how Mum and Dad had always lauded Sienna as the darling of the family, yet Tiger was always the one being rewarded with the fabulous lifestyle. Every time Tiger was maddeningly lovely and *nice* to Sienna it messed up the carefully constructed picture of the demon sister her parents had instilled in her head, and she hated Tiger even more for that. Couldn't she just be a bitch? Then Sienna would have a clear reason to hate her rather than having to invent more and more elaborate reasons. Sienna often wished Tiger would just disappear from her life and stop overshadowing her – and now? Well, now, in a funny way Sienna had her wish. Now she had no real reason to feel tied to Tiger. Sienna felt a curious sense of isolation. With no warning she burst into tears, without knowing why. Perhaps at the shock of losing . . . well, losing a part of her. Everything she had assumed about her family and her sister . . . was never as it seemed. Instead she had been playing second fiddle to a mere cuckoo in the nest for all this time.

She had one question in her head for Tiger. Why did she keep it secret? They could have been friends instead of sisters if only she had known. Sienna might have even felt a bit sorry for her that her own parents must have given her away. But in hiding the truth for so long, that opportunity was long gone. Sienna had of course wondered if she was adopted too. Usually couples adopted because they couldn't have children . . . but Sienna dismissed the possibility after she had remembered how everyone used to comment about how much she took after her father.

Sienna found herself becoming angry that she'd been lied to. Her parents obviously kept it secret out of respect for Tiger, and now they were dead she would never know the full story. She couldn't ask Tiger; if she hadn't told the truth for the last twenty-nine years then she certainly wouldn't start now.

Lance could help, thought Sienna with a flash of inspiration. If anyone could get to the bottom of it, he could. He had a way of talking to people and finding information. He could check facts and more importantly get the full low-down. Maybe he could even find Tiger's real parents for her, perhaps find out why she had been given away? Then again, why should Sienna help a cold-hearted bitch like Tiger who could lie so easily for a lifetime? Sienna reached for her phone and dialled.

'Lance? Sienna – er – Starr here . . . Listen, are you around for a coffee tonight? Yes, it's urgent. Oh great, see you at Bar Italia. Eleven? Great. See you then.'

A collective gasp rang out at the spectacular vision as Tiger burst onto the stage in the magnificent Grand Ballroom to a rousing fanfare, all megawatt smiles and sparkling diamonds with the Starrlets prancing military fashion in synchronised lines behind her, dressed in cavalry helmets and cleverly designed harnesses. The ponytails in their helmets bobbed as they flounced to the music, mirroring Tiger's own towering feather version as she strutted into position. The crowds all cheered and applauded as the

Starrlets turned their backs to the audience to reveal long shiny ponytails cheekily fixed to their harnesses at their peachy buttocks. As Tiger danced to the loud romping music, kicking up her powerful legs and then slowly stretching out her thighs from beneath her bustle, the Starrlets bobbed their tails perkily to the beat. They knew they looked fantastic and they were loving every minute. The energy was riding high and Tiger was holding it together, looking exquisite and, to Prince Romano and his unfeasibly glamorous guests, one hundred and ten per cent in control. All eyes were on her and boy did she work it. No one would have known that barely five minutes earlier thoughts of being shot to her death were the only things filling her head.

'Go girl!' squealed Nikki excitedly as the Starrlets all huddled inwards round Tiger as she strode to the horse, swiftly removing her bustle as she went. On the beat, the girls all turned, whipping out brass trumpets from the backs of their harnesses and miming to the deafening fanfare as Tiger swung herself elegantly into the saddle. They then marched into position as Tiger rode the horse to Prokofiev's *Romeo and Juliet*. The crowds erupted as Tiger sailed through the air on rocking-horseback, its hundreds of thousands of crystals sending sparkles bouncing off the ballroom walls.

Tiger playfully kicked off her heels and languorously stretched out her long legs as she rocked, peeling off her stockings and pinging them off at her toes. Inside she was trembling as her stomach muscles burned from holding the elegant position. Using one of her stockings as reins, Tiger nimbly hopped into the saddle with one manicured foot and delicately held her other foot between the horse's ears in front of her coquettishly. She balanced on the horse like a statuesque 1940s circus girl to the raucous cheers of the crowds as she leaned back like a daredevil. She had mastered this move on the rearing stuffed polar bear at home; Pepper had been most impressed.

The audience gasped in awe at the showers of crystal sparkles dancing on the walls around them as Tiger commanded centre stage like a warrior, the tall plumes flowing from her headdress dramatically in the breeze as she rocked. Her smile was radiant, her body lithe and sensual. Beneath the veneer, Tiger's head throbbed with the now-deafening sound of the audience closing in around her. No one would hear gunshot above this lot, would they? Would she die instantly? Do people hear the shot that kills them?

Faces in the front row began to loom sickeningly towards her. Were they cheering? Or sneering? She felt a bead of sweat dripping from her temples. She glanced at the Starr-lets high kicking their hearts out, and registered Georgia's face smiling back at her, morphing in Tiger's mind into a hideous Joker grin. She remembered Ocean's warnings to her. Was Georgia behind the notes? Was she going to step into her shoes for good tonight?

Hang on in there, thought Tiger to herself, just hang

on, she thought, trying to concentrate on carefully manoeuvring into an impressive arabesque. Another roll of cheers. She was relieved her legs obviously knew what they were doing at least. She caught sight of the stage manager in the wings as her hamstrings stretched out excrutiatingly. Where's Blue? There's no sign of Blue in the wings? He was supposed to be looking out for her. Tiger felt her grip slipping on the silk stocking as her palms became clammy. Sweat dripped from her brow into her eye, stinging as she held her pose. She could see four of everything, fading in and out of focus as the music pounded sickeningly in her head. Is that stage-hand pointing something at me? thought Tiger, unable to see clearly with her blurred, salty vision. He's pointing something! Where's Blue? Is something happening back there? God, I'm slipping . . .

'Pow!' came a deafening bang. Tiger screamed, tumbling from the horse as colossal jets of flutterfetti spewed up into the huge domed ceiling. The audience gasped as Tiger scrambled up and pelted from the stage under a sparkling rain of glitter, covering her face with her arm as she pushed through the path of the shocked Starrlets. The gasps turned to a swell of jeers and catcalls. Blue caught her tearing into the wings like a banshee as Georgia seamlessly stepped into Tiger's role on stage and started teasing with her horsetail to adoring whoops and applause.

'Jesus Christ, Tiger, get a grip! What the hell's wrong with you!'

'G-g-gun shot . . .'

'What on earth? It was just the fucking confetti cannons – don't you remember, you asked for them! Get your arse back out there!'

'I c-c-an't.'

'Go!'

'I can't!' screamed Tiger, looking back at the stage to see Georgia spinning her nipple tassels to rapturous applause. 'It's too late, goddammit!'

'Oh Jesus and Mary, you've really screwed up this time, babes. What the hell's got into you?' yelled Blue, shaking her roughly by the shoulders.

Unable to bear being screamed at by Blue, her rock, her ally, Tiger fled to her dressing room, slamming and locking the door behind her.

Chapter 22

Poppy clutched at her throat, feeling it constricting as she gulped for air behind the locked door. She looked at her reflection in the mirror, trying to remind herself what was real. What was happening to her? She thought she was going to die as she gasped for breath and tried to swallow. She felt a huge weight on her shoulders and chest, and a foreboding sense of dread deep within her. She felt paralysed with fear.

Poppy daren't look at the pregnancy test lying there on the floor; that little blue line on the white plastic stick like a meteor crashing through her childhood. As if the rape wasn't enough, now this? She had never felt so alone, so isolated as she stood there in the bathroom. She tried to calm her breathing down. She leaned over and splashed water from the tap into her mouth with her trembling hand, trying to swallow the cool liquid; hoping it might settle the churning feeling in her stomach. Who could help her now?

Stricken, she just stood there, rooted to the spot, unable to even cry. What was going to happen to her? She knew this had to be her punishment for what happened with Mr Rogers. She must have led him on somehow, it must have been her fault, and now this . . . this was her punishment. She should have gone to mass like she was supposed to. Perhaps if she had gone to confession none of this would have happened.

Poppy's mind raced and she sank to the carpet under the weight of her fear. How long would it take for someone to notice a bump? It was nearly four months ago since the night with Mr Rogers, and Poppy already had a bit of a podge. She had thought it was all the extra food; she had been feeling quite sick on and off for a few weeks and at first Mother had been feeding her up with lots of mashed potato, saying it would line her stomach and soak up any 'bad water'. When the sickness kept coming back, she made Poppy drink gallons of hot sweet tea as her fail safe 'cure' for everything. The thought of a cup of sweet tea being the cure for her pregnancy made Poppy convulse with panic. She pulled her school jumper over her stomach and rolled onto the carpet, letting the tears come. And they came. She was barely able to silence the sound of her sobs as they wracked her little body.

Chapter 23

'Of course, I just knew something was up before she even boarded the plane. She'd been quiet ever since that cake fight at the Three Little Pigs.'

'Uh huh.'

'Well, just after I took her down to the stage I whizzed back up to her dressing room. She'd never be any good at covering up a murder you know; she'd only left the latest bloody letter ripped in two in the bin!' Blue slammed his pink 1974 Triumph Spitfire down into third gear as he screeched into Regent's Park like Penelope Pitstop in her Compact Pussycat.

'Get away. Was she scared, then?'

'Scared of what? I haven't told you what was in it yet.'

'Oh, I assumed – well you said all the letters have been pretty weird.'

'Yes. Well, this one said something about shooting her.'

Richie was silent for a moment as they cruised down the dappled, tree-lined road, the sun winking between the cover of the green leaves. Blue had the roof down on the Triumph and it was garnering a few stares. Or rather, the boys were – gorgeous Richie with his twinkling big brown eyes and flawless skin, with the whole striking, über-groomed hulk of Blue literally shoehorned into the driver's seat next to him.

'You see, darling, because Tiger's kept the letters quiet, she can't tell anyone she thought she heard gunshot. Everyone just thinks she's losing it! The papers are having a field day with all these bloody stories; S&M vice dens, assaulting fans, missile warfare in the most exclusive tearooms this side of Paris; and now scared half to death by a ton of glitter? Nuts!' Blue pumped the brakes for a jogger weaving on the road. 'Get a "Wide Load" sign for god's sake!' yelled Blue as he passed, swerving violently.

'So you really think people reckon Tiger's losing it?'

'Course! If the Americans have been keeping their eyes on this little lot then I reckon her show's hanging by a thread. No one wants a one-woman freakshow circus as their leading lady. I know Lewis has been fielding calls from them the last couple of days. Prince Romano was not best pleased about the hiccup, and word gets round in this business. It's a travesty, it was all going so well, like a vision. I never thought I'd say this but thank fuck for Georgia, at least she put herself out there and finished off the show as best she could.'

'Yeah, shame. I mean, poor Tiger, having to be upstaged by Georgia, huh?'

'What? No way, it's impossible for a streak of piss like Georgia to upstage her. But Tiger didn't cover herself in glory that night, I can tell you that for nothing. If she just dropped the "independent lady" act and was upfront about the anonymous threats instead of always thinking she needs to take care of everything herself, we could have had this thing nipped in the bud from the start. As it is, it's way out of hand now.'

'Hmm. So she's quite fragile then?'

'Yeah, I reckon. Never seen her like this. And after everything she's been through in her life.'

'Oh?'

'Well, what I told you the other night was only – god, what *did* I tell you the other night? You were pouring the Martinis down me . . .'

'Oh you didn't have that many! But you know you can always talk to me about *anything* you know . . . a problem shared and all that.'

'Is a problem doubled.'

'Oh thanks! You saying you can't trust me?'

'Yes. No! Oh shit, sorry, no . . . oh, of course I trust you!'

'It's okay, don't worry. I know it's personal stuff, darling. Look, I didn't mean to be nosy . . . I don't know, I just feel a bit sorry for her that's all. What you gonna do?'

'Well, that's why we're heading back now with a car full of goodies! Thought some new frocks might cheer her up. Rex and Sienna have put together a BBC radio interview today so she can give some kind of chatty, endearing public explanation for her recent humiliation. It's a damage limitation thing, you know, give her the chance to show she ain't nuts. I think they're doing a tour of the house, like a kind of "opening the doors on the glamorous but hardworking life of a National icon". The last I heard, Rex briefed her to say she suffers from low blood sugar and that she passed out, and thanks to her marvellous Starrlets the show went on blah blah, wank wank. Oh, the perils of being a showgirl and all that.'

'Hmm. Smart.'

'Yeah, although it doesn't help that she's lost so much weight recently, knowing the press they'll even turn that round to make out like she's been starving herself to the brink of collapse or something sensational.'

'Wow, it really is a big mess right now,' breathed Richie, almost cheerfully. Blue regarded him with a wary sideways glance.

'Yes, well she won't be in it for much longer, I can assure you of that. Tiger's a winner. She's come this far from nothing and she's staying,' snapped Blue as he swung sharply into Tiger's driveway, sending the neatly raked gravel flying up in a mini tidal wave over the group of paparazzi camped outside. Blue yanked up the handbrake and cut the engine with a loud 'phut'.

'Oh I didn't mean – oh I'm just trying to be supportive, darling, anything that makes you unhappy makes me unhappy too.' Richie squeezed Blue's knee. 'I – I really didn't realise Tiger was in such a bad way. Honestly I didn't. She might lose her show . . . and after everything you . . . Jeez. Sorry.' Blue looked at Richie's big brown eyes. He leaned in for a kiss, but instead of the usual butterflies, he felt a faintly nagging feeling in the pit of his stomach.

'Come on then, Rex, let's get that champagne open,' urged Sienna, arranging Danish pastries on a platter in Tiger's kitchen.

'Bit early for you, babe?' replied Rex, waving a plate of croissants in the direction of the radio crew who were testing their mics.

'It's not for me, it's for Tiger,' she sighed.

'Oh yeah? Not trying to get her drunk in the morning are you?'

''Course. She needs oiling up. I imagine she's nervous.'

'Well maybe . . . but you'd better not give it to her in front of Lewis or he'll think you're trying to throw a spanner in the works,' said Rex provocatively. Sienna looked up from the artistically arranged plate of pastries.

'Now whatever gives you that idea?'

'Just saying.' He shrugged, before wandering over to talk to the radio crew.

'Coo-ee!' came the unmistakable call of Blue as he clattered through the front door with Richie in tow. 'Where is she then?'

'Who?' said Sienna, sullenly.

'Ooh, Nefertiti,' replied Blue as he stood in the kitchen doorway. Sienna looked up blankly.

'Your sister, dumbo, who else?' he retorted.

'Oh. Upstairs doing her make-up. Although why anyone

needs make-up for a radio show is anyone's business.'

'Because she's Tiger Starr, that's why. You could take a tip or two from her you know, and then maybe *you'll* be glamorous one day.'

Sienna gasped out loud at Blue's rudeness.

'Richie?' barked Blue. 'Stay down here, babes, I'm taking these up to her ladyship. This interview shouldn't take long. Half an hour tops.' With that he flounced off up the stairs.

'Is he always that bitchy?' asked Sienna, looking at Richie.

'Oh, er – I wasn't listening, sorry,' replied Richie awkwardly.

'Come in, don't be a stranger,' offered Sienna. Richie hovered outside the door.

'No, no, er, it's okay I'll wait here.'

'Don't be silly, come in, have a pastry.' Sienna held up the plates for Richie to see. He glanced at them before sweeping his eyes round the room. He seemed to recoil slightly as his eyes settled on the radio crew with Rex chatting to them cheerfully.

'Thanks but I ate breakfast. In fact, I think I left something in the car. Tell Blue I'm outside, thanks.'

'What? He'll be ages . . .' But Richie had already slipped out of the door.

'Peculiar boy,' muttered Sienna, deciding to indulge in a flute of champagne after all.

* * *

Blue knew something was wrong the second he opened the bedroom door. Lewis was in there with Tiger and the body language was flashing red alert. They were on opposite sides of the room and Tiger looked rigid as a frozen leg of lamb, with the dog clamped firmly in her lap.

'Ahh, just in time,' said Lewis sternly. Well, he seems normal so far, thought Blue, draping his armloads of dresses on the back of a beautiful antique armchair.

'Are you in on this too?' asked Lewis quietly, bobbing on his heels with his hands held behind his back.

'*Quoi?*' asked Blue, innocently.

'*This!*' roared Lewis, holding aloft a pile of pink letters. Gravy jumped down and ran under the bed for cover.

'Ah.'

'And when were you both thinking of coming clean?' Lewis hissed through clenched teeth.

'Well, Tiger − you see − er . . .' Blue was tongue tied as he tried to think of how to explain without dropping Tiger in the shit that she had pretty much concealed them from him too.

'What the FUCK were you both thinking hiding this from me?' Lewis scolded. 'Now it all becomes clear, all this . . . all this *madness*, the ridiculous behaviour.'

'Okay, but how did you find − I mean—' started Blue.

'Oh! I only found out because stupid over here asked me to fetch Gravy's new cricket jumper for the interview; although why on earth the fucking DOG needs an OUTFIT for RADIO!' Lewis bellowed, turning puce before composing himself again. 'And then what did I find stuffed in Gravy's drawer? Oh piles of the stuff! Now let me see, "I know your secret." "I know what underwear you have on today." "I know your secret" again, err, "I have a bullet with your name on it," oh and another "I know your secret." Want me to go on? There's plenty more!' The room fell silent. Gravy peered from under the bed. Tiger fiddled with her hair.

'Aaaatchoo!' Lewis sneezed. 'Tiger?' he whispered urgently, crouching down to look her in the eye. 'Now listen to me, lady. I need to know what skeletons you have in that fur-lined closet of yours. What's this secret, huh? If you have even so much as an *arm bone*—' he paused for dramatic effect, '—you tell me right now. For your own safety. I *need* to know. Got it? Now's your chance.' A deadly hush fell on the room. Tiger looked up and opened her mouth. Nothing came out. She looked away. Lewis sneezed again.

'Right, I'll take that as an all clear. Right?' said Lewis in a low voice. 'Now, I shall take care of the phantom letter writer *my* way, you hear? *Nobody* threatens you, hoax or not, and gets away with it.'

'L-l-lewis. . .'

'No buts. Aaàtchoo! Oh that bloody dog. Aaatchoo! Right, I'm going to get rid of the radio crew, you're in no fit state for publicity today.'

'Oh, b-but Sienna and—' started Tiger.

'I'll take care of them, I'll take care of it all. I wish you'd let me do that a bit more often. Aaaatchoo! Christ. Blue, fetch me a tissue, please. Aaatchoo!' Blue hurried from the room dutifully.

Within twenty minutes the radio crew had packed and gone, with the promise of an exclusive live interview from Vegas as recompense. A moody Rex followed out the door with Sienna soon after, exchanging measured hostile glares with Lewis. Blue was confused that Richie seemed to have disappeared altogether and set about messaging him.

Tiger came down into the parlour sheepishly once she knew everyone had gone. She padded across the room to the minibar in her mink-lined slippers, and started to rinse a Martini glass with vermouth, breaking the deafening silence with her clattering.

'You want one?' she asked, waving the bottle of Tanqueray over at Lewis, who was stretched out in an armchair, studying the ceiling. He regarded her through narrowed eyes.

'Oh what the hell, it's lunchtime. Scotch if you've got it,' he grumbled.

'Coming up.'

'Tiger.' Lewis paused, deep in thought. 'Tiger, I'm worried about you. I've never seen you like this. Can I be honest?'

Tiger didn't reply. Lewis continued regardless.

'Tiger, this is getting too messy. "I know your secret." What's that all about? There's no smoke without fire you know. The Americans know something's going on. I've calmed them down. Put them off the scent. But we can't have any more upsets. You know you can talk to me if there's something you need to get out in the open. I can help you. We trust each other, right?' Tiger simply busied herself pouring out a Scotch.

'Look. I'll say it again. I'm worried about you,' continued Lewis, 'I – I want to come and live with you for a bit.' Tiger dropped the ice tongs with a clang and looked up.

'What? Here?'

'Yes, here. Just for a while. I just want to keep an eye on things – aaatchoo! That bloody dog.'

'Well, I don't think that's really necessary. Blue's here.'

'Correct, and you've already been hiding things together. No, I need to be here. We'll just keep our heads low while I think about how – aaatchooo! We'll just camp out here until – aaatchoo! Hang on, I just need some fresh air for a second.' Lewis jumped up and went to the front door. As he opened it a wall of paparazzi clicked and flashed frantically in front of his face. Lewis slammed the door shut immediately and returned to the parlour, blinking.

'Okay, scrap that. I'm taking you out of here.'

'Huh?'

'A break. We need to get away from this circus for a few days.'

Chapter 24

'Ooh a Sunseeker Trideck if I'm not mistaken!' squealed Georgia, barging past from the rear and running across the gangplank. 'Bagsy the owner's stateroom!' she yelled behind her as Blue and Tiger looked at each other with wide eyes and open mouths.

'Since when was Georgia a yacht expert!' giggled Tiger.

'Intriguing!' winked Blue, mincing towards the ropes. Tiger sighed and gave him a big bear hug from behind.

'Oh darling, the sun is cheering me up already,' she declared. 'I'm feeling great. Just feel the heat! Let Georgia have whatever room she likes – after all, this was Lewis' idea. He's the one who has to put up with her gobby mouth, anyway, so god knows he deserves *some* perks, eh!'

'Ha, yeah, poor Lewis!' laughed Blue. 'Come on, darlings, all aboard the pleasure boat!' he shouted back at Sienna, Rex and Lewis who trailed behind lazily, the two men gassing about last night's big fight on Sky. 'And fuck Richie, wherever he may be,' declared Blue triumphantly over at Tiger, who was standing eyeing up the gangplank.

'That's the spirit, darling,' she agreed supportively. 'It's his loss. Fancy just disappearing like that. Look what he's missing. Silly boy,' she chuckled as she daintily slipped off her mules ready to board the boat.

'Oh, Tiger. Oh, look at this vision, my word! Oh, I think I'm over Richie already!' Tiger looked up to see the most fantastic specimen approaching. He stood a little taller than her, all broad in the chest and chiselled in the face, with a killer tan, and salt-and-pepper hair in short thick waves under his Captain's hat.

'Hello there, Ms Starr! Welcome!'

'Hi there.' Tiger beamed, proffering a manicured hand.

'I'm Captain Robert Crowe, your skipper for the weekend.' He smiled, deep laughter lines showing around his eyes.

'Superb! Pleased to meet you Captain Crowe!' she replied, unable to stop herself beaming from ear to ear as she allowed her eyes to roam over his muscular sturdy bulk.

'Robert, please. Much obliged to have you on board the *Jezebelle*. Let me help you. I see one of your guests has arrived already.'

'Hmm, that'll be Georgia. Hard to miss.'

'Georgia?' repeated Robert, a tiny flash of amusement registering in his eyes, 'Indeed, madam. Oh and might I add I'm a big fan of your work.' Blushing a little, Tiger took Robert's strong hand for guidance and tottered up the gangplank on to the luxury yacht, letting the fresh air fill her lungs and the sunshine fill her heart. 'Oh Blue, what a day for sightseeing!' she trilled behind her bliss-fully.

By lunchtime the aperitifs were well under way. Everyone had staked their claim on the cabins and were now up on the sun deck sinking green apple Martinis and shovelling back deliciously plump caviar on warm blinis. Georgia had changed into her teeniest white hot pants and highest strappy sandals and was leaning over the deck, sloshing her drink everywhere and loudly acquainting herself with everyone in the marina. Tiger, channelling Liz Taylor and wearing a thigh-skimming cream kaftan with her hair piled up under a chic turban and arms loaded with enough gold to sink the yacht, hadn't exactly been thrilled about Georgia coming on the trip for the reason that she hadn't wanted her finding out too much about what was happening in Tiger's life. However, deep down, she knew she couldn't really begrudge Georgia's presence; after all it was only natural Lewis would want to bring his girlfriend.

Lewis in turn was mighty peeved that Rex had to come, but he had thought it essential that Sienna attend to cheer her sister up; if Rex had to be part of the deal as Sienna's boyfriend then so be it. The reality was, Sienna was fuming that she had to endure a long weekend with her charlatan of a so-called 'sister', but knew that she would have to comply to keep Rex happy, who, incidentally, had been particularly enthusiastic about coming. Sienna sensed the honeymoon period of their relationship was well and truly over, so keeping Rex happy and entertained was top of her priority list. Besides, if Rex thought for one minute he was having a weekend in Tiger's presence unsupervised, he had another think coming. Sienna would be watching the pair like a hawk.

Standing on deck in a tiny black tube dress and nothing else but her long pins and bare feet, Sienna craftily eyed up Georgia in her equally revealing hot pants, unsure as to whether she was a potential rival, or a kindred spirit. Sienna suddenly became self conscious about the extra few pounds she was carrying of late. The appearance of a few curves meant she was in no way as skinny as Georgia any more. Rex seemed to be more turned on by her new curves, however, so if he was happy, so was Sienna. As she mused she hovered at Rex's elbow and made a concerted effort to keep herself on the opposite side of the deck to Tiger at all times. It was an easy task since, unbeknownst to Sienna, Tiger was keeping well away from Rex in every effort not to torment herself with the sight of him with her sister. Strangely, he seemed to be spending more time gassing to Lewis about business, boxing and broads, leaving Sienna dithering by his side awkwardly.

'So what's the plan for lunch, guys?' asked Blue, slightly listlessly. There was no doubt, thought Tiger, that Blue was unusually subdued. She guessed he was still smarting that Richie had stood him up. Despite the bravado, Tiger knew him to be a sensitive soul; in a drunken moment he had hinted that Richie might be 'the one'. Tiger suddenly felt overwhelmed with guilt as she stood there that she had chastised Blue for holding back. Instead she had encouraged him to grab the bull by the horns and throw himself into the relationship. After all, Richie had seemed so sweet, and genuinely enamoured. A girl could tell these things. Now she felt like kicking herself. She hated to see Blue suffering. Little did she know that Blue had his own waves of guilt to deal with, too.

'I vote we go to 55 for lunch,' suggested Georgia.

'We have a perfectly good chef on board in case you hadn't noticed,' sighed Lewis, helping himself to another cocktail as the waiting staff circulated with a tray of fresh Mint Juleps.

'Nah mate, let's get straight over to Nikki beach and check out the laydees!' roared Rex, rubbing his hands together. This was met with firm disapproval by both Sienna and Georgia. Blue quietly watched the ensuing heated debate unfold. Normally he would have steamed in with his queeny wit and whipped the afternoon into shape; but for now, he just sat quietly. He couldn't even sip at his Martini, for the truth was, his stomach was turning somersaults.

Paranoia and foreboding washed over him as he recounted all the things he had disclosed to Richie . . . those he could recall disclosing at any rate; private things about Tiger, secrets that nobody else knew. It was only because Richie had seemed so in awe of her, a real fan and supporter, and Blue had been so worried about Tiger, like he couldn't get through to her. And Richie seemed to get him drunk all the time too, and of course, three

Martinis and Blue's barriers always came crashing down. Well, he was kicking himself now. Tiger would be mortified that he had broken her confidence. Where the bloody hell *was* Richie anyway? He wasn't even returning his calls. Blue tried to tell himself it was all just a coincidence and it would blow over, but for now, the nagging feeling was here to stay.

'Oh come on, Lewis, we can do the Italy trip tomorrow; let's party today. We've got four more days remember. Let's do lunch now and hit the clubs later. Tiger'll get us the VIP treatment at the Caves du Roy, won't you, babes?' simpered Georgia with effortless insincerity.

'Oh, actually I was hoping to relax today. Can't we go clubbing tomorrow maybe?'

'Typical, selfish bitch,' chuntered Sienna a little too loudly.

'Excuse me?' countered Blue.

'Oh nothing. Bit of a cough,' replied Sienna, clutching Rex possessively.

'Oh. I could have sworn I heard you being really *fucking* rude about your sister. Must be going deaf.'

'Oh fuck off, Blue.'

'Sorry, dear, I don't do requests,' he bit back.

'Oh stop it both of you!' snapped Tiger, her fingers pressed to her temples. 'Look, we don't have to do everything together. You guys go off and paint the town red. I just need to rest for today and enjoy the sun. The crew will look after me. We can have our own party,' she laughed.

'Yeah, I saw how you were looking at the skipper earlier,' mumbled Sienna. Blue shot her a filthy look and minced off towards his cabin, exhaling loudly.

'Okay, that's settled,' said Lewis, taking command. 'I'll take you out for lunch, Georgia, if that's what you want. Anyone else is welcome to come. Let's give Tiger some time to herself. Maybe we can eat together on the boat tonight.'

'Fine, fabulous.' Tiger smiled, relieved. 'In that case, please excuse me while I slip into my bikini. Have a nice lunch, guys.' She gave a little wave and disappeared in the direction of her cabin.

'Er, actually I think I may stay on the boat for the afternoon,' announced Rex suddenly. Sienna looked infuriated.

'Hmm, you changed your mind at the whiff of Tiger in a two-piece,' she said cattily. 'In that case I may as well stay on the boat too. This caviar is too delicious to miss anyway,' she added, clearly determined not to let Rex out of her sight. When Tiger returned ten minutes later in her gold bikini and clutching a well-thumbed trashy novel she was somewhat surprised to find Rex and Sienna obviously settled in for the day on the sun deck, a pregnant silence hanging between them. If a hundred degrees of heat could ever feel frosty, it did now. Tiger shrugged, released her fabulous breasts from her bikini top and stretched out on her lounger, the very picture of a goddess, only looking up from her book to turn up the sound system or order more champagne and canapés.

* * *

The rain poured down, casting a blanket of gloom over the grey cobbled streets. Lance de Brett checked the street name up on the soot-coloured brick wall and pulled up his trench coat collar tightly about his neck. He hastily made his way towards the illuminated beacon of a pub sign up ahead; swinging noisily on its rusty bracket in the wind. Typical Irish summer, he thought ruefully. Lance tucked himself behind a table in the cosy pub. Even though he'd rather perch at the bar, he knew that would feel too much like he was meeting a blind date. He checked in his bag for his Dictaphone and quickly sifted through the photocopies in his folder. He pulled one out. Emma O'Connell, née Ryan. She was a knockout girl in the photo; slim, blonde, angelic looking. It had been taken in her last year of school, when she won an Avon beauty contest at sixteen. It made the local papers. Lance had no idea what she looked like now; he didn't care. She had information about Tiger Starr that he suspected would rock the boat in every sense. He hoped this was what Sienna was looking for.

The happy group tucked into a fabulous *dégustation* menu on the deck by twilight. Sienna had evidently decided Georgia was worth having as a pal, and the pair seemed to be giggling at everyone and everything. By the time the bottle of Chateau D'Yquem had been polished off with dessert, everyone was in decidedly high spirits. Captain Crowe joined them over coffee and it was unanimously decided that they would wait until the following evening to take an overnight passage to Sardinia so the ladies could squeeze in some shopping during the daytime.

Tiger felt contented and relaxed as she waved off Sienna and Georgia, who were heading off to the Byblos for a few hours' cocktails and clubbing together. Lewis and Blue were happily chatting about Saville Row tailors and comparing notes. Tiger closed her eyes and leaned back in her chair, drinking in the sounds of the cicadas and the lapping water, tinted with the sounds of chattering revellers, clinking glasses and the muffled thump of music. She felt truly peaceful as the warm summer's breeze caressed her skin and the faint aromas of sea salt and lavender wafted on the air.

'I haven't seen you this chilled out since . . . well since . . .' started Rex softly.

'I know what you're going to say,' said Tiger, eyes still closed. 'Let's just leave it as history, huh?'

'Not since we woke up together in my bed!' finished Rex.

Tiger snapped her eyes open and her face had clouded.

'I said let's leave it,' she said curtly, her body stiffening. 'Thank you, Lewis, for bringing us here,' she said loudly, terminating her exchange with Rex. Lewis and Blue smiled over at Tiger, with Rex continuing to stare at her hotly. 'What a lovely break, I feel much better. Brilliant idea, Lewis.'

'Hear hear,' said Blue, holding up his champagne flute.

'To good times!' he said, clinking glasses with Lewis. Underneath the table, Rex grabbed Tiger's hand. She tensed. He held tight until she relented, before tenderly stroking the underside of her wrist. He knew that was her weak spot.

'To good times,' he murmured softly. Their hands intertwined for a brief moment, and Tiger's eyes locked with his as they clinked glasses, a slight blush spreading across her cheeks. Lewis watched the exchange with a heavy heart.

The rain continued to pour. Lance swigged back his Guinness in the comfort of the pub and mulled over the fruits of his trip. His Dictaphone still sat there on the table; only now bearing the story of Emma O'Connell, Poppy Adams' erstwhile school friend. It was fair to say Emma was twice the woman she was in her beauty contest photograph. Maybe even three times. But boy did she sing like a songbird. The look of shock on her face when she learnt that her bookish, nerdy schoolfriend Poppy Adams was 'The' Tiger Starr; as she continually refered to her. Lance wasn't sure by the end of the interview if what she felt was bitterness, jealousy, or a grudging admiration for Tiger. No matter. He had the story, and he looked forward to transcribing the interview.

Lance now wondered how best to deliver his material to Sienna. He had school photographs, yearbooks, newsletters, public records and an interview. Following the trail of Coco, Tiger's infamous grandma, had led to a dead end. However, after Sienna had provided him with as much background as she could – her parents' names, mother's maiden name, all the dates and places of birth she could remember, it had been relatively simple. The internet made things so easy these days. Sienna could have done it herself really, he laughed to himself. But now he couldn't just give it to her on a plate of course. No, that would be too easy. He'd just give her some signposts. She needed to put in some of the work herself if he was going to let her take a cut of the money that this story would earn. Sienna needed to learn how to do the job properly. Lance didn't think she'd like the information he'd uncovered very much, but if she was so keen to play with fire then she would have to learn the hard way like everybody else, that she might just get burnt.

Lance decided he would send a nice little package to arrive at the Hunter Gatherers' office in time for Sienna's return from St Tropez. He had come to Dublin yesterday feeling a little kick at the thought of adding his own nail to Tiger's coffin after the way she had insisted on keeping their relationship quiet for seven years under the guise of 'professional complications', and wanting to wait for a special moment to make it public; only to then reject his offer of marriage. She had turned peculiar at his declaration of love, and had thrown the words 'intimacy issues' around a lot. Lance had thought that was just bullshit. He was a total mess for months after. But Tiger hadn't got off lightly – boy, had Lance wreaked his revenge through his reviews. He was determined to be a ghost that haunted her for years. Now he had the means to hurt Tiger in the way she had hurt him, and publicly; the way he knew she would hate most. And with Sienna's help, she'd never know that he was in any way behind the story that was going to ruin her.

Lance was a tough guy, but he had to admit it had been an unsettling experience talking to Emma O'Connell about someone he had loved so much and thought he had known so well for seven long years. Now he knew he'd been wrong about Tiger all along. She was simply a low-class tart who had been leaving trails of discarded men behind her for years, starting with some local boy at fourteen. Intimacy issues indeed! Promiscuous little whore, more like. The thought that Sienna would, perversely, be the one to initiate the exposé with just a few careful prods from Lance was almost too juicy and too exciting to wait for . . . and he had ringside seats. He rubbed his hands together and tucked the Dictaphone into his inside pocket, patted it affectionately, and ordered another Guinness.

'Ohhhh, I think I'm gonna be sick,' Georgia could be heard moaning loudly from the dining room the next morning. Within seconds she came staggering on to the deck, bleary eyed, wearing only tousled hair and one of Lewis' shirts, which barely skimmed her knickerless crotch.

Rex whooped with laughter as she lurched onto the main deck and hurled up her breakfast over the side.

'I'd take an educated guess that's not seasickness, babes,' laughed Rex, grabbing a satisfying eyeful as she bent over.

'Not when the boat's in the port, no,' huffed Georgia, righting herself and collapsing onto a lounger, trying in vain to smooth down her dishevelled platinum bob. Seeing Rex leering across at her, she mischievously stretched out her lethally long legs and slowly propped them up on a neighbouring chair, fully intending to torment him with a whisp of a view of pussy.

'What time did you get in last night then?' Rex asked.

'Last night? Huh!' came Blue's voice as he sashayed onto the deck, clutching a plate of croissants. 'You mean you didn't hear them clattering around at five this morning?' he said, raising an eyebrow in Georgia's direction. 'Good god, girl, I can see the black hole of Calcutta from here. Put it away, will you!'

'You're just jealous,' she mocked cheekily, crossing her legs.

'Yeah I know,' agreed Blue. 'So did I miss anything? Any fit men there last night?'

'Ooohh . . .' Georgia sprung up again and hung her head over the side of the boat, panting, last night's myriad cocktails threatening to haunt her again. Rex and Blue couldn't help but laugh.

'Misty? Is that you?' came a disembodied voice from

the harbour. 'Misty? Is that really you?' Georgia came away from the side, eyes wide and skin white as a sheet.

'I know it's you up there! Misty! It's Carrie!' Rex and Blue looked at each other and mouthed simultaneously, 'Misty?' Georgia took a deep breath and casually sauntered over to the side of the yacht.

'Hey, Carrie! What a surprise. You're still knocking around then?'

'Yeah, baby! Business is booming!'

'Shhhh! Keep it down, bloody hell!'

'Sorry! Listen, we thought you were gone for good! We've all missed your bony ass. The high rollers still ask after you, you know.'

'Yeah yeah, keep it down. How come you're out and about so early anyway? You're not usually up before lunch.'

'I was just nosing, I heard a rumour that Tiger Starr was on this boat and I was hoping to get her autograph. And then I see you instead! Dumb rumours as usual. But how cool to see you again! Like fate!'

'Yeah, fate.'

'So who's up there? Room for one more?'

'Er, not exactly. Tell you what, I'll meet you for a coffee and we can catch up. Usual place, in say, forty minutes?'

'Cool. *À bientôt, ma cherie.*'

Georgia turned back to the deck to see Blue and Rex looking up at her incredulously.

'What?'

'Oh nothing . . . Misty.' Rex stifled a laugh.

'Oh don't be ridiculous, Carrie's an old friend, she's er – a trolly dolly. Does a lot of flights to Nice. Misty's just her nickname for me. We all have them, don't we?'

'Do we?' asked Rex, looking at Blue.

'Well, I hear yours is "King Kong",' sniggered Blue.

'I'm flattered!' said Rex, looking rather chuffed.

'Oh I can see you're both in a stupid mood, I'll see you later.' With that, Georgia flounced off in the direction of her cabin. Blue and Rex exchanged knowing looks before dissolving into sniggers again.

'Are you gonna tell Lewis she used to be a hooker, or shall I?' asked Rex after a few minutes of general hilarity.

'Oh don't. We mustn't say anything.'

'What? Don't you know anything about Lewis? He'd be spitting if he thought we knew something he doesn't. I have to work with him remember. He's a nightmare at the best of times, let alone when he's pissed off about something.'

'Maybe he's already acquainted with Misty.' Blue shrugged, stuffing warm croissant into his mouth.

'Lewis? I'm not sure that's his style!' laughed Rex.

'True . . . he doesn't strike me as someone who pays for it. But you must be able to tell from the technique in bed or something, surely?'

'Nah, you can't tell. Some hookers can be quite boring in the sack actually, too concerned about what they look like from every angle. Like they think you're secretly a movie mogul and you're gonna leap up and give them a part in your next film and make them a star or something. Either that or they're bored shitless.' Rex realised Blue was staring at him, taken aback. He reddened a little, realising what he had said. 'Oh come on, every bloke's tried a bit of brass at least once in his . . .' He trailed off, sensing Blue's eyebrow couldn't arch any higher.

'Well, this man certainly hasn't!'

'Only because you're a queen! I tell you what, I wouldn't mind giving Georgia a go.' Rex smirked provocatively.

'What?'

'Yeah, you know, see if she goes faster when there's money in her box!' Rex fell about laughing.

'You're appalling. Well, I think she's been riding Lewis hard.'

'I bet she has!'

'Not like that! I mean, rinsing him for money, clothes, apparently moved in to his apartment after a month.'

'Hmm. I know the feeling, mate. Poor Lewis.'

'Ahh,' sighed Blue, smacking his lips. 'Who knew this weekend would be so entertaining? Georgia "Misty" Atlanta, bless your cotton socks!'

Shortly before dinner that night the yacht left the harbour and powered off in the direction of Sardinia. There was a tangible air of expectancy as everyone eagerly anticipated the delights that would be waiting for them when they arrived on the shores of the beautiful Italian island tomorrow. Blue had done several fashion shoots on location there over the years and was relishing the thought of visiting for pleasure rather than work. It would be a treat after his exhausting day of shopping and sunbathing with Tiger. Much to their delight old actor Elliott Walkern had popped his head up from the neighbouring yacht that afternoon whilst the pair were having a pitstop on deck, and he had invited Tiger and Blue over for a civilised teatime cocktail. They had a blast with Elliott and his fellow movie star pals, but left swiftly after the salty old dog started chasing Tiger round the sunloungers. Blue had now worked up quite an appetite, and his mouth was watering at the thought of the fresh lobster which was about to be served.

'Evening all!' Tiger said brightly, sweeping into the dining room. An audible gasp escaped into the air.

'Oh wow, don't you look fresh,' breathed Blue, taking in her outfit; a stunning taupe body-con number that clung to her curves and offset her light olive tan, teamed with her favourite skyscraper Sergio Rossi heels and even more gold jewellery. She had her hair in Raquel Welch mode – voluminous waves and tumbling down her back. 'God, if I was straight,' Blue muttered, leaning back in his chair. There was a moment of silence as homage was paid to the vision of high voltage sixties Riviera glamour. Sienna kicked Rex under the table and he closed his gaping mouth.

'So! I hope we all had a lovely day.' Tiger smiled, bracelets jangling and clinking as she pulled her chair up to the dining table between Lewis and Blue. Georgia and Sienna sniggered by way of reply.

'Something wrong?' asked Tiger, shaking out her napkin and laying it across her lap.

'Oh the twins here have been thick as thieves all day,' groaned Rex.

'Hmmm. Best friends now eh?' Tiger smiled. 'Good, that's nice.'

The girls giggled again. Tiger shrugged and daintily sipped her aperitif.

'Oh, Georgia has had quite a day of seeing friends, haven't you love?' Blue smirked. Georgia's sniggers evaporated rapidly.

'Eeeeuww!' squealed Blue, suddenly leaping up from the table.

'Sorry, darling, I must have just knocked it over by accident,' said Georgia smugly, patting the spilt ice-cold champagne roughly from Blue's crotch.

'Thanks, I think I can see to that myself,' he replied, snatching the napkin away from her.

'Okay you two, enough. Let's just enjoy our supper shall we?' suggested Lewis, looking at Georgia mysteriously as the waiters paraded into the dining room with an array of silver salvers.

A fine feast of lobster, dressed crab and brandied gambas was rapidly devoured, followed by a selection of digestifs. Lewis eased himself into the full Cognac menu, and Rex excused himself to go to the bathroom. Sienna and Georgia embarked on a giggling stream of gossip while Blue went up to the wheel room for a little navigation demonstration from Captain Crowe. Feeling like she had energy to burn, Tiger rose and crossed to the saloon, changing the music to something a little more lively.

'Oh good idea, let's have a dance!' said Georgia, jumping up. 'That's if I can stay up straight while the bloody boat's moving.'

'Cor, I thought it was me! I thought I'd just had too much brandy! I feel so nauseous!' remarked Sienna.

'Nope, this boat's definitely bumpy, babes,' laughed Georgia. 'Anyone have any seasickness pills?'

'Sure, I'll go and fetch them,' offered Tiger, disappearing off upstairs as Georgia whacked up the volume.

Tiger hummed to the music as she tottered up to her cabin, the thumping beat still loud from the floor below. Now where did I put those tablets, she wondered to herself, surveying the room. Finally her eyes settled on her Chanel tote, which contained everything within its Tardis-like capacity. As she bent over and rummaged in the huge bag she felt two firm hands circling her waist.

'Oh Blue! Stop it, that tickles,' she laughed, scrabbling in her bag for the packet of tablets.

'I thought you'd be pleased to see me,' murmured Rex in Tiger's ear as he bent over her. She froze.

'Oh Rex, behave. Get off, I'm looking for something.'

'Aren't we all, babes,' he replied, tightening his grip and inhaling the sweet scent of Tiger's perfume. She wriggled to free herself but he just pushed her, face first onto the bed.

'What are you playing at?' protested Tiger, laughing uneasily and twisting herself round to face him. He wasn't laughing. She felt faint as he pushed himself up close and her heart leapt involuntarily as she felt his breath on her neck. He lay on top of her. No words passed between them for a moment. Tiger felt her heart pounding as he leaned in slowly, very slowly, to kiss her. She whipped her head away to one side, but not before his lips had brushed hers softly. Her red lipstick left a soft smear across his cheek. Closing her eyes she felt his manly bulk on her, his rock-hard cock prodding her through her dress. She felt wet between the thighs and almost dizzy with desire as she lay still for a moment. Then with a burst of strength she jerked up and pushed him away angrily. Rex staggered back but immediately lunged in again and grabbed both Tiger's arms, holding them firmly up above her head and pinning her to the bed, staring down at her with eyes of steel.

'Wooh!' squealed Georgia, staggering around the saloon downstairs to the thumping music.

'Oh I feel sick,' complained Sienna, holding on to the wall.

'Oh just drink more, you'll get used to it. I've done this loads of times. Either drink or shag your way through it. Come on, Lewis, baby, join in the fun! Where's Rex anyway?'

'I mean it, Georgia, I feel really queasy,' said Sienna

miserably. Lewis downed his Cognac and stood up. 'I'm going to help Tiger find those tablets for you,' he said kindly, guiding Sienna to a chair. 'You just sit still and watch the moon out of the window. Don't take your eyes off it okay? It should help with the sickness.'

'Okay,' said Sienna, her face now a terrible shade of green. Lewis headed straight for Tiger's cabin, trying to stave off the sinking feeling in his gut. He had tried to give Rex the benefit of the doubt this weekend, but he had seen the electricity flying between him and Tiger. He trusted Tiger knew better than to even think about rekindling the flame.

'Rex, this is stupid,' snapped Tiger. 'It's not funny any more. Stop playing games.'

'This isn't a game. I know you feel the same. Don't fight it.'

'I feel *nothing*! Get off me! My *sister* is downstairs. How could you do this to her?'

'Sienna? But what about us?'

'There is no '*us*'. You have Sienna, remember.'

'Maybe I don't want her. I want a woman, a strong woman. I want *you*. I had you for a moment, I want you back.'

'How dare you! You made your choice!'

'No, *you* made it for us, remember?' Rex hissed, tightening his grip on Tiger's wrists.

'I had to, I – Sienna – you wouldn't understand. Anyway,

you moved on quick enough. You could have chosen someone who wasn't *family*!'

'Sienna means nothing!'

'How can you say that! You made your bed, now lie on it! That girl adores you. If you hurt her, I'll kill you. Blood is thicker than water.'

'Oh listen to Don Corleone here.' Rex laughed mockingly and simply pushed his knees apart further, so that Tiger's legs spread wider. He shoved his erection down on her. Tiger struggled to banish sickening flashbacks of Ed Rogers pinning her down from her mind. A smear of white powder trickled from Rex's nose. Tiger felt rage welling inside her.

'What are you *doing*!' spat Tiger through clenched teeth. 'You're off your face! And while Sienna is downstairs!'

'Ha! She's no Snow White I can assure you.' Tiger felt sick to the stomach at his words.

'Whatever she is, she's only metres away right now. She worships you. Don't break her heart.'

'What do you care? She doesn't speak too highly of you.'

'I beg your pardon?'

'Oh, I get to hear all sorts,' he laughed, lunging to kiss Tiger as she struggled and bucked wildly to free herself.

The door to Tiger's cabin was ajar as Lewis approached. As he pushed it open, Sienna came panting up the spiral staircase.

'Wait for me, Lewis, have you seen Rex any . . .' She stopped mid sentence as she saw a flash of Tiger and Rex in the cabin. Lewis pulled the door shut immediately, but it was too late. A nano-second of Rex in his unmistakable striped shirt rolling around in apparent ecstasy with Tiger was enough. Sienna's face crumpled in slow motion, before she pelted back down the stairs in floods of tears. Lewis felt a red mist descend in front of his eyes. Barging through the door to the cabin he flew across the room and grabbed Rex by the shirt collar, pulling him roughly to his feet.

'Oh thank god!' puffed Tiger panic stricken, immediately rolling from underneath Rex and catching her breath.

'Get out there and explain yourself to your girlfriend,' snarled Lewis in Rex's face, pushing him roughly against the wall, one hand up at his throat.

'That woman's a fucking animal!' roared Rex, pointing at Tiger. 'She couldn't keep her hands off me!'

'You bastard!' Tiger gasped loudly from the bed, anxiously wringing her bruised wrists. In a second Lewis registered the lipstick smeared across Rex's cheek and dropped him without a word. He looked down at him on the floor with disdain, the tic starting in his cheek, before turning to Tiger, looking horrified as she sat on the bed heaving for breath.

'You stupid—'

'He's lying!'

'You stupid bitch!' Lewis growled.

'He jumped on me!' Tiger wailed as Rex slipped from the room unnoticed.

'You have to have everybody, don't you!' Lewis cried out, flying towards her and grabbing her roughly by the arms as she tried to leap up. 'Everyone has to fall under your spell!'

'No! You've got it all wrong! He crept up on me and pinned me down!' she squealed, struggling to free herself but falling back on the bed. 'Get off me! Let me go, you animal! You're just as bad as Rex!'

'No, *you're* the animal! I saw how you looked at each other after dinner last night! He's your sister's boyfriend! You're just acting like a bitch on heat!'

'No! You've got it so wrong! Don't be like all the others!'

'Like hell have I got it wrong! I gave you everything! I gave up my work, my life—'

'How DARE you!' screamed Tiger hysterically, thrashing about and managing to wriggle a hand free. She brought her talons slashing down across Lewis' cheek.

'Just let me go!' yelled Sienna into the wind, struggling against Rex and Georgia's grip as they tried to sedate her by shoving a Valium in her mouth.

'Don't do this, babes,' said Rex in a low voice.

'I'm jumping overboard, leave me alone!' cried Sienna, tears running down her cheeks as she collapsed to the deck, convulsing with sobs.

'I'm going to get Lewis,' said Georgia gravely. 'We have

to turn this boat round.' Rex grunted and turned back to Sienna.

'Babe, what you saw – she just jumped on me, I was fighting her off. You know I only have eyes for you. Trust me,' pleaded Rex as Sienna bawled into her dress.

'I want to go home!'

'Babe, we're in the middle of the ocean.'

'I'm swimming home then!' Sienna cried as she struggled to stand up. Rex yanked her down again.

'Come on, babe. Let's just get to Sardinia and I'll take you straight home.

'But tonight—'

'Forget tonight, let's just lock ourselves in the cabin. You don't have to see anyone.'

'Well . . .'

'I've got a couple of grams on me. We could have our own party. Come on, babe, you're with me on this aren't you?'

Georgia heard the commotion before she saw it. Tiger and Lewis were screaming and yelping, and Georgia could hear things being thrown. As she peered through the crack in the cabin door, she watched the pair fighting like animals; rolling around, groaning, hissing at each other, pinning each other to the bed. With one last howl, Lewis flung a sobbing Tiger heavily on to the floor and stormed towards the door. Georgia backed into the corridor before freezing as Lewis slammed his way out of the room. Seeing her standing before him, Lewis pushed her out of the way and he staggered back downstairs, his face and neck covered in smears of make-up, scratches and bite marks. If she hadn't just witnessed the terrible brawl with her own eyes, Georgia wouldn't have been able to tell if Lewis had just been fighting or fucking.

Georgia followed him anxiously down to the saloon. At that moment Blue came wobbling down the stairs. 'Ooh that was fascinating,' he gushed, flopping down onto a sofa. 'I need to get me a Captain.' Sensing an atmosphere he looked round and saw Rex huddling a hysterical Sienna off to their cabin, and a shocked Georgia staring over at Lewis who was standing out on deck, visibly shaking.

'Did I miss something?'

By 3 a.m. Georgia woke from her fitful sleep and realised she was alone in her cabin. Great. She had every right to be pissed off at Lewis and Tiger, but everyone else seemed to be acting like the victim in all this. She rolled out of bed and padded out to find Lewis. Predictably he was out on the deck, a large whisky in his hands.

'What are you doing out here?' Georgia asked over the hum of the engine.

'What are *you* doing out here?' Lewis countered.

'I came to find you,' she replied.

'You're naked.'

'I just got out of bed.' Lewis stared into his whisky before taking a swig. Georgia put her hand tenderly on his shoulder and slid onto his knee. Lewis pushed her away roughly.

'Put some clothes on.'

Georgia was lost for words. An awkward silence fell as she just stood there shivering in the cold sea breeze, looking at him.

'What's the matter, babes?' she asked after a minute, crouching down to look up into his eyes and putting her hand on his arm.

'I'm not your "babes",' he replied, shaking off her hand. 'Let's . . . let's finish this thing.'

'What?'

'It's not working, Georgia. *We're* not working.' Georgia stared at Lewis, open mouthed for a moment, suddenly feeling sick. She stood and stumbled backwards.

'But—'

'I'll put you on a flight from Sardinia tomorrow.'

'Wait, but . . . is this to do with the Misty thing? I can – I can explain,'

'Oh that? Hmmm, Rex couldn't wait to tell me about that today. No, don't trouble yourself with that.'

'Oh, good because—'

'Because it was over long before that. I'm just relieved I now know for sure I've made the right decision.'

Chapter 25

Sienna stared at the transcript on her desk, her eyes blurring in and out of focus. She had been reading and re-reading the same line for half an hour now. She forced herself to go over page four again.

EOC: Oh, it was round the school like a forest fire. Fourteen years old and pregnant? We were all shocked. We knew something was wrong because she'd just disappeared one day. We had a maths test, and we thought she was skiving . . . but no, that was it . . . she was gone.

LDB: So who told you she was pregnant?

EOC: Well, it's what my parents told me. We were all told to keep away from her, you know. We all thought it might be catching . . . oh, you know how it is when you're that age. But Poppy came back one day to get her books and things and I – I spoke to her. I couldn't resist, she seemed different somehow. I don't know, more . . . mysterious in a way. I guess I just wanted to see if she was just the same old Poppy.

LDB: Who was the father?

EOC: We weren't really told exactly. She was a dark horse, that Poppy Adams. Always got good grades you know, we all thought she just used to stay in working, but she was obviously out messin' around with boys. It was such a surprise. We never knew she had it in her to be a – tart like that. Of course my mum said it was her punishment from God that she fell pregnant. That she wasn't a good Catholic. Looking back, she even had a thing for lovely Mr Rogers. We all used to tease her about it. Always thrusting her chest at him, wearing tight gym shirts, she was. He left the same week Poppy left. Went back to Australia apparently. A funny rumour went round that he was the father and some of us got into trouble for spreading gossip. Terrible really, poor Mr Rogers was a terrific teacher – he'd never have lowered himself to messing around with a girl like Poppy. No, we all reckoned the father had to be one of the yobs from the local boys' school. They all showed an interest in her – or her chest, more like.

LDB: And so what happened next?

EOC: What do you mean? When she left?

LDB: No, after you spoke to her when she came back to collect her stuff. Did she tell you anything?

EOC: Um, not much, all she said was that she was going away, being sent to boarding school.

LDB: She didn't tell you anything about the baby herself?

EOC: Oh yes! Yes, she told me she had already chosen a name. She seemed quite excited about that.

LDB: And what was the name?

EOC: Robin. I remember because there was a Robin Hood film out at the time. Although she didn't say if that was why she'd chosen the name . . .

LDB: Did you see her after that?

EOC: No. She went off to her boarding school in England somewhere. Probably the best thing for her. Keep her out of trouble and all. I think she was going to give little Robin away you know, just between you and me. How else would she be able to go away to boarding school? And it made sense that her family wanted to get the bejesus out of Tipperary after the shame she brought them.

LDB: Did she keep in touch?

EOC: No. That was it. Well, I mean, I've seen The Tiger Starr *in newspapers and magazines since then of course! But she doesn't look anything like Poppy. Like a different person. Although looking back it doesn't surprise me in the slightest that a girl like that would take her clothes off for money.*

Sienna couldn't bring herself to turn the page and read any further. So Tiger was her sister after all, lock stock and barrel. Sienna didn't know whether to be relieved or disgusted about it. Particularly now she knew what the big secret was. That the cold-hearted ice queen had given away her son after getting knocked up by some unknown boy at fourteen, the dirty whore. Well, if Sienna had a nephew out there, she was damn well going to find him.

The words on the page in front of her blurred again as her mind wandered. Where to start? She couldn't rely on Tiger to tell the truth any time soon about the son she gave away. And Sienna had already used up all her free favours from Lance just to get this far. Forget the detective act, there had to be a quicker way of flushing her nephew out, and Sienna knew just the way. Bob Bell may have eaten her for breakfast once before, but now she felt ready to play the game properly.

Chapter 26

'I need some more of the big pink ones, darling.'

'You can say that again,' said Blue, sliding the dish of jumbo pink Swarovski crystals across the shag-pile carpet of the parlour to where Tiger lay, stretched out in her black satin *déshabillé*, silk stockings and fluffy mules. She grunted a distracted thank you as she delved into the crystals with one hand, whilst keeping her eyes on *Whatever Happened to Baby Jane?* playing out on the mini cinema screen set into the wall. A towering spike-heeled shoe was perched on a silver tray on the carpet in front of Tiger like a sculpture, with beautiful clear and pink crystals snaking their way up the heel and spreading out towards the toe.

This was a favourite 'work and pleasure' past-time for Blue and Tiger; sitting peacefully in front of a good film whilst rhinestoning all manner of costume pieces. Since the drama of St Tropez, Tiger had wanted to reclaim some modicum of reserve about her life; so keeping herself safely at home and well away from the public eye seemed a step in the right direction. Besides, she needed to focus one hundred per cent on Vegas now. She was past the slow jog and was now shifting up two gears before the final sprint for the finishing line. Her own Vegas show, for Chrissake! Finally it had hit her. She was already psyching up.

It proved a welcome antidote to the black well of anger she had been teetering on the edge of since the St Tropez trip. Anger at what Rex had done to her. Anger that Lewis and Sienna had both misjudged her so badly. Anger that she had been tarred with the wrong brush yet again, anger that nothing had changed in all these years. The dark shadows of her past were reaching for her, threatening to prise open the Pandora's Box of memories and emotions she had kept firmly locked up for so long. Tiger knew she couldn't afford that possibility – it would surely swallow her up. She just had to be pragmatic and deal with today's mess if she were to survive.

Tiger certainly had enough of that mess to deal with. She was still reeling from what Rex had done on the yacht. She had played it back in her mind so many times over, and each time she felt like she had just witnessed someone's mask slip. She had known Rex for ten years and she just didn't recognise him back there on that boat; he had been just a bizarre champagne, cocaine and lust-fuelled cartoon of himself. She couldn't reconcile the two personalities. And now Sienna wasn't even talking to her. All Tiger could do was to keep calling and leaving messages, and pray that Sienna would figure out the truth in her own time. If nothing else she was a smart girl.

Tiger had been kicking herself mentally that straying into a social scenario with Lewis had proved so disastrous. If only she hadn't agreed to the trip. The pair had been forced to clear the air the moment they had reached Sardinia. Tiger was still offended at how Lewis could have been so wrong about her, but both had agreed on one thing – neither wanted to drop their working relationship after they had put their hearts and souls into it for so long.

Lewis was now esconced in Tiger's pad as previously promised. Strangely, since he had moved in, Tiger still found herself regretting having kept herself so distant from Lewis for the last fourteen years. She hardly dare admit that he was pretty good company around the house. Since their fight he seemed to be making an effort to be more agreeable, setting their disagreement to one side. He had fantastic stories that were aired after his nightly bourbon and even Blue enjoyed his dry humour. Tiger and Blue giggled between themselves that they felt like kids on the *Jackanory* rug when Lewis started with one of his tales late at night. It was almost as though his presence made everything safe somehow; she hadn't even received a pink letter since she had returned to London. Tiger hoped it wasn't the calm before the storm.

The temporary living arrangements weren't appreciated by everyone, needless to say, and tensions ran high between Tiger and Georgia back in the rehearsal studio. Georgia had taken her split with Lewis pretty badly. But since her naked ambition hadn't dissipated a jot in the face of her romantic failure, and since she could hardly blame Tiger for any of it, she was still as professional and hardworking in the studio as her jealousy would allow her to be.

Tiger bravely continued to put sticking plasters over the situation. Meanwhile, she gave Lewis and Blue strict orders to keep her fully occupied with work. Gluing rhinestones to her stage shoes was about the only thing she could do this evening to keep herself safely distracted from the siren's call of that terrifying Pandora's Box.

'Another hour and I'll have this baby all finished,' said Tiger, squinting as she carefully daubed spots of glue onto the silk of the shoe on the tray before her.

'I'm nearly done with the other one,' said Blue. 'I can finish yours too if you like.' Tiger looked up alarmed, and snatched her shoe up, clutching it to her bosom.

'You must be joking! This is my therapy!' she gasped, smiling.

'Spoilsport,' huffed Blue. 'More champagne?'

'Go on, top me up.' Tiger nodded, stretching out and yawning languidly. 'Boy, rhinestoning is hard work.' She grinned, flexing her biceps theatrically.

'Oh I love this bit,' said Blue, as Bette Davis slapped Joan Crawford up on the screen. 'Yeah! Right in the chops! Oof!' squealed Blue, clapping his hands together.

'Hmm! Some pent up aggression there, darling?' asked Tiger, amused.

'Oh you know. Bette's the best.'

'Our usual ten quid says you were dreaming of doing that to Richie.'

Blue was silent.

'Hand it over,' said Tiger, holding out her palm.

'Oh, alright. Maybe I'm still a bit sore.'

'Sore? You've been a bitch since St Tropez.'

'More than you?'

'Yeah! Quiet as hell! It's awful! I'm used to your wise-cracks and put downs. When you're flat my world stops spinning. You're like champagne without the bubbles!'

'You're kidding? I didn't know it was that bad.'

'I can read you like a book, sweetheart.' Blue averted his eyes uncomfortably.

'Oh my god he really hurt you,' Tiger whispered, the familiar wave of guilt washing over her that somehow she had encouraged her best friend to back the wrong horse in Richie. For a moment Blue looked deeply troubled as he fiddled with a rhinestone.

'So anyway. Screw Richie. What's up with Libertina? You two should be together. I like her, she's cool.'

'Euuugh!' groaned Tiger loudly, slapping her hand against her forehead. 'I really like her too! But I've got the reverse Midas touch these days. Everything I touch turns to shit.'

'Meaning?'

'She thinks I just want a fling. Nothing serious.' Tiger sighed loudly.

'And do you?'

'I'm not sure. Probably . . . you know me.'

'Oh Jeez. Yep, you're right, you're hopeless. Can't keep a man, can't keep a woman . . .' Blue nodded.

'Oh, tell you what, since I'm on the floor, why don't you just kick me while I'm down here, babes?' They both burst out laughing. Blue knew it was time to drop the subject.

'You know, you should take some make-up tips from Bette!' he joked, a fiendish glint in his eye. Tiger regarded the character of Baby Jane thoughtfully, up there on the movie screen in her two inches of dry, caked panstick, smeared lipstick and smudged black kohl pencil as she ranted at Joan Crawford.

'You know who Baby Jane is, darling?' Tiger said slowly as a wicked smile crept across her face.

'Who?'

'Rosemary Baby!' Tiger held her breath. Blue paused before shrieking and rolling over in peals of laughter. Tiger slapped her stockinged thigh and hooted. Gravy bared his teeth and started to growl.

'Easy now!' giggled Tiger, stroking the dog affectionately. 'Ooh, maybe that was an omen! Creepy!'

'Don't tempt fate, darling,' said Blue ominously. The growl swelled into a full rumble, before Gravy launched himself violently at the picture window, squaring up to the glass and barking and yelping his head off as ferociously as a miniature Yorkshire Terrier could. Blue and Tiger exchanged worried glances.

'Blue, are – are you okay? You've gone white!'

'I'm, I'm fine,' he stammered. 'I just thought I saw a figure go past the window, that's all.'

'Oooh! Maybe it's the ghost of Richie!' Tiger sniggered. Blue wasn't laughing.

'Right! What's going on!'

'Lewis?' gasped Tiger and Blue in unison as they turned to see him standing in the doorway, clad only in his silk dressing gown. Tiger's eyes were instantly drawn to his toned, muscled calves.

'Someone's out there,' insisted Lewis as Gravy started flinging himself at the window between barks. Lewis turned on his heel without another word, and returned a moment later wielding an axe.

'What the—' shrieked Tiger in horror. 'Where on earth did that come from?'

'I knew your stalker wouldn't be able to stay away,' declared Lewis, steely eyed. Unflicking the catch on the picture window he leapt out onto the patio, axe held aloft and dressing gown flapping behind him in a gust of wind.

'Oh, Superman eat your heart out,' murmured Tiger. As she turned to Blue he grabbed her and pulled her roughly away from the window and towards the back of the room, scattering dishes of rhinestones across the floor as he went.

'Blue, what is wrong with you? Let go!' giggled Tiger, perplexed as Blue positioned her behind her *chaise*, putting the scene of Joan Crawford throwing herself from her wheelchair up there on the movie screen in Tiger's full view. Blue had broken out in a sweat and his hands shook nervously.

'What's wrong, babe?' asked Tiger.

'Maybe you should keep your head down. I'm worried,' warned Blue, edging back towards the window. 'I think I know who might be out there.'

'Look, I think you're all over-reacting.'

'No, I think I screwed up and said some things . . . look I think I may have given too much away to . . .' A chilling scream pierced the night air.

'Woah. I should call the police!' said Tiger.

'No!' squealed Blue. 'No, I think I know . . . I don't think it's anything to do with the threats, I think it might be R—'

'Here's your letter writer,' boomed Lewis, appearing at the picture window with not so much as a Brylcreemed hair out of place, his arms tightly holding the wrists of a tracksuitclad figure.

'You!' gasped Tiger and Blue in unison.

Chapter 27

Sienna beamed as the sales assistant passed over her purchases, all beautifully presented in sleek white expensive bags embossed with the distinctive Yves Saint Laurent logo.

'Thank you, ma'am, enjoy your day.' The store manager smiled as Sienna tottered towards the door. 'And don't worry, we'll call you as soon as the python-skin shoes arrive in store,' he added discreetly. Sienna felt a million bucks as she swept out of the shop, laden with her spoils She had decided that she would reward herself with a couture spree the second she got her promotion at Hunter Gatherers and claim some nice new trophies to mark her first official ascent up the professional ladder. She had even been jammy enough to con Rex into footing her retail therapy bill as a kind of 'advance bonus'. The fact that she had managed to extract the pledge from him as he teetered on the brink of orgasm between her firm tits one night just went to prove how canny she was becoming.

Sienna hailed a black cab and sped towards the Ritz to meet Georgia for a lunch pit-stop. The pair had become inseparable buddies since St Tropez, and Sienna couldn't understand why they hadn't discovered each other sooner.

It was a fact they were a handsome couple and garnered stares and wolf-whistles wherever they went, what with a combined 136 inches of inside leg between them and a calculated gimmick of dressing like twins. They had truly found their match in each other; equally as ambitious, equally as cunning, and each nursing a perfectly healthy resentment of Tiger Starr. Sienna intended to reveal to Georgia later today her master plan for publicly exposing her sister as the ruthless liar and heartless bitch that she knew she was. Tiger's fans deserved to know the truth, and Sienna deserved to find her nephew. She wanted to keep the impact of the big *dénouement* as a surprise for Rex when he opened the newspapers on the big day, so for the moment she was positively bursting with excitement to tell her new best friend about her ingenious plot.

Sienna scrabbled in her handbag for the precious three-hundred-year-old antique silver cocaine spoon with carved skull handle that Rex had given her after St Tropez, and she shovelled herself a little scoop of Colombian marching powder from the vial in her lipstick case. Holding an embroidered handkerchief daintily at her nose to conceal the tiny spoon, she sharply inhaled before sinking back into her seat and grinning from ear to ear as a blissful wave of confidence washed over her. This was the life. The cab swung up to the entrance of the Ritz and a handsome young doorman swooped to open the door with his shiny black leather-gloved hands. His dark eyes discreetly grazed over Sienna's fabulous figure as she elegantly stepped out of the cab and flung a crisp twenty through the driver's window with an order to keep the change No more public transport for Ms Starr, she was well and truly in a new groove and she was staying.

'Oh look over there! Guess who just went into the Ritz a second ago?' said Honey Lou breathlessly as she pounded her way down Piccadilly arm in arm with Blanche.

'I dunno. Brad Pitt?'

'No, silly! Georgia!' said Honey Lou. 'Isn't that just so glamorous? I mean, the Ritz for lunch!'

'Huh. That girl's up to something,' grumbled Blanche. 'How can she afford the Ritz on a chorus girl's wage?'

'Well . . . she usually has other means, doesn't she.'

'Hmm. You know what, Honey,' drawled Blanche with a smirk, 'you're absolutely on the nail with that. There are some women who never pay their way in life, an' she's right up there leading the pack. It's freeloaders like her who give the rest of us a bad name.'

'I thought her and Lewis split up though?'

'Exactly. But Georgia will always find some other mug to foot her bills.'

'You don't like her much, do you?' said Honey Lou meekly as the girls turned the corner into a side street.

'Does anyone? I just have a nasty feeling in my gut about her. She's dodgy, alright. Her insincerity is embarrassing around anyone she thinks might give her something, and then in the dressing room? She's—'

'She's a royal asshole.'

Blanche sucked her breath in dramatically.

'Honey Lou Parker! That's some dirty language coming from a lady! What would Pepper say?'

'But Georgia *is* terrible! She's so nasty to all of us when she's in one of her "moods". And have you heard the way she speaks to Tiger when she thinks no one's listening? She's so disrespectful. Two-faced. She's quite happy to accept the wages Tiger pays.'

'Yup.'

'But it's weird you know, it's like Frankie's under her spell. I think some of the girls are almost . . . frightened of her.'

'Are you?'

'Hmmm – no. Well, maybe. Just a bit at first, when I was new. But definitely not now. That kind of bitchiness and jealousy won't get her anywhere. She just makes me laugh now.'

'Good. Because if she does anything to you, you just come and get me, okay?'

'Oh sure. I'm fine, don't worry. I feel like one of you now anyway.'

'Good. The Starrlets are a happy family and that's the way we like it. We look after each other. And that's why we have to look out for Tiger when we get to Vegas.'

'Oh I think Tiger's pretty fearsome. She wouldn't take any shit from anyone. I think she just humours Georgia half the time for a quiet life.'

'Well, let's just say I just have this funny feeling about Georgia, like something's in the air. That Prince Romano show was too weird. It was like Georgia had a hand in it somehow. You saw how she just stepped in . . . I could be wrong, but it was like she already had a little routine planned out . . . almost like she'd been expecting it, right?'

'Yeah, that was weird now you mention it. But then she's been itching to take Tiger's place ever since I can remember.'

'True. And you know what, something's not been right with Tiger for a few months now.'

'Well I wouldn't know about that, I'm pretty new . . . but she does seem so – so *unhappy* at times. Can you believe that? She's Tiger Starr! Ugh, that Georgia. How can anyone be so nasty to someone who's just worked damn hard and done well for herself from nothing? And God knows Tiger's helped *us* enough.'

'Exactly. We gotta look out for her. We gotta look out for each other, girl.' Blanche shuddered and grabbed Honey's arm protectively as they strode their way across the road towards Soho.

The girls had become firm friends over the last few weeks, largely wanting to escape the increasingly neurotic atmosphere pervading the dressing room courtesy of Georgia Atlanta, but truly bonding after discovering a mutual love of Josephine Baker one night over a bottle of wine and a movie at Blanche's tiny apartment. Once Blanche and Honey Lou had made their connection they became thoroughly excitable about the idea of forming a 1930s-style duo together. They wanted to call themselves The Fabulous Baker Girls, and craft some amazing Josephine-inspired acts. Who knew, if they worked hard and did a good job, Tiger might even put them in one of her shows as a feature! She'd already been more than generous with her time and advice. But boy would it take some hard work to get the act together; being a Starrlet meant long, exhausting hours as it was, but both Blanche and Honey shared a good work ethic and believed that going the extra mile would always pay dividends.

Their first project was to devise an exquisite birdcage routine, inspired by Josephine Baker's own incredible rendition of an exotic bird singing on its perch. But Blanche and Honey wanted to put their own unique stamp on it. They had decided they would mirror each other with one dressed in black feathers and plumes and one in white to reference the black and white silent movies of the time. They then wanted to commission a sparkling birdcage that would revolve slowly as it was suspended mid air, so that they could create beautiful synchronised poses hanging from the bars and swinging on their perch as they rotated. They were now making excellent use of a rare day off to nip into Soho for fabric samples and crystal-colour charts, in order to put together some first drafts for costume designs. They were determined to create something gorgeously fabulous that would show off everything they had learnt with Tiger. Something to make her proud of them.

'So what do you make of the day off then?' asked Honey, breaking the silence.

'Pepper said something about an incident at Tiger's house last night,' said Blanche. 'Apparently Lewis is going to come and talk to us on Monday, like a regrouping kind of thing. Pepper used the word "morale". I think she was referring to Tiger being distant recently, because she said that after last night everything would be back on track as a team, and right back to normal after the last couple of months.'

'Blimey. Whatever happened last night must have been serious.'

'I guess we'll find out soon enough,' sighed Blanche as they passed an *Evening Standard* seller on the street corner, waving his newspapers above his head. 'We always get to hear the story one way or another,' she added uneasily.

'Your name's not on the list. Sorry, madam, there's nothing I can do.'

'Starr. I can see it on your list, there,' said Sienna jabbing the clipboard irritably.

'I'm afraid Ms Starr arrived half an hour ago,' said the tall blonde matter-of-factly.

'I'm her sister,' said Sienna, squaring her six-foot frame up to the blonde and staring her in the eye intimidatingly.

'I'm sure you are,' replied the blonde, looking Sienna up and down disbelievingly.

'And this lady here is Georgia Atlanta,' continued Sienna. 'My *sister*, Tiger, assured me she had left both our names as her guests.' Tiger had in fact called Sienna that very afternoon after lunch to invite her to Demimonde, the newly opened members' club on Berkeley Square. She had a celebration planned which she wouldn't reveal details of. Sienna had only just started taking Tiger's calls again, and she demanded information on the phone before committing to the invitation, but Tiger insisted on them all simply meeting for a glass of champagne. Something about 'getting things back to normal'. Intrigued, Sienna had accepted, on the condition she could bring her new best friend, Georgia. She wondered if this was going to be Tiger's feeble attempt to apologise for making a move on Rex in St Tropez. Too little, too late, thought Sienna smugly; but there's no harm in drinking the bitch's champagne if she's offering, is there?

'Right, let me look at my list again,' huffed the blonde, 'Nope, sorry I can't see – oh wait, actually I do have a plus 2 scribbled at the bottom here as it happens, but no names. Simple misunderstanding.' The blonde nodded to the gorilla next to her and he unclipped the red velvet rope and motioned Sienna and Georgia within.

'Thank you so much.' Sienna smiled at the blonde, waiting until she was over the threshold before leaning in close and adding, 'By the way, you could use a breath mint.'

As the girls entered the sleek, plush dark wood reception of Demimonde against an eerie collage of dark forties Weimar jazz which filtered through the walls, they were greeted by slim, chic hostesses in identical immaculate tuxedos, towering black stilettos, and finger-waved hair, Dietrich style. All very innocuous until it became apparent that half of them were in fact male. It was hard to tell. They all looked so beautiful. Beautiful make-up, beautiful hair, tall, lithe and androgynous. Trust Tiger to pick a place like this, thought Sienna. As she turned to Georgia, she caught her eyeing up a pretty blond boy with kohl-lined eyes and a beauty spot who whisked her coat away with his leather-gloved hand and a quick flutter of his long eyelashes.

The pair were ushered into the busy bar, which was decked out like an ancient French clip joint, with authentically ripped and aged flock wallpaper and hundreds of iron candle sticks that might have been bequeathed by Marie Antionette herself. The walls vibrated and the candle flames jolted with the incongruously deafening electro music which boomed and farted from concealed speakers in the velvet-covered ceiling. People were slinging back oysters and caviar at the booths as though they were on the *Titanic*, and little pots of snuff were being taken around on silver trays by the Dietrich army. The small dance floor was packed and sweaty.

Sienna scanned the room but couldn't see any sign of Tiger or her crew. She dragged Georgia over to a stunning

Mae West look-alike mixing cocktails behind the bar and asked where she could find Tiger Starr. Mae West replied in a low, gruff voice that Tiger was in the private area and to knock three times at the wooden door. Sienna smiled, clocking Mae's Adam's apple, and complimented him on his amazing outfit before dragging Georgia back in the direction they came from to a small *Alice In Wonderland*-sized door. She knocked. Three times. A tiny confessional-style window slid open and a pair of watery blue eyes peered out questioningly. The window slid shut. Sienna waited. Nothing. She knocked again. Three times. The window slid open and the blue eyes peered out again.

'I'm Sienna Starr, I'm Tiger Starr's sister!' she bellowed through the window. The door opened and a hand reached out and motioned the girls inside. Spotting Tiger's pink hair instantly, Sienna marched over to her table angrily.

'Bloody hell!' she shouted in her sister's ear. Tiger span round in her chair.

'Wow! Hi! That's not much of a greeting is it? Oh hi, Georgia.' Tiger nodded kindly.

'Jesus, what's with this place! It's easier to get in to the friggin' French Foreign Legion!'

'Oh you should have called me, I'd have come and got you at the entrance.' Tiger smiled.

'Yeah, yeah. I'm sick of having to tell everyone I'm your friggin' sister. I have a name too you know.'

'Okaaaay,' said Tiger, bemused. 'Why don't you relax, have a glass of champagne!' she said, pulling up chairs for the girls. Sienna nodded over at Blue, Lewis, Hartley and Pepper before slumping down into her seat. She scanned the room, recognising a couple of actors, a singer and a supermodel. The decor was distinctly more 'Opium Den' in here.

'I'm really pleased you came, Sienna,' said Tiger, smiling. 'Thank you.' She reached out to squeeze Sienna's hand. Sienna kept it clamped shut in a fist. 'You look nice, the pair of you. Very smart,' persevered Tiger. 'I especially love your dress, Sienna. Your figure's looking fantastic. Jessica Rabbit eat your heart out.'

Sienna scowled at the compliment and crossed her arms over her front. She didn't need reminding about her new curves, especially in the face of Tiger having lost most of *hers*.

'Yeah cheers, I owe it all to champagne,' said Sienna, brushing off the flattery, and wondering why her sister seemed unusually relaxed and happy. 'So what's the news then?' Sienna asked, cutting to the chase. Tiger handed over a couple of glasses of Taittinger and pushed a bowl of fresh strawberries and peppercorns across the table towards the two girls.

'Well,' said Blue dramatically from across the table, 'Lewis caught Tiger's stalker on the prowl in her garden last night!'

'Oh?' said Georgia.

'Stalker?' asked Sienna. 'Didn't even know you had one.'

'No, you wouldn't, would you,' said Blue, 'since you don't

pay too much attention to your sister unless you're getting something from her.'

'Okay, guys, this is supposed to be a celebration,' cut in Lewis, holding his hands up in the air.

'Yeah sure,' said Sienna, sneering at Blue, 'so who's this stalker then? That weird little guy who turns up at your shows?'

'God no, I feel so terrible about him. I was convinced it was him, and I feel so bad now. I knew all along he was just a sweet little man,' sighed Tiger, looking genuinely upset.

'So who was it in the garden then?'

'Rosemary Baby,' said Lewis.

'Who?'

'Rosemary Baby!' said Lewis, Blue and Tiger in unison.

'Didn't I meet her once?' Sienna sputtered. 'With your friend, Tiffany . . . ?'

Tiger nodded sadly.

'Rosemary Baby? Like the film? About the spawn of Satan?' smirked Georgia, doing her best not to catch Lewis' eye. She was still giving him the silent treatment.

'Er – in a manner of speaking,' said Blue, trying not to snigger. 'Rosemary Baby is an old washed-up performer with a bad case of the green eye. But now, the ugly mo' fo' is in custody awaiting trial. Last we heard she was locked in a cell, screaming to the warden that she was a superstar who needed her yoga mat. But at least she confessed to the anonymous letters and everything.'

'Letters?' asked Sienna and Georgia in unison, arching their eyebrows higher with each twist of the tale.

'Er, look, we aren't publicising the extent of the stalking,' interjected Lewis awkwardly and shooting a look at Blue. 'Let's just say, Tiger's been targeted for a few months and now we're just looking forward to things getting back to normal and being able to concentrate on the shows. Tiger wanted to have you here Sienna, to share in the celebration of the end of a dark period,' said Lewis, raising his glass in Sienna's direction.

'Like I said, I'm really glad you could make it.' Tiger beamed.

'To good times ahead!' squealed Blue over the music, clinking everyone's glasses noisily. Sienna clinked glasses and smiled broadly.

'To Tiger,' she said. 'I do hope you enjoy this evening, dear sister.'

'Oh thanks, Sienna! That really means a lot,' said Tiger, visibly touched. 'It's just a huge relief, to be honest. I'm going to let my hair down tonight.' A leer crept across Sienna's face. Tiger didn't notice. 'I'm glad you came,' she continued, reaching out and placing her hand on Sienna's arm. Sienna was getting excited. Excited at the thought of the look on Tiger's face in the morning when she saw what was waiting for her in the newspapers. Excited that by the looks of things she would be reading the headlines with the biggest, fattest hangover of the century. Enjoy, dear sister, enjoy, thought Sienna, washing back her champagne happily.

Chapter 28

Tiger woke with a start as Gravy jumped up onto the bed. The sun was blazing through the window. She had forgotten to draw the blinds last night. The birds were singing outside. Loudly. Tiger's head was pounding as she wracked her brains, trying to remember coming home. All she could say for sure was that it had been a great night. She'd have to check her bar bill later to see just how great it had been. She rolled over and buried her face in the cool side of the pillow, expecting Blue to come in any second with a glass of water and a hair of the dog and any gossip about who he'd pulled at the end of the evening.

Tiger felt as though today was the first day of the rest of her life. No more letters, no more suspicion, no more paranoia, no more 'what ifs', no more 'whodunnits', no more 'I know your secret!' As if! A tinkle of laughter escaped her lips at the absurdity of getting herself in a lather for months over the obsessive games of some washed up, chinless, titless wonder who should have bought a one-way ticket to the nuthouse a long time ago. If only Tiger had known it was Rosemary Baby sniffing around, she would have called Tiffany Crystal and let her wait in the garden for her personally! Tiffany would be thrilled to know that nasty piece of work would soon be rightfully behind bars. Deep down, everyone knew that Rosemary had tried to kill Tiffany. It was a travesty she had not been brought to justice but now that would change. Funny how good things come out of bad, sometimes.

Tiger felt thirsty and wondered when Blue would be up – and if he fancied going out for breakfast. She reached out to dial his room from the phone next to her bed. No answer. Maybe he was already up fixing breakfast, she thought hopefully. Tiger cuddled Gravy and snuggled under the duvet, determined she was going to have a relaxing day off after all the drama of the last few months. Her eyelids felt heavy. She was so tired, she felt she could sleep the whole day. Maybe she would . . .

'What do you have to say for yourself?' boomed a voice through her sleepy fug. Tiger jolted and snapped her eyes open to see Lewis standing at the foot of her bed.

'Lewis! Did you just come in without knocking?' Tiger gasped, quickly pulling the silk sheets up to her chin and grabbing Gravy, who was growling protectively. 'What are those?' she asked, regarding the pile of newspapers in his arms with suspicion. Lewis dropped them onto her bed with a heavy thump. His breathing was even, but heavy and furious. Tiger sat up and reached out gingerly for the top of the pile.

'Needless to say your publicist has officially dropped you as of this morning,' he said flatly. 'I have no idea what the Americans will have to say about this, when they hear there's yet more scandal. So. Is it true?'

Tiger's eyes skimmed over the headlines, her vision blurring as she scrabbled through the pile frantically. She picked out words here and there. 'Tiger Starr's teenage pregnancy scandal!'. . . 'schoolgirl disgrace'. . . 'heartlessly abandoned baby boy' . . . 'living a lie' . . . 'the sleaze beneath the glamour', Tiger shook her head in disbelief, unable to speak.

'I asked you, is it true?'

'N-n-n . . . w-w-w . . .'

'Exactly. I gave you the chance to tell me. Thanks.' Lewis stormed from the room, slamming the door so hard it ricocheted in its hinges. Gravy hid under the bed. Tiger felt the familiar sensation of her throat closing as her breathing became shallow and frantic. The pounding in her head was increasing, the pressure at her temples unbearable. She leapt up to the window for air but stumbled and fell. She lay there on the carpet, panic stricken, gasping for breath, unable to scream, unable to cry.

Poppy Adams regained consciousness after an exhausting twenty-four hours. She ached all over. As she blinked her eyes open she focused on the shiny hospital walls. Mother had gone, and Poppy was alone. She felt shattered. Through her emotional daze she knew she just wanted to hold her baby. As she struggled to get comfortable a nurse came bustling in through the door and prodded and poked around painfully for a bit. Poppy didn't know what was happening but submitted, eagerly anticipating holding her baby.

Once back on the ward and concealed behind green curtains, another nurse came with a cup of hot sugary tea.

'I didn't ask for a drink, I just want to see my baby, please,' said Poppy feebly, clutching at her painful breasts.

'You need some sugar. Now drink the tea, there's a good girl.'

Poppy sighed and took a tiny sip.

'Okay, I've had some tea, now can I see my baby, please,'

'Has your mother not come to see you?'

'No. I must have fallen asleep after—'

'Yes, of course you did, dear. That usually happens.'

Poppy could hear talking from behind her curtains and a baby crying from across the ward.

'Can I just see my child, please,' she asked anxiously.

'You will have to speak to your mother. I'll call her to come and see you.'

'I don't want my mum, I want my child!' demanded Poppy, angrily. Another baby started crying in the ward.

'Calm down and drink your tea, I'm fetching your mother now.'

'My baby! What have you done with my baby?' screamed Poppy as the nurse hurried out of the cubicle, swishing the curtains shut behind her.

'My baby! My baby! Where have you taken my baby?'

Poppy's cries and screams echoed through the wards unanswered.

'Blue! I need Blue! Lewis, where's Blue? He's not in his room. Bluuuuue,' Tiger wailed from the top of the stairs, clinging to the banister. Lewis appeared at the foot of the stairs.

'Blue? Oh, he's the one who caused all this, didn't you know? Why don't you read his little note. Here.' Lewis climbed the stairs and threw a sheet of lined notepad paper at Tiger.

'*Darling I can't live with myself. This is all my fault. I told Richie about your ordeal. I was so worried about you I needed to talk to someone. He must have gone to the press. I thought I could trust him I'm so sorry I've ruined your life, I'm beside myself. I know you will never forgive me for breaking your confidence . . .*' Tiger couldn't read any further. She ran to Blue's room and checked under the bed for his leopard-skin luggage set. It was gone. She flung open the wardrobe and was confronted with an empty space where his clothes had once been. She ran to his ensuite bathroom and saw that his toothbrush was gone. Staggering back to his bed she dissolved in tears on the floor, clutching his duvet to her cheek. Why, why, why was everything happening like this? It was all wrong! She had never felt so alone. Lewis looked on, stony faced, from outside the door.

'Where's the kid now?' he asked.

Tiger wiped her tears from her cheeks as her shoulders shook.

'I c-can't deal with you now. You need to g-give me forty-eight hours,' she stuttered.

'Yeah right. Oh, by the way, you got another anonymous letter this morning. Seeing as Rosemary is in a cell and has no way of sending one, I'd take an educated guess she gave a false confession. She's obviously so desperate for fame she's realised the only way she'll ever get herself talked about is to be a notorious stalker. Unless there are any more skeletons you'd care to tell me about?' Tiger stared in utter disbelief at the piece of pink paper. As she struggled for breath, the floor seemed to fall away from beneath her, the colours before her eyes draining to black. The darkness seemed so inviting; Tiger let herself slip away into unconsciousness.

Chapter 29

Sienna hummed as she smudged another layer of smoky kohl onto her eyelids. Leaning back from the ornate bathroom mirror she fluttered her long lashes for the full effect. Vampy, she thought, as she turned up the sound system a notch. Rex had paid for her to have top-of-the-range speakers concealed in the ceiling of her bathroom and she was enjoying the luxury every time she had a bath or a girlie pampering session. Tonight she was meeting Rex and Georgia for drinks at a fine jewellery launch party in Mayfair. All she needed now was her set of emeralds to complete her look and she was ready to go.

Shortly after the bombshell of yesterday's newspapers, Rex had made a short and snappy announcement over breakfast that he had terminated Tiger's account with immediate effect, and promptly asked Sienna what she thought to the idea of starting to work on Georgia's profile. Sienna thought it an excellent idea. Overall, she was rather delighted that her handiwork seemed to have tied up a lot of loose ends for everybody and was working out rather well. She was pleased Rex and Georgia seemed to be getting on, too – Sienna had always thought it important for your friends to like your boyfriend.

Accordingly, Rex had taken Georgia for a meeting at the expensive Kube Hotel in Knightsbridge last night to start working out a PR strategy. Personally Sienna had always thought the place was swarming with high-class hookers, but then if Rex was taking Georgia there she must be mistaken. Sienna had gratefully taken the opportunity to spend the night at her own flat, wanting to have a girlie evening on her own and have a think about how best to go about finding her nephew. It would be a lot easier now he had probably read the newspapers himself, she thought. She was hoping Rex might have called to wish her sweet dreams last night, but he didn't; Sienna guessed he had probably been shattered after an evening talking business with Georgia. Well, Sienna would now give him a night to remember to make it up to him, poor lamb.

Sienna heard loud banging and she rolled her eyes up at the ceiling. The neighbour upstairs had taken to complaining about her music. She turned it up another notch to make a point. Shovelling her make-up into her handbag, she saw a little white wrap, and remembered she had a couple of lines left from the weekend. Waste not, want not, she thought, emptying the contents onto her marble windowsill and quickly racking up a huge line. The banging continued. She polished off her chemical hit and dabbed her nose daintily. More banging.

'Alright alright!' she yelled up at the ceiling and cut the music dead. She realised the banging was coming from her front door.

'Jesus, don't tell me he's actually come downstairs to complain,' she muttered under her breath, traipsing across the hallway. She opened the front door and stared.

'Can I help you?' she asked in a surly manner, wondering who the fuck this woman in a headscarf was. Maybe one of the neighbours had ordered a takeaway and given the wrong flat number.

'Sienna, can I come in?' asked a familiar voice. Sienna stood, bewildered, for a few seconds and watched as the woman pulled off her scarf to reveal pink hair pulled back from her pale, gaunt face.

'Tiger?' Sienna ventured, shocked by her appearance. She stepped aside and watched transfixed as Tiger made her way into the hallway; scrawny in her plain work-out gear, short in her ballet pumps, and haggard without her make-up. She looked terrible – as though she hadn't slept – and her eyes were bloodshot and swollen. She had a solemn expression. Great. Sienna did not want her sister messing with her buzz right now.

'Hey,' said Tiger. 'Sorry for dropping in on you like this. You look nice. Going out?'

'Yeah. I need to leave in about ten minutes actually, so can you make it quick?'

'Oh, right. Yes of course. Well, I need to share something with you . . . I guess you read the newspapers.'

'Might have done.'

'I thought you might have rung to talk to me about it . . . ?'

'Heh. I thought you should be the one calling me actually.'

'I couldn't be sure you'd pick up the phone to me.'

'No, you're right. I wouldn't have. So, have you come to tell me where my nephew is then? Only, you need to make it quick, I have things to do tonight.'

'I wanted to explain. . . tell you the truth. The thing is . . .'

'Don't even think about telling any more lies, Tiger. Just tell me where I can find him. I have a right to see him and tell him the truth about what his mother's like. He deserves to know.'

'Look, maybe I should come back when you have more time, I'm not sure this can be rushed.'

'No way, I want this over with.'

'No no, I should come back—'

'Just get on with it, you lying fucking bitch!'

Tiger stood silent for a moment and blinked, her eyes visibly filling with tears at Sienna's tangible venom. Tiger took a deep breath.

'Sienna, you don't have a nephew.'

'Excuse me? But the interview that your school friend—'

'You don't have a sister either.'

'What? Are you on something? What are you talking about?'

'I'm not your sister.'

'Oh come on, this is getting ridiculous—'

'I'm your mother.'

They say that when you are about to die your life pulls up before your eyes – a little home movie to accompany you through your last remaining seconds. Right now, Sienna felt the world about to crash down on her, a quick-fire family slideshow playing behind her retinas, flashing up scene upon scene, but each now coloured with a different hue; each now tinged with the possibility of an entirely different reality. She staggered slightly and put her arm out to the wall. Tiger reached out.

'No. Don't touch me. Don't come near me,' Sienna whispered. She stood for a moment wobbling on her heels, thinking. 'Now, just run that by me again. You're my . . . mother? But what about Mum and Dad? You're not my *mum*!'

'Sienna darling, I know this is a lot to take in. Mum and Dad were my parents, but they were your grandparents. After I had you they took you away from me to bring you up as their own. We moved to England and I was sent away to boarding school. I had brought shame on the family. I was only fourteen, I couldn't even . . . I wasn't even allowed to . . .' Tiger trailed off as Sienna was now crying loudly, clinging to the wall as she shook.

'Wait!' Sienna shouted through her tears, suddenly angry. 'You're lying! You're twenty-nine! You're only ten years older than me! Stop lying!' she choked.

'No, darling, I'm thirty-three. I've always lied about my age. As soon as I turned sixteen I ran away from boarding school to Spain for a few years to get away; I couldn't bear you being so close and not being allowed to see you learn to walk, or hear your first words. It was a nightmare time. I got myself into so much trouble, with bad people. I just wanted to self-destruct, to try and forget the pain of what had happened. But, I came back. I came back a different person, Sienna. I changed my appearance, my name, my age, I needed to be someone else, I couldn't put the past right. Besides, I knew that was the only way Mum and Dad would feel it was safe enough to let me near you, *they* wanted to re-write history, so that's what *I* had to do, too, for them to let me still see you.'

'But why lie about your age?'

'I had to do everything I could to make sure you'd never suspect anything. I just spent a few years being eighteen. I never celebrated birthdays . . . no one ever noticed . . . or cared. My god, if you'd ever had any reason to even suspect anything . . . well you might have thought I actually wanted to give you away. I could never let you think I wanted that. I'd rather play the game so Mum and Dad would let me see you occasionally than risk them cutting me off from you completely.'

'They said you were in London working, and you didn't want to see me!'

'Of course they did,' said Tiger. 'They were protecting you. Why do you think they never had pictures of me in the house? They disowned me. I was an embarrassment. I was their dirty secret. And they never liked the idea of my performing. It just confirmed their views that I wasn't a good Catholic girl. I won't pretend I'm not angry at them, Sienna. For nineteen years I've carried the anger around in my heart and when they died I knew I'd never get closure; that it would haunt me forever, what they did. I wanted to tell you a thousand times but I didn't want to hurt you or colour your memories of your grandparents. Whatever they did to me I know that they loved you so much. You were the apple of their eye. You have no reason to be angry at them. But we have a chance to make a fresh start *now*, we—'

'Wait! But – they wouldn't have *lied* to me for all these years? Everyone said I looked like my dad . . .'

'No! God no. You take after your granddad, yes it's true . . . I brought this . . .' Tiger scrabbled in her handbag and pulled out her passport. 'Here. Take a look in the back at my age so you can see the proof for yourself. In a weird way, shaving four years off my age kind of worked in my line of business.' Tiger let out an uneasy laugh. 'You know, all the stars lie about their ages. Only my reason wasn't for vanity. Here. I want you to look, I need you to see that I'm not lying.' Tiger held out the passport for Sienna to take. She recoiled as though Tiger were holding out a glowing hot poker. How had she missed Tiger's date of birth when she looked in her passport before? Well, she wasn't looking for it . . . she remembered nearly being caught by Blue and having to put the passport back as soon as she saw her place of birth as Clonmel. How could she have been so stupid! A humungous clue had been right there in front of her nose like a big, pink, velvet elephant.

Tiger knelt down and put the passport on the floor in front of Sienna's feet. Sienna's carefully applied smoky make-up now coursed down her cheeks in rivers of black. She hesitated before picking up the passport and checking the back. She let out a tiny wail and threw it across the room, covering her face with her hands as she sobbed.

'Go away!' she snivelled. 'You've done too much! I can't take this. You liar! I wish Mum was here! My real mum!'

'Sienna, *I* am your mother! Please!' Sienna collapsed to the floor as she sobbed. So this was what Lance had meant when he told her enigmatically he wasn't giving her everything on a plate. He must have figured it out for himself! He knew! The bastard! He knew he was getting his cut of the money anyway. He'd probably been watching the whole car crash with fascination. Of course Sienna was in so much of a hurry with her stupid story and the thought of bringing Tiger down she didn't check things out properly. Now she'd brought her own house of cards tumbling down spectacularly. Oh boy, had she scored an own goal this time! She had single-handedly orchestrated the reveal of her own seedy secret.

Sienna looked about her and felt her world fragment around her as she sat there on the floor. Everything that she'd ever thought was real suddenly took on a new meaning. All Tiger's visits, conversations, all providing new answers . . . and yet more questions. Sienna knew she had to stop thinking, it was all too much to take in. She now deeply regretted that line of cocaine earlier; she felt like she was on the edge of a cliff, and she didn't know which side was reality any more.

'You need to leave,' said Sienna quietly, trembling there on the floor.

'I'm not leaving you here like this,' said Tiger.

'Get out!' screamed Sienna suddenly, flying up at Tiger with her fists. Tiger cowered and backed towards the wall, small and childlike in front of Sienna's wiry six-foot frame, bristling with anger.

'Oh my god! You're a whore!' spat Sienna. 'Pregnant with me at fourteen? My dad some nameless local boy? I bet you had 'em all didn't you, lifting your skirt behind the bike sheds like some dirty tart. You probably don't even *know* which one my father is do you! I bet—' Tiger suddenly lashed out like a cornered animal and slapped Sienna hard. Her cheek reddened immediately and Sienna drew back in shock, hands leaping to her face.

'God – sorry – Sienna I didn't mean—' started Tiger.

'Oh my god I hate you!' hissed Sienna, trembling. 'I hated you as my sister! And I hate you even more now! A stripper for a sister was bad enough, but now a whore as my mother?' she screamed.

'No, it wasn't like that! Please let me explain!' Tiger knew deep down she could never explain. How could she tell her daughter she was born out of such cruelty and violence? Tell her daughter she was brought into the world because of a rape upon an underage schoolgirl? That her father was some *Lolita*-loving gym teacher who had coolly groomed an innocent fourteen-year-old until he got his prize? Or that her parents knew and colluded with the school to hush it all up after the father was arrested and deported? Tiger could never tell her daughter the truth. It might destroy her. It had almost killed Tiger, slowly but surely.

'To think I even took your stage name!' raged Sienna. 'Ugh! I can't even get away from you in my head now, knowing you gave birth to me.' Sienna lunged forward and returned the slap to Tiger's face. Tiger flinched but stood and took it. Tears rolled down her burning cheeks.

'You're not my real mother!' screamed Sienna. 'You'll only ever be that woman who gave birth to me! You gave me away didn't you! You just didn't want me. Mum and Dad aren't alive to tell me the truth, so you know you can just lie and cover up, like you've done for all these years.'

Tiger shook her head as she cried. 'They took you away from me, and they took away the name I gave you. They gave you the name Rose against my wishes. I wanted to call you Robin. They couldn't even do that one little thing for me,' she whispered. 'There was never a day that went by when I didn't think of you.'

Poppy had heaved the last of her suitcases into the taxi. She made her way back up the garden path to the front door where her mother stood, watching proceedings with a stony face. Her dad was nowhere to be seen.

'Okay, that's me all packed,' announced Poppy, quietly.

'Good. The driver knows where St Mary's is, he'll drop you at the gates. He's already been paid.'

'Okay. So ... I'll see you when we break up for Christmas?'

'You'll go to Auntie Mary's in Kilburn for holidays. She may be old but she knows how to discipline.'

'Oh.'

'It's for the best. No distractions. Now you have to work hard. Get yourself some good grades and make something of your life. You're lucky, you have a second chance now – a chance to pay for your sins – turn your life around. Just you remember that as I'm slaving every hour God sends to pay for your second chance. You really have no idea what pressure you've brought upon the whole family; how much I personally have to pick up the pieces of your behaviour. You owe it to all of us to step up to the mark, young lady.'

Poppy looked down at the path and scuffed her shoe on a stone awkwardly.

'Can I see Robin before—'

'Rose. She's Rose now. Don't you forget that. I don't think it's a good idea for you to see her, you'll probably just upset her anyway. She'll be safe with us. We have to put the past right now. It's for the best.'

'But ... just a hug for my baby.'

'She's your sister, remember. Now go.'

'But . . .'

'Goodbye, Poppy.'

'Right . . . bye then.' Poppy looked up and leaned in for a hug but her mother was already closing the front door. As it clicked shut, the taxi driver beeped, and revved the engine impatiently. Poppy beat a lonely retreat back up the path, heartbroken and churning with nerves. She climbed into the taxi and as it pulled away she looked back at the house, at the parlour window, hoping to see a curtain twitching on her departure at least. Nothing. As she settled back into her seat with a lump in her throat, Poppy knew she would never return to her old life ever again.

Tiger leaned against the grand iron railings outside Sienna's flat, shivering in the crisp night air with tears streaming relentlessly down her face as the last thirty minutes replayed in her mind on high speed, over and over and over. She had never for a moment expected Sienna to take the revelations well, but Tiger had truly been played the Joker card when Sienna finally revealed it was her who had sold the stories to the newspapers. That had really knocked Tiger sideways. She supposed she should have been relieved that it hadn't been Blue's loose lips that had broken the story. But the irony of the situation wasn't lost on her. She had asked with trepidation if Sienna had been behind all the anonymous letters too. Sienna simply said she now wished she had been that person, but regrettably, no. Tiger had been shocked. Sienna's hatred for her was so pervasive, and Tiger just didn't know who was who or what was what any more.

Tiger had tried to explain as much as she could in as little time as possible, but how could she tell the whole truth when she didn't want to tell her daughter she was the product of a brutal rape? So most of the secret was finally out, and for what? Tiger had now been disowned by her daughter, much like she had been disowned by her own parents. Sienna had then literally thrown Tiger out on the street. As her own parents had done. Tiger felt a huge hole within; where the lies, secrecy, and the terrible reality had sat and gnawed away at her for the last nineteen years. She had been able to deal with it for as long as she had her daughter nearby. But now Sienna had rejected her that had all changed.

Something had to fill that black hole where the secret had once been, and all Tiger felt now was rage, desperation, grief, and an acid bitterness filling her up and threatening to drown her. Shaking with sobs, she realised that the terrible wailing sound echoing through the street was coming from her. People were staring at her as they passed, straying out into the road to avoid walking too near her, as though she were some crazed, inebriated tramp. Tiger sank to her knees, clutching at the railings, bent double with sobs. She had nothing left without her daughter in her life.

The door to the house suddenly slammed and Tiger looked up hopefully. Through her blurred vision she could make out Sienna's heels stepping down the marble stairs to the gate. Tiger tried to scramble to her feet but stumbled. Sienna stopped at the railings and towered over Tiger.

'Get up off the floor you pathetic creature. Do I know you?'

Sienna stalked off as Rex's distinctive orange Lamborghini screeched up to the pavement a few doors down. Tiger watched Sienna jump in, slamming the door with a heavy muffled thud as she was whisked off in to the night, with Tiger left crying there on the pavement alone, feeling like there was nothing left in her world to lose.

Chapter 30

The gloved hand flicks carefully through the pages of the scrapbook in quick succession. The last page is closed, and the book is held for a moment. One hand strokes the cover hesitantly, before it is hurled into the lethargic log fire across the room. Imbued with energy, bright flames leap up to lick at the book, bubbling and mutating the cover. The pages within hiss musically as they burn bright, then curl and turn to ash, before the flames retreat into the embers once more. The silhouette of a figure is faintly sketched out by the moonlight that trickles through the window, a suitcase is fastened loudly with a zipper and hoisted to the front door. The figure leaves the room and is lost into the night. The defaced images of Tiger Starr left pinned to the wall sing their silent song of sadness, obsession, cruelty, passion; while the remains of her likeness smoulder in the embers, reduced to smuts of carbon.

Chapter 31

Scores of feathered showgirls paraded in perfect forma-
tion, all tits, teeth and long legs, high kicking their way
across the screens. Lewis had lost count of how many
times the loop had played on the plasma screens mounted
in the arrivals lounge. He averted his eyes and instead
concentrated on the hypnotic flashing neon patterns
beaming out from the slot machines in an attempt to relax.
Bored and even more anxious within thirty seconds, he
checked his watch impatiently for the hundredth time.
Tourists, revellers and a few stag parties were steadily
flowing into the airport lounge. The tic in Lewis' cheek
started as he tried not to think about the possibility that
Tiger hadn't got on the plane after all. He hadn't heard
anything for sixteen hours since she called to announce
Vladimir was driving her to the airport.

The last two months had been a rollercoaster for Lewis.
Tiger had been catatonic for days after she returned home
in the early hours of the morning having confronted
Sienna. Tiger had then been silent for days. She remained
shut in her bedroom mostly, not eating, reading any press
or answering any calls. Lewis was juggling the ravenous
media and paparrazzi single-handedly, with the skill of a

circus acrobat. Then, something happened to break the stagnant silence. Lewis had come home one evening with a Trois Petits Cochons cake; just another of many little gestures in an attempt to put a smile on her face. As he walked in through the front door, he was confronted with a shocking scene; furniture, mirrors and windows were smashed, walls were scratched and scored and curtains ripped.

Lewis had dropped the cake right there on the vintage parquet floor and had run through the house screaming, praying the intruder hadn't attacked Tiger. But there had never been an intruder. Lewis found Tiger curled up in a ball in the mess of her own making, shuddering with tears amongst shards of broken mirror in the wrecked bathroom. All up her legs and arms were long scratches and gouges as though an animal had been clawing at her, and blood was all over her hands. That night Lewis had never seen so much anger in one person as he saw in Tiger. Her whole story came pouring out. Everything. Lewis had been shocked to discover Sienna was Tiger's daughter but that had only been the start. Tiger had wept and shook as she screamed and railed against her past, pausing only to claw at her throat as she struggled for breath with panic. It was like watching a demon forcing its way out of her. Lewis had been floored by what he heard; his mind reeling as so many pieces of her jigsaw puzzle seemed to click into place for him after all these years. Lewis had held her tight throughout that long night. He listened to her, wept with her, took her punches when another surge of anger came, held her in his arms when she tried to hurt herself, and lay beside her when she collapsed in yet more tears for her lost daughter.

As the sun came up marking a new day and Tiger began to finally expire with exhaustion, Lewis had dutifully cleaned her scratches with antiseptic lotion and dressed them, before putting her to bed – a Valium secreted into her cocoa so she could sleep peacefully. Immediately he called in glaziers to fix the broken windows and interior designers to clear the house and set about redesigning some new themes for each room. He showed them all Tiger's precious old books so they could see what kind of things she liked. By the time Tiger awoke twenty-four hours later, her house was purged, stripped back to its bare walls ready for redecoration. Everything damaged had been removed. That was what Lewis wanted for Tiger.

From that day forward he took things very slowly. He never mentioned that night, ever. Instead, he encouraged Tiger to eat, and to carry on talking if she needed to. He smuggled her incognito out of the house via the back garden wall and took her for late night strolls and chats and fresh air. He kept everything to a routine and didn't let her talk about work. Another pink letter arrived for her, which Lewis promptly and quietly handed over to the police. Without hesitation he installed a discreet security team to guard her and her home. Tiger's cuts healed and she gained a few much needed pounds. Eventually, after a few weeks, when Lewis thought she was far enough away from that terrible night in her house, he had encouraged her to tell her side of the story to the press. A Sunday tabloid had already discovered that Sienna was Tiger's baby – the story would run and run if Tiger didn't stop it. He put it to her that it would be a good opportunity to tell the facts on her terms, and with dignity. Furthermore it would show that she wasn't running away in shame should she decide to go ahead with her year-long Vegas show. It was a long shot, but Lewis simply had to keep the faith that she would see it his way and get back in the saddle for the show. Right now it was the best thing for her to do, if she wanted to move forward in her life . . . and if she ever wanted to make the pain she had suffered worth something, instead of letting it destroy her.

Lewis had kept all the arrangements running smoothly in Vegas and had played down the scandal. He certainly didn't reveal anything of the carnage that had been laid bare behind closed doors. The Vegas producers were happy to be reassured that there had simply been some phoney tabloid story again. They weren't even bothering to read them any more. Tiger was getting stellar previews in America and that's all they cared about. Of course, if Tiger jettisoned the show now he would be in shit up to his eyeballs; but all Lewis cared about was keeping her options open for her, so at least she was left with choices about her future. Knowing just how many choices had been taken away from Tiger in the past, Lewis was determined for that not to happen for her again.

Tiger declared after much thinking that she would not be giving over her story to the press, moreover that she just didn't feel ready for Vegas. It was a bleak outlook for Lewis; he sweated bullets but kept the faith. Somewhere along the way, his confidence must have started to rub off on Tiger and within a week she had changed her mind. She had realised she wanted to take control of her life again, like she had when she returned to London as Tiger Starr fourteen years ago. Lewis immediately helped Tiger to find a top female broadsheet journalist, and the story was a huge success; sensitive, eloquent and erudite. Tiger hadn't really wanted Sienna to learn the circumstances of her birth from a newspaper but as Sienna had disowned her, what choice did she have? And as much as she wanted to sugar coat it for her daughter's sake, Lewis had persuaded her that honesty was the best policy. Without naming names she revealed that she had been raped by a much older man, an adult in a position of authority. That she had wanted to keep her child regardless but that she'd had no choice but to abide by her parents' decision. Lewis was inundated with requests to use Tiger for radio and chat shows, women's magazines and lectures. She politely declined. She had said her piece, and she had regained some control; she hadn't done it for the notoriety. But she still wasn't ready for Vegas.

One person who still hadn't surfaced after the latest

revelations was Sienna. Lewis knew deep down this would always hold Tiger back, but was powerless to reason with her. Sienna had fiercely maintained a block on all contact, but Tiger wanted to be on call for her in London in case she ever changed her mind. Tiger worried that if she left the country, she might lose that faint glimmer of hope of her ever getting to see or speak to her again.

Lewis had now been in Vegas for a whole week with Pepper, Blue and the Starrlets, checking all the set ups for Tiger's proposed three-month schedule of rehearsals with her girls, before the Vegas producers and the director was expecting her to join them out there. Lewis had tracked down Blue and told him everything, begging him to come back on board. Now that Tiger seemed more stable, Lewis had wanted to reintroduce her friends and close circle to her life, and her closest confidante Blue was an essential part of keeping her strong. All the while, Lewis still kept the faith that Tiger was getting back in the saddle. Finally, his prayers were answered when yesterday he had received a call to say she would fulfil her commitment and come to Vegas. Tiger explained how she felt she had let her daughter down throughout her life, and she was determined not to let anyone else down. Lewis had been on the verge of a heart attack until that point, and nearly choked on the phone as Tiger had told him her decision.

Now as he paced up and down the arrivals lounge, his heart was sinking rapidly as he realised she must have lost her bottle. One or two tourists were excitedly weaving their way past with their luggage – it seemed that they were the last stragglers who had been on that flight. Lewis sighed and turned to leave, wondering what on earth his next move would be on the show. It was doubtful he would ever work again. Not after he had been sued for major breach of contract at any rate. No one would trust him professionally any more. Everything he had put his heart and soul into for all these years would be gone. Not to mention Tiger. If they didn't work together, what was left? It wasn't like she saw him as a friend, only a manager. She would have no more reason to see him. Lewis wandered over to a slot machine, shoved in a few coins and tried to swallow back the lump in his throat. Rows of cherries blurred in front of his eyes as he mechanically played his few dollars. After barely a minute, he felt his stomach churning as he tried to push the horror of his situation from his mind.

'Hey, watch that hatbox! You can't put anything heavy on it!' came a loud voice echoing over the noise of the slots. Lewis jerked his head around to see the most fabulous creature tottering her way across the floor, hair bouncing on her shoulders as her hips wiggled, a porter wheeling a trolley piled high with luggage beside her.

'Tiger!' Lewis cried out, striding towards her, quickly breaking into a run.

'Oh man! I fell asleep on the flight and then had to spend half an hour touching up my hair and make-up after we landed,' laughed Tiger. 'Couldn't let anyone see me looking less than showroom, darling!'

Lewis couldn't stop a huge smile from spreading across his face as he picked her up in a bear hug and swung her around.

'Woah there! Now that's a welcome!' said Tiger. 'Most unlike you! Have you been drinking?'

'No . . . for the first time in my life, I – I missed you, that's all.'

'Oh, eeeeuww! Porter? Can I have the old Lewis Bond back please? Moody Lewis I can handle but soppy Lewis? Jeez. Come on you, let's get to the hotel, I could murder a Martini.'

Chapter 32

The gloved hand calmly passes over a passport to the heavily made-up brunette at the check-in desk. Tinny, muffled flight announcements echo through the vast hall against a backdrop of chatter and the odd squeak of trolley wheels as they are pushed with their stacked cargo. The brunette opens the passport to the photograph page with her pink plastic talons, studies the information for a second, then looks up from beneath long, spidery lashes thick with clumpy mascara.

'Good morning, Mr Hunter. Are you travelling alone today?'

A smile creeps across her coral pink-painted trout pout, lips dripping in gloss as she takes in Mr Hunter's handsome chiselled jaw and black velvety eyes.

'Yes, just me,' he replies in his deep voice.

As Rex Hunter waits in the departure lounge he yawns. He had no sleep last night. He had far too much on his mind, and far too many last minute preparations to make.

'This is the last call for flight VG321 to Las Vegas. Please go to gate 43 immediately,' crackles the tannoy. Rex folds his newspaper up, knowing that first class will be called any minute.

Chapter 33

Tiger sat quietly in her vast, luxurious, dressing room as the world busied itself around her. Cherry and Brandy were hurriedly steaming and plumping a mountain of feathers in the corner. Mario was busy teasing Tiger's curls to perfection while Blue paced up and down, bellowing orders to Hartley through his walkie-talkie. Gravy snored on the enormous cream leather couch in the centre of the dressing room as he curled up peacefully next to Ocean, who was gassing with her agent down her mobile whilst artistically decanting Tiger's numerous bouquets of flowers into bronze vases and screening the well wishing cards. She particularly had her eye out for any pink letters, as Lewis had briefed her to do. Lewis had also installed a liberal sprinkling of hefty goons outside the dressing room to watch over Tiger. No one would be getting past them to that dressing room, or anywhere near Tiger backstage in fact. It gave everyone peace of mind knowing that she was safe from physical attack, and happily the air in the theatre tonight was electric.

The plasma screen relay up on the dressing-room wall was focused on the spectacular stage, all sparkling and ready to be filled with showgirls. Tiger could just make out Lewis on the screen, prowling around behind the curtain, gesticulating wildly to the stage manager who was nodding sagely. Tiger wondered if this was what the eye of the storm felt like. Her opening night in Vegas and she was cool as a cucumber. Scarily in control. She had never felt so clear-headed as the madness unfolded around her. Nothing, but nothing could beat the anticipation and thrill of an opening night.

Tiger had felt at home in Vegas the moment she set foot on terra firma three months earlier. Lewis' warm welcome, and seeing Blue and Pepper and the girls had confirmed in her heart she had made the right decision; she was in control again and turning her back on the drama and bad memories. These last three months of rehearsals had been gruelling, but Tiger had thrown herself into them with gusto, enjoying being back at work. She had pushed herself to exhaustion every day, so she could sleep her way through the demons that came into her room at night, taunting her with memories, and the pain of her daughter's rejection. Despite nursing a broken heart underneath her smiles, Tiger clawed back her strength again bit by bit. The truth was, she was more determined than ever that she would one day be someone her daughter could be truly proud of. With that thought firmly in her mind, she was one hundred and ten per cent driven.

All the hard work of the last three months had certainly been worth it, as for tonight's big opening she was on peak form, as sleek as a racehorse, as focused as a jet fighter and as polished as the crown jewels.

'Hey Tiger, are you in a world of your own, or what!' drawled Ocean, with a dramatic flick of her wild blonde mane.

'Oh, sorry. I was just going through that opening routine in my head again.'

'Oh man, I'm sorry. Tell me if I'm annoying you and I'll disappear. I know how important it is to have time to yourself in the dressing room.'

'No! It's fine, sweetheart, to be honest I'd rather have my friends near me tonight.'

'Well, I just wanted to tell you there's a bouquet here from that actress Libertina Belle! It says on the card she's in the front row tonight and . . . ahem, perhaps you should read the message yourself, looks like she's certainly thinking of you in a special way! Do you guys know each other or something?'

Libertina looked around her as the huge auditorium filled with a steady stream of excited guests, all dressed in their finest cocktail attire and clanking their jewels as they took their seats. She peered over the top of her shades at a group of men who had recognised her and were nudging each other excitedly. She winked lazily back at them and blew a kiss. Turning her attention to the glossy souvenir programme that had been left on each of the front row seats, Libertina flicked through the pages and swallowed back the lump in her throat as she thought what a long way Tiger had come from nothing.

Settling back in her seat she let the rumbling hum of the audience wash over her along with the tangible excitement that wafted on the air with it. It wasn't something she really experienced in the world of television or film. She liked the feeling of it. Taking a sudden sharp shove to her shoulder, she whipped her head round. 'Pardon me, ma'am,' apologised a smart gentleman profusely as he took his seat behind her, blushing as he recognised who he had just barged into. 'These aisles are narrow. I'm so sorry, Ms Belle.'

'That's okay, no problem. Enjoy the show,' she drawled loudly, waving her hand dismissively and smiling. As she turned back to her seat, someone caught her eye. She went in for a double take. Sienna? Libertina tensed immediately. She recalled meeting Sienna briefly at the Savoy show a year ago, except the once fresh faced, skinny streak of oatmeal Libertina remembered now looked tired, wan and nervous as she furtively made her way to her seat. Oh, Sienna was all designered up, alright, and had developed some killer curves but beneath the expensive glamour she looked pale and ill. What had Rex been doing to her the past year? Libertina was alarmed by Sienna's presence. Knowing what had gone down between her and Tiger, Libertina guessed she wasn't exactly here as a welcome party. The two women's eyes met as Sienna struggled to take her fur coat off. A flicker of recognition lit up in her eyes before she hurriedly looked away and resumed rear-ranging her outfit. Libertina was thoroughly unsettled.

'Tiger Starr, the Starrlets and ladies of the chorus, this is your ten-minute call,' blasted the audio relay, cutting through the idle chitchat. For a second a pin could be heard dropping in the dressing room as all eyes rested on Tiger, who was calmly sitting at her mirror, inspecting her make-up and sipping at her Martini. Blue bit his knuckles, waiting for her to speak. She took a deep breath.

'Okay girls, tighten me up and tie me off!' Tiger roared, rising from her chair to cling to the wall. Cherry and Brandy leapt for her corset strings, winking at each other as they pulled in opposite directions.

'We made it, my darling,' murmured Blue as he surveyed the proceedings and turned the music up. Once in her shimmering corset, he clipped Tiger's huge spray of creamy tail feathers securely into the back, then stood to one side for Cherry and Brandy to spray her liberally with diamond powder. Job done, the girls bustled out of the room effi-ciently, heading for the wings laden down with Tiger's quick changes for the first half and enough spare tit tape to sink the *Titanic*.

'I'm going down with the girls to check the chorus line presets, darling, you do your breathing,' said Blue.

'Wait,' said Tiger softly. 'One last check?' Blue hesi-tated, not because he didn't want to look at Tiger, but because his eyes were welling up already. He pinched the bridge of his nose and forced himself to look at her.

'Fucking fantastic,' he said, choking on the words. Tiger flung her arms around him.

'Thank you for coming along for the ride with me,' she whispered. 'I'm sorry it's been bumpy.'

'Darling, it's been worth it,' he snivelled into her shoulder. 'I'm just so grateful you forgave me.'

'Oh sweetheart, we've been over that. It's all settled.'

'Oh get a room you two,' laughed Ocean.

'Mama mia, watch ze hair!' squealed Mario, rushing over to tease Tiger's curls again.

'C'mon guys,' said Ocean, clutching Gravy under her arm. 'The leading lady needs her last couple of minutes for her prayers. Blue, get your butt down to that stage. Tiger baby, I'll be outside the door to lead you down when you're ready . . . Tiger? Are you okay?' Tiger was discreetly dabbing a tear from her eye.

'Oh Christ,' said Blue, 'Mario, tissues – now!' He clicked his fingers. 'Darling, are you okay? What's wrong?'

'Oh it's . . . I'm okay, it's just . . . I wish my daughter were here to see it that's all.' Tiger choked on her words as she tried to compose herself. 'I just wish I could make her proud . . .'

'Now stop right there,' said Blue, grabbing a wad of tissues from Mario and shoving it under her nose. 'Blow,' he ordered. Tiger snivelled into the tissues. 'Listen to me, darling. You have nothing to prove. You hear? You did what you had to do by telling your side of the story. It was the right thing. Sienna just needs time. The truth is out there now, that's the main thing. And my god, we are all so proud of you. But the most important thing for you right now is for *you* to be proud of you. You hear me?' said Blue, rubbing Tiger's arms firmly. Tiger let out a little sob.

'Oh Jesus – Mario get some cotton buds – the make-up's going to smudge any second,' ordered Blue. 'Don't you dare cry, Tiger, you look perfect and you're going to ruin your face if you start crying. Now come on.' Tiger nodded her head and sniffed deeply. 'Good girl. Do you want us to stay here with you until you go on?'

'No, darling, I'm fine. I really need two minutes on my own. I'm okay.'

'Okay, chop chop, guys, let's leave the leading lady to it,' squealed Blue, clapping his hands together. Mario, Blue and Ocean left the room to allow Tiger her last crucial moments of privacy.

Down in the spacious wings Blue went through his check-list with Hartley, and quickly scooted round the stage with the deputy stage manager to check all the giant powder puffs had been concealed in amongst the scenery in the right places. He saw Ocean up above leading Tiger into the flies to be strapped into her harness, just as the Star-rlets poured into the wings from the dressing rooms having their last little warm up, flexing their ankles, stretching their thighs out, and wiggling their heads about in their giant powder puff hats. Enormous racks of quick costume changes were suspended above them, upon which were hung myriad headdresses, backpacks and tails, and next to which was Tiger's own rack of quick changes. Cherry and Brandy were hanging out next to the team of chorus line dressers and wiggies, at whom Hartley was now barking orders. Lewis was sitting intently by the backstage monitors with Pepper, biting his nails as Pepper hissed her 'break a leg' wishes to the dancers. The sixty-piece band were winding up their warm up in the pit.

Out in the audience Libertina gripped the arms of her seat nervously as the house lights lowered. Blinding searchlights flashed dramatically around the auditorium, and applause and gasps rippled as a delicate rain of glitter fell from the *trompe l'oeil* sky above their heads. The band blasted out their opening bars and an army of chorus girls in merkins, pasties and headdresses appeared upon long catwalks that rose in the aisles, parading elegantly in sequence between the audience to whoops and cheers. As they snaked their way towards the enormous semi-circular stage the vast shimmering festoon lifted, revealing a stage set straight out of 1950s Hollywood with mirrored staircases, golden filigree gazebos and twinkling stars. Even Libertina let a gasp escape as she was transported back in time to the golden age of glamour right there in her seat.

A glitter pyro exploded in a twinkling puff centre stage, and Tiger appeared, being flown down from the sky as she flapped huge fans of fluffy cream feathers, with star-shaped swings being lowered down behind her upon which four of her leading Starrlets were perched. God, she looked incredible, thought Libertina, her heart fluttering a little. The lines of chorus girls and the remaining Starrlets were now fully assembled on stage, dressing the staircases and gazebos, posing like exquisite statues to receive Tiger centre stage. All around Libertina the audience were rising to their feet already. She shook her head in disbelief at the spectacle and wiped a tear from her eye.

'Oh man that was fun,' puffed Tiger in the interval, collapsing onto the couch and high-fiving Ocean who came in behind her clutching Gravy, followed by Cherry and Brandy trundling their trolleys full of discarded costume and feathers. The girls immediately started allocating everything back to its rightful hanger before laying out the next sets of costumes in order.

'You okay, Blue?' asked Tiger.

'Oh yes! Come here, darling, I just can't get over how fabulous you were! The whole thing looked like some unbelievable dream!' said Blue, leaning over and squeezing Tiger hard.

'Hey, you'll never guess what, Lewis gave me a hug back there at the end of the first half!' said Tiger, jumping up with elation. 'Has that *ever* happened before?!'

'Oooh, one of these bouquets is from Lewis, by the way,' chimed Ocean, 'I forgot to tell you. And he left a really sweet card. Here.'

'Wow! He must be softening up.' Tiger smiled, reaching out for the card. She stood for a moment reading it. Her eyebrows rose as she blushed deeply; she could barely keep the broad smile from her face. Lewis had always been her rock but in recent months he'd emerged as far more that that. He was her hero. 'Right, who's ready for round two?' Tiger said happily as she settled at her dressing table and prepared for a change of make-up. Ocean smiled to herself as she watched Tiger stop to tuck Lewis' card in pride of place in front of her mirror. *We've had a long journey. I'm here for you for ever. Congratulations for your opening night. You are magnificent. Lewis x*

Libertina sat back down in her seat as the house lights went up for the intermission. Her throat was sore from cheering so hard. Not needing a voice any more husky than it already was, she wondered if a little liquor would ease her throat. Outside in the bar she ordered herself a Manhattan and wandered across to the gift shop. She didn't normally go in for souvenirs but she had ten minutes to kill. There was a whole window display given over to Tiger. Libertina felt a deep yearning creep through her as she scanned the little trinkets and posters in their display cases, all bearing Tiger's logo. Her yearning was coloured with resignation. She had always sensed there was only one person Tiger's heart belonged to – even though Tiger didn't know it herself. It was so obvious to anyone on the outside that she and Lewis were meant for each other.

Hell, if you work that hard for that long to keep your hands off each other then you must have something real special you want to protect. It was obvious from the way Tiger was so desperate for his approval; she simply adored him; he was always in her mind. He was clearly also a man who used a hard exterior to hide his true feelings . . . and not just to hide those feelings from Tiger, but from himself. Libertina had done her best to keep any romance strictly casual and non-exclusive between her and Tiger, to try and protect herself. But as with all affairs, someone always gets hurt and all she had done was to torment herself, instead. Libertina eventually selected and paid for a little silver star-shaped compact mirror, encrusted in rhinestones. A smile curled across her full lips as she decided that was exactly how Tiger had to be seen in her eyes; a beautiful, frivolous luxury.

'Ladies and gentlemen, the show will resume in three minutes,' boomed the tannoy. Libertina made her way back to her seat, clutching the compact in its candy-striped paper bag close to her heart.

So far so flawless, thought Lewis as he paced in the wings. He was knocked out by how much happier the Starrlets had seemed without Georgia. Her decision to leave the troupe to become a feature act in her own right under Rex's guidance had amused Lewis, and had furthermore been a convenient development in paring down Tiger's team and removing bad apples. Lewis suspected the kind of 'features' Rex would be developing with Georgia probably weren't suitable for the theatrical stage. He couldn't say he was sad that Rex had resigned from the team after the exposé.

The show was unfolding beautifully, and as it fast approached the grand finale, Lewis found himself more excited than he had ever been before. He was truly enjoying watching the spectacle; and he had never felt so proud of Tiger or their achievements as he listened to the applause and cheers surging through the theatre from the audience. He would normally be out in the frontline, scrutinising Tiger, thinking *Push! Excellent! Clients! Brand! Media! Deals! Business!* Only now he was standing in the wings, he had a view from behind the scenes. He had been watching from that vantage point for some months now; and he had a glimpse of someone entirely different who he hadn't opened his eyes to before. Sure, he knew Tiger Starr the superstar inside out, but now he was seeing Tiger the human being.

Tiger waited in the flies, shaking with adrenalin and nervous excitement as the stage crew opened up the door of the glitterball in anticipation of the grand finale. She took a deep breath and climbed in, letting Cherry and Brandy arrange her voluminous train around her before hopping onto her birdperch. Her hand gently stroked her yellow diamond roaring tiger brooch that she had pinned at her breast for luck. It looked magnificent amongst all the diamonds of her corsetry. The band was blasting at full pelt, the audience cheering them along as they romped their way towards the grand crescendo for the finale. Tiger steadied herself with one of the velvet handles within the glitterball and gave a nod to the stage hands.

'Knock 'em dead, girl,' shouted Ocean excitedly over the music, blowing a last kiss. The crew got the all clear over their headsets from the stage manager before heaving the door shut. Tiger heard the automatic locks click into place and her world became muffled in her airtight glitterball.

Tiger's heart pounded as she reminded herself this had been teched for months, and she had rehearsed this epic number countless times herself. She felt the stage hands banging on the door twice as their all clear for the prop to be lowered and submerged in the pool ready for the grand reveal. The band seemed awfully loud, even through the glitterball, Tiger thought idly. She shuffled uncomfortably and felt fabric bunched up under foot. Damn, Cherry and Brandy must have left some ruffles caught under her heels, she thought irritably. She wriggled from her perch and struggled to crouch down in her corset and rearrange her outfit. She jerked as she felt the glitterball begin its descent, and held her hands up to her padded walls to steady herself. As she crouched there, she registered a weak shaft of light emanating from the door, subtly puncturing the blackness of her velvet padded cell. Jesus. Tiger froze in disbelief, her mouth turning dry as her mind raced frantically. How could a watertight seal let light in? As she stood her eye caught something poking out from the lining of the padded door. Her stomach churned as her fingers went straight to the rip in the padding and pulled out an envelope. Pink. Ripping it open she pulled out a wafer-thin note. Gulping, she held it up to the weak light only to decipher a spider's scrawl upon it.

You're not as watertight as you think you are, babe. It's been fun. Love Always, Rex

Rex? The pink letters? Surely not Rex? How? Why? The glitterball shuddered a little as it made contact with the pool. Tiger dropped the note like a hot coal. It dissolved to nothing at her feet as freezing water began pouring and bubbling in from the door, soaking her as the glitterball steadily plunged deeper into the pool. Nobody heard Tiger's cries for help above the deafening band. She slammed her fist onto her panic button and felt it fall from its panel, exposing cut wires. She screamed in her padded cell as the water rose higher by the second.

Rex Hunter calmly stuck his Mustang convertible into gear and pulled away at the lights. The audience should be really going nuts by now, he calculated, looking at the clock on the dashboard and smiling to himself as he cruised down the Strip amongst the flashing neon lights of uptown Vegas. Well they'd be getting a finale to end all finales tonight. He figured Tiger would have read the final note by now, and should be getting her pretty little feet wet right about . . . now. It would all be over in about three minutes, and by the time she was revealed to the audience in all her lifeless glory, he'd be well on his way to the airport.

It had all been so easy. Getting into the theatre earlier that evening by posing as a bearded flower delivery guy was a masterstroke. All he had to do was to 'get lost' and find his way to the backstage area, climb into the flies to the prop and slash the seals on the door. With his intimate knowledge of Tiger's shows he knew approximately when the stage manager would do his last minute check of the props. All he had to do was make sure his sabotage occurred after that. He'd also made sure to dig out the safety alert in the door and leave his special little message. He was out of there in two minutes flat. There could be no proof he was the saboteur. He had even prepared his note on rice paper – knowing it would leave nothing once it had dissolved in the water – just the empty, fingerprint-less envelope it had been delivered in.

Now he was on his way back home, happy in the knowledge he had avenged another woman who had humiliated him. Rex knew it was impossible for anyone to hold their breath underwater for several minutes, especially if precious energy was wasted struggling. Good. It was time for Tiger to go. If he couldn't have her, no one else would.

All Rex ever wanted was a strong woman. Someone he

could respect. Tiger was the embodiment of that. Smart, independent, beautiful, sensual, passionate, she had class, she was a lady, and she took no prisoners. Ten years Rex had waited patiently for her; his goddess, his fantasy, his everything. He couldn't quite believe it when she had jumped on him after her Savoy show, any more than he could believe it when she had brushed him off so casually. Like she was saying goodbye to the gasman. And with a watch! Like he was just another one of her adoring fans to be patronised! Oh, he pushed her after that. He watched her falling to pieces very slowly and elegantly with every threat, every letter; and just when he thought he might have finished her off, she got back in the saddle. The more she fought, and the more he pushed her, the more he found himself enjoying the game.

Rex had enjoyed watching her pain and torment burning away at her insides as she watched him with Sienna, and when he saw her begin to disintegrate, he twisted the knife even further. St Tropez had been tremendous fun. Even he hadn't anticipated how that would turn out. He had enjoyed filling Sienna's head with hatred for her; it hadn't taken much to manipulate a silly young girl like that. Just the odd prod in the right direction.

Hiring Richie as his stool pigeon had been the true masterstroke of course, giving him access to blow-by-blow reports and updates on Tiger's decline. Most satisfying. He'd briefed Richie to get close to Blue as a means to getting close to Tiger. That was until the plan backfired and Richie went and developed real feelings for that camp bastard. Oh, then Richie had backed off the job like an Italian tank and even told Rex he had grown to like Tiger too much to continue informing. It was quite a curve ball; Rex certainly hadn't bargained on a desperate cash-strapped ex rent-boy suddenly developing scruples. When Rex got back to London he knew he would find Richie and make him sorry for not finishing the job he had been paid good money to do. That's after he whisked Georgia off for a filthy weekend. God, she knew a few hot tricks in bed. Rex felt a twinge in his crotch as he drove. She still wasn't a patch on that hot bitch Tiger though, he thought with frustration.

Rex had to hand it to Tiger, she had fought her corner admirably. If only his mother had done that. The years upon years of beatings his father meted out and still his mother did nothing. Sometimes Rex swore she'd have held him down for his father if it meant she was let off a thrashing for the evening. She may as well have thrown the punches herself, the bitch, thought Rex. It used to bemuse him that everyone thought his father killed her. Nobody ever thought that angelic, downtrodden little Rex did it. Even Rex had blocked it out of his head and re-written his own history . . . almost.

Only once in a while, he couldn't keep that one memory from popping up any longer. His eyes clouded as he recalled pushing his mother down the stairs with his own hands that night, sheer anger overcoming him as she began to assist the hundredth beating of the year. The vision of his mother falling swam in Rex's mind as he pushed his foot down on the accelerator pedal and turned onto the freeway. Ah, the 'fall'. It had such grace and an almost ethereal quality to it, thought Rex, replaying it in his head in slow motion as he cruised in his car. His mother had almost flown, with her arms outstretched like Jesus, her eyes bulging with shock and disbelief. Of course the stupid cow couldn't do anything properly; she broke her neck and just lay there, clinging on, feeble and pathetic with the fingers of one hand twitching. Most unbecoming. His father had just stared at Rex in shock, like his little punch bag of a son was going to turn on him next. With adrenalin coursing through his veins, Rex had challenged him fearlessly. But his father ran. Ran down the hallway and locked himself in the bathroom, the coward. Rex had calmly walked down the stairs, and had looked at his mother lying and trembling at his feet. He knew he had to do the right thing. Put the dog out of its misery. The iron on top of the pile of freshly pressed bed linen was the closest thing to hand. He was twelve. Rex never had been able to stomach a weak woman since.

Tiger was clinging to the velvet ropes of her perch for dear life, hoisting her chin above the freezing water. She felt sick at the thought that the frogmen down in the pool had no idea what was going on literally feet away. They were there in case of mechanical malfunctions. And they were oblivious to the impending disaster within the glitterball walls. Tiger guessed she had maybe ten seconds left before she was completely submerged. She knew she had to calm her breathing and concentrate. Once the band segued into 'Carmina Burana' and the tabs lifted, the glitterball would make its return journey out of the pool, as though pushed up by fountains and water jets. Tiger prayed she could make it through. Water bubbled at her nose and she took a deep breath, unsure if it would be her last, before letting her head slip under the surface.

Blue, Lewis, Ocean and Pepper were grouped together in a huddle backstage, watching spellbound as the prop disappeared from view into the pool. The animal handlers had settled the Bengal tigers onto their podiums and were hurrying back into the wings before the tabs lifted. On cue, the fountains sprang into a beautiful dance as the curtains pulled away to reveal the final scene. A gasp went up in the crowd at the aqua fantasy as the tigers reared up, roaring dramatically. The light show was exquisite, programmed in time with every choreographed spray and jet of water.

'Crack open the champagne, Hartley! We've done it! We're there!' squealed Blue, jumping up and down as *oohs* and *ahhs* rippled through the audience.

'Maybe we should wait . . .' started Hartley.

'Are you kidding?' interjected Lewis, loudly. 'This is a fucking victory!' he bellowed, grinning from ear to ear.

Blue stepped back to look at Lewis in utter amazement. 'Steady on, Lewis!' he laughed.

'Well, I just wanna toast us all when Tiger comes out of that glitterball,' said Lewis, 'Are we the mother of all teams or what? This finale will have everyone out of their seats alright! Listen to them all out there, it's incredible!'

Tiger shuddered as her body fought the desperation to inhale. She thought her lungs were about to burst. Maybe this really was it. The end. She had nothing left to live for any more anyway; she had done what she set out to do, to reinvent her life, pay for her sins, make a success of herself. Except that her dream that her daughter would one day be proud of her would now never happen. Tiger knew she couldn't manage another second. Her mouth fell open and cool water washed in. Rex's final note flashed in front of her eyes, his face appearing before her laughing, morphing into the face of Ed Rogers, his hand over her mouth suffocating her as he raped her. Was this really the final curtain? Drowning in an eight-foot Fabergé egg-shaped glitterball? Was she really going to kick the bucket in a fucking glitterball? On stage? In front of her audience? Blackness spread through her, inviting her in. Her fingertips felt cool and light above her head. She gave herself up to the peaceful euphoria that washed over her.

Rex shoved his foot down on the accelerator to overtake. The glitterball should now be lifting towards heaven, taking the leading lady with it, he thought to himself with a smirk. The Starrlets and the sixty-strong chorus line would all be parading down below her on the stage. Knowing everyone would be blissfully unaware of what was in store gave Rex the pang of a hard on. He imagined Tiger, struggling to the bitter end. He wondered if he was in her thoughts as she drowned. He could hardly wait to hear it on the news.

Lewis was in danger of looking emotional as the glitterball ascended. His eyes were misty. Blue shuffled over and squeezed him on the shoulder.

'I never thought I'd say this,' started Blue, as he followed Lewis' gaze towards the prop, 'but I think what you've done for Tiger is . . . well it's love. The way you've picked her up. You had her back, all the way you know. You held her up. Tonight, this is just . . . wow. And you got her here. I only wish I could have . . .'

'Blue, you have meant more to her than I ever have,' Lewis burst out, keeping his eyes on the stage. 'Tiger and I just work together, remember. I'm just her manager. She's extraordinary, and I only wish I could have had . . . just a tenth of the closeness you two have had. She told you everything from the start. You're the closest person to her. Man, I just didn't have the balls to lay my feelings out there. I was too scared. The feelings I had – have for her – are just too much. So I wanted to be the one to show her off to the world instead. Shit, I guess I just ended up controlling . . . I never wanted . . . I just wanted to be near her, I had no idea how huge she'd become . . . be careful what you wish for, Blue. It was too late for me to say anything from the first moment I started working with her.'

Blue stared back at Lewis, his mouth open.

'You have been her right hand for all this time, Lewis,' said Blue slowly and clearly. 'She has been devoted to you for all these years. She lives to please you.'

'No Blue, she has been doing it all for her daughter. To one day make her proud. To put things right. I was just reading the map in the front of the car while Tiger drove at the wheel for the last fourteen years. And everything was for Sienna, I can see it all now.'

'No. You're missing something. Tiger lives to please people, and help them. That's what she does. And you are one of those people. You can't say you've ever been easy on her, yet she's stuck by you like glue. You're each other's rock. And what you did for her these last few months ... that's called love. It's not too late to say something,' said Blue, trying to catch his eye. Lewis simply stared at the stage, the tic in his jaw starting. Whatever window of emotion Lewis had opened, he closed off again just as quickly as he always did. He stood next to Blue and gave him a warm thump on the shoulder as they watched the stage intently.

Tiger's stomach hurt from retching up water and her lungs burned in agony. She felt dizzy and disorientated as water lapped around her waist. Only one thought entered her mind as she shivered violently and tried to stay upright; she was damned if she was going to emerge for her stay of execution looking like she'd just bobbed up from the *Titanic*. No, there was only ever one way to make a comeback and that was looking fucking fabulous. Her hands leapt to her soaked and matted pink curls. She knew the world would have to know sooner or later . . . she ripped off her pink wig and let her dark hair fall to her shoulders, shiny and wet. If people wanted to see her stripped bare? Well, that's what I'm gonna give 'em, she thought, frantically trying to rip off her waterlogged costume before the door swung open for her big reveal. No make-up, no pink hair, no diamond-encrusted costume . . . just Poppy Adams. She felt ready for the biggest truth of her life.

Libertina laughed loudly as 'Carmina Burana' reached its thunder-cracking crescendo. Only Tiger could do camp like this and get away with it. All three spotlights focused on the door of the enormous glitterball as towering fountains of water shot into the air noisily and white tigers reared up baring their fangs. Beams of pink light illuminated the water as the glitterball door slid open to thunderous crashes of drums, timpanis, roaring tigers and water jets. There stood Tiger, shimmering and completely naked like an apparition from the heavens, the spotlights giving her wet silky skin an otherwordly glow. She was stunning. And brunette! The audience was silent. Then came a noise like the rumbling of a volcano as five thousand people stood up from their seats before erupting into a cacophony of gasps, squeals, screams and cheers, clapping their hands, and stamping their feet in rapturous approval. Libertina noticed Tiger seemed to have her eyes closed, as if in a daze. She must be overcome at the reaction, thought Libertina affectionately. Suddenly Tiger dived fifty feet into the water below, drawing gasps from the crowds and more elated cheers. Libertina's knuckles went white at the spectacle. She had no idea this was the kind of thing Tiger had been training for. She looked over at Sienna, only to see her sobbing uncontrollably.

'Okay, girls, go to bar sixteen, and close in around the pool, keep fucking smiling, and five six seven eight and GO!' barked Blanche on stage, making an elegant spin from her central position so the audience couldn't see her bellowing her commands.

'Honey Lou, we're getting Tiger out of the pool, this is all wrong!' Blanche yelled to her second in command. The two girls pirouetted through the middle of the Starrlets to reach Tiger, who was floundering in the water.

'Shit, babes, hold on to me!' screamed Blanche, grabbing Tiger's wrist. Honey Lou grabbed for her other wrist and together they pulled Tiger out onto the stage, panting and spluttering.

'I nearly – drowned – I haven't got the – strength—' gasped Tiger.

'Right, Honey, let's get her on our shoulders and parade,'

yelled Blanche. 'One, two, three, four and up! You just sit and smile, Tiger!'

The two girls emerged from behind the Starrlets with Tiger upon their shoulders like their glittering trophy. She beamed and winked and played Lady Godiva as Blanche and Honey Lou paraded her elegantly across the stage. The audience were going nuts. The Starrlets then huddled around Tiger and with an almighty push thrust her up onto the velvet swing that hung down from the Fabergé egg. 'Can you do it?' hissed Blanche.

'I'll do this even if it finishes me off,' whispered Tiger, nodding down at her dance captain and gritting her teeth.

'We'll always catch you, Tiger,' murmured Blanche, motioning for the Starrlets to stand back as the glitter-ball rose, taking Tiger into the sky with one last enor-mous rousing crescendo.

'I'm standing outside the Strip's newest show, *Night of A Thousand Starrs*! What a show! Tiger Starr looks set to conquer Vegas with the epic production we saw tonight! Fans and . . .' The radio reporter's voice turned to white noise in Rex's ears as he sped towards the airport. This couldn't be right. How could Tiger's show be a slam-dunk success? She should be dead. He frantically reached over to fumble with the radio and flashed his lights aggres-sively at the truck in front, which was slowing down. Bugger this, thought Rex, swerving to undercut the truck. As he reached for the radio again he heard the deafening parp of the truck before he felt it ploughing into the side of his Mustang.

'Security are all over the stage now with the cops,' re-assured Lewis as he patted Tiger dry with a towel, just as Blue was talking animatedly to a police officer over by the dressing-room door.

'But – it was Rex! I just don't – Lewis, he tried to *kill* me?' she whispered. 'I can't work out if I was dreaming it all, it's just all so ... *surreal*. Did I really read it right?'

'Don't start questioning yourself. We'll nail him,' said Lewis tightly. 'Jesus, I can't get my head round it. That was the most unbelievable performance I've ever seen ... and you were dying in front of us. I didn't even ...' Lewis choked on his words.

'Oh darling, stop!' Tiger's lip wobbled and a single tear rolled down her cheek. 'It's over now,' she whispered. 'It's over. I survived.' Lewis knelt down beside her and kissed her cheek tenderly. Neither of them saw Libertina standing across the room at the door with Blue, watching intently.

'Lewis?' said Tiger, softly.

'Hmm?'

'I think I've paid for my sins now.'

'Oh my beautiful one. You had none to pay for in the first place. God, Tiger, there's something I need to tell you ... I've wanted to tell you for fourteen years. Tiger, I lo—'

*   *   *

The Mustang careened into a tailspin as the truck jerked away again. Rex tried to steer into the spin. Cars honked and screeched behind him as he rotated at high speed towards the central reservation. The car ricocheted off the metal and turned itself over, spinning through the air like an elegant acrobat. Behind him, traffic swerved in its path to avoid the disaster as the car crunched to a landing upside down, smoke rising into the night air from the undercarriage and fluid vomiting from the engine.

'Tiger? Lewis?' ventured Libertina from across the room. Lewis shrank back from Tiger and coughed awkwardly.

'Oh my darling, I didn't see you there,' said Tiger warmly, hurriedly pulling on her quilted silk dressing gown. 'Wait, I'm coming over for a hug.'

'No, dahhling, stay there. Look, I didn't want to spoil a moment between you,' Libertina continued, flashing an apologetic look at Lewis, 'but this just couldn't wait—'

'Oh?'

'Yeah. I brought someone with me. I picked her up downstairs . . . she didn't know if it was okay to come and see you. I said you'd wanna see her.'

'Oh right. Well . . .' said Tiger cautiously. 'Well it's just I can't really see fans right now until all the stuff with the cops—' Tiger stopped as Libertina stood to one side and Sienna stepped forward. Tiger's jaw fell.

'Tiger? I mean . . . M-m-m-mum? Can I call you that?'

Sienna was shaking. 'I came to . . .' She tailed off to stare at her mother as Tiger stood in silence, trembling.

'I had to see you . . . to tell you I – I came all this way to – I just couldn't believe I was actually watching my mum up there tonight. You were amazing,' Sienna whispered, tears beginning to run down her face. 'I'm sorry. I know . . . I read the story in the paper. I know the truth now. I know everything. You were just a kid. I'm so sorry . . .' Sienna bowed her face and cried into her hands. Tiger's face crumpled and she leapt forward, flinging her arms around Sienna, squeezing her tightly. The two women wept in each other's arms, rocking from side to side as they sobbed uncontrollably, both saying their sorrys over and over and over again as Sienna buried her face in her mother's thick, dark hair. Lewis and Libertina exchanged glances and without a single word pulled back towards the door to leave Sienna and Tiger alone. Libertina looked up at Lewis and touched his arm lightly. 'I didn't mean to interrupt, dahhhling. Only Sienna was pulling away, she was scared she wouldn't be welcome,' she whispered. 'But . . . now you need to finish what *you* were going to say to Tiger yourself, too.'

Lewis looked away, a flash of embarrassment in his eyes. 'We'll see.'

'Don't lose her. Look, I should go. Could ya just tell Tiger we'll talk soon? Oh and hey, look after them both, Lewis.' With that, Libertina planted a soft kiss on his cheek and pulled away, her job done.

No sooner had Libertina left the room than a police officer approached the doorway.

'Sir?' he asked, politely.

Lewis nodded 'How's it going?' he asked.

'Yeah, we're making progress. I just have to let you know I've been called out to another job, some huge pile up on the way to the airport, a truck and a convertible or something. Probably fatalities by the sound of it.'

'Oh boy. Poor folks,' sighed Lewis.

'Yeah. These kids with their flash cars. So, I'll leave you in the capable hands of my deputy, he'll be up in five minutes. Good night, sir.'

'Great. That's great. Thanks, Officer,' said Lewis, giving a nod before stepping from the dressing room. As he reached for the door handle, he watched as Sienna stood back from Tiger, and overheard her say: 'I'm so proud of you, mum." Lewis softly pulled the door shut, leaving the pair safe from the outside world.

Twelve months later

Tiger Starr's final night in Vegas was the party of the decade. The stars had turned out in their droves for her finale performance. In the front row sat Libertina Belle with fellow actress Rosalee Jones. Libertina could barely stop herself from proudly waving around the huge rock on her left hand at every opportunity. Not only had Libertina outed herself on national television but after meeting Rosalee on the set of her latest blockbuster she had found herself proposing after only six weeks. The pair had just been married by Elvis in the Say *I Do* Drive Thru chapel and couldn't think of a more fitting way to celebrate than to watch Tiger's show before jetting off to Mustique, away from the gossip-hungry paps eager to track down the newest hot couple on the block. Lesbians were the latest big thing.

Tiger was looking the picture of a goddess as she bumped, grinded and shimmied her way through the show to adoring cheers and whoops. She had kept the brunette look for the last year, and regained her glorious firm curves. The show had been a runaway success, fully booked for ten shows a week. But now Tiger was ready to bring an era to an end this evening. She had a queue of movie directors eager to line her up a few parts, and she felt a change of scenery would be perfect timing. She could always find a protégé burlesque star to nurture if she felt the need. Although she knew she would never, *ever* hang up her own diamond g-string. It was her life and it was in her blood.

Pepper was still going strong and that night was displaying as much energy as she had twenty years back. Over the last year she seemed to have cultivated a new career as a professional gambler in between shows. No one could beat the old broad at Texas Hold 'Em and she was living a high old life. Pepper planned to plough the profits into opening a new burlesque lounge as soon as she found the perfect venue; a dream she daren't even have thought about fifty years ago. Whoever said life ground to a halt at eighty obviously wasn't living in Vegas.

Not long after the opening night a year ago, Tiger had put Gravy on stage with her to collect her stockings between acts. The little Yorkshire terrier now had his own newspaper column, along with his own sweater range and organic dog biscuit line.

In fact there had been a few additions to the stage crew, off stage as well as on. The Starrlets' dressers had a new addition in the shape of Sienna, who cheered Tiger on from the wings every night. Sienna was looking incredible now. She was happy, clear skinned, drug-free and tanned, and even more Amazonian than her mother, with positively illegal curves. Under her mother's nurturing eye,

Sienna's champagne-Charlie lifestyle had been ditched a long time ago, along with her life in London. Sienna had been relieved to make a fresh start with a little sixties condo in Vegas which she shared with Honey Lou and Blanche. With Blue's guidance, Sienna had found her niche styling and costuming her flatmates for their late night shows, which they performed in the lounges as The Fabulous Baker Girls. Tiger had helped get them started by speaking to a few of her contacts, and she hoped one day to put them in her own show as a feature act.

Secretly Sienna fancied a little go at treading the boards herself and often danced in front of her mirror in her creations when Honey Lou and Blanche were out; using some of the moves she had picked up from Tiger. There was no doubt she had a natural flair. It was in her blood, alright. It had felt like a long, hard year, but both Tiger and Sienna had worked hard to piece themselves back together, with mutual help and support. It hadn't been plain sailing by any means, and there was still a lifetime of questions to be answered and worked through; but the two women now shared a bond as mother and daughter. That, they both knew, would never be broken.

Neither Tiger nor Sienna had attended Rex Hunter's bedside as he lay in intensive care for three months after the crash. When he regained consciousness he had been arrested, shortly after being informed he was paralysed from the waist down. He was released without charge, following a lack of any conclusive evidence, but his subsequent breakdown meant he was soon on a one-way ticket to a high security mental hospital.

Georgia Atlanta hadn't shed any tears over Rex despite their brief fling. He was obviously no use to her now. Within weeks of his crash Georgia was already in Los Angeles, planning her megastar acting career. She hadn't hit the big time yet, although she was now selling hundreds of thousands of movies as Georgia Jism, and even had a number one in the adult movie charts with *Gang Bang Slutz IV*. She knew the perfect mainstream movie part would be out there for her one day. She just needed to find herself in the right director's bed.

Lewis had finally managed to find the words he had wanted to say for so many years. Tiger had fallen into his arms immediately, and despite a stormy and passionate relationship over the past year, the handsome pair were still going strong. They were *the* showbiz couple everyone wanted at their party and movie premiere. Lewis still pushed Tiger to be the best she could be and still delivered stinging critiques of every performance. Tonight, they had rowed furiously before the show over Gravy's stage outfits – Lewis still not quite believing that Gravy needed three costume changes per show. However, by the finale Lewis was grinning from ear to ear as he watched his beautiful lady out there on the stage, imagining the incredible make-up sex they would have in the dressing room after the show.

Tiger and Blue were still inseparable, only Blue now lived in his own house, so he could accommodate his ever-increasing wardrobe. Richie had contacted him shortly after the show had opened, begging to be taken back. Blue had agreed. He had never known that Richie had been hired by Rex, and Richie's attack of conscience didn't extend to telling him the truth, especially now that Rex was safely tied up in a straitjacket. Regrettably Blue decided he didn't fancy Richie any more and after a disastrous vacation together, Blue packed him off back to London. Blue was now dating half of the hottest new boy band, fresh out of LA.

Lance de Brett now had his own 'Jerry Springer' meets 'Parky'-style TV show back in England. Despite him enjoying moderate success, neither Tiger nor Sienna ever tuned in.

Rosemary Baby, meanwhile, was cleared of sending the letters to Tiger but still served six months at Her Majesty's pleasure. The subsequent unravelling of her many years of benefit fraud proved to be her undoing. Released from Holloway prison twenty pounds heavier and no less ugly, Rosemary had developed a taste for the short-lived fame she had enjoyed, posing as Tiger Starr's stalker. However, with nothing but her own dubious talents to rely on, she soon found herself laughed out of every respectable theatre and venue in Europe. Eventually Rosemary ended up in Amsterdam, in a seedy sex show off the main drag. It might not be the superstardom she craved, but at least she was still performing. Even if – for now at least – the donkey got top billing.

Ebury Press Fiction Footnotes

Turn the page for an exclusive interview
with Immodesty Blaize . . .

What was the inspiration for Tease?

It was Paul O'Grady who got me thinking about novels after he gave me a hilarious vintage book about life in a burlesque grindhouse. Since I was a fan of Jackie Collins, *Dynasty* and all things campy and tongue in cheek, I wanted to pick up the gauntlet of writing a bonkbuster set in the world in which I live. I have seen the surreal, bizarre and beautiful in my job, and met all manner of fabulous, eccentric, extraordinary, or downright rancid characters along the way, so I had no shortage of inspiration!

Like you, Tiger is an international showgirl who has helped reinvent burlesque, but how do you define Burlesque?

It's a little like asking how do you define music, or how do you define theatre . . . It means different things to different people, and is a genre that has transformed and developed immeasurably over the last two centuries. Its popular roots are to be found in early 19th century British music halls, at a time when the genre was about parody, satire and bawdy comedy.

What I perform (and what Tiger performs) is classic American burlesque striptease and European showgirl acts, the type that were popular in the mid 20th century. Around this time, a burlesque show was essentially risqué, ironic cabaret, with bawdy comedians, stripteasers, chorus lines and specialty acts. The stripteasers were often huge legends, as famous as the movie stars of the time. The shtick was also as important as the strip, but the erotic undertow was essential. My own shows are similarly big elaborate theatrical spectacles with a variety of acts, in which I also perform with my dance troupe, my 12 piece big band, and huge props and sets; pure classic glamour.

Why do you think it has such an enduring appeal to modern audiences?

My shows attract a large female audience as much as a male audience. It is a form of erotic entertainment that appeals and is accessible to both sexes. The women love the glamour and love to come to the shows dressed up; they really tap into their own inner showgirl. The shows are enormously glamorous, funny and camp, but, ultimately, they are pieces of theatre. They offer fantasy and escapism which I think is an antidote to our modern social climate.

Ironically we have spent so many decades thinking about the future, predicting the future, anticipating a better future, that now I believe there is a trend for looking back to the glamour of the past with the benefit of rose-tinted spectacles. In the noughties we have a very 'quick hit' culture, and everything is so accessible now . . . except the past, we can never actually re-experience that. Perhaps that's why there is so much allure in recreating the classic, perceived 'halcyon days' of a time that is gone forever, its memory preserved in black and white stills and moving picture, it is otherworldly.

I think also the overwhelming accessibility and use of

sex in our media is also why people gravitate towards the concept of seduction and tease. But the bottom line is: a fabulous glamorous show full of beautiful women disrobing has always been popular, and always will be!

How did you come to be a showgirl?
It was an organic thing; there was never one 'Eureka' moment. Pieces of the jigsaw puzzle fell into place over time: dance classes as a child, my obsession with Parisian showgirls, a mother who looked like Wonder Woman, watching *Gypsy* and falling in love with Mazeppah, discovering Betty Page in my teens and all the pinup queens, feeling out of place with my hourglass shape in a time of super waifs and heroin chic, working as a stripper for a few months when I graduated from university, being told I looked like Modesty Blaise by the gas man, being an artist and being able to design my own costumes, working in film as a producer director and honing the art of the mise-en-scene . . . as long as I was creating my crazy fantasy worlds, in whatever way I could.

Both you and your character have the most wonderfully elaborate stage acts but did Tiger get some of the spectacles that you yourself would like to perform? (Diving tigers for example?)
Yes, Tiger performs at my favourite UK venue, The Savoy Theatre. That's next on my list of theatres to perform at. I'd also like her automated roaring black panthers for my

Blaizing Angels! I allowed her to borrow some of my acts too though . . .

Dream-casting time: aside from you, who in your head would play Tiger Starr in a movie version of *Tease*?
Monica Belucci, although Salma Hayek's striptease in *From Dusk 'Til Dawn* was jaw dropping: the beauty, those curves, all rendered me speechless.

What about Lewis?
Jon Hamm or Clive Owen – that old fashioned, uber masculine charisma.

And Libertina?
Megan Fox.

Who are your favourite authors?
Ian McEwan. Haruki Murakami, Evelyn Waugh, Lewis Carroll, Djuna Barnes, Henry Miller, Charles Bukowski, Terry Southern, Toby Litt, Will Self, Jacqueline Suzanne, Jackie Collins.

Confession time: which classic novel have you always meant to read and never got round to it?
Herman Melville's *Moby Dick*.

What are your top five books of all time?
Evelyn Waugh *Vile Bodies*

Emile Zola *Nana*
John O'Hara *Butterfield 8*
Toni Morrison *Beloved*
Jilly Cooper *Riders*

Which book are you reading at the moment?
Me Cheeta, the autobiography

Do you have a favourite time of day to write?
Ideally I like to write late into the night say from 10pm
until 3 or 4am, then review my work and make amend-
ments as soon as I get up, when my brain is fresh as a
daisy and in a practical headspace.

A favourite place?
Anywhere comfortable. I tend to go to my house in the
South of France. I have my room with a view and I sit
at my 1930s writing bureau, or when it's sunny I sit by
my pool with a dirty martini. It's more *Dynasty* that way.
If it's a late night I'll lounge on my bed with my little
dog; I get terrible backache that way though, hunched
over to the early hours tapping away!

What's your writing process? Are you a planner?
I cannot write a word until I have storylined every chapter.
I need to have my 'map' in front of me. That way I don't
get distracted by the fun details and lose the plot, literally.

Which fictional character would you most like to have met?
Rupert Campbell Black from *Riders*!

Who, in your opinion, is the greatest writer of all time?
Tough. Just one? I'll plump for the phenomenal talent of Hemingway.

Other than writing and performing, what other jobs or professions have you undertaken or considered?
I used to work as a producer/director. It was all complementary to what I do now for obvious reason . . . and so much of my inspiration on stage has come from cinema.

What are you working on at the moment?
I am writing the second novel with which I'm having great fun! I am also embarking on some really exciting projects with EMI, who I signed with earlier this year. The first of those will be the movie of my annual *Tease* show, which will be in cinemas on general release later this year, and available of DVD in 2010. I shall unveil my latest act I've been working on to mark the occasion!

...er is a high-powered barrister, the scourge of the divorce courts, hoping to become a QC – to "take silk" – after her next high-profile case.

Her daughter, Isabelle Cissé, is a talented graduate launching herself on the London fashion scene, full of dreams and ambitions – and still smarting from her parents' divorce.

Blonde, beautiful Victoria Crabtree is the mistress of a wealthy Italian garment manufacturer, bored with being a kept woman, hungry for security and stability with the man she loves.

Three women – three generations set on a collision course. Their lives and conflicting ambitions become tangled as Christine handles the divorce case that could give Victoria the man she's wanted for her own for so long – but which could wreck her daughter's career at the same time.

Praise for Rupert James and *Silk*:

'Sexy, funny, compelling, *Silk* sizzles' Tilly Bagshawe

'Taking on the gossipy tone of the very best Jilly Cooper novels and giving it a modern twist, this is a 21st century bonkbuster with attitude.' *Elle Magazine*